Collision Course

Collision Course   Joe Broadmeadow

Collision Course

By Joe Broadmeadow

[signed] Joe Broadmeadow 4/2015

All rights reserved. No part of this book may be used or reproduced, stored in or introduced into a retrieval system, or transmitted, in any form, or by any means (electronic, mechanical, photocopying, recording, or otherwise) without the prior written permission from the author or publisher. This is a work of fiction. Names, characters, places, and incidents either are the product of the author's imagination or used fictitiously.

Text Copyright ©2014 Joe Broadmeadow
JEBWizard Publishing
All Rights Reserved
ISBN-13:978-1497321458
ISBN-10:149732145X

Acknowledgements

No one writes a book alone. It is a collaborative effort of many people. Some help by reading and offering suggestions, some by giving you the time to write.

I would like to thank the following for their immeasurable assistance in making the book a reality.

Ms. Kelsey Broadmeadow, ESQ. (coincidentally my daughter), for her patience and assistance in answering my unending questions on the many legal intricacies of the book.

Dr. Edwin Pont for his greatly appreciated assistance in helping me craft the medical terminology. Edwin is also one of the finest people you could ever meet. His becoming a member of our family has made us all the better for it.

Any errors in the medical or legal aspects are all my misunderstanding of their explanations.

Michael Campbell, a profoundly positive influence on my life almost from the moment of birth, for his reading and suggestions of the draft versions.

Chief Anthony Pesare, Middletown Police and retired Major, Rhode Island State Police. For his insight, advice, critiques, and willingness to take time to read my manuscript, I am forever indebted.

To Jeff Slater, a friend of over forty years, for the amazing cover design. Jeff's creativity is inspiring and greatly appreciated.

To those Officers, Agents, Troopers, and Prosecutors I had the honor and pleasure to work together with, thank you for the experience of a lifetime.

For Defense Lawyers that everyone loves to hate until you need one, thank you for showing me the reality of truth.

And to my wife, Susan for giving me the time to write and the support to let me believe I could.

Dedication

To the men and women who wear the badge and try to make a difference, few will ever really understand, or appreciate, what it takes.

Prologue

Innocence

Life wears away our innocence. For Anthony Machado, those he trusted most slashed it from him; fileting Anthony's humanity.

"Father, can I help you?"

The older priest, kneeling in front of the young altar boy, looked up. "No, no, everything is fine, just helping Anthony adjust the cassock. It's a little big on him."

The young priest looked into the terrified adolescent eyes. "Anthony, isn't your Mom coming here to get you soon?" The boy remained motionless.

The older man rose up, facing the newly ordained priest. "Father" the words slow and deliberate, "I said everything is fine! Anthony is helping me pray the Rosary for our Holy Father tonight. His mother is picking him up in the morning. You may go," motioning Father wanson towards the door.

You do not argue with the Pastor of the Church, let alone one thought likely to be the next Bishop of the Diocese of Providence. The young priest turned reluctantly away, walking towards the door. "I can come back later and help if you'd like Father."

"No," the Pastor replied, taking a moment to calm himself, "there is no need. This is something we need to do. Anthony will benefit from the experience. Please attend to your other duties."

Father Jim Swanson would never forget the look in Anthony's eyes, or the look in the Pastor's.

"Please close the door on the way out, we need time to prepare, and I will not tolerate any more interruptions."

The sound of the latch echoed through the church.

Lost

One week later, Father Jim was hearing confessions. The door to the confessional opened. A penitent came in and knelt.

Father Jim slid back the privacy screen.

"Bless me Father, for I have sinned."

Father Jim knew the voice. He knew what was coming. He did not want to bear this burden.

"Father…"

The details horrible, the sadness overwhelming, yet the boy continued until he said it all.

"Father, he told me there is no penance for this, no forgiveness. He told me it was my fault, but I wanted to, to ask for… I, I begged him, I tried to get him to stop."

The door swung open, and he was gone.

Father Jim came out of his side of the confessional. The Pastor stood there, watching the boy leave.

"Did Anthony not receive his penance? He seemed in a bit of a rush to leave."

"Of course he did. Father, would you excuse me please," heading towards the sacristy. Jim wanted to go after Anthony, to do something to help him.

"You will hear my confession," commanded the Pastor, stepping into the confessional.

Father Jim hesitated, trying to think of a reason not to comply. He could not. The right to confession is a fundamental tenet of the Catholic faith. Seeking forgiveness is the first step to redemption.

God promises the Sacrament of Reconciliation.

There are several elements to the Act of Contrition in the Roman Catholic faith. They include the priest, the penitent and God.

One has to have faith in the process.

Faith, he thought, this is what my faith compels me to do. This is why I became a Priest. This is my obligation.

He returned to the confessional, closed his eyes, and waited.

"Bless me Father, for I have sinned..."

Father Jim tried to grasp the words of the Pastor, this emotionless recitation of unimaginable evil. He sought a reason to forgive, some hint of genuine sincerity to permit absolution. He could find none. He knew they lacked other essential elements, genuine contrition and an intent to sin no more.

On the other hand, could he really be sure? Why is faith not absolute?

Father Jim went through the motions of giving absolution and assigning penance to the Pastor.

Penance?

What penance could there be for this? How can you absolve someone of destroying innocence? Go and sin no more indeed.

Jim waited a few minutes before leaving the confessional, hoping to avoid any additional conversation.

The Pastor was waiting.

"I want to thank you for your understanding and patience with me, Father. I am sure this will be easier for you when you are more experienced. By the way, I planned to inform you of this later after I had spoken to the Bishop, I am removing Anthony from serving as an Altar boy. It seems he was never been properly baptized. I doubt his mother will ever help him meet the requirements."

"But Father, we can get his mother's permission for someone to sponsor him. We can deal with this issue. Why should Anthony suffer...?"

"No, that will not be adequate."

Father Jim just stared at the Pastor.

"Please see to it that he is removed from the schedule and replaced accordingly. I plan to discuss this with the Bishop. He will have to receive the Sacrament of Baptism, before he can receive Holy Communion. It is important that the requirements of doctrine are met, wouldn't you agree Father?"

Jim felt lost, his faith confronting an irreconcilable contradiction.

Why does God barter redemption, in exchange for confession, instead of preventing the taking of innocence beforehand? Is the need to use temptation so critical to measuring the sincerity of the faithful? At what cost?

Why impose this obligation on me? Why use me as the instrument nullifying this abomination? If this is his will, I may never understand. I do not think I ever could.

1: Hijacking Justice

June 22, 2006

United States Attorney Robert Collucci stood on the courthouse stairs addressing the media.

Coming on the heels of his announcing his candidacy for the United States Senate, Collucci was reveling in the media attention.

"My office sought and obtained an indictment of East Providence Police Sergeant Joshua Williams on Civil Rights violations while acting under color of law," pausing to enjoy the effect.

"I secured the assistance of the Justice Department's Civil Rights division in seeking this indictment. This office assumed responsibility from the Rhode Island Department of the Attorney General insuring the matter would receive its proper attention."

The implication was not lost on the reporters.

"As long as I am the US Attorney, we will continue to fight for Justice for everyone. This pattern of racial profiling and civil rights violations by police officers will not be tolerated."

Collucci, looking directly into the cameras, continued. "The evidence in this matter is clear and convincing. The Government will prove that the defendant, Sergeant Joshua Williams, acting under color of law, executed Anthony Machado for the simple reason of being a black man."

Pointing at the courthouse. "Inside this building, Justice for Anthony Machado is at hand. My platform in this office, and in all my future endeavors, will be Justice for everyone. Thank you."

The reporters shouted questions; Collucci smiled and waved them off.

Josh Williams, sat in the office of his attorney, Harrison "Hawk" Bennett, watching the news feed.

"Can you believe this?"

"Believe it, my boy? I am counting on it." Reaching for the remote, he switched off the TV. "Collucci is an arrogant, self-centered, manipulative bastard, and those are his good characteristics. Not to worry, I am going to use those very traits to bury that son-of-a-bitch."

2: *Plans and Deceptions*

March 14, 2006

"Hey, wanna make some money?"

Anthony "JoJo" Machado looked up from the park bench and saw David Anthony Ventraglia, known as Divothead, walking towards him. Ventraglia was not alone. JoJo considered Divothead to be one of his few friends; he didn't know the other guy, and didn't much care to meet anyone.

JoJo trusted no one.

"Yo, Divot, I always need to be making money, what we gonna do?"

Anthony 'JoJo' Machado's heritage was a mystery, born on or about June 6, 1983 in Providence, RI.

He and Mom were found by an inquisitive dog attracted by the smell of blood; the plaintive howling drawing the attention of a curious neighbor with the decency to show concern and dial 911.

JoJo's mother, Altagracia Manuela Medeiros, was a progeny of a sexual assault upon her mother, the father known only to God. Raised in the foster-care system of RI, she was also a victim of sexual abuse.

Altagracia, not quite age one, and two other siblings, ages two and four, were placed with DCYF, the Department of Children, Youth, and Families after being discovered abandoned in an unheated apartment.

The children were brought in for medical evaluation. The older two could say their first names; they called the infant "little one."

A nun who cared for the child created a splendid name. Altagracia, High Grace, the Virgin Mary will guide her, Manuela, so God is with her, and Medeiros that would allow her to blend in with Fox Point.

She was a good Sister, terrible psychic, unless irony was her intent. No one would ever compare JoJo's mom and the Virgin Mary.

Altagracia carried the burden of a too-fertile reproductive tract and decreasingly low criterion for her sexual partners. She was an all-too-common victim of the lack of conscience, or sense of responsibility, by many men. JoJo was the only one of five children she actually managed to bring up by herself.

Rumor had it JoJo bore a resemblance to a former parishioner of St. Domenicks Church. The man died trying to pull people out of a burning building in Providence; once again, unexpected heroism depriving a child of the potential for a different, more fulfilling life. A short time later, Altagracia was sober enough for a day to realize she was pregnant, again.

People often wondered why DCYF chose to leave JoJo with his mother.

Many assumed the others were female. Removing them from the dysfunctional parenting of Altagracia improved their chances for a better upbringing, in an environment that encouraged planned parenthood. Perhaps they believed it was worth risking one, while saving the other four, considering the budget constraints. A pessimist might argue risking them all was a better bet, letting evolution select the fittest.

Resource limitations force Social Service agencies to choose between a known evil and an uncertain one.

3: *A Different Path*

JOJO'S nickname came from his mother's habit of saying, 'Yo,Yo' to everyone she greeted, sounding like she had downed a twelve pack.

Which, in all probabilities, she had.

The name attached to JoJo as a youngster playing basketball at the Boys Club. JoJo's mom, whenever she showed up, would yell "JoJo, that's my boy. JoJo, watch him man, he is going to the NBA."

While JoJo's father failed in being a physically meaningful presence in his life, he made up for it as he had left him, genetically at least, a sense of duty and responsibility. Those that knew JoJo said he was genuinely kind, caring kid and avoided trouble.

JoJo never went to the NBA. Instead, he went to another organization known by its initials, the United States Marine Corps, USMC. He enlisted at 17, having managed to keep himself in school long enough to graduate.

He realized early on that he did not want to live like his mother or most of his friends.

The Marine Corps lived up to its reputation and broke JoJo down only to rebuild him in the manner of a Marine. He was selected for, and completed, Reconnaissance training. It seemed a career in the Corps was tailored made for JoJo.

Two tours in Iraq and three tours Afghanistan categorically eliminated that possibility.

Wounded early in his first deployment, he recovered quickly and applied the lessons to the next four tours. He suffered more wounds, but he made the bastards work for it.

His luck ran out on a mission to some remote outpost known as hill 181.

Sergeant Machado and two other Reconnaissance Marines received orders to establish an observation post to monitor and disrupt the Taliban's infiltration routes from Pakistan.

The Recon Marines left the Forward Operating Base headed west, away from their intended course. The idea, to mislead the Afghans about the mission.

Of course, the Afghani likely assumed this, so it was an exercise in futility in Sergeant Machado's mind. Nevertheless, Gunny Scotton usually got his way.

Three kilometers out of the base, turning a slow, wide, 180-degree arc, setting flares to locate anyone trailing them, they headed to the real objective, Hill 181, one-half kilometer from the Pakistan border.

Arriving at sunset, the Marines deployed their equipment, set rotating watches, and settled in. Sergeant Machado took the first watch with Corporal Sanchez; Gunny slept.

Just after 2200 hours, Sanchez spotted movement 500 meters away, three figures carrying weapons.

Machado decided to wait and see if additional groups followed before taking out this group. Better to kill as many as you can at once than take them on piecemeal.

The group moved slowly down the trail, smoking, noisy, probably high. Despite denials by the Taliban religious leaders, many of the fighters were addicted. Drug use was rampant.

The Marines detected more movement further up the trail, four more individuals; one carrying what appeared to be a Stinger Surface to Air Missile launcher. Sergeant Machado now had a very good reason to wake Gunny.

Twenty-four years to the day Gunnery Sergeant Michael Scotton joined the Marine Corps; his twenty-two-year-old son graduated from Officer's Candidate School at Quantico, VA., and was accepted into Marine Aviation training, on his way to becoming a Marine Super Cobra helicopter pilot.

On First Lieutenant Michael Scotton, Jr's twenty-fourth birthday, during combat operations in Afghanistan in support of the First Marine Division, he was shot down and killed by a Stinger missile,.

Gunny Scotton would strangle Machado with his bare hands if he let them get past and did not wake him.

When Gunny heard what they had, he smiled, and said, "Okay, we're going to go kill most of them, but I want the bastard carrying the Stinger. Alive."

Machado knew better than to argue.

Scotton selected an ambush point on the trail, positioning Machado and Sanchez to take out the lead and rear of the group, reserving the Stinger bearer for himself. He told Machado and Sanchez to wait until he rolled the concussion grenade into the middle of the group before opening up.

As the group of Taliban entered the kill zone, Scotton pulled the pin on the MK3A2 Concussion Grenade, released the safety handle, counted to three, and rolled the grenade beneath the feet of the fighter just in front of the one carrying the Stinger. The grenade went off. Separating the Taliban fighter from his genitalia; sending him "weaponless" to Allah and the seventy-two virgins. The explosion knocked the Stinger from its bearer's hands, rendering him unconscious.

Machado and Sanchez followed their instructions to the letter.

Then there was one.

A mostly deaf, partially blind, twenty-two-year-old illiterate, unsophisticated, brainwashed Taliban, who would be better off if he died, became a temporary "guest" of the Marines. They quickly secured from the area taking the Stinger, and the one remaining fighter, with them.

Moving quickly to a newly established position, they set up to look for any movement or indication of Taliban following them. They saw none.

Scotton moved off alone to a separate area with his prize.

The Taliban fighter, legs and arms tied, began to stir. Scotton let him regain the remnants of his physical abilities, Allah the merciful should have spared him. As he recovered, Scotton began his interrogation. Among the Gunny's many talents was an uncanny ability with languages. He began by smiling, welcoming the Taliban, in fluent Pashto, to his home, and then cutting off the fighter's thumbs.

To say the man was screaming, or more correctly trying to though the gag, is a flagrant understatement. Scotton then asked a series of questions, while running the blade over the remaining fingers. The man was whimpering and begging for his mother. This seemed to drag on for hours. In spite of Scotton's threats, the man retained the ability to count to eight.

Scotton learned, the group was not the rear security team, but the point of a larger force massed just on the other side of the border. One quick radio broadcast of no more than 10 seconds duration and Marine Aviation and Artillery would send Allah a few hundred more Martyrs. Unfortunately, Pakistani pride and politics outweighed the lives of US forces. As long as they remained on that side of the border, they were untouchable.

Suddenly, Machado saw a change come over Scotton. The Gunny started pacing back and forth, conversing, pleading, and crying out, to an unseen presence. Scotton finally looked back at the Taliban, ran at him; bayonet raised, screaming, and sliced the rope binding his arms. Eyes are not made to open that wide except in the presence of absolute terror.

The man fell to his knees, looked up, and yelled some Pashto version of "You fucking asshole," as he lunged at Scotton. The Gunny shot him dead with his M9A1 9mm sidearm. He looked at Machado and said, "Michael told me to let him die a warrior, how can I argue with that?"

Machado and Sanchez exchanged glances. Sanchez, trying to lighten the moment, said, "Fuck Sarge, it's not like he could thumb a ride back to Bumfuckistan."

The Marines began policing the area for anything the Taliban might use against them, preparing to move out. Just as they readied themselves to leave, death decided it wanted three more.

The Rocket-propelled grenade round, reaching the limit of its range, caught Sanchez in the chest, knocked him on his ass, and fell, without detonating, to the ground. Sanchez looked at Gunny and Machado and rolled himself onto the round.

Nothing happened.

Gunny Scotton laughed and said, "Sanchez, get up, dumb ass, you look like a monkey trying to fuck a football. It's a fucking dud."

"Fuck!" Sanchez grimaced as he tried to stand up, "I think my ribs are broken."

Scotton came over, probed a bit until Sanchez started swearing in Spanish. "Listen, son, you just have to be tough. We cannot leave anything behind, so suck it up and let's go."

Grabbing Sanchez by the arm, the Gunny said, "One other thing, I speak Spanish as well. If you ever say something about my mother again, I will shove a working RPG up your ass, comprende' Pancho?"

Machado hoisted the communication equipment and started down the trail. Sanchez in the middle, Gunny covering the trail as best he could. They went about three kilometers; Machado motioned for them to stop.

He saw movement ahead.

Sanchez set up a position to cover them. Scotton moved off to the flank, while Machado kept on point to identify the target.

He did not have to wait long.

The group of Taliban moved quickly. Machado guessed they knew their lead team was compromised, and decided to intercept the Marines. The Taliban knew these hills and mountains so well they seemed to be able to materialize out of nowhere.

Sanchez spotted the sniper, leaving him no choice. He squeezed off a burst of fire, cutting the man in half, eliminating the threat but alerting the larger group to their presence. Gunny threw five fragmentation grenades into the middle of the group and beat feet back to Sanchez and Machado.

"Sanchez," Gunny pointing to the likely route the Taliban would use to get to them, "keep their fucking heads down so Machado and I can get around them. We'll set up crossing fire positions and take 'em out."

Sanchez smiled and set his weapon on full auto, readied extra ammo, and waited for them. "Aye, Aye, Sarge, I got it."

As Gunny and Machado made their way to flank the Taliban, a burst of fire told them Sanchez was at work.

Then it all went to shit.

They heard Sanchez screaming. Gunny pointed Machado towards the top of the rise and ordered him to continue while he went back for Sanchez. As he made his way down the reverse slope, a round caught him just above the knee, broke his leg, and sent him rolling down the hill, almost landing on top of Sanchez.

Machado made his way to the top and looked down onto a group of ten Taliban, the taller one, standing in the middle, was clearly the leader. They were all listening as he spoke; gesticulating towards Sanchez's, and now Gunny Scotton's, position.

Machado took him out with one round to the head, and then managed to kill or wound seven more before bailing from the position. Now that they knew he was there, he would move somewhere else.

The Hajis would assume he'd go help the wounded Marines.

He was going to do that, but not directly.

If Gunny Scotton and Sanchez were alive and conscious, they were still dangerous Reconnaissance Marines, not taken easily. If they were dead, Machado could not fix that, but he would take out as many of the bastards as he could.

Machado moved away from his position to the rear of the Taliban. He came upon two wounded fighters and insured they would not recover. Grabbing an AK-47, he moved further off and began firing the Taliban weapon. The AK-47 has a very distinctive sound, readily identifiable by anyone familiar with the weapon.

Machado was going to use the Taliban's lack of field immediate communication to draw the others to the sound of the weapon, which he hoped they would assume was their own.

Moving a hundred meters away from his original firing position, he watched as three more Taliban cautiously made their way to the ravine bottom. He pulled the pin on a frag, threw it at the Taliban, and then moved perpendicular to his position. The grenade went off, killed one of the fighters, wounded the other two, one severely.

The lightly wounded fighter moved towards Machado's last position, trying to lure Machado into a direct confrontation. *These bastards aren't pussies,* Machado thought, as he moved ninety degrees to the right.

The Taliban, surging with adrenalin, ignoring the intense pain from his wounds, yelled for Allah's help, and ran over the top of the rise. Firing quickly, spraying the area with automatic weapon fire.

Machado rolled to his left, firing back, catching the guy in the left shoulder, spinning his body. The weapon continued to fire as the Taliban spun down to the ground.

Two rounds caught Machado. One bullet passed through the lower leg muscle, the other through Machado's upper-right shoulder. The rounds exited without hitting any bones. Neither was fatal, as long as he stopped the blood flow, but they were painful.

Machado fired once more, killing the Taliban fighter.

Machado knew he needed to get back to Corporal Sanchez and Gunny Scotton. If they were dead, he did not want the Taliban defacing the bodies. If they were wounded but alive, he did not want them captured.

Using his field medical kit, he wrapped his wounds as best he could, slowing his blood loss. Once he was back with the other two Marines, he would do a more permanent job.

As he worked his way to a position, he spotted two more Taliban setting up a mortar. Taking them both out, he made his way to the mortar. Machado lobbed a few rounds into the surrounding hillsides before dropping a grenade into the mortar tube, rendering the weapon useless.

Returning to his original approach, he peered over the top and saw Sanchez, with a compress field dressing on his shoulder, putting a splint on Gunny's leg. Making his way down the slope, he counted fifteen dead Taliban.

"Will you look at this Sanchez, the fucking prodigal Marine returns." Gunny Scotton smiled, looking at Machado, "Where the fuck have you been while we were killing these bastards?"

"Killing the rest," Machado replied.

The Marines tensed as the sound reached them.

The mortar has an unnerving sound, deep and guttural. One feels it as well as hears it.

You know the round has left the tube. You can run. But which way? If you run back, and the trajectory is long, you are dead. If you sit still, and the bastard knows his stuff, you are dead. You make yourself small as possible, a part of the earth, and hope...

Machado regained consciousness.

He heard the sound of the wind; but there was no wind.

He saw Gunny Scotton lying on the ground next to Sanchez. He tried calling to them. He could not hear his own voice. Just the whistling sound of the wind.

Machado started to move towards the two wounded Marines. With each motion, he felt searing pain. From his shoulders to the small of his back, he felt as if he was on fire. Reaching back, his hand returned covered in blood.

Painfully making his way to Sanchez, he checked for a pulse, it was weak, but he was breathing. Gunny Scotton began to stir and tried to rise up. One hand torn to pieces, covered in shrapnel wounds from his feet to the top of his left shoulder, and his right eye swollen and distended.

Sounds slowly returned. He heard more rounds incoming.

Crawling towards Sanchez, spitting blood, Scotton ordered, "Go find that mortar, Sergeant, I'll take care of Sanchez, if they fire with the same trajectory again we're screwed."

Machado made his way towards where he thought the mortar was set up. Gambling the guy would be firing a pattern out further from his position, trying to bracket the Marines. He heard another round, and it gave him a fix on the position. The round arced further east, giving Machado the opportunity to focus on killing the bastard and not worrying about his two friends.

Rising slowly to the top of the rocky tableau, he caught sight of the mortar. There were five Taliban. Two were operating the mortar; the other three were in the process of setting up a DsHK 12.7mm machine gun.

They were trying to lure the Marines back to their position, get them to attack the mortar, and then take them out with the heavy automatic weapons' fire.

Not bad, not going to work, but not bad, Machado thought.

The two mortar men carelessly left their AK-47's out of reach, making them less of a direct threat when he opened fire. Planning his attack, Machado would take out the machine-gun team first, and then go after the mortar men. It would take them time to react to Machado's initial assault. Enough time, Machado hoped, for him to eliminate them before they got to their rifles.

Then, for once, chance intervened in a positive way.

The three Taliban working on the machine gun, laid down their weapons, walked over to the mortar position, and began arguing.

Machado's elimination of the leader left a void.

Quickly revising the plan, Machado threw two frag grenades into the group and opened up on them in full-auto mode.

Not as economical as his previous work, but equally effective.

Moving down the slope, he retrieved some Russian grenades from the dead, used them to destroy the mortar and machine gun, and headed back.

Making his way back to Gunny and Sanchez, Machado set up the communication net and called for a Medical Evacuation chopper. Using the encrypted channel, he provided their position and situation. The response was as expected. Within minutes, several Super Cobra helicopter gunships and a Huey transport chopper arrived on scene.

Hoisting Sanchez onto the chopper first, then Gunny Scotton, Machado threw off his pack, weapon, and helmet and jumped in. The chopper pilot began climbing out. The force of the liftoff threw Machado headfirst into one of the supporting pillars, knocking him unconscious.

The medic, working on Sanchez and Scotton, looked over, saw Machado was breathing, and continued to work on the more severely wounded Marines. He would get to Machado when he could.

On arrival at the Medical Station, the staff evaluated the Marines. Machado regained consciousness, but was having trouble moving his right arm, difficulty speaking, and was unable to follow simple commands.

The doctors managed to stabilize Machado and ordered him transported to the airfield. Within an hour, he was airborne to Germany.

JoJo served his last tour.

4: *Welcome Homeless*

On December 24, 2004, Staff Sergeant Anthony Machado received an Honorable Discharge from the United States Marine Corps. A consequence of his designation as medically unsuitable for duty due to wounds suffered on 5 October 2004 in Combat Operations, Helmand Province, Afghanistan.

Staff Sergeant Machado received the following decorations for actions while serving in Iraq and Afghanistan.

Navy Cross

Bronze Star with "V" Device

Purple Heart with three Oak Leaf Clusters

The citation for the Navy Cross reads as follows:

The President of the United States of America takes pleasure in presenting the Navy Cross to Staff Sergeant Anthony Machado, United States Marine Corps, for extraordinary heroism while serving as an Assistant Squad Leader with First Reconnaissance Battalion, First Marine Division, I Marine Expeditionary Force Afghanistan on 5 October 2004, in support of Operation ENDURING FREEDOM. Sergeant Machado was assigned a part of a three-man reconnaissance patrol in the hotly contested Kajaki region of Helmand Province, tasked with locating and interdicting the Taliban's infiltration routes. Machado, along with two other Force Reconnaissance Marines, engaged Taliban fighters in an ambush, killing twelve and destroying a Stinger missile launcher. A heavy volume of small arms and machine-gun fire then poured in on the Marines from three enemy positions. All three Marines were wounded. Despite suffering a concussion and neck and shoulder fragmentation wounds from 73-mm blasts, Sergeant Machado exposed himself to the unrelenting barrage of enemy fire, taking up several positions to engage the enemy with his rifle and grenade launcher and protect his two wounded fellow Marines. Despite being wounded twice more, Sergeant Machado continued to engage the enemy, leading them away from the injured Marines. His unhesitating actions resulted in the elimination of all enemy combatants. Sergeant Machado then contacted evacuation helicopters and transported the friendly casualties to a landing zone 1000 meters away. Refusing to seek treatment for his own wounds, Sergeant Machado steadfastly held his position providing protection for his fellow Marines until the responding support elements safely evacuated the patrol area. By his decisive actions, bold initiative, and complete dedication to duty, Sergeant Machado reflected great credit upon himself and upheld the highest traditions of the Marine Corps and of the United States Naval Service.

At the award ceremony, Machado received heartfelt thanks from Gunnery Sergeant Michael Scotton and newly promoted Sergeant Emilio Sanchez, both of whom recovered from their wounds and returned to full duty.

On June 6, 2005, JoJo received a letter from the Veterans Administration regarding the application for full disability due to injuries suffered in combat. JoJo looked at the envelope, opened it a skimmed through it.

Sergeant (Retired) Anthony Machado

United States Marine Corps

101 Third Street

Apartment 21

East Providence, RI 02914

RE: Claim 564573USMC-2004, Application for Disability Eligibility

Dear Sergeant Machado,

Review of your application is complete, and the result of this inquiry is as follows. Per the requirements set forth in applicable Federal Statutes and Department of Veterans Affairs Regulations, all requests for determination of disability eligibility must meet stringent requirements...

JoJo did not understand most of it. He tried to read it all but only caught part of it. The last part read,

Review of the medical reports indicates the injury contributed to, but did not cause, the current diminished cognitive brain functionality.

A review of the petitioner's prior medical history indicates the primary cause of the condition was pre-natal alcohol and drug use by the birth mother commonly identified as Fetal Alcohol Syndrome. This

condition indicated by a progressive, long-term, deterioration of brain and cognitive functionality.

The injury suffered aboard the helicopter exacerbated, but did not cause, the condition.

Determination:

It is the determination of this agency that the petitioner's request for a 100% disability is denied, and the petitioner is designated as 20% disabled.

Petitioner is eligible for the applicable disability payments based on this designation retroactive to the date of discharge from the United States Marine Corps. Enclosed is a check in the amount calculated from the date of eligibility to the end of the current month. Subsequent disability payments will be sent to the address on record on the 1st of each month.

The decision may be appealed by filing the appropriate documentation with the Veteran's Administration with 90 days of this notice.

JoJo cashed the check and threw away the letter.

5: *A Time to Kill*

To everything, there is a season... a time to kill, and a time to heal; a time to break down, and a time to build up. Ecclesiastes 3-1

It is unnatural to kill, despite our human propensity for it.

One of nature's great mysteries is why we evolved to be so efficient at something that can haunt us.

March 15, 2006 started in the usual way for East Providence Police Sergeant Josh Williams, an early-morning 5k run, followed by breakfast at Julie's Kitchen in Riverside Square, and then picking up his partner, Lieutenant Christine "Swiss Cheeks" Hamlin.

Christine Hamlin, born into a well-to-do family in Rumford, RI on June 25, 1952 in the midst of the Korean War, was not your typical cop.

Her father was a major corporate adviser on several Boards of Directors for companies with significant military contracts. Warfare had enriched Chris's life.

Chris went to the Wheeler School. Her parents wanted her to go on to a quality college where she would engage in some esoteric educational pursuit, marry a man of proper upbringing, and provide several grandchildren. Chris wanted to go to medical school. Her parents thought this a waste of money. Chris enrolled in a two-year Registered Nurse program.

Furthering her quest for independence, she joined the United States Air Force. Assigned to Viet Nam, accompanying casualties back to the U.S., she soon realized that neither medicine, nor the military, was the career for her.

Honorably discharged from the Air Force, Chris looked around for a civilian job. She saw a recruitment notice for Police Officers with the City of East Providence and filed her application. Accepted into the Academy, due to pressures that Police Departments hire more females, she graduated at the top of her class. Most of the other recruits, all males, attributed this success to everything except dedication, intelligence, and ability.

"Morning, Cheeks."

"That's Lieutenant to you, smart ass."

"Sorry," sitting ramrod rigid in the car, "good morning, Lieutenant Cheeks, Sir, or Ma'am or whatever the hell gender you really are."

"You know, smart ass, I could always reassign you to Cunts and Runts."

"Bullshit, who else would put up with your mood swings, hot flashes, and whining about how much you hate whatever poor sap you've convinced to sleep with you lately? It is a guy, right, or are you changing teams to open more possibilities?"

Detective Lieutenant Chris "Swiss Cheeks" Hamlin was 54 years old, with thirty years on the job. She had survived the days of "what kind of broad wants to be a cop?"

It took time and balls.

She bore three compounding burdens when she joined the department. She was female. She was pretty, and she was intelligent. Most men dislike smart women. They feel threatened. Most assume attractive women succeed only because of their sexual appeal. It is genetic. Chris's mere presence reminded them of these weaknesses.

She made her mark on the department early on. All she needed to do was kill two armed robbery suspects holding a 14-year-old girl hostage. Shooting both while they were distracted. She managed this, despite being shot in the ass by an enthusiastic, but poorly disciplined, Patrol Officer.

The Officer suffered a premature discharge. The round ricocheted off the ground, dispersing most of its energy, went in one side of Chris's ass, fragmented into pieces, and exited the other side, Creating several holes in both cheeks.

As the two bad guys flinched and looked towards the source of the sound; Chris took that moment to aim and fire. She made her kills.

Earning her the irreverent nickname, 'Swiss Cheeks' and acceptance on the department.

Chris then went to her knees, screaming. She started crawling towards the officer, who compounded the error by trying to approach her and apologize.

Chris threatened to emasculate him with her bare hands. Some of the cops entertained the idea of holding off the rescue guys to see if she would actually do it, but wiser heads prevailed. Nonetheless, her legend made.

That is the way it is with Cops. One unlucky call, one moment, as long as they survive, defines them.

The unlucky Officer, from that point on, known as 'Swiss Cheek's Butt Boy.'

Josh headed towards the station.

"You are so damn funny. I don't understand why you don't have your own comedy series. Drive to the station, let's pick up the evidence and get to Court."

"Why the hell are we wasting our time on this, it's a freaking sale of Alcohol to a Minor, there's not going to be a trial. That idiot won't spend money on a lawyer, let's just go there, and file the charge. What's the big deal?"

"Josh, why are you trying to avoid this, you've been bitching about it since the subpoena was served, is there something you need to share?"

"Well, now that you mention it, we already drank the evidence."

"What the hell are you talking about?"

"Remember last month after we hit that house for the stolen guns? You said, and I emphasize you, 'I need a beer, go get me some'. Like all of your instructions, I took that to heart as a lawful command."

"Yeah? And I don't like where this is going."

"Well, in order to save the city money, and being environmentally conscientious not wasting gas driving to the liquor store, I just grabbed the six-pack out of the refrigerator in the back room. It happens to be the one scheduled to be in court today. I never expected to go to trial. We throw the shit away all the time, well, at least the cheap shit."

Smiling his best altar boy look.

"You fucking lazy, dumb ass, nitwit. Didn't we agree to stop drinking stuff that has goddamn chain of custody tags on them? Didn't we? Okay ace, go buy another six pack, and let's hope we don't need it."

6: *March 15, 2006, 4:00PM*

On the drive back, Chris said, "Josh, I swear to god, if I didn't like you so much, I'd find a way to put you in Traffic or School Resource Officer or something. I cannot believe you did that."

"Did what?" he smiled. "You told me to buy another six pack. I did! The case settled right?"

"Settled? The six-pack was cold with a freaking receipt stuck to it, dated today, for Christ's sake."

"Cheeks, I did not lie. The esteemed member of the bar asked me, 'Is this the same beer you seized on the night of the incident?' I can answer that honestly, it was, in fact, the same beer...Becks."

"You know what he meant."

"No, I do not. Who am I to infer or interpret? I answer the question asked, using the common American version of English, with all its nuances and hidden meanings. I truthfully answered his question."

"How the fuck do you lie with a straight face?"

"I beg to differ. I did not lie. I answered the question. Shame on him for not phrasing it properly."

"Josh, this is going to bite you in the ass someday, how can you not know that?"

"Years of practice, Cheeks. And wait a minute, you like me?"

"Not at the moment, ass-wipe. Josh you're a good cop, don't get caught up over stupid shit."

"Cheeks, I appreciate the concern, but you and I both know this is a big fucking game, sometimes we win, sometimes they win, but the one sad fucking truth is, the lawyers always get paid. That's why the able counsel for the defense in this case will be paying our bar bill later..."

7: Sergeant Josh Williams

Josh Williams was born on July 25, 1972 in Cumberland, Rhode Island

He had many friends, but no one closer than Charles Akerley. Josh and Charley were together almost all the time, from the moment they got up in the morning until they went to sleep.

Josh and Charley grew up together from the G.I. Joe stages through the discovery of girls and beer. Charley was the charmer, using his looks and charisma to talk many young girls out of their jeans. Josh was shy and reserved and settled for those rejected by Charley as 'two-baggers.'

Josh found himself awkward around girls; often exaggerating his exploits to Charley, so he would not have to listen to him. He and Charley graduated from Cumberland High School in June 1990.

Charley originally wanted to join the army, but one of his unprotected sexual exploits proved fruitful, so he got married, and joined the working class.

Josh had other plans and never looked back. Accepted at Providence College, he spent most of the first semester at Billy's cafe instead of the library, and decided to join the United States Air Force after a rather somber review of a spate of questionable decisions.

****

September 1990

Instead of his Intro to Calculus class, Josh was sitting at the bar of Billy's Café. It occurred to him that perhaps it was time for a change.

Josh headed out to his car. Heading onto Route 146 North, he decided he needed some fatherly advice, however, not from his father.

He knew that answer.

Jumping off at the Washington Highway exit, Josh headed into the Albion section of Lincoln. Josh knew John Flanagan would be at Lillie's Lounge.

Josh would catch him as he was on his first Scotch, before the Viet Nam, Marine Corps, or any other of Flanagan's fables began. Flanagan did two tours in Viet Nam. He served six years in the Marine Corps. Josh heard the stories so many times he could tell them himself.

Josh's father was also a Marine. He developed a comfort level with the stories, the nightmares, and the need to tell someone.

As a small boy, Josh listened in terror, as his own father relived in his nightmares, terrors of the jungles, ones that earned Silver Star, two Bronze Stars, and three Purple Hearts. There were many.

As Josh got older, nine or ten, he would try to help as his mother held his father while he thrashed, screamed, cried, begged, called out names of the dead, until collapsing in exhaustion. Now this has a name, then it was just a family's private burden.

Josh arrived and went inside. Flanagan was, as expected, on his first Scotch. "Isn't this special?" Flanagan said. "The wannabe doctor has seen it fit to visit with us little people. Give me only un-begotten son a beer, Jerry, he looks so educated, doesn't he?"

Josh smiled; he knew better than to challenge Flanagan in the belittling game. "I think I'd like to try one of those Dewar's and water you are so fond of."

Sometimes the road to perdition starts with an enjoyable indulgence. Oft times the path conceals itself.

Flanagan smiled and asked, "What's the problem now, Josh? Girlfriend dump you? Dog died? Got a grade lower than an A on a test?"

"I haven't been going to classes. I am so far behind the best I could end up with is academic probation just to stay in the school."

"Hmm," Flanagan picked up the Scotch, pointed at the glass, "there are no solutions here, my boy, just more questions. Maybe a change of course, so to speak, is in order."

Josh picked up his own Scotch, took a drink. "Not bad, I like it."

Flanagan put the drink down, looking at Josh. "You have choices, good ones, bad ones, and ones that can go either way. I have taken them all. No one can tell you the way, sometimes it is not evident until years later. Only you can figure that out."

Josh sipped the Scotch again "You know, fuck it, it. I'll join the Corps and see where that takes me."

Flanagan smiled. "I will tell you where that will take you, Parris Island and not much further. Look, Josh, I love the Corps. If we were in a war like the ones your uncle, father, and I fought I would say go for it. In war, you want to be with the best. All you need is a little discipline in your life, maybe the Corps will do that, or maybe it will take away that desire to learn, to be something."

Josh finished the Scotch and ordered another round.

Jerry glanced at Flanagan, who nodded in consent, and then made the drinks.

Putting his arm around him, Flanagan said, "Josh, it took me five years before I would have a second Scotch at one sitting. It will hurt if you lack experience, go slowly kid, go slowly."

Josh smiled back. "Look I know my limits, I can handle it…"

Flanagan put up his hands and said, "Kid, you haven't even mastered puberty yet, let alone found your limits. Hell, I haven't found mine yet. Jerry here fought in the Civil War for chrissakes and he hasn't even found his limit. Just be careful and don't let youthful exuberance take you places you aren't ready to go."

Josh nodded, "Thanks John. I know you've been around, hell that is why I came here. I will think about it." Looking behind the bar he said, "Hey Jerry, when you were fighting with the Confederates did you get to meet General Lee?"

Flanagan laughed. Jerry shook his head and sighed, "oh great, an up up-and-coming Flanagan, just what this place needs."

Flanagan then launched into an explanation how the US Marine Corps could have single-handedly won the war in Vietnam if the politicians had just taken the chains off.

Josh pretended to listen, but was lost in his own thoughts. The adrenaline from all of these questions running through his head was wearing off. He decided to leave.

Josh stood up, wobbled a bit, regained his balance before anyone noticed, and said goodnight to everyone. Walking outside he started towards the front lot, realized the car was in the back lot, and walked there.

No car.

What the hell, he thought. I parked it right here like I always do.

A memory flashed by, white truck in his favorite spot. He went back to the front lot, hmm, Flanagan was not lying. Scotch is powerful stuff.

Finding the car, he jumped in, took a deep breath, and pulled out onto Albion road. He headed towards the bridge over the Blackstone River. He almost went the wrong way at the rotary, recovered, and continued to the bridge.

The weather in September can be deceptive, warm and sunny during the day, dropping off to that damp cold sometimes worse than winter. Wet roads, particularly bridges, freeze suddenly. This month was unusually rainy and cold.

The front wheels crossed over from the roadway to the metal bridge structure. Josh could feel control slipping away. As the rear wheels caught, the momentum forced the front of the car to the right, Josh steered into the skid, somewhat recovered control, then made one of those decisions that hindsight revealed as wrong.

Deceived by the car moving in a straight line, Josh stepped on the accelerator in an attempt to get the car off the bridge.

He succeeded, and failed.

The car gained additional momentum, came off the bridge surface, hydroplaned on the wet roadway, and collided with a huge oak tree at the corner where the road went to the right, and Josh did not.

Josh's head hit the steering wheel, opening up a nasty gash above his right eye. Head wounds bleed a lot. They always looked worse than they were. This looked fatal.

A car came by, and an older couple got out. "Oh my god," the woman yelled, "Harry, go call for a rescue." She came over to Josh and put a scarf onto his head trying to slow the bleeding.

A moment later, Josh could hear sirens, and then looked up to see the face of Flanagan staring at him.

"Okay, kid, lesson learned I hope, let's stop this bleeding and get you fixed up."

Rescue arrived, put a more sophisticated compress on his head, and took him to the hospital. Flanagan followed the rescue and was in the ER with him when Josh's father came in.

Edward Williams was the Town administrator in Cumberland, having retired from the Rhode Island State Police as a Captain. He was not happy.

Williams knew Flanagan from their time in Vietnam and went over to speak with him. He then went to speak with Josh. After that brief conversation, Williams talked to the attending physician, advised him that it was apparent his son had been drinking, and asked if it would be better if he were stitched up without the benefit of a painkiller; in order avoid any risk of problems due to the alcohol. The physician, also a friend of Ed Williams, agreed.

That's the thing about Rhode Island, one degree of separation.

Josh never said a word as the doctor put in 15 stitches. He knew better. He created the problem. He would bear it as well as he could.

He needed to change.

The next morning Josh and his father spoke. Josh still was not quite ready to be forthcoming about his school situation but listened as his father talked about taking responsibility for decisions and the consequences.

The repairs took six weeks. Six weeks of begging rides to school, six weeks of depending on friends to get him out of the house.

The day he got his car back, Josh received a notice from Providence College to meet with the Academic Committee. They would determine if he would continue in school.

He reverted to his old habits. Josh was an optimist, but he could fall into dark moments. He recalled reading about Winston Churchill visited by the "Black Dog."

The Black Dog was riding shotgun this day.

He headed to Lillie's Lounge. Jerry was not working, and Josh knew Flanagan was away fishing. It didn't matter. He would have one drink and head home. It was 4:30 in the afternoon.

At 7:30, Josh decided he had enough. He was slow to this realization. He headed out of the lot, down onto the bridge, right into Deja vu.

The car did not slide this time until it was almost across, but it slid nevertheless. The right front quarter of the car came into collision with the supporting bridge abutment. Josh's chest hit the steering wheel; at least there was no blood this time.

Josh got out and checked the damage. This time he bent the right fender onto the tire. He managed to pull it far enough away to drive the car.

Arriving at home, he flirted with the idea of saying the car was hit at school. However, he knew calls would be made; attendance records checked, increasingly specific questions asked. It would all come out.

His mother saw the car as he pulled in. She called Josh's father. They were separated at this point due to some indiscretions on Edward's part. Williams came over.

It was a brief encounter.

Josh withdrew from school the next morning and found the US Air Force recruiting office in Pawtucket. On October 10, 1990, Airman Josh Williams reported for Basic Training at Lackland Air Force base, San Antonio, TX.

His timing was perfect.

Upon completion of his training as a Security Police Officer, Josh was the beneficiary of a grand, all-expense paid, tour of Saudi Arabia, Bahrain, and Qatar during the first Gulf War. He spent a year with Air Force Office of Special Investigations, leaving after his second enlistment with the rank of Staff Sergeant. His work in OSI exposed him to investigative Police work and he looked to join a real police department.

During his time in Saudi Arabia, he also managed to obtain a Silver Star, breaking the cardinal rule against volunteering.

On 1 February 1991, freshly arrived newly promoted Airman First Class Josh Williams arrived at the Security Police Weapons System Security Unit, King Abdul Aziz Air Base, Saudi Arabia. Josh's first assignment, Security Alert Team, responsible for base perimeter security. The Gulf War was in full swing and combat operations out of this base were at a peak.

On 3 February 1991, while assigned as reserve SAT team, Josh saw two chopper pilots and a Flight surgeon heading towards a Medevac helicopter. The Captain came over to Josh and ordered him to contact Special Operations command. They were heading out for a downed pilot and needed a Para-rescue jumper for security. Josh did as ordered. The reply did not make the Captain happy.

"Next available PJ is thirty minutes out on an inbound aircraft, Captain."

The Captain looked at Josh, "Who's in charge here?"

Josh pointed at the Sergeant sitting in the Weapons Jeep.

The Captain went over to the Sergeant. "We need a security escort, can you spare somebody?"

"I don't know, Sir, I'd have to get clearance from my Lieutenant."

"I don't have time for this horse shit, I got a downed pilot in Indian country and I've got go get him now!"

"I'll go Sir," Josh said, "I was thinking of volunteering for PJ training, I'll go."

The Captain looked at the Sergeant, "Well?"

The Sergeant, relieved it was out of his hands, said, "Okay, Williams, go."

By the end of the mission, Josh held a better appreciation for the warnings against volunteering.

Tracking the beacon from the downed pilot, they located him quickly. As the chopper set down, they took incoming fire. The pilot yelled he was calling for a gunship; they would have to come back.

Josh could see the injured pilot and the two Iraqi soldiers trying to drive off the chopper to get to him. Josh took his weapon, jumped out, and ran to cover the man. He managed to kill one of the attackers and wound the other. Before the gunship arrived, several more Iraqis attacked them, but Josh continued to hold them off. Once the gunship made a strafing pass, the Iraqis left the area.

Josh carried the injured pilot to the Medevac chopper as it landed, loaded him in, and climbed aboard.

Back at the airbase, the Security Police Lieutenant was waiting for him. He started to lay into Josh for leaving without proper authorization. The Captain from the Medevac came over, informed the Lieutenant how foolish he would look for dressing down an Airman the Captain was recommending for a Silver Star, and then shook Josh's hand.

"Guess I picked the right one to take with me, didn't I?" he said to Josh.

"That may be Sir, but I think I've learned my lesson on volunteering."

"You did well, son, you did real well. That pilot would be dead or captured if not for you, thanks."

"You're welcome, Sir." Snapping a salute and walking towards his quarters.

Josh received the Silver Star, as promised by the Captain, and never volunteered again. Honorably discharged from the Air Force, he returned to home.

Joining the PD

After returning to Cumberland, Josh reconnected with his friend Charley, who, having become civilized, found he enjoyed domestic life.

He and his wife had two children and another on the way. He obtained an Associate's degree in Criminal Justice and joined the East Providence Police Department. Charley wanted Josh to join as well.

In true Rhode Island form, Josh told Charley he wasn't even sure where East Providence was. Charley insisted, going so far as to fill out and file an application in Josh's name.

Josh learned of this when he received a notice for the police entrance examination at the East Providence High School.

On August 21, 1998, he took the oath as a Patrolman on the East Providence Police department, quickly rising to assignments in the Flexible Patrol Unit and Narcotics Squad. He spent time with the Organized Crime Drug Enforcement Task Force, assigned to the FBI, before returning to the PD as the Special Investigations Unit assistant commander working with Lieutenant Hamlin.

Josh worked for Hamlin as a young Patrol officer when she was a Patrol Sergeant assigned as Supervisor on the midnight to eight shift. He learned a lot from her and held a great deal of respect for her. She adopted him as her special project. They made some excellent arrests together. Working as her assistant commander was a dream job for him.

The SIU consisted of Lieutenant Hamlin, Sergeant Williams, and four detectives. There was a somewhat informal organization of two teams, one led by Hamlin and one by Williams. However, that was just for purposes of administration. In essence, they worked in whatever form was necessary to accomplish their goal.

They focused on the serious cases. Assisting Major Crimes, targeting drug trafficking, burglaries, weapons, and other special projects assigned by the Chief. If it needed a focused, deliberate, concerted effort, they caught the assignment.

8: *Love and Litigation*

May 2001

Josh and Sgt. Hamlin stood outside the door of Courtroom 9, waiting for the Judge to finish the hearing. They needed a search warrant signed and Judge Bannon was the Sergeant's favorite.

He always used the same line when looking at the warrant, 'I look to see if the address is mine or the Bishop's, if not I sign it."

Cops love Judges like this.

Hamlin brought Josh along to introduce him. It was important to know the right Judges.

Hamlin said, "Alright Josh, I'll do the talking, you just listen."

Josh was not paying any attention. His focus was on a young, attractive woman having a discussion with one of the Assistant AG's.

"Hey, hey," Hamlin said, "I am talking here." She noticed his focus was elsewhere. Looking over to the two engaged in conversation, she added, ""Whoa there big fella, keep it in your shorts. She's out of your league."

"Wanna bet?" Josh smiled and walked over to the two. "Hi Jerry, and?" Smiling at the young woman and reaching out his hand.

"Oh, hi Josh," noticing Josh was ignoring him. "This is Keira Walsh with the Public Defender's office."

"Hi, Keira, Josh Williams, East Providence PD."

"Nice to meet you, Officer." Shaking his hand, "Now would you mind if we continued our conversation?"

"Not at all," Josh replied, "I'll pick you up at your office. When do you get out?" Smiling and waiting for the answer.

The assistant AG rolled his eyes.

"I meant my conversation with Jerry."

"Oh, that. Okay, but when do I pick you up?" Not the least bit put off.

"Really, I don't think it is our interest, yours or mine, to pursue this conversation. So, if you don't mind…"

"I agree this isn't the place for that. However, I know a nice place on the Hill for drinks and appetizers. Come on, what could be the harm?"

Josh noticed a slight smile on her face.

"Will you go away if I say yes?"

"Immediately," Josh answered, "but I will be there at the office waiting for you as soon as you tell me when."

"Jesus, Keira, just say you'll meet him. I need to get back to court."

Keira looked at Josh, smile growing a bit broader, "Okay, five o'clock. We can walk to the Hill from my office."

"Leaving as we speak, thanks. I am looking forward to it." Josh said, walking backwards and into Sergeant Hamlin.

"Oops, sorry Sarge."

Hamlin shook her head. "One date and you are all done."

"Wanna bet, again?" Josh laughed.

9: Setting the Stage

March 14, 2006 11:35 AM

Machado eyed the guy with Ventraglia. He wanted nothing to do with meeting new people, it always ended badly for him.

"JoJo, I got us a sweet one this time. See this here is my man CK. He hooked me into the best deal yet, so you in or what?"

"I told you, man, I'm in as long as nobody gets hurt"

"Well then my simple friend...."

"Yo, motherfucker," rising from the bench, glaring at Ventraglia, "I ain't fucking simple man, my mind's messed up, but I know what the fuck I'm doin'."

"Whoa, whoa, chill, I'm just messin' with ya. Okay listen," motioning JoJo to come closer, "we gonna rip off the Cumberland Farms on Taunton Ave."

"Rip? You mean like walk in with a gun, dude, no fucking way, I ain't in for that shit, I seen enough guns in my life."

"No, man, this is where it is so fucking sweet man, CK works there. Tomorrow there's gonna be a shit load of cash there cuz all the welfare checks is out, the owner cashes them for his customers."

"So, how the fuck we gonna do this if the owner is gonna be there? Too fucking risky man."

"Listen, the owner trusts CK. He's gonna leave at 4:00 to get his brother at the airport. CK will be there alone, with the safe open cuz he needs to get at the cash."

JoJo shook his head.

"Yo, man listen, motherfucker, all you gotta do is be the lookout; let me know if the cops come by. I will go in like it's a real robbery, he gives me the money, and off we go, gone in seconds. CK waits a few minutes to let us get the hell away from there and then calls the cops."

JoJo sat looking at Divothead and then CK. "How the fuck do you know this motherfucker won't keep some of the money and rat us out? The fucking cops never believe me so if we get jacked up we're screwed."

"Wait man, there's more. CK told me the cheap motherfucking owner never got the cameras to work so there won't be anything for the cops to look at. I told you man, this is sweet." Ventraglia glanced around nervously.

"I don't know man, the fucking cops drive by there all the time checking out the bitches hanging at Bovi's. What if one of them sees us?"

"JoJo, I got a plan for that too. Before we go in, I am gonna call 911 on a fucking hot cell phone, tell them there's a shooting at Kent Farm. All them bastards be running there to be heroes, then we hit the place. And if you see one that does come by, you give me a heads up, I hide in the back with CK until they go, and we're back on."

JoJo smirked. "Man, missing that chunk out of your head didn't mess you up none, did it? Okay, I'm cool, let's do it"

What JoJo did not know is that as close as Divothead and CK seemed, there was bad blood between them. Funny part of it was Divothead would never even remember why.

CK's boss was once the victim of a vicious assault by Divothead and friends. Spending several weeks in the hospital gives one time to think. He couldn't very well complain about being tuned-up for owing the wise guys money. But he would find a way to get back at the wannabe punk they used. Piece of shit wouldn't stand a chance without his four friends.

When he bailed his worker out, and found out whom he'd been hanging with in Intake, he saw his chance.

Divothead was about to feel the revenge of a patient man.

10: David Anthony Ventraglia

David Anthony Ventraglia, aka 'Divothead', was born in Providence, RI on October 13, 1965, the son of Anthony David "Tony D" Ventraglia and Maria Pellegrini Ventraglia.

Anthony David, whose intellectual pinnacle was the juxtaposition of his first and middle names for his son, held big plans for himself as muscle for the mob. He thought everyone feared his brutality and enormous strength. He thought himself invaluable to 'Raymond', the infamous local boss of the mob.

He thought wrong.

He disappeared when he became a liability.

Almost 20 years after he vanished, they dug up his bullet-ridden body. There were many who believed he fed the fishes, but that was in the movies, in this real mob hit they went with a less imaginative, but equally effective, hole.

This one happened to be right along the bike path in the Riverside section of East Providence. One of the two men convicted of his murder, despite the lack of a body, decided to reveal the burial spot.

The cops thought it was because he confronted his own mortality. Perhaps he believed it a form of penance. It was more likely a last grasp of a self-important ego trying to reclaim his idea of relevance.

David Anthony Ventraglia managed to survive his father's involuntary absence and his mother's death from alcohol addiction.

However, he did not survive them well.

He still dreamed of being a 'wise guy' in the tradition of the mobsters of Federal Hill, the Providence home to the local crime "family." Ventraglia hung around with the wannabes and Hollywood mobster types, acting as if it was the Providence of the 50's and 60's.

He was not very successful as a criminal genius, spending several stints in the Adult Correctional Institution. He was always on some form of parole or probation.

In the course of his criminal pursuits, he managed to acquire the nickname 'Divothead,' resulting from an unfortunate selection of a robbery victim.

Ventraglia and a friend were leaving one of the downtown bars where he portrayed himself, to the drunks and hookers, as a mobster. They noticed a guy walking alone down Empire Street and decided he was an easy mark. The associate went for the getaway car; Ventraglia stalked the victim.

As his partner pulled past and slowed down, Ventraglia ran up brandishing a small pocketknife, and said in his best intimidating voice "Give me your wallet, asshole, and all your money, now!"

Unfortunately, for Ventraglia, what he believed to be a well-dressed, helpless old guy, was not. The assessment of the target well off the mark.

The 'victim' turned out to be a retired Marine Gunnery Sergeant, in the habit of parking in an area where he did not have to pay, running to the gym for a remarkably intense work out, then walking back to the car.

The Marine was in the habit of carrying a somewhat shortened nine-iron. Just in case.

Primarily for dogs, just as effective on idiots.

Something Ventraglia failed to note and, more importantly, compensate for in his attack plan.

When the Providence Police arrived on the scene, Ventraglia was lying on the sidewalk bleeding and unconscious, a rather significant chunk of his scalp removed, still clutching the knife.

The accomplice wisely chose to leave.

At Ventraglia's arraignment on the Robbery charge, he yelled out, "I was assaulted, look at my head, I am a victim here."

The District Court Judge, reviewing the circumstances of the injury, said, "Well, next time stay away from Jar-head Golfers, they leave big divots."

The courtroom collapsed in laughter and Ventraglia became 'Divothead'.

Divothead also managed to endear himself, in a bad way, to several police departments, in particular the East Providence Police. There was a genuine battle in the EPPD Detectives Squad room over who would have the pleasure of telling David that daddy spent his final moments as a target, and the last twenty years as compost and fertilizer a mere 100 yards from the dump the Ventraglia called home.

Detective Joe McDaniel was a thirty-seven year veteran of the East Providence Police Department. Since Ventraglia caused McDaniel years of headaches with his penchant for Burglary and B&E's, McDaniel won the honor.

Detective Sergeant Edward Grady, Rhode Island State Police, the person technically assigned the Ventraglia Missing Person case, went with McDaniel. This would amount to the total effort made by the State Police to locate Ventraglia.

No one believed him missing and there were too many places to dig for mob victims.

Grady and McDaniel went to Ventraglia's apartment and knocked on the door. They saw the cardboard covering the side window move.

"What the fuck do you want?" An invisible voice yelled out indignantly.

"Hey Divothead, for once I don't have a warrant for you. Just open the door, we have news."

"Listen, you fucking dinosaur, I told you don't call me that. Why don't you and that fucking gorilla trooper go hump each other someplace?"

"David," McDaniel said in his best grandfatherly voice, "is that better? Come on out here, we don't have to come in, I have something you need to know being as it is Father's day and all."

Ventraglia came out and stood on the stairs. "Now what, did one of them bitches complain I knocked them up?"

"No, that's not it."

"I know. One of those bitches I did knock up wants more money."

"Well David, it would be nice if you did pay some child support, but that's not it either."

McDaniel was grinning ear to ear.

"Then what the fuck do you two assholes want? I ain't got time for this."

"Well David, I have grand news for you on this Father's Day." McDaniel was smiling so widely his ears were practically behind his head.

"We found your father!" McDaniel said, holding his hands to the sky, "Praise God, Daddy has been found! Can I get an Amen brother Grady?"

At this point, Sergeant Grady was reconsidering his thought about being here as a good idea.

Ventraglia staggered and sat down. "Where, where is he, where has he been?"

"Well, David, turns out he was never far from you, it's like he was watching over you all this time." McDaniel was on a roll now. "Yup, he was so close but couldn't tell you." McDaniel was enjoying this.

"I knew it, I knew it," tears welling in his eyes, Ventraglia glared at the cops. "He was hiding out so you bastards wouldn't try to turn him into a rat, I knew it. When can I see him?"

McDaniel, pausing like a dramatic Shakespearean actor and holding his hands as in prayer, said, "Ah David, ever loyal, ever faithful, ever delusional, son of long absent Anthony, yes, yes you can, you can see him just by looking at those trees lining the bike path over there and the pretty flowers as well." Gesturing towards the bike path as if pointing it out to Divothead for the first time.

Ventraglia looked up, confused. "What the fuck did you bastards do with him? If you bastards did something I will kill you all and your motherfucking families too." Ventraglia was back on his feet, fists clenched.

"David, David, please, calm down, relax. Your father has finally made a positive contribution to God's good earth. Have you not seen, not appreciated, those trees and flowers, rabbits and squirrels, creatures of all sorts along the bike path?" McDaniel grinned, took a step towards Ventraglia, backing him into the wall. "Well thanks to your heroes, nature has been feeding off your asshole father's dead body for the past twenty years. Ever since his good friends shot him and buried his fat ass over there. As a matter of fact, several thousand dogs have probably taken great relief shitting on his grave."

McDaniel stepped off the porch, turning back at the ashen Ventraglia.

Grinning and raising his hands, McDaniel backed down the walk like a political candidate leaving a rally, "Happy Fucking Father's Day."

As they got back to the car, Grady was choking on laughter, McDaniel was smiling, and Ventraglia was screaming like a maniac.

McDaniel turned to Grady "now that's how us real cops practice community policing, with sympathy and compassion at such a tragic time."

11: *March 15, 2006 4:15PM*

Ventraglia drove to Gemini Drive, calling JoJo on the cell phone from the rear lot. A short time later JoJo came and got in the car.

"You ready man?"

"Shit man, I am a fucking war hero, I'm always ready."

"Okay, the shotgun is under the seat, the shells are in the bag next to it, load it."

"Load it, what the fuck it got to be loaded for man, this is a fucking set up ain't it?"

"Yeah, but we got to act like it's real, we may have to cap a round for show, make it look better, just do it man, you remember how?"

"Fuckin A man, I could take it apart and put it back together blindfolded."

"Listen, after we do this, you can take it apart and sing the fucking Marine Corps song for all I care, just load it man."

"It is a hymn."

"What, him, what the fuck you talking about?"

"It's the Marine Corps Hymn, H Y M N, not song, what are you stupid?"

"Jesus Christ, who gives a fuck?"

Slumping into the seat, looking out the window, Machado thought *I do, or at least I did.*

Divothead drove through the back streets to get onto Pawtucket Avenue, heading north to the intersection of Warren Avenue, known as Moore's Corners.

Traffic was heavy as usual for this time of the day and he caught the red light. Divothead started to pull through the parking lot of Brook's Pharmacy to get around the light.

JoJo, his head down loading the weapon, wasn't paying attention.

"Shit!"

JoJo looked up and saw the cruiser parked in the lot.

"What the fuck man, they already know, motherfucker ratted us out. I told you not to trust that fucking greenhorn prick."

"Will you calm the fuck down, that fat motherfucker sits there all day making believe he is doing something, he only gets outta the car to drag his fat ass into Gino's for lunch. He ain't even looking at us."

Ventraglia pulled into a parking spot where he could watch the officer in the rearview mirror.

"Get out of the car, go inside, and buy something, act fucking normal."

"Act fucking normal? I am holding a fucking loaded shotgun and there's a fucking cop twenty-five feet away that would love to put a nigga notch on his belt. You act fucking normal, I am outta here."

"Listen to me JoJo, if you don't get out of the car and go in the store, that asshole might suddenly think it odd that we pulled in here and then left in the same direction. Just listen to me and go inside, here's ten bucks, buy something."

JoJo got out of the car, trying not to look at the officer, and went inside the store. He came out a few moments later and threw a paper bag on the seat.

Divothead pulled out of the lot and headed back onto Pawtucket Ave. Both of them kept glancing back to see if the cruiser moved.

It did not.

"See, just be cool man, listen to me I am a master at this. What the fuck did you buy anyway?"

"I don't know, I just grabbed the first thing I came to, toothpaste, I think."

"Toothpaste, what the fuck JoJo, look and see."

JoJo opened the bag and said, "V, A, ah, I don't know what it is man, some fuckin' tube of shit."

"Let me see that," grabbing the tube from JoJo "what the fuck man you bought Vagicil, fucking crotch rot shit. What the fuck am I gonna' do with that?"

JoJo laughed. "Yo, brush your teeth with it man, they rotten. No wonder that girl behind the counter looked at me weird," laughing to himself.

Divothead drove passed the Fire Department Station 1, turning onto Grove Avenue. JoJo kept looking back, checking and watching.

"Yo, man, stop turning around, you're making me nervous."

"Just making sure man, I am the lookout ain't I?"

Divothead drove by the store and tried to look in to see if CK was out front. He couldn't see him, so he called on the cell.

"Yo."

"Yo, ready dude?"

"Yeah, just do it, I'll be in the back at the safe, come back there."

Divothead hung up "Dude, ready to make some money?"

JoJo smiled and said, "Fuckin' A man, let's do it."

Divothead dialed 911, sealing their fate.

12: *March 15, 2006, 4:45PM*

"911 operator what it the nature of your emergency, Medical, Police, or Fire?"

"Yo, there's a dude shooting man, he shot some fuckers, uh, people."

"Where are you sir?"

"Kent Farm, man, hurry."

"Sir, Kent Farm is where, what City?"

"Yo, East Providence man, off South Broadway."

"Hold one sir"

The 911 operator connected the call to the East Providence Police & Fire Communications Center.

"East Providence Police and Fire."

"911 operator 25, I have a male on the line reporting a shooting at Kent Farm off South Broadway, go ahead sir."

"Yeah, ah, some dude is shooting man, he's on Gemini, black dude, big motherfucker, and he's got a fucking AK or something."

"Okay, stay on the line with me sir."

The dispatcher put out the call, "301, 303, 3S1 report of shots fired, Kent Farm, Gemini Drive, Black male armed with a rifle, multiple victims, respond Code 3."

"Sir, I have cars on the way, can you describe him"

Divothead smiled at JoJo and winked. He thought the female dispatcher sounded black and he could not resist himself.

"Yo, Bitch, some fucking nigger is killing white people, get over there and help."

Divothead hung up.

"Why the fuck you gotta do that man? Brothers got enough trouble with the fucking cops."

"Come on man, lighten up, just having fun fucking over them bastards for all the times they fuck with me, let's do this."

In the distance, they could hear the sirens as the cops converged on Gemini Drive. "That'll keep the bastards busy for a while; they won't even know we were here." Divothead smiled with great satisfaction.

Pulling behind the store, Divothead punched a number into the cell phone, handing it to JoJo along with a small blue dust mask. "Just push send, I put in my number. If you see any cops, just call me."

"What the fuck is the mask for man?"

"In case you have to come inside the store, JoJo. Jeez man you know this shit."

JoJo took the phone and watched Divothead put on gloves and then the mask. Divothead took the shotgun and they got out of the car. Divothead kept the shotgun along his side away from the street. They walked around to the front of the store; JoJo went to the sidewalk at the edge of the lot, trying to act normal.

Divothead went inside.

JoJo could hear the sirens as cruisers headed to Kent Farm. He looked back at the store and saw someone looking out at him from the window near the cash register. *That's strange*, he thought, *Divothead said CK would be alone*. He walked closer to get a better look.

He could see a young girl looking out. *What the fuck is going on?* As he started towards the door, he saw the girl duck down.

A moment later, he heard the first shot.

JoJo's instincts took over and he ran inside. As he came in, he saw Divothead turning towards an older male. The guy held a handgun, trying to aim at Divothead.

JoJo saw the shotgun muzzle flash and watched as the guy's head went missing in the pink spray.

He dove on top of the young girl, using his body to shield her. "Don't worry; I won't let him hurt you." He could feel her shaking, she was sobbing.

JoJo glanced over the counter and saw CK, holding a knife in his right hand, running towards Divothead.

Divothead brought the shotgun around and fired chest high into CK. The force knocked CK into the display case, bounced his body back, and he fell face down.

Once again, the all too familiar pink spray misted the air, the smell of gunpowder and blood filled the room. CK's body continued to twitch and squirm. The final dance with death.

"Get the money, JoJo."

While quick to surmise the robbery was a setup, he failed to draw the logical conclusion that there was in fact, no money.

Never had been, never would be.

JoJo came around from covering the young girl and looked at the two bodies. The owner's head was missing a significant portion of its original form. CK was squirming and twitching. JoJo knew death throes when he saw them. He had seen these many times. Still, he was in shock.

Divothead came up to the front of the store, saw the young girl cowering on the floor, and he raised the shotgun...

"What the hell are you doing? Let's go, man!"

"Yo, bitch is a witness; she'll talk to the cops."

"Man, no way, you can't do this."

Divothead aimed the shotgun, JoJo moved in front of him, grabbed the weapon, easily removing it from Ventraglia's hands, swung the butt stock, connecting solidly with the side of his partner's head.

Divothead went down to his knees, clutching his head, looking at his hands, in shock, trying to understand the blood... looking up at JoJo, "What the fuck, motherfucker, I'll fucking do you too," lunging for the shotgun.

JoJo kicked out with his right foot and put Divothead down and out.

Taking the weapon, he walked over to the girl, bent down to her. She was shaking uncontrollably.

"Run."

She did.

JoJo took the shotgun, went out the front door, as he passed the dumpster, he lifted the cover, pushing the shotgun down under the trash.

Then he ran.

13: *March 15, 2006, 4:50PM*

Interrupting the quiet of the day, three alert tones came over the radio followed by the voice of the dispatcher,

"301, 303, 3S1. Report of shots fired, Kent Farm, Gemini Drive, Black male armed with a rifle, multiple victims, respond Code 3."

"Three Lincoln One," the voice of Lieutenant Charley Ackerly came over the radio using the call sign for the shift commander.

"Three Lincoln One stand by," dispatch replied, "further info on shooter, last seen..."

The radio became a mess of unintelligible noises as several cars all tried calling at once. Then, momentary silence.

"Three Lincoln One to dispatch you stand by, I am on Gemini now and there is nothing here, nothing, got it, tell those damn cars to slow down, do you still have the caller on the line?"

"All units, from Three Lincoln One, slow down, nothing showing on Gemini. Caller hung up, Lieutenant. No other calls."

"Three Lincoln One, have two units, and only two units respond here and look around. Pull the 911 recording I'll be in the station in five minutes."

Ackerly made one more loop through the parking lots just in case. One of the marked units arrived and Ackerly pulled up alongside him.

More alert tones.

"302, 307, 3S1, Three Lincoln One " the dispatcher, one of the good ones, was rattled, "Armed Robbery , shots fired, Cumberland Farms, Taunton Ave at City Hall, witness says two people shot in the head, suspect on foot, east toward Broadway, light skinned black male, 6 foot, blue hooded sweatshirt, witness says suspect armed with sawed off shotgun."

The dispatcher paused a moment, then added, "Three Lincoln One, we are getting multiple calls on this one, suspect running towards Six Corners."

Every cop now knew the first call was bullshit; this was the real one, the other a pathetic ruse.

14: *Fate in Motion*

"Now we get to do some real work, Cheeks, and we are right there." Josh jumped on the accelerator and the car stalled. "Fucking moron city mechanics, can't they even tune a car properly?" Josh restarted the car, headed onto Grosvenor Avenue, and there he was. Josh threw the car into park and was out the door.

The guy in the hoodie saw the unmarked car for what it was and ran. It was clear he was holding something under the sweatshirt. Josh yelled into the radio for cars to move onto Grosvenor to cut him off. As he did this, he remembered all those times he told people, *Don't yell into the radio, it makes it unreadable.* Yet he continued to yell locations. Adrenaline is a compelling chemical.

The suspect seemed injured; there was a strangeness to his movements, a stiffness in one leg, and an awkward running motion.

Josh thought, *Maybe he has the shotgun down his pants?*

Nevertheless, he was still quick. They ran from John Street onto Grove Street into the parking lot. As they neared Saint Domenicks, he heard a radio broadcast of a suspect in custody. Strange how that could be since Josh was gaining on the guy and still had him in sight.

Maybe there was a second suspect? No time to think about it, his guy was right there in front of him and Josh was gaining ground.

15:   March 15, 2006, 5:00PM

As the girl ran out, she was on her cell phone calling 911, hysterical...

The dispatcher at EPPD Communications center was not having a good day.

Divothead staggered to his feet, moved unsteadily to the front door. He heard the sirens and knew he needed to get out of there. Moving to his car, he jumped in, started it, and tried to drive inconspicuously out the back lot. As he approached the road, a young, white, female, soon to be ex-employee of the store, appeared in front of him.

He reacted badly.

Instead of stopping, he jerked the wheel to the right and hit the gas pedal. While Divothead was not conscientious about vehicle maintenance, even a poorly maintained Camaro can go fast.

The car jumped the parking barrier, bouncing violently, and forcing Divothead's foot even harder onto the accelerator. The car shot across the road, T-boned a telephone pole, adding more damage to Divothead's injuries and quickly terminating his escape.

16: *March 15, 2006, 5:05PM*

The first car on the scene was Officer Donald "Straphanger" Jones. Born in New York City, he bragged that growing up in the Big Apple made him immune to violent scenes and bloodshed. He bragged nothing would bother him and, in the ways of working in a small city police department, so far managed to avoid direct contact with anything approaching what he was about to encounter.

Entering the front of the store, he came around the cashier's counter, saw chunks of skull, brain matter, blood, and proceeded to distribute his morning breakfast all over his uniform, the floor, and the freshly delivered bread in the display.

Two more officers arrived and made their way through the store, looking for suspects, and trying to avoid being hit by Straphanger's breakfast shrapnel.

Deciding no living persons, other than cops, occupied the store, they radioed the information to dispatch.

Dispatch responded that the female caller, still on the line, was behind the building and the suspect was involved in a crash.

The officers ran outside. Straphanger was not sure if yesterday's dinner was going to join in abandoning ship, so he decided to secure the crime scene from outside the front door.

As the other two officers came around the building they saw a smoking Chevy Camaro against the telephone pole, a male lying in the street, and an hysterical young girl, screaming into a cell phone, kicking the male in the head.

Running up to the girl, they pulled her away from the now whimpering male. "Hold on sweetheart, what the hell are you doing?" asked Sergeant David Harriman.

"He was going to shoot me, that guy had a rifle and was going to shoot me but the other guy stopped him," sobbing, trying to get the words out between deep breaths.

Sergeant Harriman looked at Officer Wiley, who was searching Divothead for weapons. They both started scanning the area, weapons drawn. "What other guy?"

"The black guy, he told me to run, he helped me, he saved my life," she continued sobbing and sat on the curb.

Harriman radioed for a rescue and told dispatch they had a white male suspect in custody.

Dispatch broadcast additional information that a witness saw a black male enter the store with something covering his face, when he came out he was carrying what appeared to be a rifle.

Questioning the girl, Harriman tried to get a handle on what went on.

"Okay, sweetheart, listen to me, I need you to calm down and tell me what happened, nobody can hurt you now, just tell me what happened. How many were there?"

"One, or two, I don't know I'm not sure," she replied, "but the black guy helped me, and he stopped the guy that shot Mr. Subedar and CK, from shooting me."

"Tell me what you remember from the beginning." Harriman said, putting his arm around her to calm her down.

"Okay," taking a deep breath, "I was standing behind the counter looking out the front window; I saw a black guy in a blue hoddie sweatshirt walk to the end of the parking lot and stand there."

"What was he looking at?" Harriman asked

"He kept looking up Taunton Avenue then back at the store, like he was waiting for something to happen. I think he saw me looking out and he walked towards the store. That's when the door opened and the white guy came in. He was carrying a rifle and wore a blue thing on his face. He yelled something and that's when I heard Mr. Subedar yell 'Fuck you asshole' and heard the shot."

The girl looked over at Ventraglia again and tried to kick him, Harriman grabbed her and said, "Okay sweetheart, I think you've made your point to his head, he ain't gonna be feeling too well for a long time."

"What did the black guy look like?"

"He was taller than me, I don't know, I was trying to hide."

"So you think there were two guys involved? This guy here," indicating the still moaning Divothead, "and the black guy?"

"I think so, but why would he help me? I don't know if he was part of it, but...well...I don't know. I think Mr. Subedar was expecting something to happen."

Harriman looked at Wiley. "Why would you think he was expecting something?"

"Well, CK never works at the same time as me and Mr. Subedar told me that if anything went on I was to just hide behind the counter."

"Did you ask him what he meant?"

"Yeah, he told me that he was only talking 'just in case' and that I shouldn't worry." She put her head down and wiped her eyes.

"A few minutes later CK got a call, went over and talked to Mr. Subedar. Then CK went to the back room and Mr. Subedar started doing something to the bottom of the display at the end of the magazine area, only, it was weird, he wasn't really doing anything, just sort of pretending to, that's when the white guy came in."

Over the radio, Sergeant Harriman heard the pursuit call by Josh. He tried to radio the conflicting information about the second suspect to the units involved. The channel was full of excited chatter, transmissions blocking out others.

He managed to get out some info on the subject, black male, armed with a shotgun. He tried to add that the second subject may not have been part of the robbery and possibly tried to intervene and stop it. He asked dispatch to repeat this for the pursuing officers.

His request never made it over the air.

Always at the moment when the most critical information is available, is it impossible to get it to the people that need it.

Rescue arrived and began treating Divothead.

The radio call for shots fired at the church came moments later.

17: St. Domenicks Church: 5:17PM

The suspect sprinted up the stairs and into the church. Josh radioed he was still chasing a suspect fitting the description. Entering the front door, he requested units set up a perimeter.

Churches are always shadowy, perhaps to enhance the mystery, or the fear, depending on the particular religious flavor. Saint Domenick's was no different, dark wood pews and altar, minimal lighting, dim candles illuminating the statutes.

Father Swanson, now the Pastor, heard the door open and saw JoJo run in and dive behind the altar. He recognized JoJo right away; one does not forget a face you see in your mind every night for 15 years. The nightmare of memories burned into his heart.

Father Jim partially closed the door. He watched JoJo crouch down and pull something from his sweatshirt. He could not quite make it out.

Oh my God, he thinks Father MacLoughlin is still here, or he's coming for me. Mary Mother of God why now, after all this time?

Another sound drew his attention to the front of the church. He watched Josh come in, low, fast, weapon drawn. *Thank God,* he thought, *Josh must have seen him come in. He'll stop him.*

Josh drew his Sig Sauer. The Sig has nice low light sights, fit well in his hand, and gave him the confidence needed should the opportunity arise.

At that moment, it did.

Movement.

Blue hooded head behind the altar moving toward the Sacristy.

"Stop right there you motherfucker or I will blow that fucking hood off with your black head in it."

While the language was a tool to get the guy's immediate and complete attention, Josh thought of the irony of such words directed at an individual on an altar in a Catholic Church.

Josh long ago come to see the fallacy and contradictions of organized religion. However, 6 years of CCD and Church every Sunday is a hard habit to break. He felt an ingrained discomfit with the words, spoken in anger, here on a platform many viewed as sacred.

It seems time slows down during a dramatic event; this is a misperception by the mind unaccustomed to such matters. The truth is the brain comes alive. It focuses its innate resources and power, creating a more in-depth and complete record of the activity.

The mind's ability to gather, evaluate, and record is exceptional and rarely fully used, except when facing what could be its sudden and immediate termination.

Nothing brings clarity like an unwelcome opportunity to die.

Twenty-five feet separated Josh from someone he believed shot two people.

Father Jim heard Josh yell, heard the words spoken in anger. *Why would anyone use those words in a Church?* He began to open the door, hesitated. JoJo was looking at him. *He knows I am here.*

Josh moved closer, aiming his weapon.

Father Jim saw JoJo starting to move again. *My God, he's pointing a gun.*

Then he heard the voice, it sounded older, but held the same sadness from all those many years ago...

"I tried to get him to stop, I tried to get him to stop..."JoJo's eyes pleading with him, again.

Father Jim pulled back, deeper into the sacristy.

Josh drew closer, focusing on the guy's hands. Eyes betray emotion, falsehood, and fear. Hands will kill you. Looks cannot kill, trigger fingers do. The guy, looking from Josh to the sacristy, perhaps measuring his chances of making it out of there without being shot. He was talking, but Josh could not make it out.

Was there someone else there? Josh wondered.

He looked at the guy's legs, one bent in the classic sniper crawl, knee angled away from the body, sliding him forward, and the other straight back with the foot trying to contribute to the motion. "Which part of don't move motherfucker aren't you getting, asshole?" Josh yelled again, "stop moving now or you are a dead man."

The guy slowed his movement.

Josh came closer.

Something was wrong, *where were his hands, where the fuck were his hands?*

Josh saw a flash of metal moving from under the guy's leg.

Look for the hands, the hands will hurt you. Look for the hands. He thought.

He saw the hand moving, holding something, lifting it towards him, the body twisting as it rose off the floor.

Josh heard the voice, clearer, pleading, almost sobbing.

"I tried to get him to stop; I tried to get him to stop."

The man was crying.

Father Jim closed the door.

The click of the latch echoed throughout the church, Jim's mind flashed back to an earlier evil.

The noise startled Josh.

Was it a misfire? Is he trying to fire the weapon, why the fuck won't he stop moving?

Josh looked through the sites and brought his aim to center mass.

There comes a time in every potentially fatal encounter, when the instinct to survive asserts itself. Potentiality replaced by inevitability. The decision made; all that remains is the mechanics of the process.

Josh aimed, took a breath, and squeezed. Thirteen pounds of trigger pull is all it takes for the first round, less for the next ones.

Josh fired three rounds, saw the impact, saw the involuntary jerk of the body, saw the pink spray from the round that hit the head, smelled the powder burn, and the blood.

Father Jim heard the yelling…and then shots.

"I tried to get him to stop." JoJo's plaintive last words directed to Josh, before he stopped moving.

Father Jim opened the door a bit and looked out. He saw Josh leaning over JoJo, trying to stop the bleeding, and doing CPR. He could hear Josh yelling, "Don't you die, don't do that to me…"

Father Jim once again did what he did on that terrible night so long ago. He quietly walked back into the residence and waited for them to come find him, where he would deny knowing or seeing anything. For this, he knew there was no absolution.

Chris Hamlin came running in.

"Josh, Josh!" she yelled.

As she moved closer, she saw Josh leaning over the guy. *What the hell was he doing?* She thought.

She yelled, "Josh, what the fuck are you do..."

Then she heard him.

"Don't you die, don't you do that to me."

She realized he was doing CPR, trying to save the guy.

As she got closer, she saw the dark, blood pool under the hood, saw the shattered right side of the head, saw the bubbles in the chest with each of the compressions.

"Josh, Josh, stop, stop," she touched his shoulder, "he's gone."

"Why the fuck did he do that, why did he make me shoot him?" Josh was yelling, "I told him to stop, I tried to get him to stop...."

Echoing JoJo's last words.

"It's okay, it's okay. You had no choice, come on with me, let's go outside."

Several other officers arrived and started securing the scene.

A cell phone rang.

The officers looked at the body, at the cell phone in JoJo's hand.

They looked towards Josh and then turned away, trying to look busy.

Chris took Josh outside and sat on the front stairs. "Look at me," she said, "you did what you had to do, you had no choice, he shot two people, he would have shot you, it's okay, you'll be okay."

Sergeant Adam Stevenson, Internal affairs, came over to Hamlin. "L T, can I talk to you for a moment?"

"It can wait until the shooting team gets here. I want to stay with Josh."

"No, L T, it can't wait."

"Josh," she said gently, "I will be right back."

Josh continued to stare off into the sky, shaking his head.

When they moved a distance away, Stevenson asked, "Did you see a weapon in there?"

Chris was angry. "You fucking leech, you haven't been here thirty seconds and you want to fuck him over? He just killed someone for God's sake, show some compassion."

Stevenson glanced over at Josh.

"We have another guy in custody, but no weapon yet, and he has a major fucking fracture in his skull."

"Good," Chris said, "I'd open the prick up myself if he was here."

Stevenson continued, "There's more, the witness says he," motioning his head toward the church, "may have tried to stop the robbery."

Chris looked at Stevenson, confused. "What the hell are you talking about?"

"Lieutenant," Stevenson said, "according to the witness, the guy in the church, the one Josh just shot, tried to stop the robbery; he clocked the guy we have in custody with the shotgun."

Chris could not quite get her mind around this. How could this be?

****

I always knew it would come to this.

No matter how I tried, I cannot break the hold, no escape.

I went halfway around the world only to die 100 yards from where I grew up.

Williams was only the instrument of my demise, not the cause.

Why don't they ask me, look into my heart, past the physical damage, look what I did.

I was wrong, I knew it was wrong, but I did a good thing. I have done many good things.

But not enough.

I do not hate him; I believe he thought he was right. Maybe, just maybe, he should have given me the benefit of the doubt.

Then we would both be better off.

Or would we?

****

18:   Revelations

Sergeant Harriman called for a female officer to transport the witness to the station for a statement.

Her name was Cheryan Pincince, age 17, the niece of Mustafa Subedar's girlfriend. He instructed the officer to contact the girl's parents and get them into the station as soon as possible. Whatever happened here was no ordinary robbery.

Bureau of Criminal Identification, known as BCI, arrived at the store. They were now dealing with two shooting scenes, three homicides, one officer involved shooting, and a related car accident. Sneaking out early was out.

Detective Frank Mooney and Detective Lieutenant Mark "Dad" Pereira held fifty years collectively processing crime scenes. Thirty-two of the years belonged to Pereira. He grew into the nickname "Dad" since he was old enough to be every Officer's father, with the exception of Joe McDaniel.

Sergeant Harriman gave the detectives details, two dead, victims of an intense, life altering, experience with the business end of a shotgun. He did not recall seeing any expended shell casings, but one of the shooters was lying next to a semi-automatic handgun.

Harriman also told the detectives of the unusual account by the clerk, making them aware this was a strange one.

As they gathered their equipment, they could not help but notice a pasty-white looking Straphanger Jones leaning against the dumpster. Nor could they ignore him.

"Hey, Straphanger, they tell me you added some color to my crime scene in there, what the fuck is wrong with you man?" Det. Mooney loved to torture cops with weak stomachs.

"Fu...ahh..fu....ah, shit, fuck you, Mooney." Jones again convulsed with dry heaves.

"Jesus Christ, Strap, get a grip, it happens to a lot of guys, right LT?" Smiling at Lieutenant Pereira.

"Oh, yeah, sure," shaking his head. "I would not give my breakfast back to no body. Get it? No Body." Pereira laughed. "Hey Strap, I think I see a piece of bacon on your shoe." Causing a new wave of dry heaves.

Mooney walked over to the still distressed officer. "I think you need a new nickname there, Strap. How about Yak Man?" laughing as he starting photographing the outside area.

The Detectives began documenting the scene, chuckling at the various sounds emanating from outside.

Pereira stuck his head out the door, "When you're done doing the worm dance over there, make yourself useful. Check around the perimeter and the dumpster, maybe we'll get lucky and the asshole will have dropped his driver's license."

Lieutenant Perreira smiled and shook his head, *What's the world coming to when a cop can't appreciate a good shotgun blast to the skull?*

Pereira began video imaging the scene inside the store. Near the front counter, he could see blood on the floor. Next to this area was a small blue dust mask, torn strap, blood spatter on the strap and inside of the mask.

Moving into the main area, Pereira saw a male victim, dark skin tone, perhaps of Middle Eastern descent, lying partially on his left side, right arm at a forty-five degree angle to the body with the hand resting on a blue steel, small frame, semi-automatic handgun.

The hammer on the weapon was cocked, the magazine was in place, and there was a single shell casing lying just behind the victim. Pereira guessed it was a nine millimeter, but that could wait.

The top of the victim's skull was missing from a point just above the eyebrows to the point just prior to curve in the back of the skull. Fragments of the skull, brain, skin, and blood were sprayed against the inside wall of the store.

Moving towards the back of the store, Pereira found the second victim. This was a young, white, male, perhaps twenty-one or twenty-two years old. He was lying face down, the left arm curled underneath the body, the right arm extended with the hand clutching a four-inch locking blade knife. The body surrounded by a pool of blood in various stages of coagulation. The body appeared intact with the exception of an approximately baseball sized exit wound just below the shoulder blade. The wound was asymmetrical, with various tissues, rib fragments, and viscera evident.

There was assorted tissue and blood spatter on the floor, display counters, and wall behind the victim. Pereira shot the last of the initial video and motioned for Mooney to start collecting the evidence.

While the BCI detectives worked inside, Straphanger Jones sufficiently recovered, or run out of undigested food, to make himself useful. As he walked around the front of the store, he saw the blue dust mask lying next to the dumpster. His initial reaction was to ignore it, but then it occurred to him it seemed an odd place for such an item.

Opening the cover of the dumpster, he peered inside. As he looked over the edge, Lt. Pereira came out of the store to get some additional equipment. Jones looked into the dumpster, saw a barrel of a shotgun pointed up in his general direction, and screamed. He dove to the ground, directly into the various piles of vomit he so fortuitously placed there.

Pereira, intrigued by this, walked over to capture the still screaming Jones on video.

"He's in there, he's in there." Jones was yelling. "He pointed the shotgun at me." Swimming vigorously towards Taunton Avenue.

Pereira lifted the cover on the dumpster, saw a shotgun absent a critical component for being considered imminently dangerous, namely a person with a trigger finger. He continued to video Jones while trying to think of the most appropriate soundtrack to select for what was sure to be a sensation at the next cop party.

19: All the Right Things

The next few hours were a blur to Josh.

He kept playing it over in his mind.

I saw the gun. I heard the misfire.

The guy kept moving, wouldn't listen to me.

How could this be?

I thought it was a gun. The guy pointed it at me, didn't he?

There was no gun. Josh knew that now. Knew it was a cell phone.

Josh began to have doubts.

Did he screw up? Did he kill an innocent person? What the fuck is going on?

Chris Hamlin came in with Josh's wife, Keira. She embraced her husband and looked him over. "Josh" she said softly "it's alright, you're okay, and that's all that matters."

"What the hell does that mean," Josh exploded "that's all that matters, you think I fucked up? You think I shot one of your innocent victims of police brutality?"

Chris was confused. *What the hell was happening with these two?*

Keira Walsh Williams was thirty-four years old with a Boston College Law JD and successful practice as a Criminal Defense lawyer. She did volunteer work for the Innocence Project.

You could not find two more diametrically opposed people then Josh and Keira, but they were together three years. They seemed happy. She avoided cases involving her husband's department and it seemed to work.

Yet Josh was angry, borderline crazy, glaring, fists clenched.

Chris walked between them. "Keira, give me a minute with him it's been a tough morning."

Keira turned, looked back, "Fuck you," and walked out.

"That would be a fucking change wouldn't it, you fucking bitch."

Chris reached out and slapped Josh. No idea where it came from except she knew she hated that word.

Josh looked her, shocked "What the fuck, Cheeks...."

"Don't you ever use that word again!"

"What the fuck. Are you a nun now? Suddenly you have standards? You fuck anything that is breathing at the start of the process and now you're gonna lecture me about being fucking proper?"

Chris slapped him again and kicked out his legs. Josh looked up.

"I am going to say this one more time, I have no idea what's going on here, but I do know one thing. You will never use those words when referring to your wife again. Is that clear? If I ever hear you use that word about her again, lying on your ass will be the least of your worries. Is that clear?"

Josh started to sob.

Chris realized she made a mistake. She should have asked Josh first. There was something going she did not understand.

"Josh, I'm sorry. I thought seeing her would help."

Josh sat back down and buried his face his hands. "I don't know, I don't know." Chris sat down next to him and put her arm around him. "Talk to me Josh, maybe I can help."

20:   *Voluntary Confessions*

Joe McDaniel was tired. Ventraglia was just about broken, but he could not keep his focus on him. He worried about Josh.

More often than not, it was the cops who really cared that ate their guns. It is one of life's ironies that the type of personality that made the most compassionate and effective cops made them the most vulnerable.

Josh was one of them. He cared.

He did things right.

Did everything he could to give JoJo a chance to give up.

Unless he found a way to cope, it would eat him alive.

McDaniel found his own way; he wanted to point Josh to that. He was troubled knowing that he could not.

Nightmares are personal demons, finding their own solutions.

So he went back to doing what he did best, getting people to admit to things that they prefer to keep to themselves.

With few exceptions, everyone possessed a trigger that compelled the truth, or at least a version of it. Sometimes it was a latent guilty conscience, sometimes, a misplaced sense of accomplishment.

Often it was just weariness, McDaniel's stamina outlasting theirs.

When Ventraglia started talking, McDaniel listened dutifully and wrote it all down. He made sure Ventraglia signed the Waiver of Rights form. Another detective witnessed the signature and filed it. He made sure Ventraglia initialed each line in the statement and signed it. He offered to add or change anything Ventraglia said needed to be.

He also knew it was bullshit.

The forensics told a different story. The cloned cell phone showing the calls to Machado and 911, the shotgun traced to a B&E McDaniel knew Ventraglia committed. However, it was enough to tie the moron into a felony murder wrap.

All of which was recorded on the video camera, embedded in the wall of the interrogation room. The recording device, under lock and key in the Internal Affairs division, was inaccessible to anyone.

Anyone, that is, except Joe McDaniel.

When one has been a police officer as long as Joe McDaniel, you accumulate favors. Some of these favors cross generations.

On a cool summer evening in 1971, an East Providence Police Officer spotted two young males in the back of a closed business. Getting out of the car and approaching them, he saw one of them drop a screwdriver. The officer grabbed the kid and pushed him against the wall, as he did this the second male jumped on the officer, trying to get to his gun.

The officer, hanging onto the weapon with one hand, was fighting for his life. A patron of Bovi's came out, saw the fight, and went inside to call the station.

Joe McDaniel was the first car on the scene, running to the officer he heard him yell, "They're trying to get my gun, Joe, the fucks are trying to get the gun."

McDaniel used his blackjack on the head of the kid on the officer's back, and then took out the front teeth of the other one.

McDaniel pulled the toothless one to the ground and cuffed him. The other one was unconscious.

A month later, Joe McDaniel went to court and convinced the prosecutor to drop the charges on the youths so they could enlist in the service. They both did, served in Viet Nam, and returned to start an alarm and video surveillance company.

Flashing forward to 1985, the new police station was under construction, Joe McDaniel persuaded the owner of the company contracted to install the video cameras to provide him with a key to the system. Joe McDaniel locked many people up, but he never forgot they were human. He took care of those who made mistakes of judgment, not for any other reason but his humanity and understanding of human behavior.

The key might come in handy someday if a good cop was in trouble or justice needed some help and was about to be denied.

That day arrived.

He thanked Ventraglia for his 'honesty,' stood up, and left the room.

Sometimes a little truth is all one needs. The public defender would have to reveal all the truth to compromise the lies in the statement, which in and of itself would incriminate the son-of-a-bitch.

How is it in the trick box, asshole?

Handing the documents to the Captain of Detectives, McDaniel said "Hey Cap, we got this wrapped up, I am buying at Bovi's, see you there," and winked.

The Captain, who was in diapers while McDaniel was already on the job, nodded, put the documents in the investigative file, and left.

McDaniel went to his desk and retrieved the key.

A short while later, he returned, wearing the police issue raincoat, black side out, and a Richard Nixon mask. He entered the interrogation room and inflicted such pain on Ventraglia as to make a Gestapo interrogator cringe. Moreover, he did it without any blood, the raincoat being a protection from the relaxation of Ventraglia's bowels that often issued from these moments.

The janitor would be pissed, but not surprised, about the extra time required to clean the room.

This did not change anything, McDaniel thought. But, God help me, it felt right.

21: *Reports and Findings*

The Medical examiner's report was the usual mishmash of terminology, visceral descriptions of tissue conditions, and organ damage evaluations

Three hyper-velocity Black Talon 9mm rounds worked as advertised. One penetrating the brain, two fatally damaging the pericardium.

The skin, muscles, and bone shield the heart. The pericardium, a tough sack surrounding the heart, protects, lubricates, and holds it in its position.

When punctured, the pericardium fills with blood and compresses the heart, preventing it from performing its critical function. It causes an abrupt loss in blood pressure leading to unconsciousness and death in a few minutes.

Briefly, the M.E. concluded that the victim, Anthony Machado, aka JoJo, was a twenty-four year old, light-skinned, black male, five foot ten inches, one hundred sixty five pounds, in good general physical condition. Machado's body showed evidence of several previous significant injures including the following;

Gunshot wound with skull fracture and significant residual scarring on the left front of the head.

Muscle and surface damage to the upper left leg consistent with an explosive device injury with evidence of second and third degree burns.

Gunshot wound to the lower left abdomen.

Extensive scarring on the upper and lower back consistent with shrapnel from an explosive device.

These injuries had been treated and healed as best as could be expected considering the nature and extent of the wounds. The leg wounds causing limited mobility of the limb.

Mr. Machado died of multiple gunshot wounds to the pericardium resulting in Pericardial Tamponade.

The M.E. ruled the cause of death to be Homicide by Gunshot. It was for the Grand jury to determine whether the shooting was a justifiable homicide.

22: The Tavern

Bovi's Tavern is a landmark in the City of East Providence. Some would say it is a tired looking building, others would say it has charm. One thing is certain; it is a rarity in its longevity.

It sits at what is undoubtedly the most confusing intersection of streets in the State of Rhode Island, if not the United States. This area is known as Six Corners.

Bovi's has served generations of locals and countless others from all over the world. Monday night Big Band and Jazz tradition, begun back in the 50's, is a musical legend among aficionados and the tradition continues to this day. Portraits of the many musicians that played here, pictures of the championship softball teams, and newspaper stories of the history that is Bovi's cover the walls.

There is a distinctive, if unofficial, differentiation between the day-to-day crowd gathering after work, the late night crowds on Fridays and Saturdays, and the most interesting of all, the morning and early afternoon clientele. Each group possessed a unique character. Some were able to cross over and move between all of them; most were content with being a part of their own period, so to speak.

Throughout the saga of the Bovi's epoch, there have been legendary members of the frequent drinkers club. Some of whom are memorialized by plaques or nameplates affixed to their favorite chairs, or over the bar at their favorite spot to stand. It was for many, something for which to aspire.

Many of the customers are from the public safety services of the City of East Providence, as well as other towns, cities, state, and federal agencies, which contribute to the cosmopolitan mix that makes this place unique.

Much good-natured ribbing takes place between the cops and firefighters. All in the camaraderie of those that share an intimate view into the hell that is their workplace.

Josh Williams, Chris Hamlin, and Joe McDaniel were members of this intimate, albeit non-exclusive society.

Francis Patrick O'Malley, Gunnery Sergeant, United States Marine Corps (Ret.), was the current cornerstone of the afternoon contingent, accompanied by his loyal and faithful, if imaginary, friend. The friend bore a name that changed, sometimes daily, sometimes over two or three days, and sometimes in the middle of their conversation.

Frank O'Malley was proud of many things, one of them for being the sculptor of the divot in David Anthony Ventraglia's head.

Frank O'Malley was a creature of habit. 35 years in the Marine Corps will do that to you. He would walk in the door at 13:00 most days, except Sunday.

If it were at the beginning of his financial windfall that was his pension check, he would drink Guinness. This would go on until his budget for good beer was exhausted then he would switch to Miller, Bud, or whatever Lite. He would order his last beer at 3:30; sip this one until 4:15, rise from "his" seat, bid farewell to his imaginary friend, and head out the door.

On Sunday, he would come in at 12:15 wearing a shirt and tie, carrying a copy of the Sunday letter published at St. Domenicks.

Parishioners, and Father Jim Swanson as well, never saw Frank at Mass, yet he always held the letter and raised his first glass in a toast, in which all present were required to participate, to "the Glory of God and the United States Marine Corps."

He lived by the budget. He once made the mistake of exhausting his money prior to the deposit of the next check and forced to rely on the charity of others, he never let it happen again.

However, Francis also bore a secret. Francis loved to read. He read, and more importantly, remembered everything he read. His ability to do this won him many free drinks. He would bet he could read any article in the newspaper and recite it word for word. He never made a mistake, even after he consumed what for most would have been a week's worth of beer.

O'Malley was engaged in conversation with Jimmy the Rake, and the empty stool between them, telling one of his oft-repeated stories of his days as a Marine.

"I wish he'd come up with something new to talk about." Karen said. "I could tell all those damn Marine stories."

"Want to hear a real good Frank story?"

"Ah, I suppose, he's not gonna demonstrate farting again, is he?"

"No, a real story, a story about Frank you would never believe if I told you. Watch this." Josh paused a moment while Frank engaged in conversation with his invisible friend, then walked over to him.

"Excuse me, ah..."

"His name is Adam!"

"Ah, Adam," addressing the empty chair. "Might I have a word with Frank?" Smiling he turned and said, "Frank, tell Karen here the most romantic thing you ever did for a woman."

Frank's eyes lit up. He sat up tall and straightened his shirt. He smiled; a tear came to his eye. Taking a deep breathe, he held it as if to savor the memory, then slowly exhaled.

"Karen she was beautiful, the most beautiful woman I had ever seen. She came into the bar at 20 Water Street in East Greenwich. I haven't always hung around in Bovi's, you know."

"I know the place Frank. Did you have a date with her?"

"No, no, that's the best part. It was one of those moments, one of those times when two people, directed there by forces more compelling than anyone can imagine..." Frank paused, looking out the window, and then turned back to Karen.

"Two people, well, they connect, they look at each other and just know that this time, this moment, and this encounter would be remembered for the rest of their lives."

Karen looked at Josh. He was staring into his drink; he looked like there were tears in his eyes.

My God, their actually sharing something with me, she thought.

Frank took a long sip from his drink, finished it, put it down and looked at Josh.

"Why do you make me remember this, why do I have to feel this all over?"

"Frank, it really is one of those stories that reminds me of our humanity, Karen will understand."

"No she won't, they all break your heart...I have to leave."

"No, no Frank, next one is on the house. Please, just tell me, I want to hear."

She poured Frank a tall one, the one he only could afford for the two or three days it took him to go through his good beer budget.

"Okay," taking a deep breath, exhaling slowly, then downing half the beer, he continued.

"She sat a few seats over from me. She ordered a Chardonnay and kept looking out at the boats. I assumed she was waiting for someone."

Frank drained the beer.

"I can't do this, Josh, I have no idea why this still hurts...but...I just can't."

"Karen, give him and I another one on me."

Karen looked at Frank, saw as sad face as she had ever seen on a man, she felt sorry for him.

"Bullshit, drinks are on me. Well, symbolically anyway," pouring two more drinks for them and a special soda for herself, "Please, Frank, I want to hear this."

"Well, I am not much of a pick 'em up easy guy, but she was just so damn beautiful, I thought I'd give it one good try."

Josh bowed his head, turned, and focused on looking out the window.

Karen looked at Josh. *Was he, holy shit, is he, is he, what the fuck, he's crying, what is going on?*

"I walked over and introduced myself," Frank said, forcing Karen to look back at him.

"Hi, I'm Francis Patrick O'Malley, could I sit here and talk, we are, after all, only on this planet for a short period of time". Pausing again to take a long drink, "I know it sounds stupid but it was all I could think of...she was way out of my league, Karen."

Frank looked down into his drink for a moment, "She looked at me with the most exciting, and saddest, eyes I have ever seen."

'Please, I'd like that,' she said, 'I just brought my father's......I mean my boat in, my father died last month, and I am not sure it's tied up properly.'

"I said I'd be happy to make sure it's tied up. I know a few things about knots."

Josh turned to face them, "Of course he said that Karen, the Marine Corps is, after all, part of the Navy."

Frank glared "Yes it is asshole, the Men's department. You smart ass, fairy humping, fly-boy…"

"Stop! God, you two, I want to hear the rest of the story."

Josh turned back to the window.

Frank took another drink of his beer and smiled. "So I went out and retied the boat, I came back in and sat down. We talked for hours, we talked about everything, she was brilliant, she told me she was here to finish selling off the rest of her father's things and then she stopped and became very quiet.

I asked her what was wrong.

She said she just wanted to talk about good things. She told me she was glad I came over to talk with her, it made her feel safe.

I thought to myself, this is the first time in my life I was listening to what a woman was saying, rather than looking for clues on how to get her knickers off."

"You know I have always loved that word knickers."

"Shut the fuck up, Josh" Karen and Frank said in perfect, if unrehearsed, unison.

Josh raised his glass, lowered his head, and resumed his observations of the wrong way traffic on Taunton Ave.

"Karen, we decided to get a bottle of wine and go out to her boat, it was docked at the last slip, past the bright lights, and the sky that night was breathtaking. She started to point out constellations and stars and…Well, frankly, I was in love. I know this sounds stupid and you can't imagine this ever happened to me but it did."

Josh farted, loudly.

"I will take that drink away, you fucking pig, you asked him to tell the story, it is a wonderful story, let him continue, please, just be quiet and it is open bar for you two."

"I am sorry, I am trying to help my friend here, and I know this is hard for him, should I get my own drink?"

"Yes, dammit, get your own fucking drink; make me one for God's sake." Karen came around the bar, sat next to Frank and put her arm around his shoulder.

"Thank you, Karen, and I thank that Jewish guy with the holes in his hands, the one that brings so much comfort into this world, that you quieted my misguided, unromantic, insufferable friend over there."

Josh poured Frank another tall one, made himself a Ketel One on the rocks, and poured Karen a giant 7&7.

"Hey, I am the one that asked you to tell the tale, even I know a good story," resuming his observations of Taunton Avenue.

"Have you ever felt...well, like you have known someone forever?"

Karen put her head down and started to sob. "No, dammit, no, and I so want to..."

Frank put his arm around her, way around her, trying to fake surprise at finding her right breast in his hand....

"Frank, I want to hear this, but you can speak with a broken arm."

"Okay, Okay, I was caught up in the moment." removing the arm to a less invasive position. "We just connected, we talked, we stared at the sky, and eventually she said something that broke my heart."

"Oh, my, God, what Frank, what?"

"She looked at me and said because of what happened to her father, she went to have certain testing done...oh this is not easy..."

"Frank, it's okay. Please, just tell me...."

"Well, she said she had been diagnosed with, man, I can't believe after all this time it is so hard to say......She said her Father died of a rare form of Colorectal cancer that was so aggressive it was generally diagnosed post-mortem. She told me she was tested genetically and the markers indicated a 90% chance of developing it."

"I have to tell you I was devastated, I kept thinking here I am forty-four years-old, meeting a woman that makes me look at her as human and not just a goal for my personal sexual satisfaction, I finally meet the woman of my dreams and she, well, she tells me she is probably going to die young."

Karen began to sob.

Frank put his arm around her, careful to avoid any even slight indication of touching the wrong spot.

"Karen, the rest of the night was magic, we held each other, we kissed in a way I have never even imagined and then she finally told me what she was afraid of.....It was so silly, so simple to overcome, so minor when compared with the magic of being together."

Josh turned around, looked at Karen, and said, "As big an asshole as I can be, this is something even I cannot joke about..."

Karen looked at Josh and then back at Frank.

Frank drank from the beer, bowed his head, breathed deeply.

"Karen, she told me she was raised in a Catholic family and joined a convent when she was 18."

Frank paused again, wiping his eyes, "She had never been with a man. She took my hand, held it to her heart, and whispered, 'until now...well I never wanted to be."

"She put her arms around me, buried herself in my chest, and sobbed the words, 'now he will be doing an examination, a damn examination of my, well, my ass, and that will be my memory of my first time...'"

So, Karen, I took her in my arms, I carried her down below. She looked at me with those sad, beautiful eyes, and her clothes just fell away. I was amazed at her body, she was stunning, she was so beautiful...and then I thought...what kind of God would do this to such a beautiful person...why do we put faith in a mystical being that would inflict her with a fatal disease..." Frank paused to finish the last of the beer, waving the glass at Josh.

Josh quickly poured him another and refilled his Vodka.

"She looked to me with those eyes that said I want you, I want you to be first, I want you to be what I remember. I thought for the first time in my life about someone else before myself, how can I make this good for her, not about me, how can I make her happy...."

Karen held Frank's hand, looking through her teary eyes.

"Frank, I never knew this about you. You care. You are, well, human."

"Karen, I know I come here and talk to my friend, act the fool, and most people think I am just crazy, but there was a time when I had a moment....a moment that just changes your life...."

Karen held her glass up to Josh and shook the ice cubes in it.

"Okay, but we are splitting tips."

"In this fucking place, with Cops, Firemen, and drunks, oops sorry Frank."

"No, no, that's what I am; I have been practicing for many years. I am glad you have a whole class description for me."

"Between you and your other cop and firemen friends, the sum total of my tips is three dollars and twenty-five offers for becoming a friend with benefits."

"Frank, is she still alive, do you see her?"

"In my mind, and in my very soul, I do. She is forever there, she touched my heart, she changed me forever."

"So, what happened?"

"We went down below, we were amazing together, it was incredible, and then that one moment of clarity, when the perfect thought occurs, that one chance to do something for another human being that no one will ever be able to do again, that one chance to be unforgettable."

Karen was openly weeping.

Josh walked over to the other side of the bar and was picking out a song on the jukebox.

"So I thought, with all she's been through, all she has endured, all she gave up devoting herself as a Bride of Christ, whatever the fuck that means,....soon she faces an examination, a violation of her person that has no compassion, no feeling, no....well......love behind it"

The music on the Jukebox started.

Frank bowed his head.

"Frank," Karen said in a whisper, "what did you do?"

"Well," draining the beer, "I figured some Groin-o-cologist was gonna be sticking his finger in her ass so I rolled her over, lubed up ole Woody Johnson, and blazed the trail."

...and the music played, 'I see a Bad Moon arisin'...'

A few moments later, the owner walked in. Karen had Josh and Frank cornered, swinging a pool cue, screaming, "You fucking phony, lying pieces of shit, I am going stuff this up your ass!"

The owner, having vast experience in these matters, decided now would be a good time to go to the bank for change. Karen had everything under control. He turned around, got back in his car, and went for a long ride.

23: *Trying to Help*

The phone rang in the SIU office. "SIU, Sergeant Williams."

"Tell Hamlin to call her friend at the AG's, there's something you need to know." The line went dead.

A moment later, Hamlin came in.

"So, how's my new secretary doing? Go get me a coffee and the newspaper, and then go clean my car."

Without looking, Josh replied, "Sure, whatever you need…"

Hamlin stared, "What's this, no smart-ass reply? No fuck you Lieutenant go get your own coffee? Can it be you are housebroken?"

Josh glanced up, "Sorry, Lieutenant, I was just thinking about how long it's taking for the AG to put this in front of the Grand jury. I mean it's been 6 weeks now, I can't stand sitting here answering phones anymore."

Hamlin sat down, looking at the files on her desk for a moment, "Come on Josh you know it takes time. Want me to reach out to someone?"

"Oh yeah, I just got a call, didn't leave a name. He said tell Hamlin to call her friend at the AG's office there's something you need to know."

Hamlin, annoyed, stood. "And you were going to tell me this when?"

"I didn't think anything about it, just somebody fucking with me."

Hamlin took out her cell phone, walked over to close the office door, and made the call.

24: *Politics and Payback*

"Are you fucking kidding me? What the fuck do the Feds see in this? This is all bullshit because of that political whore Collucci. Son of a bitch wants to be a Senator and thinks this bullshit will help him. Thanks Tommy, I owe you one." Hamlin clicked off the cell.

Josh stared at Hamlin, "Now I know this day is about to go downhill, what the hell was that all about?"

Hamlin went over to his desk and sat on the corner, "The US Attorney's Office requested the shooting not be presented to the Providence County Grand jury. They're also moving to take Ventraglia as a Death Penalty case."

"And why would they do that?"

"Because that political whore of a US Attorney knows he isn't getting reappointed under a Democratic President and has decided to run for the Senate. What better way to get free press, and political capital, than by taking a witch hunt civil rights case against a cop and a death penalty case for the three murders."

Josh just shook his head.

Hamlin stood up and walked to window, "By not letting the Providence County Grand jury return a No True Bill on the shooting and putting the case before a Federal Grand jury, he gets to make a big splash on his 'Justice for Everyone' campaign. It is a slam-dunk.

The district is primarily minority, distrusting of the Police, and they tend to favor the Death Penalty. He will make it look as if he is preventing a cover-up for taking on the "code of silence," adding fuel to the fire. He charges the white cop and kills the white bad guy. As a bonus, he gets his face splashed on all the local and national news stations."

Reaching for her portable radio, "Code of silence my ass," pointing the antenna towards the office door, "you can't get some of these guys to keep their mouth shut for anything. Too busy kissing some politicians ass trying to get promoted."

Chris was fuming. "I'll tell you something else; this is payback for you locking up the Bishop's brother on that DUI. Bet you did not know this, Collucci is the Bishop's first cousin. You're getting your ass handed to you for politics and payback."

Josh got up and started towards the door.

"Where are you going?"

"For a ride, I need to sort this out."

"I am coming with you; I have some people we need to see that will help us."

"Us? Chris, I do not want you drawn into this. It's my problem, I'll think of something..."

"No, this is our problem partner. Look, I know there is all sorts of shit going on in your life. Some of it I can't help with, but this I can. You would do the same for me. Lose the martyr syndrome. Let's go talk to a defense lawyer who will bury this bullshit case. I know just the guy."

Built in 1913 in downtown Providence, The Turks Head building's iconic, Fu Manchu mustachioed, Crescent emblazoned, Turban wearing figurehead, looks out menacingly from the curved front of the building over the Financial District as if ready to pounce on unsuspecting passersby.

Josh and Chris headed into the Westminster Street entrance and up to the seventh floor. Entering the first glass doorway to the right of the elevator, no indication of the occupant other than an etched image of a hawk, a hanging bell on the doorway rang.

They came into a small, unoccupied reception area. A voice from an inner office said, "Be right out, make yourselves comfortable."

Looking around, it was apparent that comfortable was a relative term. In addition to the one desk and chair, there was one other chair covered with law books and files, a small table and lamp, and several boxes of files piled in front of a ceiling to floor bookcase jammed full of Law Books and, of all things, binders of comic books.

The phone on the receptionist's desk rang. Again, the disembodied voice said, "Would you mind answering that? Just take a message."

Josh looked at Chris, smiled, walked to the desk, and picked up the phone, "Hello, Law offices."

"Wow," a female voice replied, "Hawk found one that can use multi-syllable words. Wait, what is this? You are male. Has Hawk changed teams? Hmm, May I speak to the good barrister."

Josh answered, "He asked me to take a message."

"He?" the woman asked, "He? Don't you even know his name? Well no matter, you will not last long. My guess is you are just there while the latest bubblehead recovers from breast augmentation surgery. Tell him to call his former wife, number 3 to be precise, and tell him to please call today."

"I'd be happy to; may I have today's number?" Josh replied, smiling at Chris.

"Ah, I see. A smart ass as well. Listen to me whatever your name is. Dispense with the sarcasm, tell Mr. Bennett, that is his name, to call Mrs. Bennett the third, tell him to call today, got that?" Abruptly hanging up.

Josh saw a notepad and wrote, *Call wife number 3, you should have stopped at number 2.* Showing the note to Chris, he placed it next to the phone.

Josh sat on the corner of the desk while Chris started looking at the comic books. She pulled one from the shelf, held it up for Josh to see, 'Buxom Bombshells from Mars,' and started to leaf through it.

The voice called out from the back, "be right there." A moment later, a young woman with unearthly blonde hair, bearing a remarkable body double image of the comic book cover, proportionally at least, came into the office, and straightened her skirt. She took up a position at the desk, adjusted the nameplate that identified her as Tiffany, looked at Josh's note as if written in a foreign language, shrugged her shoulders, and put it on the corner of the desk.

She then looked at Josh, smiled, and said, "Do you have an appointment with Mr. Bennett?"

Chris walked over, took out her badge and ID and flashed them in the woman's face. "This says we don't need an appointment. Shouldn't you be in class, or homeroom, somewhere?"

The girl, now even more confused than normal, said, "My Pilates class is after work, not during work."

"Ah," replied Chris, "well, Tiffany, would you please inform Mr. Bennett that Lieutenant Hamlin and Sergeant Williams are here to see him on a very important and confidential matter. You do know what that means, right?"

"Of course I do," looking offended. "It means Mr. Bennett will close the door so if anybody comes in they won't hear you speaking to him. He closes the door all the time for this stuff .I don't listen anyway. I have things to do, you know."

"I am sure you do Tiffany, now please, let him know we are waiting."

Tiffany then went to the computer keyboard and began typing, one finger at a time.

"What are you doing?" Chris asked.

"My job, I am supposed to log in all visitors in this computer so we can track Mr. Bennett's time." Returning to screen and concentrating on trying to spell, 'lootenant', as Josh looked on amused.

Josh, smiling at this compelling interaction said, "So Tiffany how long have you been Mr. Bennett's, ah, secretary?"

She looked up, ignoring Chris, smiling at Josh. "I am not his secretary, I am his legal assistant. I went to Wentwood Technical School for Legal Assistant Professional training."

Josh said "Ah, so you are L A P certified then, hmm, impressive." Looking at Chris, "Lieutenant, this is a professional L A P certified assistant, please be respectful." Turning back to Tiffany, "Please forgive her, she studied at some small girl's school and doesn't have your level of educational credentials."

Tiffany nodded and said, "I didn't get, what was that, credentials? But I do have a certificate of completion. Mr. Bennett thinks I can get into law school someday with my experience here. Please wait and I will see if Mr. Bennett is available."

Chris looked at her and said "Tiffany, you tell Mr. Bennett that I said he is available and I am coming in there one way or the other."

Tiffany stared back towards Chris, Josh got between them and whispered, "Tif, can I call you that? Try to be understanding." Gesturing to Chris, "she is an older woman and going through the change." Winking at her.

Chris, close enough to hear this, said, "Josh, will you knock it off, we need to get in there."

Josh smiled. "Not to worry L T, my friend Tiffany is going to get us in, right?"

Tiffany nodded and went into the back office; a moment later, she came back and told them they could go in. As she passed Josh, she whispered in his ear.

As they went down the hall, Chris looked at him and asked, "What did your airhead friend say?"

Josh smiled and said, "She told me she turned up the air conditioning because she remembered when her Grandmother went through the 'change."

"You know smart ass, I am glad you find yourself so damn amusing."

25: The Hawk

Harrison "Hawk" Bennett liked to say his nickname came from his predator-like instincts evidenced by his survival of three tours in Viet Nam as a member of a Special Forces "A" team. His time in Nam earned him a Silver Star, Bronze Star, and three Purple Hearts.

Brave heart he was, but the name came from his single-minded pursuit of women.

He possessed three other important characteristics.

He was brilliant.

He was charismatic.

He did not give a shit what anyone thought.

Chris and Josh walked into the back office. On the wall was a poster of Jimi Hendrix, a Viet Cong flag bearing several holes, and a worn, faded Green Beret.

Bennett, his back to the door, was swaying to the music of Marvin Gaye's "Sexual Healing."

"Hey Chris, wanna fuck?' Bennett said, without turning around.

"I am pretty sure she wouldn't want to fuck a dinosaur like you, asshole." Josh interjected.

"You mean, my boy, again." Bennett answered.

"No, ever." Raising an eyebrow at Chris and back at Bennett "What the fuck would anyone see in you?"

Bennett, turning to look over his shoulder, said, "Hmm, Chris, is this your latest project, a retarded Neanderthal?"

Josh looked at Chris, then back at Bennett, and then saw the smile start to cross her face.

"Very fucking funny, what'd you think I was going to do come to the rescue of your dubious chastity and punch this dried up old fart?" Josh folded her arms and leaned back on Bennett's desk.

"I would encourage you, Mr. Neanderthal, to reconsider those actions. You might find yourself embarrassed." Bennett replied.

Josh just shook his head and laughed.

"No really," Bennett moved closer, "never ever underestimate someone like me."

Josh rose from the desk.

"Don't do it Josh, he is not as he appears." Chris warned.

Josh laughed, "You mean he's not a septuagenarian dinosaur? He can't even..."

Josh never saw the hands move.

Next thing he knew he was bent over the desk, arms pinned behind him, with Bennett mimicking a prison shower scene.

"What the fuck! Let me go, you motherfucker or I'll..."

"You'll what Mr. Neanderthal, teach me a lesson?" Bennett smiled. "I doubt very much I can learn anything from you right now."

"Okay Tarzan, enough with the macho man act, let him go he needs your expert legal assistance, not a lesson in humility." Chris said.

"Not until this young man expresses appropriate remorse and respect for his elders," Bennett replied.

"I'll show you respect you motherfucker, I am gonna, ouch, son of a bitch that hurts, okay, okay, you win. Can you show me how to do this?" Josh conceded.

Bennett released the hold, turned Josh around and took his hand, "it takes a big man to admit his mistake and seek guidance from those responsible for his humiliation..."

Josh interrupted "I wasn't humiliated, I was...."

Bennett resumed his prison shower motion. Josh and Chris both started laughing.

"Okay, I stand before you a humbled, humiliated, and chastised person seeking," looking at Chris. "What is it I am seeking here?"

Chris walked over to Bennett, "The US Attorney is trying to fuck Josh over in order to get elected to Congress, we're not going to let that happen are we Hawk?"

Bennett walked over to the desk, leaned back, and closed his eyes, pausing for a moment.

"Okay Josh, I don't know what you did to put yourself in the target cross-hairs of Mr. Collucci, and I don't care. That son-of-a-bitch is a boil on the ass of society and I would like nothing better than to lance it with a fucking bayonet."

"But wouldn't the bayonet hurt society's ass more than the boil?" Josh asked, smiling.

"The Neanderthal has a sense of humor, there may be hope for him yet," Bennett replied, "okay, let's go somewhere and you can tell me the story," walking to the office door. "Tiffany, get your ass in here, I need Legal assistant professional type help."

Turning back to face Josh, "I know Chris wouldn't appreciate it, but Tiff does have a nice ass, wouldn't you say?"

"Well, now that you mention it, yes she does, too bad those assets fade with age, just look at our mutual friend here," turning to Chris and smiling.

Bennett grinned, "You know I may have engaged in a bit of underestimating myself, Josh. You apparently do have some redeeming characteristics. How is it that the old broad outranks you?"

"This old broad is ready to start dealing with the problem as soon as you two new fraternity brothers are ready," Chris said, her voice climbing for emphasis.

"My, my Chris calm down, we are going to go over to Hemenway's as soon as Tiff," raising his voice and turning towards the door, "gets her ass in here and gets my car sent up."

"Why don't we just walk over?" Josh asked.

"I would, but I will be headed home right after and thought to save myself the walk back." Hawk answered.

"Well hurry the hell up will you, I ain't got all day." Chris said.

"You'll have to excuse her Hawk, may I call you that?" Josh asked

Hawk nodded.

"She's going through the change." Josh said, smiling.

"Again?" Hawk answered

"Fuck you two," Chris cursed, "I am out of here." Heading out the door, she passed Tiffany in the hallway.

Tiffany handed her a small plastic sandwich bag with several tea bags, "My grandma would make ice tea with this blend, and it helped her get through the, well you know..."

Chris entertained the idea of shoving the bag down Tiffany's throat, but reconsidered. The girl was not responsible for Josh's idiocy; she was just trying to be nice.

The three jumped into Hawk's car and headed to Hemenways.

Hawk, Chris, and Josh walked into Hemenway's, a fixture downtown. Housed in a gleaming metal and glass high-rise building surrounded by windows, it overlooked the city.

It was strategically located within walking distance of the Frank Licht Judicial Center, the Department of the Attorney General, The US Attorney's Office, the US District Federal Courthouse, numerous business and financial center offices, and Brown University. It attracted a broad spectrum of people.

At any given point in time, Judges, Prosecutors, Defense lawyers, Cops, Court clerks, Brown professors, and the occasional tourist would be at the bar or one of the tables.

The hostess came over to Hawk, wrapped him in a very enthusiastic hug, smiled as she removed his hands from her rather nice ass. Nodding toward Chris and Josh she said, "Well, I see we have some new friends of Hawk's, don't let him use the 'I forgot my wallet' routine when the check comes, he has an open account here and can well afford it."

"Ah, Miranda, you are so considerate. When will we be getting together again? I so enjoy your, ah, enthusiasm."

"Ah Hawk, you have such high and unrealized expectations. I assume you are in between spouses to cheat on so there'd be no thrill in it." Laughing and walking towards the bar, "I am safe to assume a table near the common folk is beneath your high standards. So it's the bar of course."

As they walked towards the bar, Josh looked at the view of hostess' attractive return to her duty station, "You know Hawk, I suppose your non-stop effort at screwing anything that moves, just by the number of attempts, sometimes yields success. 'Cuz it can't be your looks or personality."

"Ah, and the Neanderthal continues to amuse. Order a drink my boy and perhaps, just perhaps, I will let you in on my secret." Hawk smiled, "Chris can attest to the power of my charms, though she will deny it."

"Leave me out of this locker room banter," Chris replied.

"She has never been able to let me go," Hawk winked, "once they been Hawked, they are done"

"If you were the last person on earth I wouldn't." Chris retorted.

Hawk turned to Josh, his back to Chris, and mouthed the words, "As they age, they regret giving me up." Turning back to Chris, he continued, "such anger Chris, I know you can't forget our time together, but it's over, let me go woman, there are others with more pressing needs."

Josh was starting to get a kick out of Hawk. It wasn't often someone could rattle Chris's cage. He thought this guy must be some great lawyer for Chris to sit here and listen to this. *Unless...no, can't be...well maybe.*

Josh and Hawk jostled for the corner seat, facing the door.

While they engaged in their manly competition, Chris sat in the seat and said something to the bartender. After hearing his response, she ordered a Single Malt Scotch in a chilled down glass.

She liked it cold, but not watered down.

"I have just the thing for you." The bartender said, flirting with her.

"That remains to be seen," she retorted and turned to look as Hawk and Josh stared at her.

"Single Malt?" Hawk asked. I do not recall that being one of your drinks. You strike me as a Light beer from the bottle girl."

"Well, Pablo, the bartender's name is Pablo by the way, suggested it when I asked for the best drink in the house, since you are buying." Smiling smugly.

"I know his name, I pay his mortgage with my bar bills. Will you and Pablo be adding a room to my bill as well, or will you just mount him in the car as usual?"

"Jealousy does not become you Hawk." Turning back to watch the bartender work his magic.

Pablo returned a short time later with what appeared to be a fish bowl full of ice with the glass of single malt seated in a depression in the ice. Spending several moments extolling the virtue of this particular malt, its various aromas and flavors.

"Any Scotsman would faint at the sight of this abomination." Hawk interjected.

"And what can I get you gentlemen? My friend Chris here says you are very good friends of hers as well." Pablo smiled.

"Chardonnay," Josh said, "Cake Bread Cellars. Might as well bring the bottle."

"What's this?" Hawk asked, "the lady with a man's drink, the Neanderthal with a lady's drink, what's this world coming to? Perhaps I should have a Cosmo."

"Coming right up," Pablo replied.

"Hold on, son," Hawk commanded, "You know what I would like, a Cold River Vodka Martini, very dry, frostbite cold," shaking his head. "Did you really think I'd drink a Cosmopolitan?"

"I wouldn't have been shocked." Pablo replied, winking at Chris and heading off.

"Okay," Hawk said as he and Josh sat down, "tell me the story, from the beginning, do not leave out anything. I want to know everything you thought, saw, smelled, heard, tasted, whatever. I need for you to let me see what transpired through your eyes."

Josh took a sip of his wine, composed his thoughts, and began to relive the day.

"Chris and I were on our way back from a meeting and we heard the initial call for a shooting at Kent Farm," Josh said, relating the moments leading up to his first seeing Machado.

"...As we pulled up, I spotted a guy matching the description of the suspect running on..."

"What was that description? Why did he match it?" Hawk interrupted, "All of it Josh, all of it is critical."

"Dispatch put out the suspect was a black male, blue hooded sweatshirt, armed with a sawed-off shotgun, last seen running towards John Street. As we came down Grove, I saw him. He saw us and ran towards the Church, St. Domenick's.

I bailed out of the car and went after him. I radioed in the foot pursuit and saw him go in the front door of the church, then called for units to seal off the building, and went in after him."

"Did you see a weapon?"

"No." Josh replied, voice rising

"How do you know he saw you, did he point at you, did he stop dead in his tracks and yell 'oh lordy there's the poh-lice, I better run to church?"

"No, what the fuck Hawk, I am telling you what I did," Josh replied.

"I know that, and I am on your side, but the US Attorney is going to look for a motive that affirms his case. He wants to find evil intent on your part that you chased and shot an unarmed man.

He wants to find that reason, sweeten it up with a racial motivation. He wants you to hand him your assumption by the white cop that the running black guy is naturally guilty of something.

Moreover, at this point, you have given him a good one. You were chasing a black person that was wearing a hooded sweatshirt, no weapon visible, who ran into a church. Not a bar, not a stolen car, not a roomful of gang members, a Goddamn Church. And that's the issue at this point." Hawk started taking some notes, motioning for Josh to wait.

Josh stared for a moment. *Hawk was right. They are going to twist this into a Rodney King encounter.*

"Why didn't you wait for the other officers? Why risk going in alone?" Hawk asked.

"I thought someone might be in the church. They leave the doors open so people can go in and pray. I was worried...."

"You were worried, but you didn't know. For all you knew he could be waiting just inside the door, hoping you would follow. I am missing the tactical decision here. Why did you go in, alone, before you were certain what you were facing? For all you knew at this point he already held a hostage.

Remember, juries watch TV. On every damn TV show in the country it takes 5 seconds for a fully deployed SWAT team to surround the bad guy. That is what they expect. We have to convince them the reality is not so immediate and what you did made sense, under the circumstances, with what you knew at the time."

"He just shot two people." Josh said.

"You believed he did, now we are getting somewhere, you chased a man, fitting the description of someone involved in a double shooting. You believe he has already taken lives; you were trying to prevent him from taking others.

That makes tactical sense, the rounds have already been fired, and talking is no longer an option. See, Josh, this is what I need to know. I need to know what you thought, why you thought it, and what you did as a result. Then, I can teach the jury what they need to know to decide things from your perspective, not some Hollywood cop fiction."

Chris picked up her drink, walked over, and stood behind Josh. "Make believe I wasn't there and you were telling me the story."

Josh smiled at her. "I was thinking about Father Jim as I went up the stairs. I know he spends a lot of time in the church during the day. You can usually find him there. I was worried this guy might come upon Jim and shoot him."

Hawk face lit up "Priests may not be held in as high esteem as they once were, but, this being Rhode Island, the most Catholic state in the country, a police officer chasing a bad guy into a church to protect a Priest can help us. Go on Josh."

Josh took another drink and continued. "I went up to the front door; the middle door had just shut behind him so I decided to go in one off to the left, in case he was expecting me to follow him. I opened the door and went in fast and low, getting behind the last pew. I could hear movement and took a quick glance over the backrest. I could see movement between the seats; he was crawling towards the front. I came around on the far side as he moved onto the altar. That's when I yelled for him to stop moving."

"In those words," Hawk said sarcastically, "calm as could be?"

"No," Josh shook his head, "I yelled 'Stop right there you motherfucker or I will blow that fucking hood off with your head in it."

"Hmm, not very eloquent or grammatically correct, but it was meant for effect not to impress him I suppose." Hawk interjected, talking a drink of the martini, "Did he respond to your instructions?"

"No, he kept looking toward the door of the Sacristy and then back at me. His legs were, well, something was not right with his leg. One was bent like a sniper, the other was straight back, his foot was moving but the leg wasn't. I noticed it when he was running also. I thought he had the shotgun stuffed down his pants."

"You noticed what when he was running? Everything Josh, I need everything." Hawk said

"When I first spotted him there was an awkwardness to his movement. He was fast but one leg didn't move as fluidly as the other one did. I thought he might have tried to hide the shotgun in his pants," Josh replied.

"Josh, these little details are the critical pieces that I need to show the jury you were acting reasonably, and lawfully, based on what you knew and saw. Information discovered later, while unfortunate, is not relevant. We need them to understand the basis you relied on to make decisions. Please go on. Don't leave anything out."

"Okay, the guy wouldn't listen; he kept trying to move towards the Sacristy door. I tried to spot his hands, to see if there was a weapon. One of his hands was underneath him and the other started to come up, first towards the door and then swinging back towards me. I yelled again for him to stop moving and, ah, wait a minute, as I am going over this I can see him now, his mouth is moving, he's talking but can't quite make it out, then he says 'I tried...',but I can't hear the rest, I think the guy's a nutcase and his hand continues towards me. He has something in his hand, I think it's a gun and raise my weapon. I aim center mass on his chest. Then I hear a loud sound, metal striking metal. I think he's pulled the trigger and it misfired. I fired, two times, and waited a moment. It is known as double tap, fire two rounds, check for effect, fire again if needed. He kept moving, raising the weapon, well," pausing a moment, "what I thought was a weapon, so I fired again, hitting him in the head."

Josh put his head down and rubbed his eyes. Chris puts her arm on his shoulder.

"I hear him say 'I tried to get him to stop' then he stopped moving."

"Oh my God, why didn't I wait another moment...?" Josh voice trailed off.

"Let me see if I understood this, you fired, and then heard him say something?"

Josh was staring blankly.

"Listen, son. I have been where you are. You start adding things you found out after the fact to what the factors were leading up to your decision to fire, and you'll end up eating your gun."

Josh looked at Hawk, "After I fired, I knew I hit him. I heard him say 'I tried to get him to stop', and then he stopped moving. It happened, just like that."

"I want you to focus," Hawk continued, "What was the noise you heard? Describe it to me in more detail."

Josh raised his head, finished the glass of wine, and continued. "It sounded like I said, metal hitting metal, like a weapon misfiring as I thought at the time. Now that I think about it, it seemed to be from more behind him, echoed perhaps. This all happened in seconds so it's hard to have much detail."

"What did you do after you fired?" Hawk asked.

"Believe it or not, I tried to do CPR on him. I didn't want him to die." Josh replied. Staring into the empty glass, "Chris came in and pulled me away. She could see it was useless. A few other officers came into the church. That's when the cell phone rang, I realized then there was no weapon, or at least what was in his hand was not a weapon. I found out later the shotgun was recovered at the other scene."

"I am intrigued by this sound. What kind of a cell phone was it? Was it a flip phone? Could that have been the sound you heard?" Hawk asked, without looking up from his notes.

"No," Chris replied, "it was an I-Phone, stolen of course, no part of that moves"

"Then what, or who, made the sound? Can you compare it to anything else?" Hawk asked, motioning to Pablo for another Martini and Scotch and filling Josh's glass with the bottle.

"I don't know, it was a click, loud, as soon as I heard it I made the decision to fire, I don't know what else it could have been." Josh looked to Chris. Chris shrugged her shoulders.

Hawk rose from his seat, "I thought you two were experienced investigators. Think, boys and girls, think. Something caused that noise. It wasn't the cell phone; it wasn't a weapon…metal on metal…a click…loud…echoes…."

Josh looked up, "a door latch, it could've been a door latch, someone closing a door."

Hawk nodded, "now you're thinking like an investigator. You said the place was unlocked for people to come in. You told me Father Jim was usually there most days, I believe, was how you described his habits. Where was he this day? I think someone was there. Someone closed a door so they wouldn't be seen, or see what was happening."

Returning to his seat he continued, "We need to have a chat with Father Jim. If he was not there, perhaps he knows of someone that may have been there. I will call upon the good father tomorrow and see what I can learn."

"I'll do it," Josh said. "Jim and I have been friends for long time. He trusts me...."

"I think that is unwise, should the good Father have valuable information I do not want it tainted by the object of Mr. Collucci's affection, namely you, having any direct involvement with potential witnesses. You say you are close to Father Jim. Have you heard from him since this incident?"

Josh thought for a moment and said, "No I haven't, but it's not like he calls me all the time or anything. Just when something is going on."

Hawk looked at Chris and back at Josh, "How many times a day do you shoot someone in his church?"

26: *An Unlikely Association*

Father Jim met Josh during his brief stint as the Police Department Chaplin.

While Father Jim was Chaplin, he would come in and ride with various Officers. Most thought the idea of a Priest being on calls was a bad idea. The last thing you need is a complete and unfiltered picture of a street encounter. This despite the fact Father Jim carried his own mahogany nightstick, knew how, and was not afraid to use it.

Josh enjoyed having Father Jim along for the ride. They would discuss philosophy, religion, Yankees vs. Red Sox. Jim being a die-hard Sox fan, Josh never failing to point out the difference in the number of Championships held by the teams. The conversations were illuminating for Josh and a catharsis for Father Jim. It was Josh's version of a personal confessional, or a close as an Atheist could come to one.

There were several occasions where Father Jim considered talking to Josh about the good Bishop, but his training on the sanctity of the confessional was too overpowering. At least up to that point.

The Bishop, William James MacLoughlin, formerly the Pastor of St. Domenick's, removed Father Jim from the Chaplin's position citing more compelling Church priorities. Thus ending the ride-along program.

The common belief was it was because of EPPD locking up the good Bishop's brother, Dennis, for DUI. The Bishop, in a testament to his faith in his faith, believed denying the Officers access to a Priest would hasten their descent into hell.

Apparently the Bishop didn't believe that his brother, driving an unregistered car, after consuming ten to twelve beers and many shots of whiskey, going off the roadway, killing a 9 week-old puppy named Purdy, being walked by 7 year-old Kathleen Ackerly, in her front yard, while her smiling parents took pictures, warranted being locked up.

Perhaps, the Good Shepherd thought he could damn them forever.

Ironically, the Church's own Lawyer did a masterful job of finding an error in the complex DUI forms and secured a dismissal.

The bigger irony being the rest of the story.

The brother celebrated his good fortune with dinner and drinks at a Federal Hill restaurant paid for by the Bishop with the charity of parishioners. He managed to liberate the keys of the Diocese's Cadillac SUV from the Bishop's jacket.

On the celebratory ride to Foxwoods to rejoice in the triumph of Justice, the Cadillac's high-efficiency headlights illuminated a large deer in the roadway. The Good Shepherd's brother, suffering from the handicap of alcohol and loss of focus due to his young, female, and well-compensated compatriot's hands in his pants, overreacted, in a different, but nevertheless consistent, pattern of family behavior.

The Cadillac missed the deer, deferring for the moment the brother's bearing the burden of killing another of God's creatures.

It was a brief respite.

It rolled.

It spun.

Once the forces of gravity, friction, and momentum returned to balance, the young woman was dead in the passenger compartment holding onto an item with which she held much experience. Perhaps it provided a familiar comfort in those last moments, in spite of being unnaturally separated from its original location and no longer functional.

The Bishop's brother, if his faith was correct, at that moment was explaining himself to a higher being. If one is required to provide an inventory of all equipment issued when granted existence, he was short one.

Poetic justice, bad luck, perhaps divine intervention, it did not matter. The accident photos were the cause of great joy among the cops.

As a token of their great esteem for the Good Bishop, he received several copies of the best of the images in the mail, as a way of helping him remember his brother's many good virtues.

Father Jim and Josh Williams maintained their association in spite of the Bishop's attempts to derail it.

27: *Confidences Betrayed*

Father Jim decided he needed to do something. Unsure if there was anything that would help.

Who would best understand the need for confidentiality? The lawyer of course They have an obligation to protect their client and the attorney client privilege was as close to the sanctity of confession as it gets in the secular world.

Father Jim called, asking for the lawyer representing Machado.

"Public Defender's office," the young voice answered, "Kelsey Campbell."

"Do you represent the Machado case?"

"Machado, which Machado, we represent a couple people named Machado."

"I may be phrasing this incorrectly, the one that was shot the other day, and died."

"Ah, well if he died we can't represent him, he's dead."

"I mean, the other guy, the other one that was there, not dead."

"The one that was where? If it's the case I am thinking about, it was a police officer that shot him, we don't represent him, the city does."

"No, the other guy in the robbery, the one that did the shooting at the Cumberland Farms."

"Ah, Ventraglia, yes we represent him."

"Well, I heard what Machado said; he said 'I tried to stop him."

There was a pause and then, "Sir, could I have your name and a way to contact you? The lawyer representing Mr. Ventraglia is not here at the moment, but I am sure he will want to talk to you."

"Of course, giving the girl his number; my name is Father Jim Swanson."

"Father," pausing to figure this out, "you're a Priest?"

"I am."

"Oh, well then I am absolutely sure he'll want to speak to you, I will call him now, expect a call back within the hour."

Before Father Jim could say goodbye he heard the connection drop. Kelsey was already on the line calling Harris.

28:   *Steven Harris*

Steven Harris came to the law by an uncommon path.

He was raised in a strict Protestant household by a blue collar, union member, machinist father and a stay-at-home Mom who were less-than-embracing of academic pursuits.

"Why," his mother would say, "waste time reading about places you will never see or things you can never achieve? Better to get out of high school, let your father get you in the union, and marry that girl Sara you are always staring at in church."

Steven loved to read. He would be up to all hours of the night reading anything he could. They owned a TV but that was only for 'family' time and certain approved shows. TV was never to be on when his parents were not there, he didn't watch it anyway.

As the time came for graduation, Steven announced he was going to college.

His mother laughed, his father looked at him and said "and who do you think is going to pay for this?"

Harris excelled in college and managed to get accepted to law school. Upon graduation, he passed the bar on the first attempt and took a position with the Public Defender's office.

He would never get rich, but he found the work challenging and rewarding. He quickly developed a reputation as a tough, well-respected trial lawyer.

29: *Fun and Games*

It was supposed to be just for fun, so they thought.

Harris came out of the shower, stopped at the mirror, and examined himself.

"You are such a pussy, get away from the mirror."

"Nice talk for a Catholic girl."

"What's this, now you have religion?"

"Equal to or exceeding yours."

"Come over here, I don't like wasting the limited time we have."

They say opposites attract, this was strong nuclear force level attraction.

They were lost.

Lost in each other's pleasure.

Lost in their own.

Compelled to ignore the conflict, in order to satisfy the compulsion.

The climax of pleasure, the addiction of ecstasy, the irresistible lure of the denied, and the pull of the undeniable.

They lied to themselves and enjoyed it.

That which is denied, is often all you believe necessary for survival.

Both determined to survive.

Two normal, intelligent, rational people engaged in abnormal, irrational behavior neither one would have even considered possible.

This was one of those relationships.

Intense physicality.

Complimented and enhanced by intellectual curiosity and compatibility. Their conversations jumping from Quantum Physics, to Mozart Sonatas, to Dante's Inferno, to their exploration, page by page, of the Kama Sutra.

Attenuated by the sheer overwhelming sexuality, risking both their personal and professional lives.

It was exhilarating, invigorating, and irresistible.

It was crazy.

It was fun.

Dangerous fun.

During these encounters, they often shared things. Things best left unshared.

The problem with taking someone into your confidence is obvious. There is no protection against their taking someone else, and their taking someone else again, ad infinitum.

Lying in bed, after sharing ultimate physical intimacies, unveiling ones darkest secrets can sometime seem natural, almost contributory to the intensity of the moment.

The conversation seemed safe, secure. However, like an image posted to the net, irretrievable.

Another layer of risk, heightening the excitement.

It was the great unspoken consensus among those that spend time in courtrooms; everyone was coloring the truth to some degree.

"Never let the facts get in the way of the truth" was a common refrain, as it was the mantra of the opposing elements of our confrontational system of justice.

The cops enhancing the probable cause for the search.

The prosecutors exaggerating the sound of the magazine inserted into a weapon, the echo in courtrooms enhancing the noise, frightening the jury.

The defense weaving a tale of a sad childhood, lack of parental control, even abuse to garner sympathy for the defendant.

It would often seem the better liar wins.

Sometimes Juries find it hard to doubt the word of a police officer over a defendant with a lengthy record.

Sometimes Juries disregard the Officers' word because of bad personal experiences with other Officers.

The better liar.

When told of Josh's recent creative testimony in the case involving Sale of Alcohol to a Minor, Steve Harris added it to his reserve of things that might come in handy.

While he hoped never to use it, information like this could prove invaluable in pretrial discussions with the Attorney General's office.

They would never suspect how he came upon it, but they would worry about its veracity. Unreasonable doubt works almost as well.

Harris' cell phone rang.

"Hey, you know the rules, no answering anything that might be traceable."

"Just looking at caller ID, I am expecting some calls about the Morin case on appeal."

"Okay, then next week, I'll be looking for someone with an appreciation for this body."

"Fuck, it's the office, I told Kelsey I'd be with a witness all day, this must be important, I have to take it."

"But, he'll find out...."

It was too late. Harris answered the phone.

"Hey, Kels, what's up?"

A short pause, he glanced up, then walked into the bathroom, closing the door. "A fucking priest," trying to whisper, "you're telling me I got a call from a priest that was there? Holy shit, literally."

"Okay, listen to me, call the Priest back and ask him where I can meet him, no, no, not at the office, anywhere but there, can Priests go to bars? Just figure out something with him and call me back," walking out of the bathroom, grabbing his clothes, "I am ten minutes from the office."

"Jesus, Steve, why don't you just tell the world the fucking address and who you are here with"

"Listen to me, I have to go, this is major, nothing to do with us. Sorry, I will make it up next time, I'll give you one of my special full body massages, the one that makes you squirm."

"The only thing making me squirm now is if this gets out, we're going to be worried about some serious issues. I can't believe this, go and I will see you later, maybe."

Steve got into his 350Z and headed back towards the office. His cell rang just as he pulled into the parking lot. "Well, where is he?" Looking around the lot, not sure what he was looking for, but he was nervous about this.

Kelsey Campbell answered, "Jeez, Steve, will you calm down for Christ sake, he's not going to take your soul. Oh, wait, you have nothing to worry about as a soulless bastard lawyer."

"Point of law, my parents were married, ergo I am not, by definition, a bastard, but I am going to be a prick when I get back to the office. Remind me to give you a raise for your amazing sense of humor." Slowing to a deliberate pace, "where the fuck is my Priest?"

"Hi, excuse me, I believe I am the priest you are looking for," Father Jim said into the driver's side window. "Are you Mr. Harris?"

"Jesus Christ, you scared the fuck out of…I mean, you startled me, your… Priestness? What the f…ah, what do I call you?" A rattled Steve said as he looked at Father Jim standing next to his car.

"I was just around the corner when your secretary called my cell phone; I told her I would walk over and wait for you here. For some reason, she tried to dissuade me of this, but I did not want to be a bother." Pausing a moment.

"You can call me Jim if you like, I will act 'off-duty' and excuse myself from, what did you call it, Priestness?"

"Ah, yeah, sorry, you just, ah, I didn't expect you to be here, get in we need to find someplace private to talk."

Father Jim went around to the passenger side, opened the door, and slid into the seat. Trying to shift around the files, documents, and Steve's briefcase until he could fit his legs in.

"Sorry about the mess, Jim. I never have anyone in the car with me,"

"No problem, my office looks just like this. Speaking of which, why can't we talk in your office, your secretary sounded very pleasant, don't you trust her?"

"Kelsey? No, no she's great, I trust her, hell I already do trust her with my life, Jesus Christ," swerving around a car turning onto Waterman Avenue, "oops sorry for the language."

Trying to his maintain composure, looking for someplace they wouldn't be seen, *The cops here are pretty sharp, he thought, and if they see me talking to the Pastor of the church where this went down, they will be knocking the door down to talk to him too.*

"Don't worry about the language, I have heard it all, and thought of a few creative phrases myself. And since, technically, I work for Jesus Christ, I will just consider that a reminder of why I am here."

"And why is that, ah, Jim?" Steve looked to the priest, trying to gauge him.

"To get the truth out of course, I saw what happen, I knew Anthony, ah, JoJo I believe he is, or was, called, from a long time ago, and I saw Josh do everything he could to avoid shooting him. And I heard what he said."

Father Jim looked out the window, watching as they went onto 195 Westbound and then took the South Main and Wickenden Street exit.

"You heard what who said, Jim?" Steve asked.

"Well, both of them," Jim answered.

"Jim, would you like a beer or wine or something? I don't want to keep driving around and I need to hear the whole story."

Jim smiled, "You know, since I have shed my priest persona and official status that would be good."

"Oh yeah," Steve said "sorry about the inarticulateness of my familiarity with the proper way to address a Catholic Priest. I was raised a Protestant."

"Well, seeing as you are a Protestant and all, please tell me you have at least one redeeming characteristic." Jim looked gravely at him.

"Ah, shit, I mean, I never paid much attention to that whole church thing."

"Well, to borrow your favorite phrase, in the name of Jesus Christ at least tell me you are a Red Sox fan!"

"Oh, well, sure, of course, that's the only fan around here isn't it?" Steve replied

"Ah my son, sorry, Priests love calling people son, there are those among us that are not, the worst of them are Yankee fans, and thus unredeemable in the eyes of the Lord."

"Well, shit then, I am on my way to Angel's wings," Steve laughed.

Jim looked at him and smiled "let's reserve judgment on that for someone more qualified."

Steve parked the car and they got out. Jim, standing at the back of the car, removed his white collar and looked at Steve, "Undercover Priest, what do you think?"

"Well, you look like a waiter at a Federal Hill restaurant; I guess it's the best we can hope for." They walked over to small cafe overlooking the riverfront.

Since the Providence 'Renaissance,' the river front area was a nice place to people watch and enjoy a drink. They found an outside table and settled in.

The server came over, smiled at Steve, and asked for the drink orders.

"What will it be Father, I mean, Jim?" Steve stammered as the server tried to figure out this combination.

"Well, under the circumstances, I would like, wait, ah sorry, whose paying for this? I don't like to waste my parish..., ah, parent's money," raising the server's eyebrows another notch.

"Oh, have whatever you want, it is on me. I'll take it out of Kelsey's Christmas bonus." Smiling back at the waitress.

"Do you have Cold River Vodka?"

Waitress shook her head.

"How about another favorite of mine, Thor's Hammer? No," reacting to the continuing denial, "Okay, perhaps Ketel One? Wonderful," noting the change in the response, "on the rocks, three olives, loose in the glass, do not stab my olives, and if you have a bottle that's been kept in the freezer, as you know all vodka should, use that, please."

Steve had not met many Catholic priests but he was starting to regret the Protestant upbringing, if Jim's performance was any indication of the norm for them.

"So Jim, you said you saw and heard what happened. How? Where were you? The cops didn't list any witnesses."

"Well, this is going to be hard for me, but...well...I left." Jim looked out over the river and shook his head.

"You left? What do you mean you left? Where were you when this happened?"

Jim looked at Steve, looked down at the ground, sighed, and stood up. "Excuse me for a moment, I need to consider something, I will be right back." Jim walked over alongside the river, looking out over the water flowing by.

Steve watched as Jim stood near the wall. *What was this about? Why would a Priest have anything to do with this? He needed to be cautious, listen to what the priest knew but do not get caught up in these things.*

Jim returned and looked at Steve for a long time. Eyes troubled, he took a deep breath and said, "Will what I tell you be confidential, or more to the point, who will you tell about our conversation?"

Steve looked at Jim, he was not sure what he had, but he knew this man took things to heart. He needed to be careful how he went about this.

"Jim, I represent a man charged with three murders. Right now in State court, but there is word the US Attorney's Office may take this case, which puts the Death Penalty on the table. I have a responsibility to insure he gets a fair trial. In doing that I am compelled to look for any reasonable doubt, any errors by the police, any information that casts doubt on the guilt of my client. If you are going to tell me information that requires me to present you as a witness for my client, I am required to disclose that. If what you have is damaging to my client, I am under no obligation to turn that over. Jim, if I can use what you have, and protect you, I will. If I can't I will at least make sure you are treated fairly."

Jim looked out at the river again, back at Steve, and into a different dimension. Steve could see his mind weighing the options.

"Okay, wherever this takes me, I will let God guide me."

Jim seemed to relax, he smiled, he leaned forward, looked Steve in the eyes, and said, "Where the hell is my drink? If I am going to bare my soul, I at least deserve that to ease the way."

"Can we get those drinks?" Steve was practically standing on the table. Almost as if that is all it required, the server appeared.

She looked at Steve and said, "Your Father wanted his Vodka frozen a bit, so I stuck it in the deep freezer for 10 minutes."

"He's not my father."

"Well, technically speaking, I sort of am, for my normal purposes," Jim laughed.

"Okay, thanks, what's your name," looking at her name tag, "ah Candy, is that your real name?" Steve asked.

"Why would I make that up?"

"Ah, that is so true," replied Steve, waiting for the server to move away, smiling and waving at her every time she turned around.

"Okay, tell me what it is you saw and heard, I will do everything I can to protect you, but like you said, we are here for the truth."

"I was in the Sacristy."

"The what?" Steve interrupted "sorry, where is the, what did you call it, Sacristy?"

"The Sacristy. A room off the altar where the Priest prepares for Mass. We store our vestments, materials, various chalices, incense, and other implements used during the Mass."

Jim gave Harris everything he could remember about that day, except how he knew Anthony Machado. He hoped no one would ask.

"Jim, how well do you know Sergeant Williams?"

"Oh, oh," Jim thought.

"I was the Police Chaplin for a few years. I used to ride in the cars with different officers. I rode with Josh quite a bit, in spite of his failings."

"Failings?"

"He's one of those Yankee fans, I never understood it. He seemed to be literate," trying to inject some humor and derail the conversation track.

Harris laughed. "You really are a diehard fan aren't you?"

"That I am, Steve, that I am. Look," fishing an olive out of the drink, "that's all I know. I wanted to tell someone about this, but I was scared and embarrassed. I am not proud of what I did, but if this can help get the truth out I am ready. I know you don't represent Josh, but perhaps you could pass this on to the lawyer that is."

"Jim, I will do what I can. My first obligation is to my client, but I know the lawyer representing Josh, he is a good one. I will get him this information. Let me ask you one more thing."

Jim tried to conceal his worry, hoping it wasn't opening up his connection to Anthony.

"Of course."

"Why not go to the police with this, or to Josh? You said you spent a lot of time with him, is there something you not telling me?"

Jim shook his head, "I was hoping to just tell you and not have to be otherwise involved. I know that is not possible now. Let's just say that if I am forced to testify some other issues, unrelated to your client, or even Josh, may come out. It would be bad for the church. My god, just my actions alone that day are bad enough."

Steve finished his drink, motioned for the check, and put his notepad back in his briefcase. "Jim, thank you for telling me this. I know it was not easy. I'll give you a ride back to St. Domenicks."

"No, I'm good. I think I will walk up to Brown University and over the Henderson Bridge. I enjoy walking; it will help me sort things out."

Steve stood up and shook Jim's hand. As they turned their separate ways, neither one noticed the man along the river. Why would they? RISD students are always taking pictures of the river and downtown architecture. This camera was focusing on human subjects.

"Who is he?" Slattery asked Waters, looking over the photos.

"Father James Swanson, the pastor of Saint Domenicks Parish, East Providence."

"Hmm, not likely a coincidence."

"Nope, the good father seems to have provided something to Harris. I think we need to have a chat with him soon."

"Should we run this by Collucci?"

"No need, he brought us here to work this. I don't need his advice, or permission, to do my job."

An hour later, Father Jim was sitting in the US Attorney's office. No good deed goes unpunished.

"I do not believe I have to talk to you," Jim said.

"Well, Father, many of your beliefs are persuasive and compelling, that one is not. I can put you in front of a grand jury and force you to testify. However, I have a more subtle, yet effective tool at my disposal. Bishop MacLoughlin, your direct boss I believe, is my cousin. We grew up together. We are very close. If I bring this lack of cooperation to his attention, you will be pastor of the prison chapel. How does that sound?"

The workings of the mind always surprised Jim. Under threat, the mind proposes all sorts of solutions to the problem. Some reasoned and practical, some apocalyptic. He was also shocked that, in spite of more than twenty years as a Priest, he was entertaining one of those options.

"What is it you want to know?"

"What did you discuss with Steven Harris? What do you know about this case?" Collucci was angry.

"Suppose I were to tell you it was a private, personal matter between us. I am a Priest after all."

"Bullshit!" Collucci moved to stand in front of Jim, "Harris doesn't belong to the church. I do not buy that crap. I want to know what you told him, all of it."

Jim resigned himself to reality; he gave Collucci the whole story. Yet, he reserved the nuclear option until he saw where this led.

When he was finished, Jim looked at Waters, then back to Collucci, "might I have a word with you, privately, Mr. Collucci?"

Waters started to object, Collucci raised his hand to stop him, "of course Father, by all means. Excuse us a moment, would you Agent Waters?"

When the door closed, Collucci smiled, "You can say whatever you want here, but I can still use it if needed."

"Oh, I realize that. I was just wondering, why no one is curious about how I knew Anthony Machado?"

Collucci stared for a bit, "We know he grew up in East Providence, right near St. Domenicks. He played ball on the CYO team. Nothing startling there."

"That is true, very true. But there could be more to it; perhaps you should ask your cousin."

"Why don't you tell me instead of playing games, Father? I am done wasting time here."

"This is something you need to hear from the Bishop, so you'll believe it." Jim stood, "If we are through, I will be going."

"Father, I hope you aren't trying to turn the support of the church against me, that won't work."

"Nothing could be further from my mind," turning and walking out the door.

Collucci was not close to his cousin; Father Swanson would not know that. *Still, there was something in his tone, Collucci thought, not cocky, confidence perhaps. Well, I suppose a call couldn't hurt.*

"Yes, hello, this is Robert Collucci calling might I speak to Bishop MacLoughlin, please? Ah, I see, well when the Bishop returns would you have him give me a call. No, nothing urgent, when he gets back is fine. Have him call the US Attorney's office in Providence. What's that? Oh yes, I work there." Slamming the phone down. *How can they not know that?*

30: *The Learned and the Liar*

Keira Williams sat at her desk thinking about her life.

How had it come to this? How had they drifted apart?

She knew her work took too much time. She knew Josh's job took too much of his. Nevertheless, they always were able to compensate, always able to find a way.

It changed when Steve Harris asked her to help on the Morin appeal, and the other cases that followed.

They began spending too much time together. Josh and Steve were of the same mold, different flavors. They did not mix well. It was a dangerous situation.

Her cell phone rang. She looked at the caller ID, Steve. *He must have heard something about the First Circuit date for argument, she thought.*

She answered the phone, "Yes Steve, when do we argue?"

"Argue? We never argue, my love," the voice betraying a serious level of intoxication, "join me for a cocktail at Bovi's, we can discuss my strategy for becoming the United States Fucking Attorney General."

"Good God, Steve, how long have you been there?" Keira asked.

"Not long enough yet, my beloved, come join me, the cops are busy locking up nefarious elderly felons for possessing hallucina, hallucine, ah, shit. Come on down or I'll drive over and drag you here."

"No," Keira yelled, "don't you leave there. I am on my way; put the bartender on the phone."

"Hi Keira," Karen, the day bartender, said, "I already took the idiot's keys. Please come take him out of here, he keeps playing the same damn song over and over on the jukebox and the boys are about to kill him."

"I'll be right there, thanks." Keira ended the call and headed to her car.

A short drive later, she arrived at Six Corners and walked into Bovi's.

"Will you look at this, my friends," Harris exclaimed as he spun around with a pool cue nearly decapitating half the amused audience, "we are joined by beauty itself. How is it that Josh Williams, the illiterate cretin, won the heart of this fair creature?"

"Okay," Keira glared at the amused crowd, "which one of you assholes talked him into buying shots?"

The crowd dispersed to their normal bar positions and tried to conceal their amusement.

"Karen, come on," Keira pleaded, "I asked you not to play along with letting him buy the drinks for these assholes." Glaring at the crowd as they averted the look, still laughing.

"I know," Karen replied, "but he is so damn cute I can't resist him," looking over at Harris as he tried to smile and stop swaying.

Keira walked to the bar, her mere look creating an opening, and smiled, turning to watch Harris' attempt to move unobserved to the jukebox.

Harris, swaying less than gracefully, came back singing Marvin Gaye's "Mercy Mercy Me" for the 25th time, dancing over to Keira to the delight of the not quite humbled crowd, using the pool cue as a microphone.

"Oh, Oh mercy mercy me...ah things aren't what they used to be..."

The crowd, imbued with a new sense of bravado, joined in. The whole bar began singing.

Keira smiled, grabbed Harris' hands, and swung him to the rhythm.

As the song ended, Keira returned to her seat at the bar. "Karen, give this idiot one more and the rest of the bar as well."

The crowd erupted in cheers.

Keira stood up, held her drink high, and said, "If I come here one more time because you assholes fed my good, but idiotic, friend drinks that make him call me, I will have you all neutered. Well, except you Frank, there is no way to cut off those big balls, Skol!"

The crowd raised their drinks in reply. Frank beamed with the special treatment, and all was right with the world.

Argio "Beansie" DiBenedictis drank his drink, but he knew he was not part of the celebration. He was tolerated in here because Josh asked them to. Nevertheless, free is free, so he acted as if he was a part of it.

The drink consumed, Keira guided Steve out of the bar. "Okay, Stevie boy, get in the car and I will take you home."

Harris started to walk past the passenger side. "Whoa, there big fella," Keira said, grabbing his arm and spinning him back to the other side.

As she did this, Harris' momentum swung him past the door. He continued on, Keira no longer able to control the motion.

They ended up with Keira's back against the car, Harris leaning into her.

"My God, those are firm breasts," Harris smiled.

Keira pushed him off, spinning him towards the passenger side door.

"And that is the extent of your experience with them, get in the fucking car."

She opened the door, pushed him in, looked around to make sure no one, in particular passing cops, saw them, got in the driver's side and left.

She should have looked behind her as 'Beansie' DiBenedictis, sitting in the outside seat for smokers, took it all in. "Beansie' got on his cell and made a call.

31: Temptation

"Nice job, Josh," Deputy Assistant General Kristin Volpe said, "I wish all my witnesses were as well prepared." Closing her briefcase and walking out of the courtroom with Josh.

"Thanks," Josh answered, "I try."

'Not hard enough, she thought, not hard enough'

"So how about I buy you a drink at Christopher's?"

"Sounds good to me." Radar warnings ringing in his mind, *'Dangerous road, this'* he thought, but knew he'd go anyway.

Sitting in Cristopher's, waiting for Kristin, his cell beeping several times, calls, texts, and emails. He ignored it.

I am not doing anything wrong.

He saw Kristin coming down the side street. She was a very attractive woman. It was impossible not to notice her. She came in, walked over, and touched him on the shoulder.

"Hey, Pucci," she said to the bartender, "these drinks are on me."

"Whatever you say, Kristin," smiling back, "lucky man there today, aren't you Josh?"

Josh smiled back at him.

The bartender delivered two glasses of wine and walked discretely away.

They drank the wine in silence for a bit. The action covering the awkwardness.

"I don't see you in here as much. Where have you been hiding?" Kristin asked.

"Not really hiding, just haven't had time." Josh smiled, raising his glass, two fingers pointed up, in the universal sign for more drinks.

"Ever come here with your wife?"

"Nah, she's not really, ah, well, truth be told, world's would collide."

"Ah, I get it; keep this place to yourself as a refuge."

"How about you, where's Mr. Kristin at?"

"Who knows? Off somewhere, wherever the company has sent him. He's an engineer for an oil exploration company." Glancing toward the bartender and smiling as he delivered the drinks. "If I am not working, I'm alone and free more often than not." Looking at Josh, then into her drink.

Radar warnings were at the highest level.

"I know what you mean. I work a lot too. My wife is always off with the Innocence Project or some other quest for justice, we never see each other. We hardly..." Staring into his glass. "Ah, you don't need to listen to my problems. I suppose I can keep you company here for a while." Josh replied.

Kristin reached over, putting her hand on his thigh, "That would be nice. Maybe we can go get something to eat later?"

"Sure," Josh answered.

What the hell, Keira's probably at the damn office with Steve Harris. Or so they say.

After another round of drinks, they decided to walk over to South Main Street and find a place.

As they crossed over the river, Kristin took his hand and pulled him close, kissing him deeply.

Josh surprised himself by not pulling away. He leaned into her. His hand found her right breast, the nipple rising to his touch.

She whispered in his ear.

"You know, I can cook pretty well. My condo is off Benefit Street."

"Sounds good to me." Josh answered. Unsure where that answer came from.

"Listen, why don't you walk over and grab a bottle of wine. The address is 685 Benefit; I'll leave the door unlocked." Kissing him again and heading across the road.

Josh stood there for a moment, watching her walk away. *Damn, she is nice looking.*

Kristin turned around, saw him watching her, and smiled. She pointed towards the city as if to command him to move.

Heading back towards downtown, Josh tried to remember the closest place to buy wine. *Where was Hamlin when he needed her? She held a sixth sense for finding liquor stores.*

The voices in his head began to debate,

What the hell are you doing? Get in your car and get the hell out of there. Are you insane? She's going to find out.

And then the counterpoint,

No she won't, she doesn't care anymore. She's spending all her time with that asshole Harris. What do you think they do with all that time?

Josh listened to the debate, found the wine store, bought the wine, and walked to Benefit Street.

It is only dinner…

32: *Argio "Beansie" DiBenedictis*

Hamlin and Josh drove along Taunton Avenue near Grove Avenue.

"So how was the trial yesterday?" Hamlin asked. "Did you manage to avoid committing perjury or any other such transgressions?"

Josh glanced at Hamlin and said, "Ah, nothing unusual, went really well." Ending the discussion.

"There's the motherfucker." Josh said and pulled behind the Chinese market.

A lone figure was walking towards the dumpsters. Josh jumped out of the car, grabbed the guy, threw him against the dumpster, and kicked out his legs, dropping him to the ground.

"Come on Josh, I was trying to help," the guy yelled, trying to avoid the punches and kicks as he lay on the ground, curled into the fetal position.

"Listen you fucking rat motherfucker; you were talking about my wife. I should fucking rip your head off and shit down your neck for even thinking you can talk about her." Josh was incensed and no amount of pleading by Hamlin could get him under control.

"Come on man, I thought you'd want to know I saw her with the other dude, what the fuck man, if you like strange dudes banging your ole lady I am cool with that, I used to watch them banging Orange...."

"You lowlife motherfucker, I am going fucking chop you up and feed you to the fucking rats at the landfill, you are talking about my wire you asshole, not some fucking nineteen year old heroin smoking gash you pimp out."

"Hey, hey, man I know, I know, I am just saying I saw the dude and he was dry humping her on the Beamer man, I don't lie to you man, you helped me, come on man, I knew you wouldn't like it, why the fuck would I make this up?"

"Josh, Josh!" Hamlin yelled, pulling him away from the whimpering informant. "Enough already, somebody's gonna see this and call it in."

Argio 'Beansie' DiBenedictis was born in Johnston, RI on October 31, 1968.

Collision Course

Joe Broadmeadow

His mother, Caroline Ross DiBenedictis, was a good, but naive young woman, who believed that Beansie's father, William 'Woody' Woodside, a draftee in the US Army, did in fact love her and held no ulterior motivations in seducing her.

On leave from Vietnam due to the passing of his father, yet not intending to attend the funeral, he sought out, and achieved, a sexual liaison with Caroline. The two having known each other for the entire time it takes to consume three drinks at the bar.

She could not have asked for a more satisfying, or fruitful, sexual experience. Given the choice, "Woody" would have concurred with the satisfying part and preferred a less fruitful one.

He would have preferred redirecting that positive energy to surviving the remaining part of his Vietnam tour.

He did not.

Argio was a creative and inquisitive youth. He developed a fascination with chemistry primarily because, given a few simple ingredients, mixed in the proper combination, he could blow things up.

It began innocently, with one of his mother's many "friends" bringing him a chemistry set. Giving him free rein to do whatever he liked so long as he remained in the basement and did not come upstairs to 'bother' his mother.

Well, Argio for the most part stuck to the bargain. Except that one time, he heard something like screaming.

He hesitated to go look, he did not want to lose his chemistry set, but the sounds were intriguing. Guttural, unnatural, and interesting. As he made his way up the stairs, they became louder, took on a certain level of familiarity, they sounded like commands, imperatives, demands, and pleadings.

As he reached the top of the stairs, he could see the door to his mother's room was ajar. He heard the familiar creak of his mother's bed, familiar from all the times she let him sleep there, but the sound was different, more driven, more rhythmical, more pronounced.

He peered in.

He had never seen this activity before, but he intuitively understood it.

His mother was face down on the pillow, her back arched due to her being propped up on her knees. A guy he knew as Uncle Johnny, or Jimmy, he couldn't remember which one, was on top, making the guttural noise.

His mother's muffled voice was both plaintive and pleasurable.

He did not know what he was seeing but he knew he was not supposed to be seeing it. As he stood there, watching, it happened.

He never knew why it made him so excited, but oh my god, it got him so excited. He never tired of it.

He never could decide if it was the fact he was seeing things he wasn't meant to, or the fact that they did not know they were being watched.

It became his obsession, his entertainment, and one of his sources of income.

He was caught once.

He lost focus, paying more attention to his own pleasure, when the door opened and the less aroused, intoxicated, older Uncle Johnny made a beeline for the bathroom.

Surprised by the 12 year old lying on the floor wearing just shorts, he let out a "What the fuck are you doin' you little prick?"

Which caused his mother to grab a sheet, run to him, and yell at Uncle Johnny to leave him alone.

Uncle Johnny slapped Argio's mother, grabbed his clothes, and left the house but not before calling Argio a "retarded pervert son of a cunt whore."

Argio was not sure of the meaning of that description, but he knew it made his mother cry.

Argio would not let that go unpunished.

He resolved there and then to exact revenge upon 'Uncle Johnny.'

Someday.

Uncle Johnny used to drive on Argio's street each morning on the way downtown.

It took time for Argio's ability to measure up to the task, but Argio was a patient person. His anger never faded.

Argio improved with chemistry over the years and with his ability to sneak into places unobserved and uncaught.

One of his breaking and entering exploits resulted his stealing two sticks of fused dynamite.

Now, mathematically speaking, one part 18 year-old pissed off psychologically scarred, sexually deviant, idiot savant plus one part penchant for detail plus one part willing assistant plus two parts fused dynamite equals a simple, workable, and dangerous plan.

Pop up the sewer cover in the middle of the street, tape the sticks to the underside with the fuse fed through the access points for the pry tool.

Stop Uncle Johnny's car by means of a diversion. Faked bicycle accident, ball rolling across the road, something.

Time the fuse, which he figured to be 25 seconds. Equal to the time it took for Uncle Johnny to back out of his driveway and drive past the house, allowing a 10-15 second window of opportunity.

Argio enlisted the services of his best friend Kenny, whose mother was a victim of Uncle Johnny's attentions. They did several trial runs by forcing a random car to stop as they counted 25 seconds. Measure how long they could delay the car, light the fuse, and run. They refined the plan, learning each time from their mistakes.

They did not allow for chance.

On the day they decided to initiate their plan of revenge, they were unaware of several factors that would alter the course of their efforts. The curse of many a well-made plan.

While Argio and Kenny refined their plan, Uncle Johnny was also busy advancing his position within the gambling empire of the mob. For the sixty days preceding this fateful day, the FBI, RI State Police, and Johnston PD were monitoring a wiretap on several telephones, one of which was Uncle Johnny's.

So, in a rather prescient manner of predicting Argio's future, at the exact moment that Uncle Johnny backed out of his driveway, fate intervened.

Uncle Johnny started up the road.

Argio lit the fuse.

Kenny rode his bike into the side of Uncle Johnny's car with impeccable timing.

Uncle Johnny stopped.

Perfect.

Not quite.

The marked Johnston Police car came up from behind Uncle Johnny.

Uncle Johnny decided that the kid lying on the side of the road, having fallen from the bike or hit by his car, was the least of his problems, started to drive off.

Irony fails in describing the next few moments.

The Rhode Island State Police marked car pulled from the next intersecting street, blocking Uncle Johnny's escape and placing the Johnston marked unit precisely where the plan called for Uncle Johnny to be.

The Johnston officer got out of the cruiser and ran to the driver's side of Uncle Johnny's car.

Kenny ran.

Argio ran.

The fuse burn timed perfectly.

Fortunately, for all concerned, the physics of blast dynamics took over. The sewer dispersed much of the blast. The Johnston police car momentarily became airborne and then returned to earth.

It took the investigators about 30 minutes to figure out what occurred, 28 of that being spent convincing the commander of the State Police Intelligence unit that this was not a mob "hit."

Kenny gave up Argio.

Argio learned a valuable lesson.

They charged him with Malicious Destruction of Property, Unlawful Possession of an Explosive Device, and Disorderly Conduct.

Uncle Johnny never drove that way again.

Argio's mom retained the services of a very effective criminal lawyer who did a masterful job of minimizing the damage to Argio.

He became a frequent visitor to Argio's mother. However, none of that could alter the path Argio followed.

Argio went down the often-unrecoverable road of probation, suspended sentences, time served, violation hearings, and actual jail time.

Argio was many things, but he was not stupid. He learned the "coin of the realm." Knowing something about someone that they did not want anyone to know and, most importantly, knowing who could best use that information.

In this, Argio was a veritable genius.

Which explains why, as Josh pinned to the wall, almost chocked out, Beansie was comfortable in the knowledge that he would live until tomorrow.

Josh let him go.

Argio slid down onto the ground. His breath was sporadic, wheezy. He wiped his face with his t-shirt and smiled, showing off his missing front teeth. At least missing was easier to take than the shades of yellow and green on the remaining ones.

Due to a most unusual set of circumstances, he owed Josh his life.

Beansie was a 'C I', confidential informant in the formal terms, and a rarity as C I's go.

He existed as more than words in an affidavit.

Many a search warrant contains references to a confidential and reliable informant. They are the key ingredient to a plausible affidavit and often the product of creative writing. Probable cause is such a nebulous, unquantifiable subject.

One Assistant US Attorney in Rhode Island often said that when Cops started talking about informants, he thought of the movie "Harvey" starring Jimmy Stewart. It was about a 6-foot tall rabbit that Stewart alone could see.

Argio always wore sunglasses on his head and a cigarette, the same one, tucked behind his ear. He said they were part of his charm. He never changed them. The same went for his attire.

When he spoke, people backed away as he sounded like he was ready to puke. In addition, he never shut up. The oddest part of Argio was that women, well women with somewhat limited opportunities, loved him. These women were admittedly heroin and cocaine users, but many retained remnants of their showroom quality. They would do anything, anyway, to anyone that Argio asked them or, more precisely, rented them.

It was one of these former beauties, nineteen years old, pretty, addicted, misused, and crazy that almost got Argio killed and placed him in lifetime indebtedness to Josh.

Her name was Melinda "Orange" Johnson. Amazing body, sparkling eyes despite the fog of abuse diming them, red hair, carpeting matching the drapes, still pretty in spite of the ravages of her love for snorting cocaine and heroin. Her perennially erect nipples always pointing up, even under sweaters.

Argio would send her into the local bars to hustle the afternoon drunks. Many of whom only achieved self-induced erections. Their best friend was their right hand, and their navigator, the one eyed monster.

She would figure out who had money and, three or four blowjobs later, be set for the night to party.

Every once in a while a truck driver, recent winner from Foxwoods, or just some local that hit Keno would get the invitation back to the apartment for the full treatment.

This was Argio's idea of the perfect night.

Once they identified the target, Argio would head back to the apartment, set up the camera, and wait in the closet.

Orange would come dancing in; doing the full Foxy Lady ballet she once excelled at, and proceed to fuck the living daylights out of the guy. It consisted of a lot of screaming, lots of "slap me, man, fuck me hard, fuck me harder, do it, do it."

Most finished in the first 20 seconds.

She did not.

Some of them cried, some of them bled, some never managed an erection again.

Some threw her off and ran out the door.

Few, if any, came back

Of course, she already took the money.

All captured on video.

On movie night, which they both loved, they would get Chinese food, a huge bottle of wine, watch every video in their collection, and then Argio, who did possess one overwhelming talent, would make Orange, juice.

There is always an exception to every rule. He came in the form of a recently emigrated, immensely strong, Azorean fisherman named Osualdo Soares.

He did not run, he did not cry. He loved it. Then, he took it to a completely new level.

Argio panicked. It is not that he did not care at all about Orange, although he did rather enjoy seeing her in pain a bit, but this was beyond that. He saw fear, he saw terror, he saw this guy turn her over, about to tear her a new one, literally.

Sometimes courage just shows up in the most unexpected moments. It was not chivalry, but Argio decided he needed to do something.

Bursting from the closet with an old baseball bat kept there for just such an occasion, he hit Osualdo on the side of the head, knocking him to the ground. Orange took the opportunity to run, grabbing the cell phone on the way out and frantically dialing 911.

Meanwhile, Argio realized that his home run swing served to distract and enrage, not incapacitate, Osualdo. Backing towards the door, Argio tried to get out. The still amply aroused fisherman, screaming a string of Portuguese invectives, tackled him. Argio quickly surmised that Osualdo did not care whose ass he sodomized.

He began to scream.

Orange managed to get enough information to the 911 operator to convince them of the urgency of the situation. Two uniform units and then-Detective Josh Williams arrived on the scene.

The officers entered the room simultaneously with Osualdo entering Argio. They intervened to prevent the completion of the act, placing handcuffs on the fisherman, and helping Argio regain his clothing. All while failing to contain their laughter.

Cultivating informants is usually a matter of smart cops recognizing an opportunity when they see it. This was a good one.

No charges filed, no one would believe it. Nevertheless, pictures were taken as insurance. It saved Argio much embarrassment and guaranteed his indebtedness to Josh.

33: *Refuge*

Sometimes we all need a place of refuge, anonymity, and solitude.

Josh enjoyed occasional solitude. He needed somewhere separate from his real life.

Whenever he needed to recharge, he came to the place where he was seen him before, but no one knew who he was, what he did.

He would find a place at the bar, pick out someone, and try to learn as much as he could by just listening and observing. Sometimes he would even follow when they left, but more often than not, he was satisfied with just watching.

Josh wondered if the act of observation affected the observed. It was a tenet of quantum physics, the Heisenberg Uncertainty Principle. The act of observation affected the object observed. You could know with certainty its velocity or its position, but not both. The act of observation caused a change.

Josh loved reading about physics; he understood very little, yet still read all he could get his hands on. Hamlin thought he was a frustrated mad scientist. It was just his natural curiosity, seeking meaning in a meaningless world...

When he thought he knew something about the people, he would look for ways to confirm it, a nametag, a business card, anything to try to confirm his conclusions. Occasionally he would grab the credit card receipt when the wait staff was busy, write down the info, and run it later. Bending the law a bit, but nonetheless an entertaining hobby. He was not wrong very often.

I have strong powers of observation and deduction.
I can read people.
I know things just by watching.
How was it I shot and killed unarmed man?
How is it my life with Keira is spinning out of control?
Josh looked out the window, watching people passing by.
More importantly, how can I fix this?

"What the hell are you staring at?"

Josh looked up and smiled. No matter what, he never let anyone think he was startled. A multi-tattooed man was glaring at him, fists clenched on the table, leaning forward.

Sitting at the table with him was another guy, drawn and jaundiced, hand shaking as he gripped his drink, and a young, harsh, woman with enormous breasts.

"Sorry, lost in thought, not staring at anything."

"Well, go get lost somewhere else; you're making my girlfriend nervous."

Now the rule Josh lived by was this was his anonymous place. No matter how compelling it was to flash his badge, point the Sig Sauer at the asshole, and tell him to go get fucking lost. He got up and walked to the other side of the bar.

He now found his challenge.

He chose to watch this group. He would figure out these morons and find a way to exact some appropriate, yet anonymous, justice.

It did not take long.

Andre the Giant, Josh liked to assign names to his 'targets,' started complaining that the guy that fixed his car ripped him off. "It's a '66 GTO for Christ sake. The bastard should have done it just to say he could. The son-of-a-bitch was supposed to rebuild the carburetor and replace the exhaust. Not bill me for rebuilding the whole damn engine. I should have done it myself." Banging his drink on the table.

"Well, Kenny," Tanya Tits said, "you couldn't very well do that in jail, could you sweetie?" Her voice a combination of pre-pubescent little girl, post-surgical throat cancer survivor, and hangover mixed with an obvious limitation of intellectual ability. On the positive side, Josh received two good pieces of information to work with, although the fact of Andre being in the joint at some point was obvious to anyone who dealt with their type.

Junkieman smiled and kept looking into his glass with occasional glances at the breasts of Tanya Tits.

Josh finished his drink, ordered another one, told the bartender he would be right back, and walked out onto Thayer Street.

Andre did not look like the type to walk far. It took Josh two minutes to find the car parked on Meeting Street.

One quick little slice with the knife and the valve stem was rendered useless. A slow leak that would take an hour or so before the tire even looked low. The spring loaded automatic nail punch working its magic on the corner of the windshield, starting a small but persistent series of cracks that would grow as the car was jacked up to replace the flat tire.

Josh returned to the bar and continued his observations.

Andre took a call. A short time later, a young Brown University student walked in. He handed Andre an envelope and Josh watched him start counting money.

Shit, a fucking drug deal, now what the fuck do I do?

Andre smiled, looked around the table, and announced, "Dinner and drinks at the best place I can find," reaching into his pocket, handing the car keys to the excited young man. "Enjoy the car kid; it's one block up on Meeting."

"Oops," Josh thought, "I must be slipping, never saw that coming."

Tanya Tits announced that she wanted a lobster at the Biltmore, to which Andre replied "Biltmore? You'se is a weiner broad, fuckin' lobster, this bitch is nuts, eh?" Looking at Junkieman for support.

"I ain't taking you to no nice fucking place; I got real bitches for that."

Not that Josh held any particular sympathy for Tanya, but even she deserved better treatment. It gave him more incentive for revenge.

Josh caught up to the kid as he got to the car. "This yours?"

The kid was startled. "Ah yeah, just bought it"

"Did you get a bill of sale?"

"No, well, yeah, kind of, why do you care?"

"I am with the State Police," flashing his badge so the kid couldn't see who he really was, "we believe this car is stolen."

"What? No way, I just bought it. The guy advertised on a flyer around campus."

"Hmm, and you can't imagine anyone would sell a car that way if it was stolen? Look, kid, I know you didn't know. Go back and get your money, if he gives you a hard time, tell him the State Police are waiting."

The kid ran back towards the pub, a short time later he came out followed by Andre. The kid, envelope in his hand, pointed up the street. Andre started towards the car and then hesitated, looked around, and went back inside. A moment later Tanya Tits came out and went to the car.

'What a fucking hero," Josh thought. "Send the big-titted airhead and maybe the cops will cut her some slack."

Not a bad strategy.

Tanya got to the car, looked around, and got in. She drove around the block and pulled up to the front door. Junkieman came out, followed by Andre. As Andre went around to the driver's side and opened the door, one of those fortuitous moments occurred.

These kind of things happen by pure coincidence.

No one could plan it.

A Rhode Island State Police cruiser came down Thayer Street. The trooper sightseeing the pretty college girls, but it did not matter.

Tanya saw the trooper and panicked. She put the car in reverse instead of Park and stepped on the gas as she tried to slide over to the passenger seat. The GTO screamed backwards, taking Andre and Junkieman with it.

The Trooper never saw it coming.

As the vehicle accelerated, the rear end hit the front of the cruiser and pushed it into three other parked cars. Andre was now the meaty center of a Pontiac and BMW sandwich. Junkieman was a hood ornament on a Lexus. Tanya, to her credit, tried to be helpful and take control of the situation. However, on reflection later in the hospital, she would realize that shifting from Reverse to drive put the focus of the action in a different direction, not for the better.

The GTO, firmly attached to the push bumper of the State Police cruiser, once again put on a convincing demonstration of its reputation as a muscle car.

In a scene later described as like a horror movie, the GTO dragged the State Police cruiser, the incredulous Trooper still in the driver's seat, Tanya Tits, most of Andre's jeans, and several outdoor tables from Andrea's, an impressive 675 feet down Thayer street coming to a stop at the exit of the bus tunnel.

In his interview with the Accident Reconstruction team, the RIPTA bus driver that executed the coup d'état on the remains of the GTO, said he thought he drove onto a movie set.

Josh hid out in the men's room when the cops came looking for witnesses. He was able to enjoy watching, and hearing, Andre as they extracted him from his metal cocoon, Junkieman placed onto a gurney that collapsed, turning the simple leg fracture into a compound one, and the outrage on the Trooper's face as he looked at the remains of his cruiser.

Josh considered the outcome a rousing success.

34: *Angel's Embrace*

Josh never drove the Mercedes. It was Keira's car. Cops do not drive Mercedes, they stop them.

Fuck it, she wants me out, well I am out, I have had it. I am not perfect like all your damn lawyer friends, I am never going to be good enough----let's see how fast this motherfucker will go.

Sergeant Michael Gabriel "Angel" Armstrong watched the Mercedes go by. He headed north on the Parkway, expecting to find the car into the wall at Asquino's Corner

He was not disappointed, and then he recognized the car.

Angel ran up to the Mercedes and looked at Josh. "What the fuck Josh, what were you doing?"

Josh stumbled, he fell down, got up, tried to focus on Angel. "Sarge help me roll this motherfucker over, I want knock that fucking tree down."

"Josh come on man, I will take care of this, son you need to slow down...."

Grabbing the shoulder microphone, he called dispatch. "S1 have 101 and 103 meet me at Aquino's Corner on the parkway."

Dispatch put out the call.

The two young cops pulled up. Angel was walking a guy towards them; they recognized Josh and looked at each other, helpless.

Angel looked at them. "Put him in the car, take him to my house, do you think you dumb asses can find that if I write down the address? Here are the keys, don't fucking lose them, got it?"

"Sure Sarge, want me to radio for a tow truck?"

"Did I ask you to do that?, Do I look incapable of doing that myself you diaper wearing, tit-feeding, piece of whale shit, did I?"

"Ah, no, but I thought that...."

"Stop right there, we do not pay you to think, we do not trust you to think, you just follow my directions to the fucking letter, got it?"

"Yes Sergeant."

"Then drive him to my house, now. Put him in the spare room. That will be the room where my wife is not sleeping. If you wake her up, or in any other way fail to follow my directive, I will skin you both."

The officers just nodded.

"Is there any part of this you do not understand?"

Both officers looked at each other and shook their heads,

"Good, get the fuck going."

Then Angel made two calls, one to Eddie's Towing on the special number and one to his wife.

Eddie's would take care of the car and his wife would scare the shit out of the two young cops so they would not dare share the story with anyone.

35: *Indiscretion*

"Jeannie, what's the harm?" Steve Harris said, knowing that Jeannie Cavanaugh could not resist. "It's only a minor document, means nothing, just a notice for God's sake, come on." Handing her the document, "It's no big deal."

Cavanaugh took the paper, looked around the office, reset the stamp to the preceding day, and marked the document as received as of the previous day's close of business.

"If anyone finds out about this, Steve, I can lose my job," she said, looking around again.

"How can anyone find out? It's only you and I. Jeannie we have known each other for years. I would never put you in jeopardy. If anyone were to ask, you can say you overlooked it during the logging process. No one will question you."

Jeannie took the document, made an entry into the daily document filing system indicating an oversight, and put the document into the appropriate case file.

"Thanks Jeannie. Let me buy you lunch next week sometime," winking as he walked to the door. Harris turned back to look at Jeannie, smiled again, and headed out of the office.

Jeannie hesitated for a moment, sat down at her desk, and picked up the phone. *The son-of-a-bitch thinks I am stupid. He will never call me for lunch*, she thought, as the line began ringing.

"US Attorney's Office, how may I direct your call?" a pleasant voice answered.

"Yes this is Jeannie Cavanaugh. I am a clerk in the US District Court; may I please speak to Mr. Collucci?"

"One moment please, I will see if he is available."

Waiting on the line, Jeannie took time to consider what she was doing. *Mr. Collucci was trying to clean up the system. I know this is the appropriate thing to do.*

A new voice on the line interrupted her thoughts.

"Jeannie," the United States Attorney for the District of Rhode Island, Robert Michael Collucci, said, "to what do I owe the pleasure of this call?"

"Well, sir," Jeannie began.

"Robert, please call me Robert," Collucci interjected.

"Ah, Robert, you asked me to call you if I was approached by any lawyers asking for me to do something, well, improper."

"Yes, indeed. You know I need all the help I can get in weeding out this incipient pattern of ethical violations," Collucci said, sounding like a line for a television news teaser.

"Well, one just did. Steven Harris, from the Public Defender's office. He asked me to back date a document." She hesitated a moment, then continued, "I did what he asked, making sure I was in view of the security cameras like you told me. I have the document here for you."

"Thank you, Jeannie. You have done a great service today. I'll have an FBI agent come over and pick up the document." Collucci's voice was almost paternal in tone, congratulating a child for a good grade.

36: *From the Government*

Josh and Chris were on their way to meet with agents from the Drug Enforcement Administration when they received a call to respond to the Chief's office immediately.

Driving back over the Washington Bridge, they headed on to Taunton Ave. As he drove, Josh sensed something bad.

"So what the fuck does El Jefe want now?"

"How the hell should I know?" Chris answered, "Maybe he wants to promote you."

"More likely he's getting fucking pressure from all the political hoes to stick me in the rubber gun squad." Josh shook his head and sighed.

"Look, whatever he does, you know he'd never hurt a cop. He's a good-guy, Josh; he'll take care of you," Chris said, touching his arm, "but just in case I am calling Hawk and have him ready to jump over here."

"My guess is he's probably jumping something already, Miss L A P certified." Josh said, laughing as they pulled into the station. They both spotted the dark-blue Crown Victoria in front of the station. Since they did not know the car, they assumed Feds.

"Oh fuck," Josh said, "those bastards better not even think of trying to take me out in cuffs. I'll give them a real good reason for it, motherfucking cop fucking prima donnas."

"Whoa, whoa big guy, the local agents know you. They would call and have you come to the courthouse. I bet these guys are from D.C. Collucci doesn't have the balls to do anything himself, and the local SAIC wouldn't tolerate bullshit."

Pulling into the lot behind the station, they parked the car and headed towards the entrance. Michael "Mick" O'Hara, a former Airborne Ranger with two tours in Iraq and a slew of combat decorations, walked over to Josh.

O'Hara was not particularly big, but he projected strength. People often made the mistake of lumping him into the muscle head category. That was a mistake.

O'Hara patted Josh on the back, his United State Military Academy ring shining in the sunlight. "How you doing, Sarge?"

O'Hara enjoyed being a cop, some aspects resembled combat, but one could function as an individual, have an impact. Michael O'Hara had done that many times.

When he retired very few outsiders would know of him, but he would have indeed made a difference.

"Listen, I saw the Feds heading into the Chief's office. You keep your head on straight and don't let them push you into something stupid."

O'Hara put his hands on Josh's shoulders, "We all know you did what you neededhad to do. Those pussies would've shit themselves just hearing the call. You are one of the best cops here; you know what matters and what's right."

O'Hara looked over at Hamlin, "I am right, Lieutenant. This is bullshit."

Hamlin nodded. "Pure Federal bullshit Mick. You hit it on the head."

O'Hara continued, "Forget those guys, you go up there and no matter what you remember there are 100 of us behind you all the way."

Josh smiled and said, "Jeez, what the fuck Mick, you almost sound comforting. I thought you were gonna kiss me there for a moment."

"Fuck you, Josh, or rather Sergeant Williams," stepping back, rising to attention, "you just remember you've got a lot of friends out here."

"Thanks, Mick, I really appreciate it." Josh smiled, looked at Chris, and then said, "Now get the fuck back on the road and try to catch a bad guy for once, will ya?"

Josh and Chris entered the reception area of the Chief's office.

The Chief's aid, Daniel Zalewski looked up and smiled. "Lieutenant Hamlin, Sergeant Williams how are you? Please have a seat and the Chief will be with you in a moment."

He rose from the desk, walked over to the two officers, and whispered, "You'll love this. When the Federal agents came in, I called the Chief on the intercom and announced their presence. He said ' really, for what, find out', and turned off the intercom. I asked the agents why they needed to see the Chief, and the lead agent said, ' a matter of confidentiality, we need to speak to the Chief directly'. So I push the intercom button again, tell the Chief what the agent said, and the Chief says, ' Dan you're my confidential aide, have them tell you, and you can tell me'." Danny's smile was contagious.

Looking around the room, he continued. "Needless to say the FBI was not happy. So," dragging the word out, "I called the Chief again, and he said ' okay, have them wait a minute. I got that other Federal Agency on the line, DEA, or ATF, or some such fucking alphabet, and they have something to tell me that's a national fucking secret as well." Danny laughed quietly and returned to his desk.

Chief Winston Franklin Brennan was an anachronism among the group of people who have served in the position of Chief of Police. He was a political realist, who maneuvered himself into the position by ingratiating himself with connected insiders. He maintained a certain level of separation from any direct involvement, except for the occasional fixing of a speeding ticket or favorable recommendation to the prosecutor's office for leniency in a minor criminal case. Each favor duly noted and indexed in a stack of cards. Most importantly, he outlived the politicians who put him in office. He served more years than any other head of a law enforcement agency in Rhode Island, including the legendary, Colonel Walter Stone, Superintendent of the Rhode Island State Police.

"Where are they from Dan?" Chris asked.

"DC, Civil Rights division." Dan answered; looking at Josh, then back at Chris.

"Son-of-a-bitch," Josh said, "fucking witch hunting pricks."

The door to the Chief's office opened and the Chief walked out, his body filling the doorframe.

"Well, come on in Sergeant. The boys from the FBI's Civil Rights division would like to speak with you."

Chris said, "Do you want me in there as well?"

A voice from inside the office said, "We'd prefer to speak to Sergeant Williams alone."

The chief turned around and said, "Ah well, my office, my rules."

"You come in as well Lieutenant; we're all brothers and sisters engaged in a noble profession."

The Chief's aide beamed a huge smile.

Josh and Chris entered the Chief's office. The two FBI agents sat at the conference table; one of them rose, walking over to Josh.

"Sergeant Williams," the agent said," I am Special Agent Theo Murray. I am from the Civil Rights division in Washington. I would like to ask you a few questions if I could. I know we aren't particularly popular with you guys, but I am just trying to do my job," smiling and extending his hand.

Josh shook his hand. *They must brainwash these people into believing they really are here to help.* Turning his back to the agent, Josh asked. "Do you want me to speak with them, sir?"

"Well, Sergeant, I won't order you to talk to them. I don't think it appropriate for me to ask you to talk to them, but in the interest of inter-agency relations, I suppose listening to what they have to ask isn't too much to expect."

Looking over to Chris, "How about you Lieutenant, what do you think?"

"Sir, I think we can all listen to what they have to say and decide from there," Chris replied.

The conversation took place as if the agents were not even in the room.

The agent who was sitting, stood, and said, "Sergeant, I am Special Agent in charge Jeffery Slattery, DC Civil Rights Division. We have a number of questions regarding the circumstances of the shooting death of an unarmed individual and your involvement. I prefer to discuss this with you privately. I assure you this is only a preliminary inquiry, and we are not here on a formal complaint."

Josh turned to the Chief and said, "Okay. I listened. I think I have extended myself sufficiently in furtherance of, what did you call it, inter-agency cooperation," his tone sarcastic. "With your permission, I will excuse myself from any further discussion."

Ignoring the agents, Josh continued. "You have all my reports, Chief. I am sure the agents here will be seeking copies." Turning to the agents, "Gentlemen, I have absolutely nothing else to add to the report and nothing more to discuss with you, not now, not ever."

Josh turned and walked out of the office. Lt. Hamlin, barely concealing a smile, looking towards the agents, added, "Sergeant Williams is one of the most conscientious, honest, straightforward cops

I have ever worked with. You probably do not know this, and likely do not care, but that asshole of a US Attorney we have here is trying to make political capital out of this, and he is using you to do it. I hope you're proud of yourselves," turning to the Chief "and I'll be taking my leave as well, sir."

"Lieutenant," Agent Slattery replied, "I resent the implications. I am here to do my job, with or without this agency's assistance, if that's the attitude you are going to take, then I will...."

Chris turned abruptly around, "You'll what? You people could not solve a fucking suicide. The problem is you have never been a real cop. You know nothing of the case other than what you choose to believe, and try to intimidate people with your fancy suits and titles. You people are like seagulls, you fly in, shit all over everyone, and then you fly back out after you have done nothing but ruin a good cop's career. There is no search for the truth; you probably have not even read the reports. You just assume that because the guy turned out to be unarmed, and black, then the bigoted white guy is guilty."

Walking to stand directly in front of Slattery, the quickness of her movement catching him off-guard, forcing him to step back, Chris continued. "You carry on with your witch hunt, you guys always do, but I can guarantee this, and you mark my words, no matter what the fuck you guys try, we're going to win this. Do you know why? Because Sergeant Williams did nothing wrong. You'll end up looking like idiots, again!"

Turning to the Chief, "and that's my contribution to inter-agency cooperation, sir!" Executing a perfect about-face, Chris walked out the door.

The Chief walked back to his desk, sat down, and reached into the top drawer. Pausing a moment, enjoying the uncertainty in the agents' eyes, he withdrew a cigar.

Propping it in his mouth, he said, "well boys, unless there are some more pressing matters we need to dispose of I am going to go smoke my cigar and head home for lunch."

Rising and putting on his jacket to indicate the discussion was no longer open.

Slattery looked at the Chief, shook his head, and said, "You know Chief, this isn't going to make your department, or you, look very good, given your lack of cooperation. I suggest..."

Chief Brennan turned to the agents, coming to his full, most intimidating, height, "Gentlemen. I have extended all the courtesies to you that I am willing. I have been doing this job for 35 years, and I do not need any advice from you on how to manage this department. In light of some of the shit your agency pulled in Boston with Whitey and crew, I would not be bragging too much about reputation. You aren't the first prima donnas from the FBI to stand here, and I am woefully certain you won't be the last."

Walking to the office door, the Chief turned, looking directly at Slattery. "I run an honest department, we don't cover up anything, if we have warts we show them, and then we cut them off. I want to reemphasize what Lieutenant Williams said, albeit in-artfully. The evidence in this matter is clear. This is a legitimate, justified, and unfortunate officer involved shooting. The fact that politics have weaseled itself in I find disgusting."

Forcing the agents towards the door, Brennan chastised them.

"Don't you find it odd that the US Attorney in Rhode Island has to import a couple of agents from Washington, when he has access to any number of qualified, and quite capable, agents in the Providence field office?" Holding his arms apart, palms up.

"We have always maintained a great working relationship with the local office. Certainly, they are capable of asking a few questions in an informal inquiry, or however you defined your presence.

I agree with Lieutenant Williams. I wonder if your conscience bothers you when you become the instrument of a subversive, politically motivated, manipulation of the judicial process."

Brennan herded the agents out the door.

"This isn't over, Chief. We'll be back with Federal Grand jury subpoenas, and your investigation better be in order."

"Son," the Chief replied, "when your master sends you back here, please maintain that same cool professionalism you just demonstrated. It so reinforces my feelings about the efficacy of the federal government."

The agents walked past the outer office desk, the Chief following behind. He looked at his aide and said, "Danny boy, make a note, new policy. Anybody coming in here from some alphabet soup agency,

Federal or otherwise, you will refer them to Captain Charland. He loves that shit, and I don't have time for this nonsense."

Slattery turned to say something, but Murray pushed him out of the door. "Let it go, Jeff. We'll come back and deal with this a different way."

37: *Pre-Trial Ballet*

Special Agents Waters, Murray, and Slattery walked into the US Attorney's office. They bore news that might prove helpful in the Williams case and were anxious to share.

Robert Collucci came in, closed the door, and looked to the agents, "Okay, so what have you got?"

"Hamlin is fucking Steven Harris, and Harris has a fiancé," Waters replied.

Collucci smiled, "Really? Well, isn't that convenient. Perhaps it is time we played hardball with the good Lieutenant and that pussy of a boyfriend. Go pick him up. Make it a good show for him, but no witnesses. We want to keep our claws in him, but invisible."

Two hours later a distraught Harris was standing in the US Attorney's office.

"So, Mr. Harris, Steve if I may," the words dripping out of Collucci.

Harris nodded.

"You do know why you're here. Nasty business this. Attempted Bribery of a Court Official, Filing Fraudulent Documents, Obstruction of Justice. As I am certain you are aware, these carry significant jail time, fines, and, of course, disbarment. Such a shame. Such a waste of a talented legal career." Collucci was enjoying this.

Harris pleaded, "Mr. Collucci, I hardly think this is a criminal matter. I offered no bribe. It was a momentary lapse of judgment. No harm intended. It wasn't even a required..."

"Shut up, Harris. I do not give a shit about you or these documents. However, it all comes down to how we manage the issue. I can minimize the whole incident or," rising from his chair, "indict and charge you. It makes no difference to me. What I want from you is information. Give me something about Hamlin. Don't worry, you will find another girlfriend. Oh, wait," smiling at Harris, "you already have one. I wonder what she would think of Sunday visitations at the Fort Dix Federal Prison."

Harris felt his knees go weak, and he collapsed in a chair. "I don't know anything about Hamlin. It was just a physical thing. I was going to end it anyway. She's, she never tells me anything. She...wait a minute, wait one minute, there is one thing. Now that I think of it, but it's not about Hamlin, it's about Williams." Harris smiled.

I cannot do this. Chris trusted me. It was pillow talk, what the fuck am I thinking?

Collucci raised his hands in a 'well?' gesture.

"I need assurances," Harris continued.

Collucci came around the desk, leaned back, folded his arms, and said, "Fine, I assure you Mr. Harris that either you give me something useful right now or you can rest assured that today will be the last day you practice law. How do those assurances sound to you?"

"Okay, okay, but if it's worth it, I walk on this right?" Harris pleaded.

"If it is valuable and accurate I assure you, there's that word again, you will walk out of here, and this little misunderstanding will be forgotten."

Harris stood up and walked to the window, looking out at the streets in Kennedy Plaza. *How many hours had he spent waiting for the bus home because his father did not want to waste gas driving to pick him up at school? He called it his 'college fantasy'. It all come to this, giving something up to help himself. Ah, well I can't be much help in prison can I?*

Turning back to face Collucci, he began "Hamlin told me Williams lied in a court hearing."

Collucci rose from the desk, "Continue, where, when, which court?"

"Well, she said he colored his testimony. She thought it was funny. However, she was worried he'd go too far someday and get caught."

"Which court?" Collucci demanded.

"Sixth Division, District Court. Some sort of an alcohol violation, I don't know any specifics."

"Go," Collucci muttered, reaching for the phone.

Harris just looked at him.

"Get the fuck out of my office now, or I will indict you and that bitch of a plaything of yours for Obstruction of Justice," Collucci threatened.

Harris was out the door, down the stairs, and in the middle of Kennedy Plaza before Collucci dialed the first number.

38: *Justice for None*

Josh walked into the office, saw Chris talking on the phone, took in the look in her eyes, and knew.

'That son-of-a-bitch indicted me didn't he?"

Chris nodded her head, motioned for him be quiet, and put the phone on the speaker...

"Anyway, we all...." the male voice paused, "...what the hell was that, Chris?"

"Nothing, I turned the volume up. They're doing work on the heating system, and I couldn't hear you." Smiling at Josh and shrugging her shoulders.

The caller continued, "The SAC told Collucci he wasn't using any of his agents for this fucking witch hunt. He could call the fucking President of the United States for all he cared. That as far as he was concerned, every agent in the Providence office was busy for the next decade."

The caller went silent for a moment. "Hang on; let me close my office door." There was the muffled sound of movement, and then the caller came back on.

"Where was I? Oh yeah. Collucci started yelling he would have him sent to fucking Podunk and the SAC said that at least he would not have to put up with the political fucking cesspool here. So you tell Josh no matter what happens not one fucking moment of any local agents' time was used in this charade and that we all know this is bullshit."

"Thanks, Kenny" Josh said. Chris gave him the 'what the fuck look.'

"Cheeks, did you put me on a speaker? Josh is listening right? Dammit Chris, I said this was between you and me."

"Sorry, Ken. My partner here just never learns to keep his mouth shut," Chris replied, giving Josh the finger.

"Well listen, the SAC wanted you to know how the office felt about this, but he also does not want anything to fall back on him. He is a good guy, ladies and gentlemen, but he is also a few years short of retirement, and he would prefer to keep his pension. Don't bag me on this."

"Kenny, I appreciate it," Josh said, "it will stay here. Thanks."

The line went dead and Chris stood up, "You didn't hear the whole call. Collucci is planning to send the rat squad to arrest you at Bovi's. He got it in his head that he'd make you look bad in front of your friends and get a little payback for the Police and Fire Unions voting to endorse his opponent."

"Are you fucking kidding me? I'll just go down to the court and turn myself in, that'll piss him off."

"I have a better idea," Chris smiled. "They want to make a big splash in the media, let's give them a fucking tidal wave."

Josh gave her an inquisitive look.

"The indictment is under limited seal. I cannot wait to find out which fucking magistrate agreed to that order. They only have 24 hours to keep it under seal. They have to try to get you quickly or the seal is broken, then they have to notify the department, and you can turn yourself in."

Chris walked over to the window, thinking. "They'll come looking for you tonight at Bovi's. Even they can figure out you will be there on a Friday. And they will find you, but not quite right away."

Josh looked at Chris and smiled, "and what exactly are we going to do?"

"Call Beansie. We need a few of his special girls and his camera expertise."

39: *I am Right Here...*

Beer *Blast at Bovi's*, the signs read.

Come join us for a fund-raiser for the East Providence Animal Shelter sponsored by the East Providence Fire IAFA and Police IBPO unions.

"Have a Beer, Save a Pussy," read one sign.

"Have a Beer, Dogs Like Pussy," read another.

Chris looked at the signs, looked at the shit-eating grin on the well lubricated, off-duty cop's face, and just shook her head.

"Hey, hey, Lou, ahh L ah T ah sir er ma'am," the officer tried to speak through the beer static.

Chris gave him a look and said, "Don't go down that road son. You want to sip your beer through a straw or enjoy yourself?"

Sergeant "Angel" Armstrong came over, put his muscular bicep over the young officer's face, and said, "Not a problem, LT. It is past his bedtime anyway. I'll take care of the little man."

How many times have Sergeants saved embarrassment and lives? Chris thought. Then, moving suddenly towards the officer, made him jump in spite of the strong grip on him.

"Thanks, Angel. How do you keep doing this?"

"When I retire, I am going to teach Kindergarten. I figure this is good practice." Lifting the officer off his barstool, hauling him over to a booth in the rear, and planting him firmly in the seat.

A few, more seasoned officers, who all benefited at one time or another from 'Angel's' embrace, immediately surrounded the officer.

Chris moved through the crowd, spotting Beansie sitting at the end of the bar. He was sandwiched between two of his very special ladies, surrounded by a whole flock of off-duty night shift cops and firefighters.

"Beansie," she smiled, "how are you this fine day?"

"Not very fucking happy at the moment," glancing at the crowd around him, "I don't do discounts for anyone, not even Cops and Firemen."

"Not to worry, Beansie," Chris smiled, "the firemen would ask for recipes, and the cops have already drank so much beer they're harmless." This drew a series of loud protests from the crowd.

"Okay boys, move on," Chris announced, "we have things to discuss, and you aren't invited."

Most of the crowd moved on, but not before one made a nearly fatal comment. "I told you she rolled that way..."

Chris was not even out of her seat before Angel was standing between her and the crowd. "Okay, LT, just a joke," glaring at the retreating group, "we all know you're not a rug muncher."

"Only you, Angel, only you," Chris laughed.

Angel smiled, nodded his thanks, turned around and knocked the offending officer on the back of the head so hard he went to his knees.

"Next asshole says anything about the LT, I am not going to protect your dumb ass, and you will regret it."

"Give them a beer on me," Chris said to Karen, "and make sure they know it."

A moment later, there was a cheer from the other side of the bar, "Thanks LT, thanks Ma'am, thank you..." while Angel stood vigilantly behind them, nodding and smiling, like a proud parent.

Beansie looked over at the cheering cops and then back at Chris, "What am I supposed to do in here, with all this, ah, protection?"

"Well, these young ladies here are?" Looking at the girls.

"They are mine," Beansie said, drawing her look back, "and I don't think we are staying," rising from the stool.

"Sit down, you little fucking weenie. These girls do not belong to anyone, let alone a piece of shit like you. I have a mind to lock you up for being an A I N. I just need the girls. I can get anybody to take pictures."

"A I N?" one of the girls said, "what's that?

"Asshole in the nighttime," Chris said, "and Beansie here is a repeat offender."

"Now, Beansie, be a gentleman for once in your life and introduce me to your friends."

Beansie looked around. There was no escape. "This is Apple," pointing to the blonde, "and this is Cherry." Looking uncomfortably at the crowd surrounding them.

"Ah, a fruit theme, rather healthy Beansie, my compliments." Looking at the girls, "you aren't going to make a lot of money tonight in the usual way, but Beansie here," motioning to Angel to come over, "is giving you a paid holiday."

The girls looked at each other and then to Beansie. Angel moved to block the view.

One of the fruit sisters asked, "What's a paid holiday?"

"You do what I tell you, when I tell you, and Beansie will pay you twice what you've ever made in the past."

"No fucking way," Beansie yelled, rising from the seat, "those bitches work, or they don't get paid."

The bar went silent, sort of.

Angel leaned forward.

Chris smiled.

Beansie sat down, negotiations concluded.

By eight o'clock, the bartenders at Bovi's already served more beer and drinks than St. Patrick's Day.

Beansie took a seat in the corner near the door, armed with his camera, and tasked with very specific instructions.

An old panel van, belonging to Vinnie the plumber, covertly delivered people from the Shaw's parking lot to the rear entrance of Bovi's in order to conceal the actual number of people inside the bar.

A small area set aside just inside the door kept free of obstructions, a designated 'smoker' positioned outside, supplied with drinks, to serve as the 'closer', Josh sitting at the one stool visible from the outside. Everyone in position.

The lookouts, sitting on the picnic table across the street, spotted the dark-blue Crown Vic, as it drove by in a pathetic attempt at covert reconnaissance. They gave the signal as the car came back around and parked.

The two agents got out of the car, walked to the door, yanking it open, strode in announcing, "FBI."

The door closed behind them and the dumpster pulled to the curb, blocking the door, awaiting the trash service truck that pulled up at that moment.

The agents, oblivious to the machinations they triggered, started towards Josh and their world went insane.

Two very well endowed young women, wearing thong bikinis, appeared at their side, held their arms, and smiled for the flashes of cameras and video.

Frank O'Malley, coming from behind the agents, put his arms around them just after the girls moved away, yelling "God bless the USA," and spilling the two Guinness beers he held in each hand on the agents' suits, while still managing to smile for the cameras.

The agents pushed O'Malley away, and began scanning the room for Josh.

Every face in the crowd was now wearing a Josh Williams mask.

Chris came over, smiled, and said, "Is there anything the East Providence Police can do to assist you?"

Behind the agents, the various signs were paraded; cameras continued to flash, and the crowd began cheering "Na, na, na, na....Na, na na na, hey hey hey, FBI."

"You think this is funny? You fucking local yokel asshole," the agent yelled, "this is obstruction of justice."

"My, my, what an attitude toward a sister in the thin blue line. If you think this is funny, wait until you see the pictures. My bet is they are on Facebook and YouTube as we speak. Might I buy you a drink, in the interest of cooperation?"

"I am going to indict your ass for this Hamlin, and lock up that fucking partner of yours."

"You go right ahead and try asshole," Chris smiled, "my guess is the prima donna political cocksuckers in FBI Headquarters will be sending your ass to some fucking outpost on Diego Garcia, when they hear this story." Chris joined the chorus dancing to "hey hey hey, FBI"

The other agent grabbed his partner's arm, turned, and tried to open the door. It opened just a few inches at first and then a bit wider, allowing Vinnie the plumber to look in and say, "Hold on boys, still taking a dump."

Forcing the door, the agents made their way to the car. Vinnie's van was inches from the rear bumper, and the trash truck blocked the front.

The lead agent then made another error in judgment, turning the siren on and off; he yelled out the window at the trash truck operator, "Move the truck immediately this is the FBI."

"Yes Sir. Mr. FBI agent," said the driver, snapping a perfect, if wrong handed, salute.

As the truck pulled away, a huge wave of fluid from inside the still exposed compaction area splashed out, covering the hood and pouring all sorts of fermenting items in the open driver's window.

Josh, who left his seat as the performance began, watched it all unfold from across the street.

It is good to have friends.

40: *Justice Derailed*

Sergeant Joshua Williams surrendered himself to the United States District Court of Rhode Island. At his arraignment, he entered a plea of Not Guilty. The court released him on his own recognizance, after he submitted to fingerprinting and photography at the FBI office.

As Josh walked out of the FBI office, he knew what was coming.

There exists in Rhode Island a controversial law known as the Law Enforcement Officers' Bill of Rights, an object of derision and complaint by politicians and Chiefs of Police.

The law's genesis was a consequence of the abuse of power by the very same politicians and Chiefs of Police, this fact often missing from the public discourse.

The latest amendment of the law allowing, but not requiring, the immediate suspension, without pay, of any officer charged with a felony. The presumption of innocence being an inconvenient burden, ignored for the sake of politics.

As Josh left the FBI office, Lieutenant Hamlin and Chief Brennan greeted him.

"I know, Chief, weapon and credentials. I'll have them brought to you," Josh said, trying to smile.

"Bullshit," Brennan replied, "I am going to have to clip your wings a bit, keep you under house arrest so to speak, but I am not taking anything from you. I believe in the Justice system in this country, not just in word but in practice as well. I do not give a crap what the other Chiefs might think. They want to suspend somebody just because it is the easy way out, let 'em. I am not doing it."

Brennan looked at Hamlin, then back to Josh. "Now Lieutenant Hamlin here is going to drive you back to the station. You take a few days off, and then come in on Monday. There are plenty of things I need help with, and you're it."

At East Providence Police Department Headquarters, every member of the department, and a huge number of civilians, waited for him in the front lot. Many carrying signs proclaiming the injustice of the indictment. Francis Patrick O'Malley held a huge sign referencing Salem Witch Trials, Japanese Internment Camps, Nazi Concentration

Camps, as well as a host of other references to history's oppressed. Most did not understand the sign. No one read the whole thing, but they all let Frank stand in front.

Josh was overwhelmed.

Chris pulled the car to the front of the station, looked over, and said, "Well, Ace, looks like you have a few friends, perhaps you should say thank you."

Josh got out of the car to a thunderous applause. Amid varying cries of, *stand tall Josh, we've got your back*, Josh leaned against the car and took it all in. Waiting for the noise to die down, he climbed onto the hood of the car, motioning for the crowd to listen to him.

"I don't know what's going to happen, but I do know this; few ever understand the pride we feel being a members of this department. Very few, unless they put on that badge, wear that uniform, stand on the shoulders of those great cops that came before us, will know how proud I am to be one of you. So, with all sincerity, I want to thank you, and say Fuck you all."

In that moment, one of those times where no one planned it, the entire crowd began to move as one out onto Waterman Avenue.

A spontaneous, heartfelt, unstoppable parade.

It snarled traffic on Pawtucket Avenue, Waterman Avenue, Taunton Avenue, and a host of side streets. It moved down Waterman, gathered more people, spurred on by the emotion of the moment.

They made their way to Bovi's, some in an attempt to ease the pain of injustice, some for the inevitable free drinks. It did not matter; they made the best of a bad situation.

The intent was not to forget tragedy in the death of a young man, but only to mitigate the revulsion of political ambition trying to destroy a good man.

41: A Message of Help

Chris Hamlin walked into the office, finding Josh already there.

"Early for a change, what's the special occasion?"

"I slept here last night. You'd be surprised how comfortable that couch in the back of the surveillance van can be." Josh yawned, sipping his coffee, and leaned back in the chair.

"Josh, maybe it's none of my business, you and Keira belong together, whatever it is, don't mess that up."

"You're right," Josh replied, standing and walking to the coffee pot, "it isn't your concern. She made her choice."

"Is this about what that rat fuck Beansie said? Christ Josh, that asshole would say anything to get himself out of shit. There is no fucking way Keira has anything with Harris. I can't believe you even imagined that's true."

Josh turned and looked at Hamlin, "I don't know what's fucking true anymore, she's been spending a lot of time, and I mean a lot of time, with him. Now Beansie tells me he saw her pick him up at Bovi's."

"Exactly, asswipe," Hamlin interjected, "do you think for one minute, if Keira were having an affair, she'd go to Bovi's? Half the cops on the department live in that place off-duty, not to mention the fire guys, lawyers, and a million others that know you both. She is not stupid. More to the point, she is not the type. Whatever she saw in you, I will never understand."

Josh returned to his desk, brought up his email on the computer, and started sorting through it.

One email jumped out at him. He did not know the address, clearly intended to catch his eye, bwareofonyfriends@hotmail.com. The subject line read, *'You are surrounded by rats'*.

He opened the message,

"Josh,

There is someone providing information to Collucci.

He says he has something he will use to destroy your credibility.

It is coming from someone close to you, another cop perhaps.

If I get more, I will pass it on. Check your email closely; it won't be from the same email address. A friend."

"What the fuck," Josh muttered.

Hamlin, looking over her glasses at Josh, asked. "Something else wrong?"

"Somebody here has a fucking real bad sense of humor, trying to fuck with me over this shit, come here, take a look."

Hamlin came over and looked at the screen display, "I don't know Josh, not many guys here would know enough to go to a onetime use email. Keep an eye out for more and forward me that email, I can trace the IP address in the header info and see where it came from."

Walking back to her desk, she paused a moment and then said, "Can you think of anything they might have that they could use?"

"I can't think of anything right now except my wife may be having an affair, and suddenly the US Attorney may have some shit on me. This just keeps getting better and better." Josh sighed, sinking back in the chair.

"Josh, there's no way Keira has anything to do with this, and she's not having an affair with Harris or anybody else," Logging into the computer, and retrieving the forwarded email message, she looked at the header information.

A short time later, after reaching out to contacts at the local cable company, Hamlin got up from her desk. "Come on, let's go for a ride. We have something to check out."

"Where are we going?" Josh asked.

"The library on Grove Avenue, the email was sent from there this morning, and they put surveillance cameras in since the fire last year."

Heading out the rear private door from their office, they ran across Chief Brennan coming up the stairs.

"And where are we off to now boys and girls? I do hope we are keeping away from any additional controversy for a bit." Smiling and drawing on his ever-present cigar, "And Sergeant."

"Yes sir?" Josh replied.

"Relax son, no need for such military formality, it's just us," the Chief continued, "don't worry about them DC agents. I read the reports. You did it by the numbers and there isn't any way they are even gonna get an indictment, let alone a jury to believe anything other than a justified shooting."

Continuing up the stairs, the Chief said, "You did a great job Josh, remember that. This department is behind you all the way." Motioning for them to continue, Chief Brennan headed into the building.

Josh looked at Hamlin, "he's like our own Buford Pusser isn't he?"

Hamlin replied, "He always plays that naive small-town Police chief act, but he is very smart, and most importantly, loyal to his cops, well the good ones anyway. He never forgot where he came from, unlike some of the brass we have here."

Getting into the undercover car, they headed over to the library. Parking in front, Hamlin looked at the external surveillance cameras and said, "If we're lucky we can isolate the time frame on the digital recordings and match them to the range of time the sender was in here. The Internet provider couldn't tell me how long the user was on, but they gave me enough with the header information to show the time the email was sent."

"I bet whoever it was, created the email address here and then sent the email. So we'll look at 30 minutes or so prior to the time stamp in the header information."

Walking into the library, they headed over to the main desk. A young woman looked up and said, "How can I help you?"

Hamlin feigned a serious look, and said, "Is Ms. Johnson in? I am Lieutenant Hamlin from the police department. We need to take her back to prison."

The young woman appeared startled and started to reply, when a voice from the back room said, "Don't pay any attention to her, Becky. Lieutenant Hamlin is just kidding. She is really here for her GED classes."

A tall, well-dressed, 60ish black woman came from the back office Carrying a pile of books and CDs. Handing them to the young woman she said, "Could you please return these to their proper locations, Becky, while I deal with the comedienne here."

Looking at Hamlin, "So how is my favorite illiterate? I see you finally found the library. Do you need to use the restroom, or are you ready to learn to read?" coming around the counter to hug Hamlin.

153

"Josh," Hamlin said "this is Vera 'Aunt Jemima' Johnson. We served together in Viet Nam. She used to do my laundry and make my bed."

Johnson smiled and said, "actually Josh that is true. Miss 'I went to a fancy girls school' did not know how to do laundry or make a bed. If I hadn't done it for her, she'd have never survived, even the guys stirring the honey pots smelled better." Letting out a huge laugh and then looking around to make sure no one noticed.

"How are you Chris?" Johnson asked

"I am well, V. We need to get together soon, how about dinner on Friday?" Hamlin said, holding Johnson's shoulders.

"At a restaurant, or do you expect me to cook like usual?"

"I'll buy the groceries and Vodka."

"Okay, I'll cook, make it around 7. I'll email the shopping list, and you can drop the stuff off here on Thursday around 5,"

Looking over at Josh and then back at Hamlin, "So what do I really owe this visit to? I am sure it's more than weaseling a dinner invitation."

"We need to look at the surveillance video from this morning," Hamlin answered.

"Okay, I'll show you where they are, but as for operating it, you are on your own. I still have a rabbit's ear antenna on my TV, and I pay for cable," turning and heading back into the inside office.

Chris and Josh followed her into the back room. She pointed to the recorder. Chris retrieved the DVD and replaced it with a blank one.

"I put a new disk in V, so the camera will continue to record. I'll get this back to you on Friday." Turning as she left the office she added, "Don't forget to send me the grocery list. Looking forward to it."

"I am putting it together now, Miss Mooch. See ya' later."

They went directly to the station and into the SIU office.

Chris took the disk from her notebook and placed it in the DVD drive.

Waiting for the program to recognize the media, Chris brought up the email header information she got from the Internet provider and looked at the send time.

The Windows Media player queued up the first MPEG file. Chris hit the play button and noted the time on the surveillance camera time/date display. Scrolling rapidly, moving the time-lapse images to one hour before the email send time.

Watching the images, she scanned forward quickly. Stopping on one of the images, she noticed a familiarity about the person. "Josh," she called, "come here and look at this, does he look familiar?"

"Ah yeah, that's Frank O'Malley. He goes there every day." Josh answered, "He has an odd way of reading email. He has the librarian print it out for him. He prefers paper. I doubt he would even know how to create an email. I created his for him. FrancisPOMalley.GSGTUSMC@hotmail.com. It's not him Chris."

Chris continued up to the time in the email header. No one entered the library except Frank.

"There's nobody else." Chris sighed, slumping back in the chair.

"Did you adjust for UTC?" Josh smiled.

"What the hell is, oh shit, I completely forgot," the notion clearer in her mind, "the email time stamp is in UTC." UTC being Universal Time Coordinated, a method for synchronization across time zones.

"So my genius Lieutenant, if the email is time stamped 14:45 UTC that would be?" Josh opened his arms in a questioning gesture.

"East coast is UTC-5, right?" Chris answered, moving back to the computer. "I've been looking at 13:45; I should look at 8:45, no wait. Frank came in at 9:00 our time. It must be before that. I need to look at 8:15."

"Ah, my little girl is growing up, she can add and subtract." Josh replied and went back to reading reports.

Flipping Josh the bird, Chris returned to the search screen, adjusting for the time difference. At 8:35, she found what she wanted. Two individuals entered within moments of each other, just before Frank O'Malley.

One was a woman, about 25 years old. Chris followed her progress from the camera on the exterior to the one monitoring entrance doors. She grabbed a few frames to create an image she could enlarge and enhance.

"Too bad they don't have cameras inside." Chris said with a hint of frustration in her voice.

"Ah, they'd have to get rid of Orwell's 1984, and all those other inconvenient references to privacy wouldn't you think?" Josh answered without even looking up.

She ignored Josh and examined the other individual. This one was male, wearing a military fatigue field jacket and dark-rimmed glasses. Something else was odd about him, but she could not quite put her hand on it. She grabbed some frames for this one and then brought both subjects up in Photoshop.

After using the available tools, two clear images emerged.

Josh and Chris studied them.

Nothing.

Switching between the full image and the enhanced facial ones, it suddenly hit her. "Son-of-a-bitch," Chris said, punching Josh.

"Hey, what the fuck is wrong with you?" Josh replied.

"Look at his pants and shoes, look at his fucking pants and shoes." Chris yelled.

Josh looked at the picture, back at Chris, and then studied the image a bit more. "They're dress shoes and pants," Josh said. "The guy is wearing suit under the field jacket. I bet the glasses are probably fake."

"Exactly," Jen exclaimed, "I bet that bastard is a Fed, he's the sender."

"Or she is the sender, and they're trying to spook me into something," Josh replied, "or they know she's trying to give me info."

"Jeez, you're a fucking conspiracy theorist on steroids aren't you?" Chris said, "Do you think Frank might remember them?"

"He might. I will ask him when I see him later. So now what, we still don't know who the woman is, or if she is even involved, so all we have is a plot line for a spy novel."

"We'll wait for more email. Since this place seems to offer the sender some level of comfort, maybe they'll send more from here, we can narrow it down."

They did not have to wait long.

Chris checked the header information and called her contact at the Internet service provider. The email came over Wi-Fi service at Starbucks on Waterman Street in Providence.

There were no cameras to help with this one.

Listen, Collucci has something about you and Hamlin. Something about a court case. I will try to get more. This isn't right what's happening and there's other things going on. Collucci is a rotten SOB. Take care, watch who you talk to. A Friend.

"So now what?"

"Maybe there'll be more." Hamlin answered. "Any ideas of what they're talking about?"

"Not a fucking clue."

"Maybe we should call Hawk."

"And tell him what? That we're getting anonymous messages. This is just someone fucking with us. It's probably Collucci, or one of the DC pricks." Josh went into the back room and came out with two beers.

"Not from evidence I hope. Are they?"

"Nah, I bought these with the money you hide in your bottom desk drawer." Smiling at the Lieutenant.

Hamlin shook her head, "Well that's no problem. I took that money from your desk anyway. Right back at you, Ace."

After finishing the beers, they decided to call it a day. Heading to the lot, Hamlin leaned on the side of her car. "Go home, Josh. Go home and see if she is there. Fix this."

A sad look embraced Josh. "It won't matter, she's gone. As soon as this is over, so am I."

"What does that mean?" Hamlin tried to talk to him, but he got into his car and left.

42: *Return Visit*

Lieutenant Hamlin sat at her desk cataloging the previous day's evidence seized by Patrol arrests. As she made entries into the department computer system, her phone rang.

"SIU, Lieutenant Hamlin," she answered.

"Lieutenant, Marion at the front desk. There are two men to see you. They say they are from the Justice department."

Great, Chris thought, now what?

"Be right out Marion," she answered and headed for the lobby.

Chris decided to take the long way, through the dispatch center. The one-way mirrored windows allowed her to look out to the lobby unseen.

As she walked through the center, Dispatcher Ginger Perez said, "Those boys might just as well tattoo Federal agent across their foreheads. They look plain foolish standing there all jarhead like. I got a mind to go tell them a thing a two 'bout messin' with my boys."

Chris smiled. Ginger Perez had been a dispatcher for over 30 years. She took a personal interest in all of her 'boys,' which of course included the women of the department as well. She taught, by instilling fear of raising her ire, all new officers in the realities of the world.

How many times had Chris heard Ginger's speech,

Listen, you are nothing but a wet behind the ears pup. I am not your secretary. I am not making excuses to your wife or girlfriend for you. I am not here as your personal maid. I will save your ass when, and if, you need it, but you will respect me and my fellow dispatchers, clear?

Some of the new patrol officers took years until they measured up to her standard. However, once you did, there was no more loyal person on your side than Ginger.

"You know, I have half a mind to let you at 'em. However, I think I have done enough damage with the Justice Department for a while. I'll just go play nice," walking out the side exit, through the records division, and into the lobby.

"Hi, I'm Lieutenant Hamlin, what can I do for you?" Extending her hand.

"Special Agent Tom Waters, Justice Department," came the reply, and he handed her a document, not bothering to acknowledge the overture of greeting.

"And this is?" Chris questioned, raising her eyebrows, and trying to stay composed.

"A subpoena," Waters replied. "I assume you understand what that entails, Lieutenant."

"Oh sure, I have ignored them before," Chris said, smiling, and turning away.

"Aren't you going to read what it requires, or do you need me to read it to you?" Waters asked, taking a step towards the door. "You are required to provide certain reports and documents to us."

"Well, Special Agent Waters and silent partner here, I will take this document, review it, and decide whether or not it is legitimate, since you produced no identification attesting to your authority to deliver said document."

"Lieutenant, you are fully aware of who we are and the agency we represent. There's no need for anything other than you complying with the court order."

Crumbling the paper in her hand, enjoying the agent's reaction, Hamlin added, "Oh, I know exactly what you represent. If, at such time, I am satisfied that the document is in order, I shall endeavor to comply fully and expeditiously."

Chris turned to the doorway. The door shot open and Ginger Perez came out, glaring.

The silent agent took a step back, startled by the appearance of the angry looking black woman. Perez was not big, but she was not tiny, and she frightened much better men than these.

"Ah, Ginger, say hi to my new friends Agent Waters and Agent Prefers to remain silent," gesturing to the agents.

"Lieutenant, we are aware of your escapades the other night. Perhaps if you have someone literate explain the gravity of the situation, you'll comprehend how serious this...."

Both Ginger and Chris took steps toward the agents, backing them up again.

At that moment, Chief Brennan came out the opposite side door. "Gentlemen, from this day forward, as a matter of professional courtesy, please direct all such matters to my attention. Lieutenant Hamlin has more important things to do then stand around here in the lobby." Looking over the agent's shoulder at Hamlin he added, "Don't you, Lieutenant?"

"Why I do believe I do, sir." Chris nodded, walked past Ginger, and into the records area.

"Ms. Perez shouldn't you be sending cars on calls, or answering 911 lines?"

"Well, Chief, I just wanted to make sure..."

"Ginger, I got it from here, thank you," waving his hand towards the dispatch center.

Perez turned back, muttering, "Empty suited phony errand boys..."

"Now Gentlemen, is there is anything else?" The Chief tried to suppress his grin.

"Chief, I don't know what kind of department you run here, but I..." Waters was angry, glaring at Brennan.

"Stop right there, son. You had it at, I don't know. You have served the subpoena, and we will comply with the letter of the law. It will take time to review and produce copies of the material. Why don't you run along and we'll call you."

Waters and the other agent headed towards the door.

Brennan watched them leave, shaking his head. *This is going to get messy he thought,* and headed back to his office.

When Brennan returned to his office, Chris was waiting inside.

"So, Chris, you want to explain what's so damn important in our report files that Collucci felt the need to send, not one, but two FBI agents to serve a goddamn subpoena."

"It's that stupid sale of Alcohol to a Minor case out of Fernando's Liquors," Chris answered.

"Please enlighten me as to why the Feds would care about that?" Brennan continued.

"Because Josh used some, shall we say, creative testimony in the hearing." Chris sighed, and sat down.

"Oh, I can't wait to hear this story, let me get some tea. I've a feeling I am going to need something soothing."

After Chris related the story of the 'evidence' to Brennan, the Chief sat at his desk for a moment and then said, "Who knew?"

"Who knew what?" Chris asked, looking confused.

"Who knew the six-pack wasn't the original? Did the Defense lawyer handle it, feel it was cold?"

"He did and he asked Josh about that," Chris answered, looking amused.

"And this was funny why?" Brennan persisted.

"Because Josh said, and I quote 'Well, in the unlikely event we lost this case, and the court required the return of the evidence, I didn't want it spoiled. We stored it in the evidence refrigerator. I am a big fan of beer you know." Chris said, a bit apprehensively.

Brennan paused a moment, "Boy can think on his feet, can't he?"

"He can do that, boss. However, that still leaves the issue, who knew? Nobody knew about the purchase except Josh and…" Chris stopped dead in mid-sentence.

Brennan looked at her with his 'do I want to know this' expression.

"I may have an idea, and I am going to kill the son-of-a-bitch if I am right." Chris was incensed.

Brennan took a sip from his tea and offered, "how about we both pretend you didn't say that, so I couldn't have heard it?"

"Not to worry Chief, I've got this under control." Chris headed to the door.

"No words in the English language make me more nervous than when I hear 'Not to worry'. Not only do I worry, but also I get very anxious. You handle this Lieutenant, and try to do it within the law. In other words, don't get caught."

"No to, ah, relax Chief," Chris said, "I am merely going to ask some questions, inflict maximum pain, and leave no marks." Chris smiled and was gone.

161

43: *Are You Kidding Me?*

"I can't believe you are sleeping with Harris." Josh laughed, shaking his head.

"Was, was, not anymore," Chris replied.

"Yeah but jeez...." Josh went quiet, "I can't believe I accused my wife of sleeping with him. I am such an asshole."

"What do you mean accused her?" Chris looked at him and slapped his shoulder.

"Remember the night I rolled her Mercedes on the Parkway, and Angel took care of me?"

"Yeah."

"Well, what got me fired up was thinking about what Beansie said, so I went looking for Harris. I found Keira's car at his office."

Chris just shook her head.

"I went in, found them in the back, and grabbed Harris by the throat. I wanted to kill him. Keira pulled me off him, tried to calm me down. I was screaming something to the effect you want to fuck him, go ahead. I don't care," Josh looked out the window of the car, "I left that night, wrecked the car, and haven't been back since."

"You are an asshole, you know that," Chris lectured.

"Why the fuck didn't you tell me this before?" Josh asked.

"I tried to tell you she wasn't having an affair. You wouldn't listen."

"Well I would have if you told me the truth about you and him."

"Look, what I do on my own time is nobody's business. It is why I never date cops. They are like a bunch of old women, cannot wait to spread shit. Harris and I made an arrangement. It worked, well it did. Now I am going to turn him into a gelding, the little fucking worm."

Chris stared out the window, "Listen Josh, maybe I should have told you, but it doesn't matter now. Go home, crawl on your knees, and apologize."

"I can't, why would she even listen to me." Josh sighed, "Forget it. I blew it. She probably has the divorce petition ready to go."

"You could try, Josh." Chris said.

"I don't even know where she is," Josh replied, "she sent me a text saying she was leaving, and I have no idea where to look."

"Listen, first we take care of Harris, then we're going to find Keira, and you can think of a way to apologize."

A few moments later, Josh pulled up in front of Harris' office, and started out of the car.

Chris grabbed his arm, "Oh, no. This time is all mine. You stay here and practice your 'I am such an asshole speech'. You are going to need it. Now stay, boy, stay!"

44: *Thanks for Nothing*

"Mr. Harris, there's a Lieutenant Hamlin here to see you," Kelsey Campbell announced. "She doesn't have an appointment, and the waiting room is full."

"Let her in Kels, it's okay." Harris went to the door and opened it, "Hi, Lieutenant, what can I do for you?"

Pushing him back into the office, slamming the door, Chris barked, "You have ten seconds to give me a good reason not to cut your balls off and shove them down your throat."

Harris blanched. "What? What is this about; oh wait...okay, okay. You found out about Emily, listen, I was going to explain."

"Emily, Emily, who the fuck is Emily?"

Harris thought, oh shit bad tactic.

"Oh, you mean the princess you're engaged to. I am a cop you moron, did you think I wouldn't find out?" She chided. "No Stevie boy, we have a bigger issue. It involves document subpoenas from the Federal Court about rinky-dink local misdemeanor cases." Chris moved toward Harris, causing him to back into the wall. She sat at his desk, put her feet up, and grinned.

"Now, there I was, being served with a subpoena by the FBI for records about a sale of alcohol to a minor. What would interest them in this case? No terrorists here. Then it occurred to me. The little twist about that case that I shared with you and, here's the kicker my former friend, no one else."

"Chris, listen. He was going to indict me on bullshit. I could not afford that, I didn't want to help the S.O.B. I had no choice."

"So you gave me up? Thanks Ace, nice to know I mattered to you." Chris stood and started for the door.

"Wait, I am sorry. It is not you he wants. It's Josh." Harris looked at the floor, "I am sorry Chris, I couldn't think of anything else to do..." his voice trailing off.

"Oh there was a choice Steve, but you took the easy way out. You did the same thing to Josh Collucci was trying to do to you. You could have stood up to him. He would not indict you. He is too busy running for

Congress.. Well, it was fun while it lasted, right up until I found out what kind of guy you are." Chris walked out the door and never looked back.

45: *Two Versions, Same Story*

On Monday, the first day of trial, US Attorney Robert Collucci stood on the courthouse stairs addressing the horde of media.

Hawk and Josh came around the corner, started up the stairs. The reporters deserted Collucci for a shot at the defendant. Collucci looked incensed at the abandonment. The reporters were jostling to get a question in. Hawk and Josh continued through the crowd.

Hawk paused, as a reporter asked, "Aren't you worried about the government's overwhelming case, Mr. Bennett?"

Turning to the reporter, he came back down a few steps, laughing. "Wow, did my worthy brother pass out a printed listing of his manufactured evidence for you, along with his campaign speech?"

Facing all the reporters, he continued, "As much fun as it would be to debate Mr. Collucci in public on this matter, I prefer to do my job in the courtroom. Mr. Collucci would be wise to emulate this. It is easy to make a speech about evidence, another thing to produce it in court."

Hawk was in his element now. He loved quests and touting at windmills. Inflicting some damage on Collucci would be fun.

"Sergeant Williams and I have every confidence the jury will recognize this witch-hunt and return a not guilty verdict on all counts. Glad to see the media is taking such an interest. I hope, at the end of the trial, you'll expose this for what it is, a travesty of justice in pursuit of political gain." Hawk headed back up into the courthouse.

"Morning, Sergeant Williams," nodded Deputy US Marshall Steve Murray. Murray, a retired Providence Police Officer, worked with Williams on a number of cases. "I have to send you through the metal detector like the common folk this morning," he apologized.

"No problem, Steve, I won't be carrying a weapon in here for a while."

"A short while," Hawk added.

Making their way to Courtroom 3, they found the spectator's gallery full. There was a mix of East Providence Officers, Chief Brennan included, a significant number of media, and a few lucky civilians who managed to get seats.

Josh looked around to see if Keira was there.

Recognizing the look, Hawk touched his shoulder. "Listen my boy; you need to focus on the trial. Their case is not very good, but it is a jury we are dealing with. Trust me, you will have time to find her and apologize later. Alternatively, you can follow my philosophy. Replace her." Shrugging his shoulders, he began pulling files from his brief case.

US Attorney Robert Collucci and Assistant US Attorney Margaret Fleming came in with Special Agents Slattery and Waters. As Fleming and the agents began laying out files and notepads, Collucci came over, extending his hand, "Mr. Bennett, good morning."

Hawk reached out, took the hand in a powerful grip, enjoying the apprehension in Collucci's eyes. "Good morning to you, sir."

Collucci tried to pull away. Hawk pulled him closer, whispering, "That's the last pleasantry you'll get from me until this is over, sir." Increasing the pressure of his grip, enjoying the look of fear in the eyes, and then releasing it.

Collucci rejoined Fleming at the government table and took some notes.

The Deputy US Marshall entered the courtroom and announced, "All rise, the United States District Court, District of Rhode Island, is in session. The Honorable Ulysses Steven Rodericks presiding."

Hawk leaned over to Josh, "Useless Rodericks. This is going to be fun."

"Be seated."

Judge Rodericks took a moment to organize his bench. "Gentlemen, and Ladies, I know you were originally expecting Judge Shore to preside. Judge Shore had a family emergency so, as the Chief Judge, I have assumed trial responsibility. I trust that is not an issue."

Not waiting for a response, Rodericks continued. "We will begin jury selection this morning. I expect to impanel the jury before the end of the day. Trial will begin first thing tomorrow. Before we bring in the jury pool are there any preliminary motions, Mr. Collucci?"

"No honor," not quite rising.

"Mr. Collucci, I realize it may have been some time since you've been in a courtroom, but in this courtroom, you will stand before addressing the court, is that clear?"

"Yes your..." as he started to rise, "Yes your Honor."

"Mr. Bennett does the defense wish to be heard on any preliminary matters."

Hawk made a point of rising, standing ramrod straight, "Yes your Honor, I'd like to be heard on my motions to dismiss based on prosecutorial misconduct as well as failure to comply with discovery."

"Objection, your honor," Collucci interjected

"Objection to what?" Roderick said. "You're objecting to his arguing a motion? I'll entertain the motion and take it under consideration."

"Thank you, your honor." Hawk began, "the defendant in this case is a highly regarded police officer with the misfortune of being involved in a deadly force incident. The East Providence Police investigated the matter, with the assistance of the Rhode Island State Police. The result of that investigation was turned over to the Rhode Island Department of the Attorney General for presentation to the Providence County Grand jury."

Pointing at Collucci, Hawk continued. "The US Attorney intervened and prevented the case from being put before the state Grand jury. This intervention was absent any compelling governmental interest or indication of any federal issues. My motion consists of three main points.

First, government attorneys had a conflict of interest in conducting the grand jury investigation,

Second, government attorneys conducted abusive and misleading questioning of witnesses before the grand jury; and,

Thirdly, government attorneys and agents interfered with defense counsel's access to a government witness.

Clearly, the US Attorney has a conflict of interest inasmuch as he turned this into a public political circus and demonstrated no compelling federal issues. During the Federal Grand jury presentation, he threatened witnesses with prosecution, or promised immunity, to compel testimony. The Government abused witnesses and forced false testimony. Lastly, the government denied defense counsel access to interview these witnesses. Some of the witnesses used to secure the indictment are not even listed in the discovery witness list. Defense had to discover their existence independently, in as much as their Grand jury testimony was not included in discovery.

This case is not properly before the court.

The case should be dismissed and referred back to the Department of the Attorney General. When, and if, the matter is presented to the Providence County Grand jury, the government will have ample opportunity to review the grand jury testimony results, and, if need be, conduct an independent investigation to determine any compelling governmental interests or violations of federal civil rights.

For those reasons, defendant moves the case be dismissed."

"May I be heard, your Honor?" Ms. Fleming requested.

"Ms. Fleming, if you insist. However, I must caution you. Under the circumstances, your written response to this brief would be appreciated as a timesaving gesture to this court. I would like to move on. I am taking the motion under consideration for now." Rodericks answered.

"Very well, your Honor, I will have it to you as soon as possible." Fleming sat, taking notes.

True to his word, Rodericks pushed through the jury selection.

The jury consisted of seven women and five men. Five black, three Hispanic, and four white.

Hawk was satisfied that the mix would insure a fair and impartial verdict. Specifically, not guilty. Despite Collucci's best efforts for an all minority jury, some masterful use of pre-emptory challenges to potential Jurors worked to Hawk's advantage.

46: *A Special Delivery*

On the second day of trial, Josh walked alone into the courthouse. Hawk called to tell him he would meet him there. As Josh came up the stairs to courtroom 1, Deputy US Marshal Steve Murray handed him an envelope.

"What's this?"

"Don't know," Murray replied.

"Who gave it to you?" Josh asked.

"Read it. I was asked to get it to you before the trial." Murray turned and headed into the Marshal's office.

Josh looked at the envelope, computer printed, one letter, "J."

As he started to open the letter, Hawk walked up to him.

"What's that?" he asked.

"I don't know," sliding it into his briefcase, "I'll read it later."

"Okay, my boy, this is where I earn my money, and you are dazzled by my legal brilliance, or not. Either way I get paid, right?" Smiling and diverting his gaze to several female reporters entering the court.

Josh looked towards the women and back at Hawk, "would it be better if I were female? Would I get your undivided attention?"

"Not at all son, I am sure you'd be an ugly woman, you'd get no attention." Walking into the courtroom and placing the files on the defense table.

"All rise."

Judge Rodericks came into the courtroom, took his position on the bench. After reviewing several documents he said, "Mr. Bennett in the matter of your motion to dismiss, I have some serious reservations about the timeliness of this. I am going to withhold any decision until I hear the government's case."

Turning to the government table, "I must say Ms. Fleming, there are some rather striking deficiencies in the government's response. I would hope your case in chief is more substantial."

Fleming and Collucci both started to rise.

"Sit, please, sit." Rodericks intoned, raising his hands, "I am not prejudging the matter, just expressing concern on the quality of the material so far before this court."

After a few minor preliminary matters, the jury members came into the courtroom. Judge Rodericks provided a brief synopsis of the trial structure. With the preliminary matters completed, the government began with its opening statement.

"Ladies and Gentlemen, my name is Robert Michael Collucci, the United States Attorney for the District of Rhode Island. I represent the government in this matter. We intend to present you with a tremendous amount of evidence proving, beyond any reasonable doubt, that the defendant Sergeant Josh Williams, acting under the color of the law, deprived Mr. Anthony Machado of his Civil Rights."

Stopping to look at several of the jurors directly, "And more importantly, his life." Shaking his head slowly, he looked over at the defense table, he pointed at Josh.

"Mr. Williams, while acting in his official capacity as a sworn police officer, shot and killed an unarmed African-American man for no other reason than the color of his skin." Grabbing the sides of the podium, "Can you imagine? The color of his skin."

Holding up a picture of a Marine in dress blues, he continued. "Anthony Machado was no ordinary man. He was a decorated United States Marine Corps combat veteran, disabled by wounds both physical and psychological, and the defendant executed him simply because he was black." Placing the picture on the podium.

"You will hear testimony, from an FBI expert in use of force and tactical operations. He will detail how Sergeant Williams, by deliberately entering the church alone, disregarded standard police practice. Based on nothing but flimsy radio reports. .

Why? That is what you need to ask yourself."

Collucci noticed some of the jurors looking at Josh. He moved to draw their attention back to himself. "Why would Mr. Williams, a trained, experience officer, enter the church alone? There were literally dozens of officers converging on the scene."

His movement causing the desired effect. "Why not wait?"

Focusing his attention on the jurors that looked at Josh.

"I will tell you why." Pausing to look at each juror. "He was chasing a running black man. In the insular police world, that is an invitation you cannot refuse. Sergeant Joshua Williams, a Police Officer, acted as judge, jury, and executioner. He took the law into his own hands, convicted a man, and sentenced him to death for the crime of being black and running away."

Back at the podium, he leaned in towards the jury.

"The defendant killed Mr. Machado for the color of his skin, forever silencing the content of his character."

Pointing again at Josh, "Mr. Machado, a US Marine combat hero, killed by this man sworn to uphold and protect the Constitution of this great nation."

Taking a piece of paper and crumbling it, "Instead, he used it to wipe the blood of an unarmed man off his hands." Tossing the paper onto the table.

"All of this, we will show you by the overwhelming volume of evidence.

You will hear testimony for a number of other witnesses, including a Priest, who saw the whole thing from inside the church.

You will hear expert testimony of how this pattern of behavior by Mr. Williams is a textbook case of Racial Profiling.

You will also hear from the defense. They will try to smoke screen the government's case; distract you with things that are not germane to this matter.

Do not let them divert your focus from the important aspect.

Mr. Williams took it upon himself to disregard standard police procedure, decide not to wait for the dozens of other officers available to assist him, enter the church alone, confront an unarmed, terrified, confused, psychologically impaired black man, Anthony Machado, and execute him in cold blood.

When the government's case concludes, your certainty of the truth in this matter will be absolute. You will also be sure of your responsibility, find Mr. Williams guilty of violating the Civil Rights of Anthony Machado while acting under the color of the law. Thank you."

"Thank you, Mr. Collucci. Mr. Bennett does the defense wish to make an opening statement?" Judge Rodericks asked.

"I will reserve my opening for later your honor. I'll wait for the defense presentation," Hawk answered, smiling at the jury, "if necessary." Hawk sat down and began writing on a legal pad.

47: *The Prosecution*

"The Government calls Detective Lieutenant Mark Pereira," Fleming announced.

Lieutenant Pereira, dressed in an immaculate dark-blue suit, approached the witness stand, turned, and faced the clerk. After taking the oath, he sat and waited.

"Good morning, Lieutenant."

"Good morning, Ms. Fleming."

"For the record, would you state your name and occupation?"

"My name is Mark Pereira. I am a Detective Lieutenant with the East Providence Police Department currently assigned as the Officer in Charge of the Bureau of Criminal Identification, or BCI for short.

Fleming questioned Pereira on processing the scene inside the church. Fleming introduced images, video, and diagrams completed by Pereira as well as other physical evidence.

"One last question, Lieutenant, is there anything you've left out as to items recovered at the scene?" Fleming queried.

"No, that is the entire list of items recovered." Pereira answered.

"So just to be clear, did you find any weapons inside the church?" Fleming continued.

"None. If I did they would have been photographed and cataloged," came Pereira's response.

"Thank you, Lieutenant, I have no further questions." Fleming returned to the table and sat. Collucci leaned over and patted her on the back.

"Mr. Bennett?" Rodericks asked, looking over his glasses at Hawk.

"Just a few, your Honor."

"Proceed." Rodericks motioned.

"Lieutenant Pereira, when you were photographing and videotaping the inside of the church, did you use ambient light or artificial illumination?"

"I, ah we, used flash on the still digital and the illumination light on the video."

"And why was that?"

"Because it was too dark, the image detail would not have been visible. It is standard photography and video-graphic techniques to use artificial illumination to provide adequate lighting for image capture and detail."

Holding up several of the photographs, "Do any of these images or video we've seen here represent the actual view of the scene with ambient light?"

"No, they were all enhanced with artificial lighting equipment." Pereira looked over to the jury, shaking his head.

"So is it fair to say that these images in no way are representative of the actual lighting conditions inside the church?"

"Objection," Fleming rose, "asking for a conclusion by the witness not established as an expert."

"Your honor..." Hawk began

"Overruled," Rodericks interrupted. "Ms. Fleming, this is your crime scene witness. I think he has demonstrated his knowledge of the mechanics of photography and is more than qualified to answer the question, continue Lieutenant."

"If I took any digital images or video without artificial lighting, the images would not be visible. The church was very dark inside." Pereira answered.

"No further questions, your honor, but I would like to reserve the right to recall Lieutenant Pereira in the future if necessary." Hawk sat down and made more notes.

"Ms. Fleming?" Rodericks asked, looking over as Collucci and Fleming huddled.

"Nothing further, your honor."

48: *In the Manner of Dying*

After several more investigators testified, the government called the Rhode Island State Medical Examiner.

"The government calls Dr. Belinda Warrish."

Dr. Warrish walked to the stand, took the witness oath and sat down.

"Good afternoon, Doctor. Would you please state your name and occupation for the record?"

"Dr. Belinda Warrish, Deputy State Medical Examiner for the State of Rhode Island."

"And how long have you been with the medical examiner office?"

"Twenty-six years."

"Your honor," Fleming looked and nodded at Hawk, "with the consent of the defense we move that Dr. Warrish be allowed to testify as an expert witness."

"Mr. Bennett?" Rodericks asked.

"No objections, you honor. I'd be happy to admit the Doctor's report as a full exhibit and agree to the validity of those findings."

"Ms. Fleming?" Rodericks asked, a bit of a plea in his voice.

"Your honor, there are certain aspects of the medical examiner's finding I wish to explore for the benefit of the jury. I will keep it brief."

"Very well, Ms. Fleming. However for housekeeping purposes, we will be taking a break at 2:00 pm, and then adjourning for the day at 4:30 pm."

"Thank you, your honor," turning to the witness, "Now, Dr. Warrish. I'd like you to examine this document. Do you recognize it?"

"Yes, it is my report of the autopsy of Anthony Machado conducted on March 16, 2009."

"Would you please read the highlighted section?"

The doctor held the report up, looked at it for a moment, then began,

"Subject, Anthony Machado, is a twenty-four-year-old, light-skinned, black male, five-foot ten inches, one hundred sixty five pounds, in good general physical condition. Subject's body shows evidence of several previous significant injures including the following:

Gunshot wound with skull fracture and significant residual scarring on the left front of the head.

Muscle and surface damage to the upper left leg consistent with an injury from an explosive device. There is evidence of second and third degree burns.

Gunshot wound to the lower left abdomen.

Extensive scarring on the upper and lower back consistent with shrapnel from an explosive device.

These injuries were medically treated and healed as best as could be expected considering the nature and extent of the wounds. The leg wounds likely limited mobility of the limb.

New injuries:

1. Penetrating gunshot wound to the chest perforating the Pericardium

2. Second Penetrating gunshot wound to the chest perforating the Pericardium

3. Gunshot wound to the skull

CAUSE OF DEATH:

Primary: Gunshot to the chest penetrating the Pericardial sac causing Pericardial Tamponade.

Manner of Death: Homicide

Evidence of injury:

Penetrating gunshot wounds of the chest:

The entrance wounds are located on the left chest, 17 inches below the top of the head, and 1 inch to the left of the midline. It consists of a 1 x ¾ inch oval perforation ranging from less than 1/8 inch thick to 1/8 inch at its widest point. This wound is consistent with a wound entrance of intermediate range. Upon inspection by the naked eye, gunpowder particles are not present on the skin surrounding the wound.

The second wound is locate ¼ inch to the left of the first penetration hole. It consists of a 1 X ½ inch oval perforation ranging from less than 1/8 inch thick to 1/8 inch thick at its widest point.

This wound is also consistent with a wound entrance of intermediate range. Upon inspection by the naked eye, gunpowder particles are not present on the skin surrounding the wound.

Further examination demonstrates that the wound track passes directly from front to back and perforates the pericardial sac, lodging in the right ventricle of the heart causing pericardial tamponade. There is no wound of exit.

Gunshot wound of the head:

There is a 1/8 inch circular gunshot wound of entrance over the anterolateral lower right forehead, above the eyebrow. To the naked eye, there are no gunpowder particles present on the skin.

The track of the wound perforates the anterior frontal skull and travels across the right anterior cranial fossa without brain tissue injury or bleeding.

The projectile then traverses the right temporal bone, and exits just inferior and lateral to the right zygomatic arch."

Looking up, "is there anything else you'd like me to read?"

"No, thank you. Would you explain to the jury, in layman's terms, exactly what Pericardial Tamponade is?"

"When the Pericardium, the sack around the heart, is punctured it fills with blood and compresses the heart, preventing it from performing its critical function. This causes an abrupt loss in blood pressure leading to unconsciousness and death in a few minutes."

"Would a person suffering the wounds you described be able to say anything before losing consciousness?"

"Well, I believe there would be a moment or so before the blood pressure collapse rendered them unconscious during which they could speak, but it would be brief."

"Even with the head wound?"

Warrish reviewed the report again. "The head wound, while causing significant damage, was survivable. My opinion is that he would have been able to speak for a brief period before his blood pressure level dropped."

"Now Doctor, let me draw your attention to another part of the report. You described previous injuries to the body."

"Yes, there was extensive prior damage, medically treated, consistent with explosives and gunshots."

"In particular, would you re-read this highlighted section?"

Taking the report, Dr. Warrish read "The leg wounds likely limited mobility of the limb," handing the report back to Fleming.

"In your opinion Doctor, would Mr. Machado have been able to run or crawl with that injury?"

"His movement would have been restricted; he could move the limb to walk, although with apparent difficulty. Running would be severely restricted as far as movement with any rapidity.

As to crawling, since that would require him to retract and extend the leg fully in order to contribute to the motion, I do not think he could crawl effectively."

"Now Doctor Warrish, did your examination of the body find any gunshot residue?"

"It did, there were small amounts of gunshot residue on Mr. Machado's chest and skull. I recovered and analyzed these with Scanning Electron Microscopy/Energy Dispersive X-ray Spectrometry. The fragments matched samples taken from the firearm used by Sergeant Williams."

"In laymen's terms Doctor."

"We used an electron microscope to locate and analyze gunshot residue. They were not visible to the naked eye. The recovered fragments compared to samples recovered from Sergeant Williams's weapon were a match."

"And Doctor, would you explain the significance of finding gunshot residue on Mr. Machado."

"Yes, the presence of gunshot residue is useful for several reasons. It is helpful in determining entrance and exit wounds and it is indicative of the distance between the firearm and victim at the time of the discharge".

"Do you have an opinion based on these findings, as to how close the weapon was to Mr. Machado when it was discharged?"

"I do, I would place the weapon with five to seven feet of the victim."

"Thank you Doctor, I have nothing further, your Honor."

"Mr. Bennett, do you wish to inquire?" Rodericks asked.

"I do, your honor, if I may have a moment," leaning over to Josh he whispered, "he was crawling, correct?"

"He was trying to; his right leg was moving and his left foot. He was dragging himself along on his elbow." Josh replied.

"Thank you, your Honor," rising from his chair, "Good afternoon Dr. Warrish."

"Good afternoon, sir"

"Doctor, is there any mention in your report of damage to Mr. Machado's arms, in particular, his elbows?"

"May I have my report again?"

"May I approach your honor?"

"Please," Rodericks answered.

Handing her the report, Warrish reviewed it for a moment and then said, "No, there were no findings of any injuries to the elbows."

"Thank you Doctor, now are you familiar with the motion made by snipers, crawling on the stomach, using the legs and elbows to move?"

"I am. I did five years as a field surgeon in the US Army after my residency."

"Splendid, Doctor, and if I may, thank you for your service."

Warrish smiled, nodding her head.

"Now, keeping in mind that type of motion, would Mr. Machado have been capable of such movement?"

"Objection, your Honor," Fleming interjected, "on what basis can this witness answer such a question"

"Overruled," Rodericks decided. "You opened this door yourself on Direct." Turning to the witness, "you may answer the question, Doctor Warrish."

"Well, his limited mobility would be specific to his left leg; he possessed full use of both arms and his right leg. I see no reason he would not be able to move in such a manner, albeit with little contribution by the left leg to the motion."

"I see," returning to the defense table and looking at his notes, "one last thing Doctor, are there any other ways that gunshot residue could end up on a victim?"

"There is the possibility of transfer." The doctor answered.

"Transfer, what exactly is that?"

"Often, particularly in police involved shootings, those involved have secondary, post-discharge, contact with the victim. They may be looking for vital signs, searching for other weapons, insuring the victim is under control."

"Is there any way to differentiate between direct gunshot residue from the discharge and secondary transfer residue?"

"If the weapon is very close to the victim at time of discharge, there would be what's known as tattooing. In essence, the hot residue burns a pattern onto the surrounding tissue. That is not evident in this matter. Also, the quantity of residue can be indicative of direct, as opposed to secondary, application of residue."

"So in this case, in your expert opinion, can you be certain the residue was directly applied to the victim and not the result of secondary transfer."

Warrish hesitated a moment, looked to the Government's table, and then answered, "Based on the quantity of residue, I do not believe I can be certain as to its source. The possibility exists it was transfer."

"Doctor, did you review all the police reports in this matter prior to conducting your examination?" Hawk asked.

"My investigators review the reports and highlight significant matters that may affect my examination."

"So, you didn't read the reports yourself?"

"No, I did not."

"Were you aware that Josh, Sergeant Williams, performed CPR on Mr. Machado immediately after the incident?" Hawk asked, looking at the jury.

"Ah, no I was not made aware of that." Doctor Warrish answered.

"Well, Doctor, now that you are aware, does it alter your opinion as to the source of the residue, or the proximity of the weapon to the Mr. Machado?" Hawk challenged.

"My opinion was based on the assumption there was no post-discharge contact with the victim by the shooter, under the circumstances you describe I would not be able to tell conclusively, absent other indications."

"Thank you, Doctor. I have nothing further your Honor." Hawk turned to the jury, smiled, and returned to his seat.

"Ms. Fleming, re-direct?" Rodericks asked.

Looking to Collucci, Fleming rose, "nothing further your Honor."

"Doctor, thank you for your testimony, you are excused." Rodericks said, "I see it is now 4:20. Rather than starting with the next witness since I assume it will take more than ten minutes, we will recess for the day."

Turning to the jury, "Let me remind you, Ladies and Gentlemen, not to discuss this case either among yourselves, or with anyone else. You are excused until 8:30 AM Monday morning. Thank you for your attention today. The Marshal will now escort you from the court."

After the jury left, Judge Rodericks left the bench. As Hawk and Josh started towards the door, Collucci came over.

"Mr. Bennett, would you like to discuss a possible plea in this matter? It would save your client from spending the majority of his good years in a Federal Prison," casting a glance at a glaring Josh.

"Kiss my fucking ass, you motherfucking political whore," Josh lashed out.

"Now, now Josh, calm yourself please. Mr. Collucci here is just starting to recognize that his case is about to collapse. I mean a number of rather harmless government witnesses have testified on the first day and they punched the first of what will turn out to be many, many holes in the government's case." Hawk smiled.

"I'll tell you what Robert, you dismiss the case right now and I can assure you we will not seek to sue your office, your pathetic political campaign chest, and your friends at the FBI for Malicious Prosecution." Hawk caught Collucci's eye, holding the gaze.

Then turning to Josh, "My boy, I think he believed we would seriously entertain such discussion. Now that I think of it he's perfect for Washington, chronically delusional."

Hawk and Josh walked out followed by a red-faced Collucci and a distraught looking Fleming.

49: Rehabilitation

Hawk sat in his office, writing notes, and listened as the phone rang, two, three, four times.

"Can you answer the damn phone, Tiffany? Please!" Hawk pleaded.

"Oh, ah, I just did my nails. They'll call back I'm sure," came the voice from the reception area.

Sometimes I wish I were gay, Hawk thought, then I'd hire male models, they must be less high maintenance.

Reaching for the phone he answered, "Law offices, how may direct your call?"

"Mr. Bennett, please, wait, Hawk? You answer your own phone. Alternatively, Jesus Christ Hawk, you're not getting ah, research assistance are you?" the caller asked. "Never mind, don't want to know."

"Why, it's my good friend from the Public defender's office, to what may I attribute this phone call?" Hawk answered, "and as a point of order, were there research being done, no one would be answering the phone." Leaning back in his chair and smiling.

"Well, I believe I have something you can use in your case, something I suspect the Government conveniently failed to provide you."

"Please continue, Councilor, you have my attention."

"How about I come over there? I can be there in 45 minutes or so," Harris replied, "one never knows the depth to which our learned brother Mr. Collucci would sink to know our strategies."

"By all means, come on over," Harris agreed and hung up the phone. "Tiffany," he yelled, "get in here. I need some quick research."

Harris arrived slightly prior to the 45-minute estimate and was amused by the disheveled, but remarkably unembarrassed, Tiffany walking from Hawk's office, retrieving her purse, and walking out the door.

"Ah, Hawk?" Harris called out. "I am announcing myself since your receptionist seemed in a hurry to leave."

"Well, the research was successful, so she was granted an early out as a reward." Hawk smiled as he came to the office door, "come on in."

Harris walked in, sat on the couch, and then jumped up suddenly, looking at Hawk, "that's not the scene of the research is it?"

"No, of course not," Hawk smirked, "I sleep there sometimes."

Harris looked at the couch, back at Hawk and said, "I'll stand, so how is the trial going?"

"First couple of days, not much to it. Crime scene and M.E. testified. They are hanging their hats on the experts on racial profiling, that comes next. I still can't believe that asshole took this to trial and expects to win."

Harris handed Hawk a file.

"What's this?"

"Read it, I think you'll see the value."

Hawk sat on the edge of his desk and began to read. Turning through the pages, his eyes narrowed and face reddened.

The forensic report from the FBI Crime lab described the various tests and procedures done to the numerous items of evidence recovered from the scene of the Robbery/Homicide. The one that caught Hawk's eye, as Harris knew it would, was the fingerprint analysis done on the shotgun recovered from the dumpster.

The examination found a number of prints. Most were inadequate to provide positive identification, lacking adequate points of comparison. However, the report noted there were partial matches to two individuals. In addition, they examiner recovered two identifiable prints. Both prints were positive matches for Anthony "JoJo" Machado. One print contained 19 matching points, the other 22. In the United States, there are differing opinions of what constituted a "positive" match, but the more the better. The two partial matches were likely David Anthony Ventraglia.

"That motherfucker Collucci never produced this in discovery for me," Hawk fumed, fanning the reports in the air. "I will move for production of this tomorrow and file a motion for Directed Verdict."

"Hawk, he isn't using this in your trial. He will argue it is not germane. He did not want to give it to me but had no choice. He buried it within records of the stolen cell, hoping I wouldn't notice until after this trial."

"Germane? Of course it is," his voice rising. "It adds more foundation to the legitimacy of the shooting. It is something the jury should know. It's...It's...."

"It's in your hands now," Harris interrupted, "use it as you see fit."

Hawk walked to his chair and sat. "Oh, I will open the day with this discovery by the defense," looking at Harris. "What do you want from me?"

"I want your guy to testify at Ventraglia's trial about the shooting, and Ventraglia will testify at Williams's trial about the robbery being Machado's idea."

"Was it?" Hawk questioned

"Who's to say?" Shrugging his shoulders. "There is only one participant in the plan that is around to tell us."

Harris smiled.

Hawk looked up, stunned. "Are you fucking crazy? I do not mind pushing the envelope to thwart the government's advantage, but suborning perjury is a line even I do not cross. Besides, trial started. The Judge will never let me add to the witness list. Especially if I just finished arguing for a dismissal for incomplete discovery."

"Look, my guy knows he's screwed. However, life in the can is a fulfillment of his wise-guy fantasies. Death by lethal injection is not. He will give the jury a glimpse of the ugly world inhabited by Collucci's victim. It will show the jury his warts and defects. It will make it a cinch to overcome the inevitable Marine-hero, minority-victim-of-police-profiling portrait Collucci will paint."

Harris paused, gauging Hawk's reaction. "I'll use this in negotiations to get Collucci to take the death penalty off the table, put it out there we've discussed the possibility of his testifying, and agree to have my guy invoke his 5th amendment privileges if you do subpoena him."

"He'll never go for it, Steve. He is a first class asshole, but he is not stupid," Hawk argued. "He'll see through this. He'll keep the death penalty on because it buys more publicity."

"He's also, deep down, a fucking coward. Juries are funny creatures. Their record of accomplishment, even with slam-dunk cases, is spotty at best. He wants a positive result, not justice.

He can spin a plea that eliminates the death penalty to the liberal sector of the district, and spin it to the right as salvaging a case, plagued by the poor investigative efforts of the local police, because of his bringing in the FBI.

Hell, he can even take a shot at the local office of the bureau. Tout his influence in Washington, his ability to produce for the district, justifying his qualifications for Congress."

Hawk smiled "You know Steve you missed your calling. You should be his campaign advisor."

Hawk looked over the file once more. He stood up, walked to the window, gathering his thoughts. "Okay, how do we do this?"

"Are you going to talk to your client first? He may not like this, coming from me. I am not on his favorites list." Steve quizzed.

"My client pays me to do what is in his best interest. In particular, when he doesn't realize it himself," Hawk replied. "I am a firm believer in the philosophy of seeking forgiveness rather than asking permission. He'll get over it."

"Well," Harris smiled in reply, "I will request a meeting with Collucci. He already refused one to discuss a plea. I'll tell him I have a Forensic psychiatrist I want to evaluate Ventraglia for an Insanity defense."

Hawk smiled.

"Exactly," Harris nodded, "he'll lose his mind and want to try to dissuade me. I'll let him and then lay this on him."

"Why are you doing this?" Hawk asked

"I let that son of a bitch Collucci bully me into something I am not proud of. If I can help out Josh and derail his political career it will be some consolation."

Hawk raised his eyebrows.

"That's the other part of the story," Harris continued, "you're not going to like this, but you need to know..."

When Harris finished the story, Hawk just stared at him for several moments. "So you really are screwing Lieutenant Hamlin, how can that be?"

"Hawk, are you nuts?" Harris was incredulous. "Collucci is going to put her on the stand and turn her into the world's biggest liar. If your client even dreams of testifying, he'll be dead on arrival, and all you are concerned with is me sleeping with Hamlin."

"Look, Steve, right after Chris decided to terminate your relationship with extreme prejudice she came here and told me the story. I was worried at first, but as I think about it, I believe I can use this to make Josh even more human to the jury. It is easy to convict a cop. Everyone has a bad cop story. It's hard to convict someone you've come to know as a human being."

"I don't know, Hawk. Collucci is good at destroying people. He will turn this into a circus of police cover-ups and lying."

"But he is planning this as a surprise. We are not surprised, but he will be." Hawk sat down, reached into his desk, and pulled out a bottle of Johnny Walker Red.

"So, Mr. Harris, are you the type to kiss and tell?" Smiling as he poured two glasses.

50: *Trial Day Two*

Judge Rodericks entered the courtroom and was halfway to the bench before the Marshal could say, "All rise."

"Good morning," Rodericks announced, "are there any matters we need to address before I bring in the jury. Ms. Fleming?"

"Nothing your honor, we're ready to call our first witness."

"Not so fast, my honorable sister at the bar, not so fast." Hawk rose and stood at his seat, "I have a matter of two motions, the second of which will not be necessary in the event the court grants my first motion."

"Proceed, Mr. Bennett."

"Your honor, based on new information available to the defense, I move for a directed verdict in this matter."

Collucci looked at Fleming shaking her head, pleading ignorance of what was coming.

"Your Honor, as is customary, we held several pre-trial conferences regarding discovery. As you know, the government is required to provide all evidence, lists of witnesses, experts, and other information it intends to introduce at trial. It is also required to provide all items that may be exculpatory in nature as to the defendant."

Turning to look at Collucci, "The government, in this matter, has failed to do so. It has failed, intentionally and maliciously, to provide my client with a key piece of evidence.

If counsel been aware of this information before trial, we would have made significant changes to our approach to this case. The government's actions jeopardized the whole judicial process."

Retrieving the report from his briefcase, "Your honor, there exist a report of an examination by the FBI Crime laboratory, regarding the shotgun recovered at the scene of the robbery."

Fleming leaned over to Collucci, "That report was in the discovery package I prepared. Did you remove it?"

Collucci just smiled, "It's not germane, argue that."

"You argue it, I complied with discovery"

Hawk noticed the discussion between Fleming and Collucci. *Perhaps I am spreading some fear, uncertainty, and doubt here. Fragmenting the team, he thought.*

Continuing his argument, "This report indicates that positive matches were made on two prints recovered from the shotgun. Those prints belong to Mr. Machado. This information is critical for the jury to have a true picture of the circumstances surrounding this matter. However, the government has chosen to withhold the information from the defendant.

The case has started. Defense developed its theory based on the reasonable assumption that the government fulfilled its obligation for complete discovery. Double jeopardy has attached. It is impossible for the defendant to receive a fair trial because of this revelation. The whole basis of the government's case was frail at best, now we find they have stooped to a new low of intentionally withholding exculpatory evidence.

For these reasons, defense moves for a Directed Verdict in light of the government's failure to comply with the full intent of discovery, thus denying the defendant an opportunity for a fair trial."

Hawk turned towards Fleming and Collucci, "under these circumstances, it is the proper thing for the court to do."

Rodericks wrote down some notes and then looked to Collucci. "How does the government respond to this allegation, Mr. Collucci?"

Collucci looked at Fleming, his eyes directing her to deal with this. Fleming started to rise, Rodericks motioned for her to sit, "I prefer to hear from the person responsible for the US Attorney's office. Mr. Collucci, would you be so kind as to illuminate the court in this matter?"

Collucci attained his current position by avoiding situations like this. He bore all the pedigree and appearance of a brilliant lawyer, but it was all show. All wretch and no vomit as Hawk liked to say.

He did not perform well when forced to think on his feet. He preferred the orchestrated, choreographed environments he could control. "With the court's indulgence, I think it best Ms. Fleming respond. She was more involved in the discovery process and can best answer this matter." Collucci pleaded.

"The court is not in an indulgent mood, sir. Your office handles these matters on a routine basis. Assistant United States Attorneys litigate cases here every day. However, you have never sat at the governments' table. You've taken a personal interest in this matter, have involved yourself in pre-trial motions and argument, so Mr. Collucci, I ask you again, how does the government respond to the defendant's motion for directed verdict?"

Collucci went on a rambling, embarrassing, illogical diatribe basing his argument primarily on the fact that the government never intended to introduce this particular report in this trial, thus making it unnecessary to include in discovery.

He argued that it was not germane. Whether or not Machado, at some point, handled the shotgun was irrelevant. He held no weapon when Sergeant Williams shot him. The prior handling of any weapon by Machado was not an element of the allegation, was prejudicial to the jury, and not exculpatory in any stretch of the imagination to Williams.

It was painful to watch.

Hawk wished they allowed cameras in Federal Court. He would get the tape and pass it out as Christmas presents to everyone Collucci stepped on over the years.

Rodericks was practically salivating on the bench.

"So let me see if I understand your argument, Mr. Collucci," Rodericks countered.

"The government's position is that the document is not relevant, but if it is relevant, it's not exculpatory, and if it is exculpatory, it's not fatal to the defendant's ability to receive a fair trial, and the jury shouldn't be allowed to hear this evidence as it is prejudicial. Is that it? There's been no harm, let's just continue our merry way?"

"Your honor, my point is..."Collucci struggled to reply.

"Mr. Collucci," the Judge interrupted, "that's exactly what I am trying to determine, you've made several points, few of which are persuasive. However, I disagree with all your contentions except, that a directed verdict may be too extreme a remedy. At least I thought you raised that issue. Perhaps I was just hoping you would, or I imagined it." Rodericks looked over to Hawk and back at Collucci.

"Mr. Bennett is it safe to assume your second motion is to compel the government to make the report available to the defense?"

"It is your honor, but I wish to reaffirm the defendant's contention that it is impossible for him to receive a fair trial."

"Yes, yes," Rodericks motioned for him to stop, "the court fully recognizes your argument and motion for a directed verdict. I need some time to consider this. We will stand adjourned for one hour." Rodericks stood up and left the bench.

The reporters in the courtroom stampeded out the door to be the first to report Collucci's evisceration.

51: *The Experts*

An hour later, the courtroom awaited the Judge's decision. Rodericks entered and assumed the bench. Organizing his notes, he looked at the lawyers, "I have taken this matter under review. The carelessness of the Government regarding discovery in this matter greatly disturbs this court. The requested documents should have been included in Pre-trial discovery. While I am not persuaded at all by the argument of their significance, they should have been provided."

Looking at Collucci, "I want assurances from the Government that there will be no more surprises in this matter regarding clearly discoverable material. I am denying the defendant's motion for directed verdict and granting the motion to compel production of the document regarding the FBI laboratory testing of the shotgun. Let me be perfectly clear. Any subsequent matters of a similar nature and I will have no choice but to grant a directed verdict. Is that clear, Mr. Collucci?"

Collucci rose, "Yes, your Honor."

"Mr. Bennett, the government will have this report delivered to you by the close of business today. You will advise the court immediately if they do not comply."

Hawk stood, looked over at Collucci, and said, "Yes your Honor. I will so advise the court."

Rodericks then ordered the jury brought back in. Once seated, he looked to Collucci, "is the Government ready to proceed?"

"We are your Honor. The Government calls Dr. Folami Kingston."

A tall, distinguished, black man came from the back of the courtroom and stood in the witness box. Dr. Kingston was seventy-six years old. He held several degrees from a variety of universities throughout the world. For most of his career, he was virtually unknown outside his academic specialty, Sociology, with an emphasis on Interracial interaction in pre-industrial America.

Doctor Kingston was the author of a controversial study of racial profiling. The conclusions rocked the conservative intellectual think tank, Wyman Janes Foundation, which funded the research.

In essence, Dr. Kingston's conclusions, disputed by all the report's co-authors, postulated that every police officer was incapable of controlling innate prejudices in dealing with blacks. This pattern of prejudice affects all officers' interactions with a person of color; including black officers by virtue of their acceptance of the police culture. His primary point being that the innate nature of police agencies foster such conduct and that this was, in fact, deliberate and intentional.

Dr. Kingston took his seat on the witness stand.

Margaret Fleming looked at the jury, and then turned to Dr. Kingston, "Good morning, Doctor."

"Good morning, Ms. Fleming"

"Doctor, would you please tell the jury of your academic and educational background?"

"I'd be happy to. My current position is Dean of the College of African Studies at Columbia University. I hold a dual PhD in Sociology and African Cultural Studies from Harvard University. I serve as a Fellow on the United Nations Committee on Race Relations. I am a Governing Board member of the Association of African Universities, and I also hold a position as Visiting Professor at the University of Venda, Thohoyandou, Limpopo, South Africa."

"Thank you Doctor, would you also tell the jury about your publishing accomplishments."

"I would be glad to," turning to the jury. "I have published over 100 articles in professional academic journals. I have several books still in print on Sociological Research Methodology, and I am the principal author on the 'Study of Racial Profiling: Patterns, Causes, and Implications sponsored by the Wyman Janes Foundation."

"Thank you Doctor. Your Honor the Government moves to have Doctor Kingston admitted as an expert and allowed to testify as such." Ms. Fleming said.

"Mr. Bennett?" Judge Rodericks looked to Hawk.

Rising, Hawk began, "Your Honor, I am confused as to what exactly Dr. Kingston, in spite of his curriculum vitae, offers the court in the way of an expert. If I understood the Doctor's initial testimony here, he has an impressive array of academic and educational credentials. However, only one of those touches on racial profiling. I fail to see how authoring one study, in which all the other authors drew different conclusions, is an adequate basis to allow expert testimony by this witness. The defense strongly objects to the Government's motion."

Judge Rodericks paused a moment, and then said, "The Court notes the defense objection, in essence, arguing to the point that the witness may be asked to give testimony as to the ultimate issue and thus questioning its value as assisting the judge and jury in deciding this matter. I am going to allow Dr. Kingston to testify under the rules as an expert. Ms. Fleming please keep to a narrow scope here. The Doctor has substantive credentials, but the court cautions about drifting too far astray."

"Thank you your Honor," retrieving a document from her file, she continued. "May I have this marked as Government, where are we, ah, Government's fifteen for identification and approach the witness?"

"So marked, approach."

"Dr. Kingston, do you recognize this document?"

Taking the document, Dr. Kingston examined it for several moments then handed the document back to Fleming, "Yes I do, it is a copy of the report I authored on the Racial Profiling practices in Police agencies."

"Your Honor, the Government moves to have the document marked as a full exhibit."

"No objection, your Honor," Hawk affirmed, before Rodericks could ask.

"Very well, document is marked Government Fifteen, full exhibit."

"Doctor, now referring to your report, can you describe the methods used and conclusions drawn in regard to Racial Profiling within Law Enforcement organizations?"

"Well, the purpose of the study was, through standard data analysis protocols and methodology, to determine if, in fact, Racial Profiling is a phenomenon within police agencies and to make a determination as to underlying causes."

Flipping through the report he continued, "We analyzed several thousand arrest reports looking for commonalities in the stated purpose, the conditions under which the encounter took place, and the background of the involved individuals."

"We also used test subjects, under double-blind study procedures, to measure changes in skin temperature and resistance when shown images of similar circumstances.

Measuring skin resistance and temperature changes has a long-standing acceptability within the scientific community. This methodology is common in research on sexual predators and pedophiles on one extreme and in product advertising on the other. It is a very reliable methodology." He placed the report down and looked at the jury.

"Doctor, as to the results of your study regarding the prevalence of racial profiling?" Fleming inquired.

"The results were conclusive. Police officers react in a more extreme and aggressive manner when dealing with black subjects. What we found particularly intriguing is that all other racial types did not have the same effect and, interestingly enough, the race of the officer was statistically insignificant."

"What do you mean by 'the race of the officer was statistically insignificant?" Fleming continued the inquiry, walking over to stand near the jury.

"In its simplest terms, it meant Police Officers reacted consistently to the testing stimuli, regardless of the officer's race. Black and white officers were equally prejudicial of black subjects. There was some differentiation among black female officers; however, even this was minimal."

"Doctor, has part of the preparation for this trial, did you have an opportunity to review the reports relating to the shooting of Mr. Machado?"

"Yes, I did."

"And did you review anything else?"

"I was provided with arrest reports of the East Providence Police Department for the past two years. I analyzed these reports using our statistical analysis program."

"And as to the analysis of the arrest reports, did you draw any conclusion?" Fleming continued.

"The incidents showed a correlation consistency with the reports analyzed during our study. East Providence officers engaged in a pattern of race based profiling. They were a much lower proportional incidence of such behavior. They were less likely than most departments, but nevertheless, profiling did occur."

"I see, and as to the specific incident involving Mr. Machado's shooting?"

"The pattern is consistent with a prejudicial assumption the subject was likely involved in criminal activity solely by virtue of his race."

"Objection, your Honor," Hawk was on his feet and angry, "this is taking on the guise of a fairy tale. The government, through this witness, has offered no foundation for this conclusion; the witness has spun a tale that since it is true in New York or LA, it is true here.

The government wants the jury to take the word of this expert, making a determination of a racially biased motive by Josh, after analyzing one report. There is no foundation here your honor, I move the testimony be stricken and the jury instructed to disregard this fallacious nonsense."

"Your Honor, Dr. Kingston is an expert in race relations and, more importantly, one of the foremost experts and researchers in the field of racial profiling by Law Enforcement. Dr. Kingston, through his well extensive academic, educational, and research background has established a solid foundation on which to base his opinions. The defense will have their opportunity under cross to challenge those, but this witness is more than eminently qualified to state his findings. As you heard him testify, he is not basing his conclusions on one report, but on an analysis of all arrest reports by the East Providence Police Department covering a two-year period. Those findings are consistent with the national research conducted by Dr. Kingston."

"Your objection is noted and overruled. You will have your opportunity in cross. Please continue, Ms. Fleming."

"Thank you, your Honor." Fleming returned to her table and retrieved a second document, "The Government moves to have this marked as Government sixteen for identification," handing the document to the clerk, "May I approach?"

Rodericks nodded.

"Doctor Kingston do you recognize this document?" Fleming inquired.

"Yes, I do. It is the report I prepared after reviewing the statements and evidence in this case."

"Government moves to have the marked as full exhibit, Government sixteen."

"No objections," Hawk agreed, again beating the Judge to the punch line.

"Doctor, would you please read from the highlighted page twenty-five?" Fleming leaned back on the table, watching the jury, hanging on the Doctor's words.

Fleming counted on the fact that somewhere in the past the minorities experienced some negative contact with the police.

"...*based on the analysis of the data relating to incontrovertible evidence of racial profiling within the East Providence Police department, the behavior of Sergeant Williams in his pursuit of Mr. Machado, into the church, alone, reflects an attitude of superiority characterized by assumptions of culpability based on race, which is prevalent within the agency and consistent with Sergeant Williams behavior in this matter.*

In conclusion, it is my opinion that Sergeant Williams's actions reflect a specific and deliberate decision to terminate Mr. Machado's life solely based on race. Any subsequent mitigating justifications were factually unknown at the time and irrelevant to this determination."

"Thank you Doctor Kingston, I have nothing further."

Rodericks looked to the jury, "Ladies and gentlemen, we will stand adjourned for lunch. Please refrain from discussing this matter. We will resume at 1:00PM. Marshal, please escort the jury."

After the jury door closed, "Doctor Kingston, you are excused until 1:00PM as well," looking to the court, "are there any other matters to discuss before I adjourn?"

"Nothing your Honor," Fleming answered.

"Not at the moment, your Honor, I am sure this afternoon will be quite different," Hawk replied, staring at Dr. Kingston as he passed by.

"I am sure it will, Mr. Bennett. I am sure it will. Court stands adjourned."

52: *Different Story*

The jury returned to the courtroom.

Hawk watched, marking lines on his pad. As soon as the jury returned, he slid the pad to Josh, "Know what that is?"

"Ah, no."

"The number of jurors that looked at you, counts going up, happy?"

"Jeez, Hawk, really?"

"I've been doing a daily count, you're on the rise. If you were running for office it'd be time to ask for more contributions."

Josh just shook his head and took out his notebook.

"Got any words of wisdom in there for me, son?" Hawk smiled.

"Are you ready for cross, Mr. Bennett," Rodericks intoned from the bench.

"Ready, willing, and adroit," rising from his seat gathering notes.

"Adroit? Perhaps you meant able?" Rodericks questioned.

"Same thing, but on steroids your Honor."

Rodericks looked at the jury. Several were smiling. *We will see, Mr. Bennett, we will see.*

"By all means, proceed."

"Thank you your honor," looking at a report, and then moving towards the witness before turning to the jury.

"Dr. Kingston, this report on Racial Profiling was it written by you personally?"

Kingston appeared confused, and then rose to the bait, "If you mean did I personally type it out, no. I have assistants for that."

Arrogance is an addicting drug.

"I am sorry Dr. Kingston, let me rephrase. Is the report the result of your effort exclusively?"

"Ah, I see. No, it was the result of a cooperative effort of a number of experienced researchers, postdoc, doctoral, and undergraduate students, as well as a number of professional research assistants."

"And did you author the conclusion?"

"I did," smiling and nodding to the jury.

"And how was this conclusion reached, was there a vote?"

"Sir, let me familiarize you with research methodology and reporting. In a study such as this, the senior research fellows each prepare an analysis of their conclusions. As the main author of the study, I prepared the overall study analysis."

"I see. Let me make sure I understand this. Is your conclusion the, ah, only valid one based on the study results?"

"The conclusion I prepared is a result of the synthesis of the data, my reading of the other reports, and the benefit of my vast experience in these matters."

"I see, thank you Doctor. Now, how many other senior researchers wrote conclusions?"

"There were seven main research fellows, including myself."

"Ah, so you are the one that breaks the tie?"

"I don't understand the question." Kingston began to fidget a bit.

"I assume that since there are six other researchers, there must have been three the agreed with you and three that disagreed. Is that not true?"

Kingston paused, took off his glasses, and wiped his eyes. "This is not a vote sir; it is a research project where we follow accepted guidelines and practices."

"I see then. Well, of the six other senior, experienced, eminently qualified researchers, how many agreed with your conclusion?"

"Once again sir," leaning forward grabbing the rail, "this is not a popularity contest this is...."

"Your honor, would you please instruct the witness to answer the question, if he doesn't understand it I will simplify it."

"Save the sarcasm, Councilor. Dr. Kingston please just answer the question."

Kingston sat up a bit straighter, looked at Hawk, and said, "All of the other researchers drew, in varying levels of intensity, different conclusions."

"I do not mean to beat a dead horse, so to speak, but just so I and the jury understand, there were seven researchers correct?"

"Yes."

"And of the six other researchers, none of them concurred with your conclusion, is that true?"

"Yes, however… "Pausing a moment, "Yes that is true."

"Is it not true that Wyman Janes, the foundation that underwrote the research, has asked for an independent audit of your methodologies?"

"They didn't get what they expected," waving a hand dismissively. "My integrity is not for sale."

"Are you being compensated for your appearance here?" glancing to the jury for a reaction.

"My foundation receives a fee to cover costs and expenses related to my review of all pre-trial documents, preparation time, and consultation efforts," removing his glasses. "My opinion is not subject to any part of that fee. It is honest, forthright, and based on facts and data," sitting back, "I resent the implication."

"Sir, I implied no such thing, I thank you for your answer. What was that fee?"

Kingston looked over to Collucci, no help there.

"Do I have to answer that your honor, I hardly see the relevance."

Rodericks looked up at Hawk, "Is this going somewhere, Mr. Bennett?"

"Your honor, I am just putting the testimony in context for the jury."

"Very well, the witness will answer the question," looking at Dr. Kingston, "no one is challenging your integrity."

"Yes sir, "glancing back at Hawk, "my standard fee for matters involving public entities, local, state, and federal, is Fifty thousand dollars. It is much higher for private institutions."

Hawk just let that sink in. Saw the sideways glances among the jury.

Strike One.

"How often have you testified as an expert witness in a criminal matter?"

Kingston was now squirming, shifting his position, "once."

"I am sorry, did you say once?"

"Objection your honor, "Collucci said, "this is bordering on badgering the witness, we all heard the answer."

"Sustained, Mr. Bennett move on."

"Yes, your honor."

Strike two.

"Dr. Kingston, do you know the name Mustafa Ali Mustafa?"

Kingston's head rose slowly, his eyes burned, leaning forward he said, "Mustafa Ali Mustafa is my son."

"Yes sir, and what does your son do?"

Collucci and Fleming were both on their feet, "Your Honor, where's the relevance here?"

"He doesn't do anything," Kingston was standing, shouting, "He's dead."

Rodericks slammed down the gavel, "Enough, stop right there Dr. Kingston, do not say anything else."

Kingston sat, hands shaking, trying to hold his glasses, wiping his brow.

"Mr. Bennett, where is this going?" motioning Collucci and Fleming to sit.

"Your honor, I am permitted to ask questions that explore anything evidencing bias."

Collucci was on his feet again, "Your Honor," glancing at the jury, "this is highly prejudicial."

"He has a point Mr. Collucci; I am going to allow this, up to a point which Mr. Bennett will get to soon."

Hawk nodded.

Collucci glanced at the jury and sat down.

Wind up.

Hawk looked at Dr. Kingston.

"Sir, I do not wish to cause you any more anguish, how is it your son is dead?"

Kingston took a deep breath, looked at the jury, trying to control the tears, "He was killed by a police officer."

Strike three.

"And was that officer white?" Hawk asked, watching the jury's reaction. "Withdrawn, your Honor," short circuiting the inevitable objection.

Collucci looked at Fleming, "How did we not know this?" he whispered.

"You didn't want to pay any more money to vet the witnesses. You found a damn report you liked and bought it without researching the person. What did you expect?"

Hawk walked over and sat. Looking at Josh, he motioned him in, "Son, I cutting my fee in half. That shit was fun."

Josh rocked back.

"Not really, but it was fun."

53: Reasonable Doubts

"What if I did shoot him because he's black?" Josh said, sitting at the bar at Hemenways.

"What are you talking about?"

"Maybe I do have deep-seated prejudice towards blacks."

"And why would that be?" Hawk raised his eyebrows, turning his head to face Josh.

"I was mugged once, well almost, at the Brown football stadium. I was 11. We went to a game with my Boy Scout troop. I went underneath to use the bathroom and an older black kid grabbed me, put me against a wall and tried going through my pockets. Someone came along, and he let me go. I ran back and never told anyone."

Hawk put his hand on Josh's shoulder.

"Josh, several hundred Viet Cong tried to kill me at one time or another. I didn't like it much then, but I don't go around trying to kill every Asian I see. Do not let this guy mess with your head. This is all psychobabble political correctness bullshit. Now enjoy the drink and forget about the trial for the moment."

"There's something else." Josh added.

Hawk turned, facing Josh, "Now what?"

"It's a long story."

"I got all the time in the world, son. My martini is chilled, and I've nothing to do but listen."

"When I was in the Air Force, right out of Basic Training, I was assigned to the Security Police Training School at Lackland. We were assigned two to a room, and I ended up with a black kid from Baltimore named Nathaniel Archibald, we all called him "Archie."

Taking a drink from his wine, Josh continued, "We took the weekend off before training started so we just kind of hung around, drank beer, and relaxed. There was this kid from Texas; he was in the same Basic Training flight, sort of a typical redneck. Anyway, one day he gets me aside and says 'why you roomin' with the nigger?"

I thought he was joking so I said, 'What? Archie, he's a great guy.' I could tell by the look on his face the guy was serious, so I just walked away, I didn't say anything to Archie, and we never had any other problems."

"So, what is the issue?"

"I should have done something, punched the guy, anything. I mean, hell, growing up in Cumberland, we didn't have much contact with minorities. I think Archie was the first black person I ever spoke to in my life."

"Josh, punching some redneck wasn't going to change his ingrained prejudice any more than it would demonstrate your lack of such beliefs. I learned a long time ago not to let the past control you, other than learning from your mistakes."

"Wait, there's more."

"Let me get another drink," waving to the bartender.

"About a year after I got on the job, I pull up behind one of our Lieutenants on a car stop. This was an old school, World War II guy about a year before retirement. Anyway, he pulled over a car with four black guys in it. As I walk up, I say 'Hey L T, what do you have?' He says, 'box of raisins, kid, niggers in a new ride." Josh paused a moment, looking at Hawk.

"Box of raisins, I get it, so?" Hawk asked.

"I laughed," Josh looked into his glass, "I just laughed. I should have walked away, got into the car and drove off. But instead, I just laughed."

"Josh, let me bring you down to earth son. If you had done that, you'd have caught all sorts of shit for being afraid, or called a pussy, or some such label. Moreover, it wouldn't have made a damn difference to that moron Lieutenant. Look, there is nothing you have ever done to indicate you hold any more prejudices than anyone else does. We all have some fear or misunderstanding of things we have little exposure to. Over time, as you gain experience with people of all colors, shapes, and nationalities, you came to realize we are all the same. Things you did or did not do at nineteen years old is not an indication of a lifetime of bias. Nor does it have anything to do with this trial, you remember that."

Josh smiled a bit and continued to stare into the wine.

Maybe you do Josh, maybe you do. I was trying to tell you I did good...trying to get you to stop like I stopped Divothead...why didn't you hear me?

54: *Those That Can...*

"The Government calls Robert Murphy."

The witness came in the courtroom doors. Murphy, sixty-eight years old, dressed in a dark-grey suit, tidy gray beard, reading glasses dangling around his neck, walked with a pronounced limp to the witness stand, took the oath, and sat down. He looked the part of a banker.

"Would you please state your name and current employment for the record?" Collucci asked, deciding to handle this witness himself, warming up for the coming big show.

"My name is Robert J. Murphy. I am a Partner at Professional Standards Consulting, Incorporated."

"Would you explain to the court what Professional Standards Consulting is and your background?" Collucci looked to the jury, measuring their interest.

"Professional Standards Consulting focuses on assisting Law Enforcement agencies, both domestic and international, in developing standards for use of force by police officers, security forces, and other agents. I spent thirty-eight years with the FBI, the last ten of those assigned to the Office of Professional Responsibility. Upon retirement, I formed Professional Standards Consulting."

"With the court's indulgence, just a few more points" Collucci said, recognizing Rodericks' growing impatience. "Mr. Murphy, what are your educational credentials and professional publications?" Collucci could see the jury was interested.

"I hold a Master's Degree in Criminal Justice from University of Chicago, a Juris Doctorate from Georgetown Law, and have published two books on Use of Force policy development. Both of which are used in a number of Undergraduate and Graduate level Criminal Justice programs, State and Municipal Police Academies, including the FBI National Academy."

"Your Honor, the government moves to have Mr. Murphy qualified as an expert in Use of Force as it relates to Law Enforcement."

"Mr. Bennett?"

"No objections, your Honor," Hawk replied.

"Mr. Murphy, let me draw your attention to Government exhibit one. Are you familiar with this document?"

"I am"

"And would you please describe the document for the court?"

"Yes, this is a certified copy of the investigative file for Case A-2013-9-2145. The Officer Involved Shooting of Anthony Machado."

"And did you have an opportunity to review this file?" Collucci looked to the jury, insuring they were listening. Juries pay more attention when they see you watching them.

Murphy nodded. "I did. I reviewed all the investigative reports in this matter."

"Did you undertake any other review of this matter besides reviewing the report?"

"I did. After doing a thorough review of the reports, I visited the site of the shooting and re-enacted the various actions reported by Sergeant Williams and the other officers at the scene."

"Now Mr. Murphy, based on your extensive background and experience, did you find anything about the reports that were of concern to you?"

"I did, if I may, a little background on appropriate use of force and the hierarchy of escalation of force would be helpful in clarifying my findings."

"Please, proceed," Collucci retreated and stood next to the jury.

"Objection, this is turning again into story telling time allowing for narrative by the witness," Hawk argued.

"Your Honor, if it pleases the court, I will elicit this testimony through questioning the witness, but as a recognized expert, he is permitted to set an explanatory basis for his finding as defined in Federal Rules of Evidence, Rule 702." Collucci responded.

"Overruled, you may continue Mr. Murphy," Rodericks concluded.

"Over time, Law Enforcement agencies have tried to build a rational, understandable, and defensible use of force model for officers. The first of these is Use of Force Continuum. The concept is of an Officer, starting with the minimum use of force, following the continuum of escalation until the lawful purpose is accomplished. These models were controversial in that some interpretations implied a requirement to follow the continuum regardless of the level of the threat present. The model, in most cases, conflicted with an objectively reasonable level of force.

Most agencies, and my consulting team, now rely on a force options model. This is more in line with court decisions. This policy provides a more realistic, and therefore safer, approach to use of force, both for the officer and suspect. By way of example, when an officer is facing an armed individual, it is objectively reasonable that he not go through a list of force options, voice command, baton, pepper spray, Taser, before resorting to deadly force, or at least the threat of deadly force.

The key point being agencies now develop and implement policies that give officers force options to deal with threats. The emphasis is still on using just the minimum force necessary to accomplish the lawful purpose, which may, in fact, be deadly force under some circumstances."

Pausing to take a drink of water, Murphy continued, "In this matter I reviewed reports from Sergeant Williams, Lieutenant Hamlin, Forensic investigators, Medical Examiner, and Father Swanson. I also reviewed the Policy and Procedures, in particular, the Use of Force policy, of the East Providence Police in effect at the time of the shooting, and the department training records."

Collucci moved to stand between the jury and Murphy, blading his body to allow him to look between them, "And did you draw any conclusions from this analysis?"

"My review of the Policy and Procedures of the East Providence Police led me to conclude they are consistent with the most up-to-date recommendations of the United States Department of Justice and latest court decisions regarding use of force. These policies and procedures are also quite comprehensive in detailing tactical methodology for responding to high-risk level incidents such as armed robberies, hostage situations, and other matters.

My review of the training records shows that the East Providence Police use a multi-phase approach to training. Combining role call instructions, memos, and monthly reviews of training and policy matters. They conduct a mandatory situational shoot/don't shoot training session using the latest in available computer-based weapon's training. The records indicated that Sergeant Williams last participated in this training process the month prior to this incident."

Pausing again, Murphy looked at Josh and then turned toward the jury, "Based on this review, I concluded several things. First, Sergeant Williams was fully aware of the policy and procedures of the department regarding high-risk situations. Second, Sergeant Williams's decision to enter the church alone, without assisting officers, nor waiting for a properly established perimeter, was in clear breach these policies. Sergeant Williams's action was a tactical error of judgment absent any compelling reason to do so. This escalated the potential for a deadly force encounter. Third, by positioning himself as a direct threat to Mr. Machado, lacking any factual indication of his participation in the robbery, he again escalated the situation."

Taking another drink of water, he noticed Hawk furiously writing notes. As he spoke, he could not control glancing at the defense table.

"To summarize, based on the facts known to Sergeant Williams at the time, as reported by him, his decision to enter the church alone, position himself within an unavoidably dangerous proximity to Mr. Machado, was a significant tactical error. These actions escalated the situation and set in motion an unstoppable series of actions, leading to the death of an unarmed man."

Josh noticed Murphy's continuous glances at Hawk and leaned over to see what he was writing. Hawk looked up and whispered, "Psychological warfare, my boy. Just planting a little doubt."

Josh smiled back, grabbed a legal pad, and joined in the fun.

Murphy continued. "If Sergeant Williams followed his training, the conclusion of this situation would be different," glancing at Josh, he reached for the water glass.

"Sir," Collucci asked in a voice measured and serious, "based on this review what conclusion did you draw from the fact that Sergeant Williams is white and Machado black?"

"Objection, your Honor." Hawk was angry, "there is no basis upon which this witness is qualified to provide such an opinion. We have listened to his qualifications as to police procedures none of which shows any foundation on which he can somehow divine motives of another person. I have every intention of exploring the opinion Mr. Murphy has crafted as to his area of so-called expertise, but I object to his being allowed to testify as if he were clairvoyant."

"You Honor, if I may..."Collucci began.

"No you may not, Mr. Collucci. You can inquire and introduce the witness's expertise in the area of police procedures and its relationship to use of force. You cannot infer anything other than factual based opinions, not suppositions." Looking to the jury, "the jury will disregard drawing any inference as to the last question asked by Mr. Collucci. The objection is sustained."

Collucci walked back to his position at the Government's table, "Nothing further, your Honor," a slight grin crossing his face. The damage done.

"Mr. Bennett, are you ready for cross-examination?" Rodericks asked, looking over his glasses.

"I am your honor."

Walking to the exhibit table, he retrieved the file marked Government Exhibit One, opening to a particular page, he looked to the bench, "May I approach the witness?"

"You may."

Handing Murphy the report, "Mr. Murphy would you read the first two paragraphs on that page?"

Murphy began to read them to himself.

"No, no Mr. Murphy, I am sorry, please read them out loud for our benefit."

Murphy looked up, over at Collucci, and then at Judge Rodericks.

"Please read them sir," Rodericks instructed.

Murphy removed his glasses, wiped them with a handkerchief, and began, *"The subject, later identified as Anthony Machado, saw our unmarked unit, turned around, and began to run towards St. Domenick's church. I immediately jumped from the car and began to chase Machado, radioing in my positions. Machado was running with a strange motion, and I thought he had a weapon concealed in his pants. Machado ran up the stairs and into the front of the church. I notified responding officers that I was entering the church and for them to set up a perimeter.*

I decided to enter the church as I knew Father Swanson was often in there during this time of the day. I was concerned there may be parishioners in there as well. The reports were that the suspect shot two individuals. As soon as I entered the church, I saw Machado hiding behind the altar, crawling towards to Sacristy. I looked around but couldn't tell if there was anyone else in the church. The only lighting was near the altar, and it was very dark."

Murphy put the report down and looked at Hawk.

"Now sir, you testified that you reviewed the policies and procedures of the East Providence Police and all the reports about this incident, is that correct?"

"Yes sir."

"And in your testimony, you said the policies and procedures were the latest and greatest, if I can paraphrase?"

"I said they met with the latest standards, yes sir."

"Now sir, the section of the report you just read aloud, is it safe to say you'd read this as part of your review?" Hawk was facing the jury, glancing back at Murphy.

"Yes I did. I read everything related to this incident." Murphy was becoming anxious, breathing quickly.

"Well then sir, in your opinion you indicated that Josh, Sergeant Williams, ignored his training, and his decision to enter the church a tactical error, I believe is how you phrased it?"

"It was an ill-conceived decision to enter the church absent any compelling reason to do so, and he chose to do this without assistance." Murphy answered, regaining composure.

"Sir, I am now going to show you Government's exhibit twelve, do you recognize this document?" Hawk stood next to the witness stand as Murphy looked it over.

Murphy tried to hand the document back as he said, "Yes, it's a certified copy of the Policies and Procedures of the East Providence Police Department," holding the document out for Hawk.

"Oh no sir, you hold on to that, we have more reading exercises to complete." Walking over to the jury Hawk turned, folded his arms and said, "Please read page twenty five, from the beginning."

Murphy flipped through the pages, came to page twenty-five, pausing a moment as he looked it over. Collucci and Fleming were trying to locate their copy to read it as well.

Hawk stepped back and looked at the two government lawyers, drawing the attention of the jury to them. Hawk looked at the jury and smiled.

"Your Honor," Collucci rose, "This document is already in evidence for the jury to review. I fail to see where this line of questioning relates to the witness' direct testimony."

Hawk started to speak but Rodericks cut him off, "No need Mr. Bennett. The defense is permitted to explore the basis of the witness's opinion. You may continue, Mr. Murphy, read the page as requested."

"Section 2, Use of Force, continued. It is the primary duty of members of the East Providence Police Department to protect lives. There may come a time where the use of deadly force is both justified and necessary. Every reasonable effort to avoid such situations, within the confines of our responsibility to the public must be taken. The following guidelines are designed to assist officers in determining the correct course of action.

One. An Officer must never place themselves in a position that escalates a situation absent a legally valid reason to do so. This would include, entering into a location without adequate backup, entering into an unknown environment without proper preparation, or failing to provide notice of intent to fellow responders. High-level threat situations are dynamic and fluid. No guideline can adequately account for all possible circumstances; however, it is paramount that protection of the lives of all involved be the main decision factor. Officers are reminded that their oath to protect the public often entails risks."

"You can stop there, sir" Hawk interrupted.

Murphy put the file down.

"Now, sir, it is also safe to say that this section is familiar to you from your review?"

"Yes, I went through all the policies and procedures in depth" Murphy answered, "It is how I formed my opinion," growing agitated.

"Would you please read the section that prohibits an officer from entering a building alone?"

"There is no such language, what there is…" Murphy answered.

Hawk interrupted, "Well then, in your testimony…"

"Objection, he isn't allowing the witness to finish his answer." Fleming interjected.

"He did answer. I asked him to read a section, and he stated there is no such language, sounds like we have a fully honest answer for once."

Rodericks looked at Hawk, "Save the editorial comments councilor, let the witness finish his answer before continuing," turning to Murphy, "sir, please confine your answers to the question asked. Continue"

"As I was saying, in your testimony you said that Sergeant Williams actions, a moment, I have it here in my notes, ah yes, you said 'was in clear violation of these policies', yet you just testified that there is no such language prohibiting an officer from entering a building alone, so which is it?"

"Sir based on my thirty-eight years of experience in these matters, my professional evaluation of the total circumstances known to Sergeant Williams, as he reported, and the language in the Policies and Procedures of his department, of which he was aware, his decision was wrong and created what became a deadly situation."

"So this is really a difference of opinion, there is no language that prohibited Sergeant Williams from entering a building alone. You just don't believe you'd make the same decision, is that not true?"

"No sir, as I stated his decision was wrong." Murphy was again agitated.

"How many incidents such as this have you been involved in?" Hawk changed course.

"I have investigated several hundred..."

"That's not what I asked sir, I wanted you to tell the jury how many incidents, in which deadly force was used, that you have been involved in?"

"Well, I was fortunate in my career, as are most in law enforcement, never to have to fire my weapon during an incident."

"So your opinions and experience are a form of hindsight?"

"No sir, I have always based my review on the facts as stated in the reports, based on what the officers or agents reported at the time, not what may have been learned later." Murphy began to perspire a bit and finished the water.

"During your career, have you been injured in the line of duty?"

"Objection," Fleming stated, "where is this relevant?"

"I am trying to put a perspective on the extent of the professional experience your witness claims, suffering on the job injuries certainly gives one experience in the risks inherent in law enforcement" Hawk replied.

"I'll allow it," the Judge said.

"Yes, a number of times, it goes with the job." Murphy answered.

"Have you ever been shot?" Hawk asked, staring at Murphy.

Murphy crossed his arms and turned slightly away from Hawk.

"Your honor, is this leading somewhere?" Collucci was now on his feet.

"With the court's indulgence, this will become apparent as to its relevance."

"Mr. Murphy has already testified as to not being involved in any deadly force incidents, certainly being shot would qualify as one." Collucci argued, trying to win the upper hand.

"Your honor, if I may, expert opinions weigh heavily on a jury. The credibility of the expert is critical. I am allowed to explore that credibility."

Murphy became even more noticeably nervous. He knew what was coming.

"Objection is overruled, please answer the question."

Murphy looked down at his hands, rubbing them on his pant legs.

"Would you like me to repeat the question?" Hawk asked

"No sir, I was shot during a training exercise," Murphy replied, his voice barely audible.

"I am sorry. I couldn't hear your answer." Hawk moved closer.

"I was shot during a training exercise," Murphy repeated, eyes narrowing as he looked at Hawk.

"And how did that happen?" Hawk took delight with this one. He knew the jury would see him for what he was.

Murphy paused, took a deep breath, and said, "During a re-enactment of an incident involving an FBI agent taken hostage during an undercover operation, my weapon discharged, striking me in the left knee."

"And sir, was there a policy in place for insuring weapons were unloaded during such exercises?"

"Yes." Murphy's voice, soft and hesitant.

"Well, I am glad to see you've recovered. Were you disciplined for this incident?" Hawk inflicted the wound, now going for the kill.

"I was suspended for thirty working days upon my recovery," Murphy whispered.

"But upon return from this suspension were you placed back in the same operational position?" Hawk asked.

"No, I was transferred to Headquarters." The answer accurate, but incomplete.

"So your new assignment was what?"

"Planning and Research," Murphy replied.

"Is that a field operational position, how long were you there?" Hawk was enjoying this. He knew Murphy as one of those behind the scenes, politically connected people that fucked-up, were taken care of, and spent the rest of their careers finding things wrong with the people doing the real work.

"It is not in the field. It is based at FBI Headquarters DC, and I was there until I was transferred to Professional Standards."

"Professional Standards, that's like Internal Affairs is it not?"

"Similar yes, we did good work there." Trying to regain some self-esteem and composure.

"And you retired at Sixty-five years of age, isn't that much later than normal for FBI agents?"

Murphy went for the bait, "Agents considered being necessary to the operation or holding special skills can be extended to age sixty-five under the discretion of the Director of the FBI. I was considered important to the Office of Professional Responsibility."

"Who took over for you when you retired?"

Murphy looked up, angry, "the position has not been filled."

"So, this position was important enough for the Director to extend you five years beyond normal retirement, and then not fill the position for three years, not to this day?" Thus sealing the witness's fate as a political hack before the jury.

"Objection."

"Withdrawn. Nothing further." Hawk returned to his seat, leaned over to Josh and said, "That's how you inflict damage."

Collucci was glaring at Hawk as he whispered to Fleming "I'll bet one of those bastards in the local office fed that to Bennett. Sons of bitches, we need to try to save this guy."

Fleming looked at Murphy; saw his drained appearance, "He's not going to be helpful. Look, damage is done. They still have his report about the incident. He did not lose all his credibility. We can save him in our summary. I say let it go."

Collucci stood for a moment, hesitated, then said, "We have nothing further for this witness your Honor." Sliding back into his chair, he leaned into Fleming, "I am going to burn Hamlin like a bug in a bug light."

55:   *A Reluctant Witness*

"The government calls Father James Swanson"

Collucci tried reading the jury reaction. This priest caught their interest. He could see it in their eyes; see the furtive looks between them.

Jim Swanson came into the courtroom, walking towards the witness box. He paused a moment to smile at Josh, entered the witness stand, took the oath, and sat.

"Good afternoon, Father Swanson." Collucci's voice betrayed his anxiety. This was going to be the nail in the coffin. All he needed to do was guide the priest along. Bennett could object. It would not matter.

It would be out there for the jury to see. There is no such thing as, the jury will disregard. It was a joke, trying to put the toothpaste back in the tube.

He was going to enjoy this.

"Good afternoon, Mr. Collucci," Jim replied, not holding the gaze, looking blankly around.

"Now Father Swanson, would you please tell the jury your current assignment within the diocese?"

"I am the Pastor of Saint Domenicks Church in East Providence."

"And how long have you been there?"

"I've been at the parish for almost twenty years, the last five as pastor."

Collucci moved over to the front of the jury, forcing Swanson to look at him, giving the jury a better view.

"And Father, were you at Saint Domenicks on March 15, 2006?"

"Yes I was."

"Where were you around 4:30 pm that day?"

"I was in the Sacristy preparing some new vestments for Mass."

"And did you see someone come in the front of the church that day, a person you know as Anthony Machado?"

"Yes, I did. I heard the front doors of the church open and saw Anthony run in, go up onto the altar, and duck down."

"And did you see Sergeant Williams enter the church?"

"Yes, a few seconds later Josh, Sergeant Williams, entered the church."

"Did you see a weapon in Sergeant William's hand?"

Jim looked over at Josh, dropped his head, and answered, "Yes."

"I'm sorry Father, could you repeat that, I couldn't hear you. Did you see a weapon?"

"Yes, Josh had a weapon in his hand."

"Could you still see Anthony Machado at this point?"

"Yes, I could see him behind the altar. I thought he was looking at me."

"Did he have a weapon?"

"Objection, calls for a conclusion by the witness," Hawk interjected.

"Sustained."

"Father Swanson, did you see a weapon in Anthony Machado's hands?"

"I couldn't see his hands, well I couldn't see both" Jim replied, trying to keep calm.

"So you could see one of his hands, correct?" Collucci was not letting him slide on this.

"Yes, his left hand."

"And did he have a weapon in that hand?"

"No, but I didn't know what was in the other hand." Jim became a bit more confident.

"Sir, I mean Father, that's not what I asked, once more, did Mr. Machado have a weapon in the hand you could see, his left hand?"

"No. However, I must tell you I was afraid."

"Thank you," ignoring the last part hoping the jury would as well. "Now where was Sergeant Williams at this point?"

"He moved to get closer to the altar, he yelled at Anthony to stop moving."

"Did you hear what he said?"

"Yes, he said...."

"Objection. Hearsay your Honor. He can testify that Josh said something but as to what he said..."

"Your honor there are well-known exceptions to the hearsay rule. One of which is independent corroboration. The reports in this matter do just that, reports prepared by Sergeant Williams. Father Swanson is testifying to what he heard Sergeant Williams say. Sergeant Williams's report is the independent corroboration."

"I will allow it, continue Mr. Collucci." Rodericks wrote some notes and looked over for Hawk's reaction. He was smiling.

"Thank you, your honor. Okay Father, let me pose the question again, when Sergeant Williams approached the altar, his weapon pointing at Machado, you heard him say something?"

"Yes, he told Anthony to stop moving."

"Father, I realize this may be difficult for you, however I must remind you, you are under oath, what did you hear Sergeant Williams say?"

Jim looked at the jury, looked at Josh, took a deep breath and said, "Josh said, 'stop right there you motherfucker or I will blow that fucking hood off with your black head in it."

"Oh boy," Hawk whispered, "I don't recall that as part of the report."

"I didn't say that" Josh protested. "I never said black head, I said head...at least I think I did."

"Well, it is out there now," Hawk growled. "What do I do? If I argue it is wrong, the jury will pay more attention, if I ignore it, they think it is true. You didn't fudge the damn report did you?" Shaking his head.

"No," Josh protested, "I put what I said, as I remembered it."

Collucci let the statement sink in a bit, and then overplayed the hand, "So let me make sure I understand. Sergeant Williams, pointing a weapon at Mr. Machado, said 'Stop right there you motherfucker or I will blow that fucking hood off with your black head in it, is that correct?"

"Objection," Hawk was on his feet, "there is no testimony as to Josh pointing his weapon. Mr. Collucci is trying to incite the jury"

"Sustained, rephrase the question."

"When Sergeant Williams made that statement was he pointing his weapon at Mr. Machado?" Turning to enjoy the jury's reaction.

"No, he was not." Jim replied, "It was pointed in the air, away from Anthony."

Collucci snapped around, "Sergeant Williams had the weapon in his hand, did he not?"

"Yes, yes he did, but it wasn't pointed at Anthony."

"Thank you Father, but nevertheless, as far as you could see, the only weapon visible was the one held by Sergeant Machado, correct?"

"Yes," Jim responded, looking at the jury.

"How close was Sergeant Williams to Mr. Machado?"

"I'm not sure," pausing a moment, "about the distance from me to where Josh, I mean, Sergeant Williams is sitting. I'm not good at guessing distances." Jim looked at the Judge, "sorry."

"What happened next?"

"Anthony, Mr. Machado, started to move closer to the Sacristy door, I heard him say 'I tried to get him to stop', several times. He sounded as if he were crying or sobbing."

"What did Sergeant Williams do?"

"He was yelling at Mr. Machado to stop moving, but I couldn't make it all out. I was moving back away from the door. I didn't want to be seen," looking at the floor.

"Go on Father, did you see Sergeant Williams do anything else?"

"No, as Mr. Machado kept moving towards me, I saw him raise his right hand and start to turn towards Josh. I thought he held something in his hand. I was afraid," looking down at his hands, "I closed the door, a few moments later I heard the shots," pausing to take a breath. "I looked out once more and saw Sergeant Williams doing CPR on..."

"A moment Father," Collucci tried to derail the answer, "did you see anything in Mr. Machado's hand?"

Hawk was writing notes as fast as he could.

"I am not sure, there may have been. I don't know."

"So is it safe to say that at the time Sergeant Williams shot and killed Mr. Machado, you closed the door and could not see what happened?"

"That is true. I did not see the actual shooting. I did see Sergeant Williams doing CPR, trying to save Mr. Machado," Jim said, trying to soothe his conscience.

"Father, what did you do after the shooting?" Collucci was going to emasculate the man now that he was through with him.

"I am not proud of this," dropping his head, "I closed the door and went to the residence."

"You never told the police what you saw, did you?"

"No, I did not."

"And you didn't come forward until after you read about Sergeant Williams's indictment?"

"Yes, I wanted to let the police know what I witnessed. I wanted..."

"I have nothing further, your Honor," Collucci finished, dropping into his chair.

"Mr. Bennett, cross examination?"

Hawk knew better than take any comfort in the smile on Rodericks' face. He was not smiling because Collucci snatched defeat from the jaws of victory. He was smiling because he took pleasure in any lawyer's failure.

Josh was not going to like what was coming, but it was necessary.

"Father Swanson, when did you first report you were a witness to this incident? It wasn't to the police was it?"

Jim blanched a bit then rebounded, this was expected. "I went to speak to the lawyer representing David Ventraglia."

"And who is that?"

"Steven Harris."

"You never went to the police about what you saw until you spoke to Steven Harris, correct?"

"Yes, I, have no way to explain. After I met with Mr. Harris, the FBI came and spoke to me. That's when I gave them my statement about being there and seeing what happened."

"Father Swanson, how did you come to know Anthony Machado?"

On one of those rare occasions, Hawk went with instinct over planning.

"He was an altar boy at the parish when I was a young priest."

Hawk knew from the eyes, there was more to this.

"How long was he an altar boy?"

"He served for three months."

Now there was no doubt.

"So you recall an altar boy from more than twenty years ago, that only served for three months? It seems odd wouldn't you say?"

"Anthony was special."

"Why was that?"

Once again, eyes betray.

"Anthony experienced some problems. His mother suffered substance abuse issues," looking at his hands, "and there were other things."

"Other things, such as?"

Hawk could see. He knew he was on to something. Instincts kept him alive in Vietnam, and they were right again.

"Anthony told me he was molested. I cannot explain more; it is under the seal of confession."

Once again, Collucci leapt before looking, assuming Jim was hiding something useful.

"Your honor, while there is some protection offered to penitents, Mr. Machado is dead as a direct result of the defendant's actions, we need to know what he may have revealed. Rhode Island law requires clergy to report matters of abuse learned as a result of confessions."

Hawk stood there a bit bemused. "Your Honor. I am gratified by my brother's support of compelling this testimony, and I concur. If Father Swanson learned of abuse within the course of hearing confession, he is required by law to report it."

Rodericks looked at some notes for a moment, "I am going to excuse the jury. This will allow the court time to consider this matter. Ladies and Gentlemen, you are excused for the day; we will reconvene Friday morning, 9:00 AM. Please do not discuss this case with anyone, otherwise enjoy your time off."

Once the jury left the courtroom, Rodericks looked to Father Swanson, "Father, are you aware of the limitation on Clergy-Penitent privilege in matters of abuse?"

"Yes, your Honor, I am. This confession took place over twenty-three years ago. The law was different at that time. I do not believe I am under any obligation to report that. Anthony is dead and it is of no benefit to him," Jim replied nervously, "I will seek guidance from the Diocese on this. However, I am disinclined to reveal anything more, with all due respect, to the court."

"Thank you for your candor, you may step down from the witness stand, for the moment, Father."

"Mr. Bennett, I am not sure I see the relevance here. If your purpose is to diminish the credibility of this witness, I do not see this as germane."

"Your Honor, if Mr. Machado suffered abuse, and told Father Swanson, it may reveal some motive for his actions in the church. The defense theory on this matter is that Mr. Machado's actions, even if we assume Sergeant Williams was lacking absolute knowledge of Machado's involvement in the robbery, were of such a threatening nature, and in total disregard of the lawful commands of this officer, that they in of themselves would be enough for a reasonable person to perceive a threat. If some psychologically significant event such as molestation, in fact, occurred in Mr. Machado's past, it could explain his irrational behavior, and support an objective perception that he was dangerous."

"And if the good Father is compelled to testify, and evokes the privilege against self-incrimination, where would that leave us, still without the information you seek and no avenue left to pursue." Rodericks closed his eyes, leaned back a moment and continued, "Mr. Collucci, what is the government's position on this?"

Collucci saw this as a way to bring even more sympathy for Machado. Not only is he killed for being black, but also a white priest failed to report his being molested by another white priest. Machado suffered for years from an uncaring, bigoted system. *This just keeps getting better*, Collucci thought.

"Your Honor, the Government needs some time to research this, however on its surface, I agree with the fact Father Swanson is under a legal obligation to testify. The Clergy-Penitent privilege offers no protection here. If Mr. Bennett wishes to pursue this line of questioning, the government does not object."

Returning to his seat, Collucci and Fleming huddle.

"Are you sure about this, Robert," Fleming asked, "if Bennett turns Swanson into a bad guy over this doesn't that ruin his credibility?"

"They may not like the priest after this, but it's not about him anyway. We got Williams's statement in. I'll push that in the summation, that's what they'll remember."

Rodericks wrote down some more notes, looked up and said, "The Court will consider this matter and entertain argument prior to resuming the trial in the morning. Mr. Collucci, please advise Father Swanson to be here, available to the court, Friday morning."

Rising to address Rodericks, "Yes, your Honor, I will have Father Swanson available at 9:00 AM," sitting back down he thought, maybe I should call my cousin the Bishop again, just in case.

As Hawk was packing his briefcase, Josh handed him a document pointing to a particular section. Hawk read it, looked up at Josh and said "Well, my boy. I never said I was infallible. How did we miss this?"

Josh shook his head, "I guess the shooting affected me more than I realized."

"Well," Hawk replied, "At least your report was accurate. Inconvenient, but accurate."

56: *Sanctuary in Sanctity*

Robert Collucci hung up the phone. This can be either the worst thing to happen, or the best, he thought.

Using the information to manipulate that wimpy priest was never in doubt. If the Bishop became a casualty, so be it. He would look even the bigger hero taking down the conspiracy of silence within the church, the cousin aspect spun to his advantage of course.

Incorruptible.

An hour later, having explained a redacted version of the situation to Fleming, he sent for the good father.

Father Jim walked into the office, determined not to be a pawn in this matter anymore. Jim glanced at Fleming, surprised to see her, nodded, turning to Collucci.

"Mr. Collucci, I need to tell you something. You are not pushing me around anymore. I will not let you use me to get to Josh. He is a good man, sir. He doesn't deserve this."

"That was two things, Jim," Collucci smiled, "or do you prefer I call you Father? I do not give a rat's ass what you think, or what you say. That cop shot an unarmed man because he was black."

"Bullshit," Jim yelled, causing both Fleming and Collucci to raise their eyebrows. "There is no damn way Josh would ever do that. I cannot believe your political aspirations are more important than the truth."

The angered tone even caught them by surprise.

"Truth? You want to talk truth there Father? How about this truth? You molested that boy. Anthony went to the other parish Priest. He told him about it. That other damn priest, yeah that's right," reacting to the stunned look on Jim's face, "is my cousin, the Bishop. He told me all about your confession."

Standing up, he walked to the window, turned, facing Jim.

"And what does our good, holy, righteous, Bishop do? Nothing. Allows it to continue, avoids doing the right thing. Runs away. Some hero of truth, Ms. Fleming, wouldn't you agree?" Glancing at the uncomfortable AUSA.

"You, seeing that as a green light, continue to molest the boy. Now you are going to lecture to me on the truth. How dare you."

Letting the impact sink in.

"I'll tell you what is going to happen. I am going in there tomorrow and argue to protect your lying asses, yours and my idiot cousin. Which is more than you ever did for Machado's."

Jim had never seen such an evil look. He was in shock.

He was willing to go to jail to protect the sanctity of the confessional. Learning the Bishop lied and twisted his confession, then discussed this with Collucci just to save himself, was too much. It was obvious the Bishop would try to cover up the truth. *So be it. I will tell them everything.* It was not absolution, but it was effective.

"And here's another thing, don't even think about trying to change your testimony. Do not think of going to Bennett with this shit. If you do, I will find out. I will indict your ass for molestation, perjury, and a whole slew of other shit. I do not give a damn about statutes of limitations. I will find a way.

And, my dear Father," narrowing his eyes, "don't think I won't bury my cousin along with you. I will take on the whole damn Church if I have do. Understand?"

Jim stood, walked to the door, as he opened it he looked into Collucci's eyes, "Mr. Collucci, the Bishop is lying to you. He has twisted the story for his own protection. I know what I did was wrong, for the wrong reasons, for an institutional philosophy I never understood. I am not proud of what I did," looking down at the ground, "but it was never about me, well, that may not be completely true, but it was not about my gaining something. I am not sure what will happen here, but understand this; my only hope of redemption is in letting the truth come out. I will no longer prevent that." Closing the door behind him.

Fleming stood and started to speak.

"Don't bother. I am through playing softball with these bastards. I do not give a shit, which one molested him, as far as I am concerned, they are both responsible. That being said, I do not want to let that testimony in. It will turn the jury's attention away from the real matter here. I also do not want to alienate the Catholic vote. They'll see this as another exhuming of old history."

Looking at Fleming, "Go to your office, prepare an argument to protect the penitent, so to speak. Rodericks is not going to let it in anyway. Greenhorn Catholic bastard wouldn't have the balls."

"I am not comfortable..."

"You're not comfortable?" Voice rising, "not comfortable with what, priests screwing little boys, priests protecting priests who screw little boys, or cops that shoot people for the color of their skin? Which is it?" Walking towards her, face reddening.

Rising to face him, "Robert this case was a stretch; you've known that from the beginning. Now this mess. It is going to turn into a train wreck."

"You want off this case? I will take over. I do not need your idealistic ideas of Justice. I am going to cause a change here. Then, I am going to cause a change in Washington."

Fleming shook her head, "I'll stay on the case. You remove me if you like, but somebody's got to remember what our goddamn job title is."

"And what is that?" Banging his hand on the desk.

Fleming stared at him, shaking her head. At the door, she paused a moment, took a deep breath,

"United States Attorney, not Lord fucking Protector." Slamming the door behind her.

57: *Damage Control*

Jim returned to the residence at Saint Domenicks. As he walked into the den, he was not surprised to find the Bishop along with the Diocesan attorney, Brian Patricks, waiting for him.

"Good evening, Father Swanson," the Bishop said.

"Good evening, Eminence."

"You know Mr. Patricks, don't you?"

"Father," Patricks nodded.

"I do know Mr. Patricks." Jim walked to the cabinet, took out a bottle of Johnny Walker Blue and offered it to his guests.

"Not for me," Patricks answered.

"I believe I will have a small glass, neat," the Bishop replied.

After pouring the drinks, Jim asked, "So am I safe to assume that this has to do with the line of questioning being pursued by Mr. Bennett?"

The Bishop nodded, sipped from his drink, eyes glancing to Patricks.

"Father," Patricks began, "as you are well aware there is significant legal precedent regarding Clergy-Penitent confidentiality. We believe that the law in this instance is clear. We are advising you to refuse to testify regarding any conversations held under the protection of the confessional." The Bishop, nodding slightly, indicating he should continue.

"In the unlikely event the court rules to compel your testimony, our advice is to invoke your Fifth Amendment protection and ask to speak to counsel."

"But doesn't that imply," looking at the Bishop, "I have something to hide, something I am concealing."

"Not at all," Patrick argued, "invoking either privilege is well within your rights, essential to the operation of the Church, and guaranteed by the Constitution. No adverse inference can be drawn for invoking your rights."

"And suppose I decide not to follow this advice?" holding the Bishop's gaze.

"Would you excuse us a moment, Brian. Father Swanson and I need to discuss something outside your area of responsibility." The Bishop stood and walked to a window.

Patricks left the room, closing the door behind him.

The Bishop turned, facing Jim. Holding his gaze a moment he began, "Jim, I know the difficulty these issues pose to one's conscience. There is not a day that goes by I do not ask for forgiveness for my weakness. However, we are mere representatives of a much greater good. The Church has built this philosophy over centuries. It has survived because it works; it protects the Church, forgives our sins, and fosters our faith. It is not for us to determine the correctness of this. We have an obligation to fulfill our vows."

Turning to the window again, "Look, you can hold whatever disdain or revulsion you feel for me in your heart, but you cannot let your personal feelings dictate something destructive to the Church. I sought help. I found peace in meditation and prayer. I found a way to resist my weaknesses. You need to do the same.

I know you walked away from young Anthony those many years ago, like you walked away when that officer shot him. However, going against your vows, damning your soul forever, losing your position as a Priest, will not undo those wrongs. They were your human weaknesses. You can overcome them, as I did."

The Bishop came over and stood next to him, "Jim, don't let our weaknesses hurt the Church. We will seek forgiveness together. We will help each other through this."

Jim started to speak, paused, and then looked at the Bishop. "You lied to Mr. Collucci. You revealed matters within the confessional, conveniently changing roles, and now you ask me to uphold that same confidentiality." Jim stood and began pacing, "Yes my dear Bishop, your cousin used that information to threaten me. Do you know what else he said? He said he'd take you down as well."

The Bishop smiled, "Jim, don't you see. He is playing us against each other. I would never discuss matters of such a confidential nature. Listen to me, we can get through this."

"No, we can't. I have lived with this long enough. I wonder how different Anthony's life would have been if I did something more."

Father Swanson dropped his gaze to the floor. "You never knew this, but I made sure you were never alone with any other altar boy after that. I spent hours watching you to make sure you had no access. It was too late for Anthony. I know you went to his house. I know many things. The things you did away from the Church on those trips with your brother," catching the surprise in his eyes. "Yes your Eminence I knew all about those, the money used, the hotels you stayed in. But they were outside my control, this is not."

Jim watched as the Bishop tried to compose himself.

"Those trips were all approved by the Diocese, there was nothing improper," glaring at Jim.

"Then why the need for the phony receipts and altered travel requests? Do not take me for a fool, Bishop. I knew someday this would all come crashing down on me. I will take responsibilities for my failings, and for not doing enough to prevent yours. However, I won't let this be used by your cousin to force me to help him put a good man in prison for something he is not guilty of."

Jim stood, walked to the door and called out, "Mr. Patricks. I need you to be present for this."

The Bishop's eyes grew wide.

Patricks entered the room, saw the distress in the Bishops eyes, and looked at Jim, "what's going on?"

"The Bishop and I have come to an accommodation," looking at the Bishop, "he will be submitting his request for retirement from the Diocese and requesting a position to allow him more time for contemplation and soul searching. In exchange, I will follow your advice as to my testimony, but up to the point of invoking any Fifth Amendment protection. If it comes that, I will testify about anything asked of me."

Jim walked over to his chair, picked up his drink, and took a long swallow.

Patricks looked to the Bishop for some guidance. The man's face was ashen.

"Since at least you and I are men of honor Mr. Patricks, I will be satisfied hearing about the resignation on the news in the morning. If it is not there, I will assume this agreement canceled. I will testify without reservation about all aspects, including matters in the confessional, by all involved." Focusing his attention on the Bishop, "If the Diocese moves to remove me from the Priesthood, so be it."

Rhode Island has the distinction of being the most Catholic state in the country. News of the Bishop's resignation ran right after the latest shootings in Providence, and before the report of the growing economy.

Jim took no satisfaction in this. He knew there were still elements of the Church that would mobilize to protect and insulate. It no longer mattered to him. He thought, 'those we saw as most worthy of our trust can become the vehicle of our dissolution.'

58: Battle Lines

Hawk and Josh walked to the courthouse. The media descended on them.

"Mr. Bennett, will you force the Priest to testify? What about the promise of confidentiality? Do you intend to take on the church on this matter? Does this have anything to do with the sudden resignation of the Bishop?"

"My, my nothing like a little battle with the Catholic Church to stir things up I always say." Hawk replied. "We really have nothing to say here. We do all our talking in the court room."

Continuing up the stairs, Hawk turned and winked for the cameras, "However, I will tell you this, moments after the jury returns the Not-Guilty verdict, if we even get that far, I will have a great deal to say about all of this. Until then, off to slay the dragon."

59: *Sanctimonious Liars*

Rodericks returned to the Bench. "Ms. Fleming, does the government wish to be heard in this matter? Are you still supporting the defense motion?" Rodericks asked from the bench.

"Your Honor, after careful consideration and research, the Government objects to this line of questioning as irrelevant.

Furthermore, we would argue that the Clergy-Penitent protection applies in this matter. The status of the penitent in this instance being deceased is of no bearing.

Compelling Father Swanson to testify on matters within the confessional is rift with risk. There is no way to limit the damage.

There may be something prejudicial to Mr. Machado that, once in front of the jury, may be impossible to redact.

As I stated in our written brief, there are numerous cases supporting the exclusion of such testimony. Tantamount here is the relevance. Assuming ad arguendo, that the Court allows Father Swanson to testify and he reveals a statement against interest of Mr. Machado, the damage would be done, yet the information is of no actual bearing on the matter before the bar.

There is nothing Father Swanson can testify to about matters heard in confession that have any direct or circumstantial evidential value in this matter."

"Thank you Ms. Fleming. Do you have anything to add Mr. Bennett?"

"Well, I am a little surprised by the Government's change of heart. Nevertheless, this may all be academic.

The protections offered by the Clergy-Penitent confidentiality cloak attach only if Father Swanson invokes them.

If I recall, he said he would seek guidance from the Diocese.

Perhaps we should ask the witness the question and see if he invokes the privilege.

I am not trying to waste the Court's time here. I think we need to have the problem before us prior to arguing about how to fix it."

"You may have a point, Mr. Bennett. Let's bring the jury in, recall the witness, and see where this leads."

Once the courtroom settled down, Father Swanson re-took the stand.

"Now, Father Swanson, do you recall the questions I asked you the other day?" Hawk began.

"I do."

"And as to the information regarding the name of the individual Mr. Machado told you molested him, will you please tell the court whom that person was?"

Jim looked over to Josh, dropped his eyes down and thought. *I have a choice here. Unveil the evil of one man, show the world that I am a coward, go back on a commitment I made to Patricks and the Bishop, not that they deserve any consideration. Alternatively, refuse and see where it goes. What is the greater good? This does nothing to help Josh, or does it? Anthony was a troubled man, perhaps he wanted to die there, at the scene of his degradation.*

The voice came to Jim at that moment.

Help him Father; he didn't do anything to me. I was dead to the world all those years ago. Let it go. The truth is what matters. No one will know the truth about me. You can reveal another truth. Any truth revealed, is good for the soul.

"Father Swanson, do you want me to repeat the question?"

"No, I just needed a moment to compose my thoughts."

Amazing how easy it is once you decide to tell the truth.

Looking to the Judge, Jim asked, "Can I explain the whole story, if I just answer the question it will be difficult to understand."

"Mr. Collucci?" Rodericks asked.

Looking to Fleming for help, her eyes conveying 'on your own here pal', "Ah, no objection as long as it is to the point." Collucci replied.

"Okay Father, continue but keep it brief."

"Twenty-three years ago, Anthony Machado came to me in confession. He told me was molested by," pausing a moment, taking a breath, "a priest within the Parish. I knew what he said to be true because I saw Anthony with the priest the night before." Dropping his gaze to the floor.

"The circumstances were troubling, but as a young priest, I was in no position to prevent what happened, or more correctly, I was not strong enough to do the right thing. I hoped I was wrong. I quickly learned the opposite was true."

He looked over at Collucci. "On that same day, the priest came to me in confession as well and admitted to the acts described by Anthony.

My faith requires me to provide absolution; my vows as a priest compel me to offer the opportunity to repent. I no longer hold that to be true."

Looking over to the jury, "I never should have walked away from that, I should have done something, but I didn't. I will live with that for the rest of my life, for that I am sorry. I never should have let Father Macloughlin, now Bishop, get away with what he did."

There was an audible gasp as the name came out, several of the reporters rushed from the courtroom.

Rodericks banged the gavel calling for order in the courtroom.

Jim looked over at Josh then back to the jury, "I think Anthony wanted to die there, where his young life was so horribly damaged. I saw Sergeant Williams do everything he could to get Anthony to stop..."

Collucci was on his feet, "Objection your honor."

Jim ignored Collucci, continued talking to the jury, "I was afraid Anthony had come for me. I believed he was there to kill me for not helping him all those years ago."

"Your Honor, this has to stop. This is not testimony. It's a speech." Collucci tried talking over Father Swanson.

"Sergeant Williams waited until there was no choice. I saw Anthony's hand come up. I believed he was holding a gun, so I shut the door. The latch made a loud sound, then the gunshots...I am sorry Josh, so very sorry," hands shaking, voice quivering.

Rodericks seemed stunned, "Father you will stop now, no more for the moment. We will be taking a short recess, please remove the jury."

As the last of the jurors left, the remaining reporters all rushed to the door, Josh stood up, walked to Jim and put his arm on his shoulder, "It's okay Jim, it's okay. Come on with me."

"Your honor, I do not think it appropriate that the defendant in this matter should be approaching a witness while they are still on the stand. Please direct him away." Collucci was incensed.

Rodericks glared at Collucci, "I hardly think the defendant in this matter would be tampering with the witness right here in front of the bench. Nevertheless," turning to Josh, "Sergeant Williams I realize you have a long friendship with Father Swanson, but please do not approach any witness while they are still on the stand."

"Yes your Honor, my apologies to the Court." Josh and Jim then walked out of the courtroom.

The reporters were waiting.

So was Deputy Marshall Murray, he ushered Jim, Josh, and Hawk into a small, private conference room.

"Did you see that?" Hawk asked.

"See what?" Josh answered.

"Useless was nice to you! When you walked up there to Jim, I half expected him to order you into custody. Instead, he acted with kindness and empathy. If you've won him over, this case is in the bag as we speak."

Hawk walked over the Jim.

"Now, Jim. I am sorry I sent you down that road. I knew there was something there. I did not intend it to cost you the priesthood. I needed the jury to see the actions by Machado, by Anthony," putting his hand on Father Jim's shoulder, "as irrational and dangerous. Anything that contributes to that is helpful, I am going to steer the questions away from this when we go back."

The look in Jim's eyes betrayed his realization that it was not over just yet.

"I am sorry Jim; I need to go into detail about what you saw. I will try to avoid any more questions about confidential matters. I don't think Collucci will want to touch on it either."

"I know he won't. He tried to get me to refuse to testify," looking at Hawk, "through his cousin."

Hawk looked at Josh then back at Jim, "who tried, what cousin?"

"Collucci. The Bishop is his cousin. He and the Diocesan lawyer came to see me last night, trying to convince me to invoke the Clergy-Penitent protection or if that failed, my Fifth Amendment rights. The FBI brought me in Collucci's office after court. He threatened to indict me. The Bishop told him I was the one that molested Anthony and confessed this to him. Can you imagine, a Bishop that would do that?"

"Wow, hold on here, Padre, tell me this from the beginning."

After Jim relayed the events leading up to the Bishop being at the residence, Hawk asked, "What did you tell them?"

"The Bishop and I held a private conversation. After that, I told them I would go along with their recommendation, if the Bishop resigned. I know a few more things about the Bishop. They would prove quite embarrassing for the Diocese, should they come out."

Hawk started to speak but Jim interrupted, "I decided that the truth was more important than any agreement with someone like the Bishop, I would testify no matter what. I owed that to Anthony and if it helped Josh, all the more reason."

"Do you think they will defrock you?" Josh asked.

"I see some of that Catholic education stuck." Jim smiled. "Who knows? It is a whole new world now; perhaps the next Bishop will decide to see things in a different light."

There was a knock on the door, Murray stuck his head in, "Rodericks is ready to resume."

The three started out the door, as Jim passed by, Josh said, "Thank you, Jim."

Jim nodded, patted his shoulder, and headed back into the fire. He now knew what it meant to have faith.

60: *Absolution*

Rodericks entered the courtroom and took the bench. "Mr. Bennett, I want to caution you on any further inquiry into matters which may, under law, be confidential. I do not want a mistrial. I allowed the line of questioning in as much as it reflected the state of mind of Mr. Machado. You are in a dangerous territory. If you cannot keep the questions relevant, and to the point, I will exclude Father Swanson's testimony. Am I making myself clear?"

"Yes, your honor. I do not intend to pursue that line of questioning. I believe we made our point about Mr. Machado's state of mind. My focus will be on what Father Swanson heard and saw during the confrontation."

"Mr. Collucci, the same holds for you, I will not allow any further inquiries into Clergy-Penitent matters. I know it may be tempting to you for reasons outside the realm of this court. I caution you not to go there."

Collucci leaned over to Fleming, "I told you he wouldn't allow it in," rising to face Rodericks, "Your Honor, the Government has no intention of pursuing that line. I would submit a motion to exclude Father Swanson's testimony as it relates to any matter except the day of the incident. His speech was inflammatory, prejudicial, and without any evidentiary value. We request the court instruct the jury to disregard that portion of the testimony."

Rodericks looked at the documents on the bench, made several notations, and then looked at Collucci, "I would concur that the testimony was close to the edge. However, I do not think it entirely without merit. The jury can give it any weight it likes. You can deal with it in summation, or perhaps with a rebuttal witness. I do not want to place any more focus on it. It is out there, instructions to disregard it may have the opposite effect. Your motion is denied. The record is noted."

"Thank you, your Honor." Collucci sat back down. Fleming could not help but notice the contemptuous look from Rodericks.

The jury returned to the court, Rodericks called for Father Swanson to take the witness stand, cautioning him that he was still under oath. "Continue Mr. Bennett."

Hawk walked to stand near the jury. "Now Father Swanson, I'd like to turn your attention to the time of the incident. Could you describe how Mr. Machado, let me rephrase. Mr. Machado was on the floor, correct?"

"Yes."

"And he was moving towards you, towards the Sacristy?"

"Yes, kept looking at the Sacristy door and then back towards Josh, I mean Sergeant Williams."

"Could you see his hands?"

"Just his left hand as he was pulling himself along the floor. I couldn't see his right hand. It was on the side away from me, and his arm was pointed back towards Sergeant Williams."

"Now Father, could you hear anything?"

"I heard Sergeant Williams telling Anthony to stop moving, he said it several times."

"Did Anthony say anything? Did he respond to Sergeant Williams?"

"He was mumbling. At first, I could not understand what he was saying. He did not seem to be listening to Sergeant Williams, he was..."

"Objection, witness is offering an opinion. He cannot testify to what Machado 'seemed' to be doing." Collucci said.

"Sustained. Confine your answer to facts Father Swanson, not what you thought, just what you saw."

"Yes sir," Jim replied.

"I heard Sergeant Williams yelling at him to stop moving, Anthony did not comply. He kept moving. He was sobbing, I heard him say 'I tried to get him to stop' several times, over and over," looking to the jury for a reaction.

"Just so we are clear Father, Machado is crawling towards you. You can see his left hand, but not his right hand. Sergeant Williams is telling him to stop moving, and Machado is sobbing 'I tried to get him to stop', is that accurate?"

"Yes, that is what I saw and heard." Jim was gaining confidence. Hawk did not like asking the next question, but it was necessary.

"Father Swanson, have you ever heard Mr. Machado... Anthony, use those words before?"

Jim face reddened, he understood why it had come to this, and what he needed to do, no matter what it cost him personally. "Yes, yes I have."

Collucci was not even listening, Fleming was trying to get his attention away from the notepad, but it came too late, as Collucci looked at Fleming, then at Jim, the answer came out.

Jim folded his hands, took a deep breath, "He used the same words in the confessional the day he told me about being molested."

Collucci simply looked at Rodericks, at a loss for the right words, and rose from his seat, "Your Honor, this testimony needs to be stricken from the record. It is prejudicial, hearsay, and irrelevant."

"Your honor, I would argue that since it goes against Father Swanson's best interest, there is an exception to the hearsay rule. Furthermore, it is relevant as it goes to the mindset of Mr. Machado which the jury can use to understand his behavior that day."

"Objection is overruled, please continue Mr. Bennett, with caution."

"Father Swanson, what was the last thing you saw before you closed the door?"

"I saw Sergeant Williams getting closer to Anthony, as he did this Anthony turned towards him. He raised his right hand. I could see something in it, but I could not tell what it was. I was very frightened. I thought he had a gun. I closed the door," Jim's voice began to quiver, "a moment later I heard the gunshots. That's when I left the church and returned to the residence." Wiping his eyes, staring over the head of the jury.

"One last thing Father, when did you first talk to the police about this?"

Jim looked confused, "Do you mean when I first told them I saw what happened?"

"Let me rephrase that, did you talk to the police the night of the incident?"

"I did. They came to the residence. I told them I was napping and hadn't heard or seen anything."

"And when did you first acknowledge to the police that you did witness the incident?"

"After I met with Mr. Harris, I realized I needed to be truthful with the police, tell them what I saw. I wanted them to know Josh did everything he could to get Anthony to surrender."

"Your honor, enough, this is beyond any acceptable standard of admissible testimony." Fleming voiced this objection, unable to contain herself.

"Sustained, the jury will disregard that last answer, and it is stricken from the record."

Hawk paused a moment to let Jim regain his composure, "Thank you, Father. I have nothing further."

As he returned to the table, Josh said, "so much for avoiding the confidential stuff, you lied to him."

"My boy, a little discomfit on the good father's part is nothing if it helps us get to the truth of this matter. You don't have to like it, but it won't matter once we get a not guilty." Hawk leaned back in his chair and enjoyed watching Collucci and Fleming in an animated discussion.

Josh shook his head, "No more of this Hawk, no more."

Hawk nodded, but he knew this was just the opening salvo.

Rodericks stared at the government table, "Mr. Collucci, do you have anything else for this witness?"

"No, you honor"

"Very well, Father Swanson you are excused, thank you for your candor."

Jim stood up, walked from the witness box, and past Josh. Josh tried to smile, but it was half-hearted. He hated what just happened to his friend.

Steve Murray was prepared again, guiding Jim out a seldom-used side exit, avoiding the reporters circling for an exclusive.

Court adjourned for the weekend.

There was blood in the water; the church wounded, sharks circling for the kill.

Later, that evening, Jim Swanson sat alone in the residence, waiting for the phone to ring.

61: What Goes Around...

"The government calls Lieutenant Christine Hamlin"

Chris appeared in the doorway, walked to the defense table, patted Josh on the back, and then took the stand.

As she took the oath, she looked intently at the jury. Some returned her gaze, a few looked away, but one was somehow familiar.

"Good afternoon, Lieutenant, would you please tell the court you current occupation."

"Certainly, my name is Christine Hamlin. I am a police officer with the City of East Providence, holding the rank of Lieutenant. I am currently the commander of the Special Investigations Unit, known as SIU."

"Thank you Lieutenant, were you working on March 15th of this year?"

"Yes"

"And did you have the occasion to respond to an incident at St. Domenicks Church?"

"Yes, we did."

"Could you tell the court how you became aware of this situation?"

"Yes sir, Josh, excuse me, Sergeant Williams, and I were driving back from court."

"Go on."

"As we came back into the city from the highway onto Warren Avenue, we heard a call for a shooting at Kent Farm."

"And what did you do then?"

"I didn't do anything, other than holding on. I knew Josh was going to head that way."

"Let me understand here Lieutenant. You are the ranking officer, Williams is subordinate. Yet, you let him determine the course of action?"

"Have you ever been in my situation?"

"Your Honor," Collucci looked to the bench," please instruct the witness to answer the question, not phrase her own."

Rodericks looked down at Hamlin.

"Your Honor, I cannot answer that question truthfully without context. I would be happy to answer one if Mr. Collucci concedes that he does not understand realities of police work. Without context, it will not be clear. I cannot answer truthfully under those conditions."

Rodericks paused a moment. He held a very low appreciation of police officers in general, taking delight in making them suffer. Yet, she made a point.

"Mr. Collucci perhaps you can let the witness establish some context here?"

"Very well, your Honor, turning back to face Chris, "Lieutenant, as the ranking officer, why did you let Sergeant Williams determine the course of action, once you'd heard the call for a shooting?"

"Because I have absolute faith in his judgment, competence, and experience. Sergeant Williams does not need any direction from me on the correct course of action," looking at the jury, "I have never known him to do anything other than what was appropriate."

Collucci lost composure, glaring at Chris, quickly recovering, "Lieutenant, that is not what I asked you."

"Objection" Hawk said. "It is exactly what Mr. Collucci asked; he just didn't like the answer. He's badgering the witness, argumentative"

"Overruled. I hardly see that as badgering," Rodericks responded. "Mr. Collucci, if the answer is incomplete, or inaccurate, ask more specific questions."

Collucci returned to the government table, picked up a report, brought it to Chris, "Do you recognize this document?"

"Your Honor," Hawk was up again, "would it be too much to ask of the government to identify the exhibit before he continues?"

"My apologies to the Court, I have just presented the witness with Government's exhibit four. May I continue?"

Hawk bowed and sat back down, Rodericks continued to look at the documents on the bench, seemingly uninterested.

Hawk leaned over to Josh, "this son-of-a-bitch does this all the time. He hates cops. He will sit there and ignore her testimony like it does not matter, or he does not believe her, useless prick. I'll object to Collucci's breathing if I have to."

"Why's he hate us?"

Hawk smiled, "He tried to get on the State Police back in the early 70's. First time boxing got his jaw broken, ear drum punctured, and knocked out," pausing for the good part, "by the first female to get into the academy."

"Oh boy," Josh chuckled, "he must really love Chris. Maybe you can get in her black belt in Karate?"

"You know, my boy, as time goes on I see more and more potential in you."

Collucci walked over to stand near the witness box.

"Lieutenant, do you recognize this document?"

"Yes, I do." Chris was going to make him work for everything.

"And?"

"And I recognize it. Yes I do." Josh was right. Answer the question as it is asked, not what you think he means."

Collucci was incensed, "Lieutenant could you please tell the court what this document is?"

"Yes," pausing a bit, looking the document over again, daring him, "it is my report regarding the circumstances of the Machado apprehension."

"Apprehension?" Collucci mocked, "You mean the shooting of Anthony Machado, the unarmed Anthony Machado?"

"No, I mean exactly what I just said," Chris replied, before Hawk could object.

"Lieutenant, would you please turn to the next to last page of your report and read the last three paragraphs," turning to the jury, "out loud for all our benefit."

"Of course," turning to that page, looking it over, enjoying the impatience in Collucci, then continuing,

"As I came up the rear stairs of the church I heard three shots fired. I ran into the church, keeping low, trying to maintain cover.

Coming up the side stairway into what is the east side of the altar, I could see Sergeant Williams bending over a subject, performing CPR.

I ran over to him, saw the damage to the subject's chest and head, realized he was beyond recovery, and informed Sergeant Williams to stop his resuscitation efforts."

Looking over at the jury, Chris put the report down and waited.

"Are you a Doctor?" Collucci asked

"Excuse me?"

"On what basis do you, as a Lieutenant on the East Providence Police department, have the qualifications to determine a person, the victim Anthony Machado in this case, was, in your words, 'beyond recovery'?"

Chris eyes narrowed, she sat up, glared at Collucci.

Hawk did not even blink, this will be classic.

"I based my evaluation on my experience, over a two year period in Viet Nam, as a nurse in the United States Air Force. I spent eight months at a forward aid station treating the wounded, and the remaining sixteen months trying to preserve casualties on medical evacuation flights back to Germany and the United States." Her anger rising.

"On many of those flights I was the senior medical staff on board..."

"Thank you, Lieutenant. You've answered my..."

"I am not finished...." her eyes burning into Collucci. "As the senior medical staff on board I, more times than I care to remember, made the call to discontinue resuscitative efforts. It was my responsibility to determine it was time to let many, many young men..." tears in her eyes, she looked to the jury, "too stop trying to save them, and to make others stop as well, in order to focus on those we might save. That is my basis for what I did." Pausing to let that sink in, "I also maintain my Emergency Medical Technician level P, Paramedic, the highest level possible."

Then it hit her, that juror. Veteran's Parkway, 1992. Car off the road, in the water. Chris and two patrol officers go in the water, pull a fourteen year-old girl from the car, not breathing.

Quick CPR and the girl begins to breath.

At the hospital, being treated for the unimaginable bacteria they inhaled from the water as they breathed life into the young woman, a thankful grandfather came to them and shook their hands.

The one degree of separation that is Rhode Island.

That should be at least one vote for Josh.

Collucci tried to resume, "So what happened after you instructed Sergeant Williams to stop doing CPR?"

Chris took a deep breath, she looked at Collucci, over to the jury, then at Josh, "I took him outside, I knew what he just experienced was going to be difficult to deal with," pausing a moment and catching the familiar juror's eye, "taking a human life, regardless of the circumstances, is hard burden to carry."

Josh dropped his head. Hawk put his arm around him.

"What about the cell phone?'

Chris looked at Collucci, tried to control her emotions, understood what the son-of-a-bitch was trying to do, but it was difficult.

"As I was trying to get Josh outside, we heard a cell phone ring."

"And where was that cell phone?"

"In Anthony Machado's hand."

"No weapon?"

"No, I did not see a weapon at that point. I also could not see his other hand."

"Lieutenant, did you remain at the scene until it was fully processed?"

"Yes, as the senior officer, the crime scene was my responsibility. Once Josh was taken back to the station, I maintained overall responsibility for the scene."

"Now Lieutenant Hamlin, I'd like you to explain the responsibilities, excuse me, let me rephrase. As the senior officer it was your responsibility to insure the integrity of the crime scene, is that true?"

"Yes, I have overall responsibility..."

"Thank you Lieutenant, it was a yes or no question." Collucci was not going to allow any more uncontrolled responses. "In this case you protected the scene?"

"Yes" Chris replied, she would wait him out.

"So there was no possibility that anything was introduced into the scene before investigators processed the evidence?"

"Yes, nothing was changed or altered once the scene was secured." Chris relaxed, she was sure there was nothing to this.

"Lieutenant were you present for the entire time the scene was under control and processed?"

"Yes I was"

"Were you surprised by any of the findings at the scene?"

This one threw her, what was this asshole looking for?

"Surprised? No. I don't know what I would be surprised by." As the words came out she knew she fell for it.

"So you weren't surprised that the victim in this matter, Anthony Machado, lying dead on the floor, after being shot by Sergeant Williams, was unarmed?"

Josh heard the voice

Why would she? I am dead, she has trust in her brothers, you'll never understand, I don't blame him, I don't blame her, this is on me, me alone, let it go, I already did.

Chris tried not to look to Josh, could not control it. She looked at Hawk, could tell by his eyes to just let it go. She wanted to fix this; it would only enhance the damage. She continued to look at Collucci.

"Just so it is clear Lieutenant, didn't you expect to find a weapon?"

"Objection, calls for a supposition, ask her what she did."

"Overruled, answer the question Lieutenant."

Useless was enjoying a bit of payback, so he thought.

"I expected the investigators to do their job. I expected them to document the evidence. I expected them to file complete and accurate reports," looking to the jury, "that is exactly what happened, that is exactly what I expected."

"Lieutenant, once you realized Machado was not armed, were you tempted to plant a weapon?"

"Objection." Hawk was on his feet, angry.

"I think it is a reasonable question, overruled." Rodericks said. "Please answer the question, Lieutenant."

Hamlin looked at the jury, "Absolutely not. The truth is the better path. That's what we always follow."

Collucci just would not learn.

Rodericks really hated women like her.

Collucci walked to the jury box, looked at the jurors, nodded his head, turned back and said, "Lieutenant, so we are clear on this, how many weapons did you find at this crime scene?"

Chris looked at him, replied quickly, "None," pausing, "but even I wasn't sure until the ME rolled the body over."

"Move to strike, your honor," Collucci said," as unresponsive."

Rodericks glanced up, "Mr. Collucci, you asked, she responded, overruled."

Collucci turned to walk back to his table, "If I may your honor, I'd like to approach the witness for purposes of identification of another document," handing a copy to Hawk.

"Continue," Rodericks replied

"Lieutenant Hamlin, can you identify this document?"

Chris took the document, she already knew this was coming, "Yes, it is a police report regarding an arrest for Sale of Alcohol to a Minor and a copy of the toxicology report in that matter regarding the sample sent to the State Toxicology Lab."

"And for which matter was this sample submitted?"

"City of East Providence vs. Fernando's Liquors, Sale of Alcohol to a Minor."

"And the toxicology report, can you read the conclusions of the analysis."

"The result indicated the sample was 5.1% alcohol by volume"

"And what was the brand name of the beer?"

Hawk stood, "Your honor, while this chemistry lesson is fascinating, I fail to see the relevance."

Rodericks looked at Collucci, "I was beginning to wonder that myself, Mr. Collucci?"

"If the court would bear with me, the relevance will be readily apparent in a moment."

Hawk sat down determined to keep Collucci off his rhythm.

"Lieutenant, the brand name?"

"Becks."

"Now, did this matter go to trial in Sixth Division District Court?"

"Yes."

"And were you present for that matter?"

"I was"

"Did you testify?"

"No"

"Who testified for the City of East Providence?"

"Sergeant Williams."

"Lieutenant, were you present during Sergeant Williams testimony?"

"Yes, I was."

Hawk was up again, "Your honor, really this is stretching it. If Mr. Collucci cannot get to the point we need to move on."

"Mr. Collucci I have allowed you a great deal of latitude on direct here, please get to the point quickly."

"I believe the next few questions will address the issue."

"During this case that City introduced the Toxicology report correct?"

"Yes, it was stipulated by the defense."

"And Sergeant Williams introduced a six pack of beer, minus one bottle, that he testified was the one seized at the time of the arrest, correct?" turning to watch the jury reaction.

"No that is not correct."

Collucci spun around, "Excuse me, did you say that was not correct?"

"Yes"

"Lieutenant, you were there for the testimony, you acknowledged that. You acknowledged that the toxicology report was introduced, but the six pack was not, is that your testimony?"

"Yes"

Collucci marched to the table, picked up the report, shaking it in the direction of Chris, "Lieutenant, I ask you again, did Sergeant Williams testify that the five bottles of Beck beer, with the evidence tag attached, were the same ones seized the night of the arrest?"

"Sergeant Williams testified the items were the same as, not the same ones, seized that night."

"Lieutenant, Sergeant Williams lied in court, didn't he?"

Hawk was up again, "Your honor, this has gone on long enough. This line of questioning is irrelevant and highly inflammatory. There is no basis for these questions, not substantiating reports to the contrary. If this case is so relevant why not have the transcript introduced?"

Collucci was apoplectic, "There is no transcript, and the trial recording equipment malfunctioned."

Rodericks tried to conceal his delight. Before him, two of his favorite targets, a female cop playing fast and loose with testimony in his courtroom, and a pompous self-important United States Attorney that, should he get elected to Congress, would likely vote against him when his nomination to the Circuit Court came through.

He knew he could pick one to ruin completely. That's not to say he could not exact some wounds on the other just for fun.

"Lieutenant Hamlin, was the evidence introduced in this matter the evidence seized during the arrest?" Rodericks smiled benignly.

"No, sir"

"So what happened to that evidence?"

"It was misplaced." Chris shifted nervously on the stand.

"Misplaced, I see. Is this a common occurrence within the East Providence Police department, Lieutenant?" looking intently at Chris.

"No, sir. Unfortunately, with some cases, in particular the non-violent, misdemeanor cases, evidence sometimes gets misplaced." Chris voice wavering a bit.

"I see, and so you decided to substitute for the misplaced evidence? Is that a common practice as well?"

"No sir, I mean yes sir, I decided," looking at Josh, "to replace the items for the court hearing. It is not common practice. If questioned about it we would have acknowledged the fact. I considered it an exhibit, not evidence."

"If questioned, I see, so you hoped not to be, questioned about it? Rodericks was smiling broadly, enjoying this.

"No, I assumed the defense lawyer would have questioned the evidence in that manner."

"Very creative, Lieutenant, you considered it an exhibit. Is there a difference in your mind between the two?"

"Yes, clearly there is. In addition, your Honor, we introduced the chain of custody of the bottle sent for toxicological analysis. This accounted for every moment from the point of seizure to when the evidence arrived at the State lab. There was no question about that."

Rodericks heard enough, "Well, I suppose if your ability to account for one of the six bottles seized is a high enough standard for your department who am I to question it," redirecting his attention elsewhere.

"Mr. Collucci, I've allowed you enough latitude, your point, what little there is of it, the court just assisted you in making it, move on."

"Your Honor," Collucci's anger rising, "I have several more..."

"Mr. United States Attorney you have no more time for this line of questioning. If you have some other areas to explore with this witness, do so. Otherwise, sit down." Rodericks' delight was electric.

Collucci stood for a moment looking at Rodericks, turned, shaking his head, and made his way back to the Government's table.

"Nothing further."

"Excuse me, Mr. Collucci, were you addressing the court? It is hard to tell since your back was to the bench."

Rodericks really enjoyed these moments. "My apologies, your Honor, no disrespect intended. The government has nothing further for this witness."

'Useless' might hate cops, but he held an greater distaste for Collucci.

"Mr. Bennett, we have about an hour or so before adjourning for the day, would you like to start now, or wait until we are all refreshed and eager in the morning?"

Hawk smiled, Useless was certainly a poster child for a lazy judiciary, yet the point made was valid.

"Your Honor, we have a number of matters we'd like to research. It has been a long day. I'd be happy to accommodate the court and begin first thing tomorrow."

Rodericks nodded, "Lieutenant Hamlin, you are excused until 9:00 AM tomorrow, the marshal will now escort the jury from the court."

Rising from the bench as the jury door closed, Rodericks left the courtroom.

"Tough day Robbie boy," Chris said as she passed Collucci.

"Oh no, my dear Lieutenant, that wasn't even close to a tough day. Not yet."

Collucci and Fleming headed out. Fleming glancing over a Josh, a slight, yet sad, smile on her face.

62: *An Unexpected Ally*

Chris, Josh, and Hawk walked back to his office. As they approached the elevator, a young woman walked over.

"Sergeant Williams?"

Josh stopped and looked at the woman, Chris moved behind her, impressing Hawk with the swiftness of the movement.

"Do I know you?" Something about the woman, a familiarity, he just could not place her.

"I don't think so," glancing back at Chris. "I have something for you, in my pocket. It's only a note."

Chris moved close to her and leaned in, "very slowly young lady, very slowly."

The woman held her left hand out to her side, reached into her pocket, and withdrew a folded manila envelope, handed it to Josh, then slowly lowered her hands.

"Jeez, Maggie said you'd be nervous, but this is like a movie."

"Maggie?"

"Maggie Fleming, my aunt, "taking in the glances among the three, "she asked me to get this to you away from the courthouse. Can I go?"

Josh nodded, looked at Chris and Hawk, and added, "thank you, I think. Did she say why?"

The woman was already on her way; she turned back, shrugged and said, "She told me she believes in the system even if everyone else doesn't."

"Well, that solves the mystery of the anonymous emails, doesn't it?" Chris said.

"What anonymous emails?" Hawk's eyebrow arching up.

"A few weeks ago, before trial started, Josh got some anonymous emails telling him to be careful, warning him Collucci had something on him."

"And you are just telling me this now because?"

"I didn't think anything of it. There were two messages and then they stopped. Chris traced one to the library on Grove Street in East

Providence. We got some pictures of Maggie's cousin there," motioning to the retreating woman. "Now we at least know one of them."

"One of?" Hawk shook his head, "Okay, I thought you two were grown out of this by now but apparently not. I need you to tell me all of it, no more damn secrets." His voice rising, "the Government's case sucks, but I've seen juries convict on less."

Hawk jammed the button on the elevator several times; as the door opened, he turned to the two of them, "Take the stairs. Perhaps this will insure that when you arrive in my office you'll be too tired to withhold anything more, and give me that damn envelope," snatching it from Josh's hands, "this way here I'll be sure to know what it says, not what you two idiots think I should know. One more thing," holding the door, "get me those images." The elevator closed.

Josh looked over and Chris headed for the staircase.

"We're really taking the stairs?"

Fifteen minutes later, they came into Hawk's office.

"Hi Tif," Josh smiled at the assistant, "is he in there?"

"He went over to see Bill Symonds, told me to just have you sit tight."

"Okay, thanks, we'll go on in."

"How are you Lieutenant?" smiling at the slightly red faced Chris, "You're not still...."

"No. I am fine, just a little winded since my good friend here decided to make it a race up the stairs," leaning on the desk.

"She's starting to show here age Tif, can't keep up with the younger generation." Josh laughed.

"Really now, do you want to tell Tiffany who won?"

"I let her win," Josh winked, "very fragile sense of self-worth."

The two walked into Hawk's office, within a few minutes Hawk returned accompanied by a tall, well dressed, gentleman.

Josh could not help but notice a reaction in Chris. *On the hunt for a new one already, he thought.*

"Josh, Chris this is Bill Symonds. Bill, Lieutenant Christine Hamlin and Sergeant Josh Williams."

They all shook hands, then made do with the limited places to sit.

Hamlin went over to Hawk's computer, "I'll bring up those images."

Hawk nodded at Chris and said, "I asked Bill to sit in for a bit. He and I worked together in the AG's office many years ago and he was an AUSA in Boston for a few years."

"I didn't know you worked as a prosecutor." Chris said, surprised, glancing up from the keyboard.

"There are many secrets my dear Lieutenant, many, many secrets. I did mostly appellate work, not many trials," handing a document to Josh, "read that and then let Chris read it."

After the two read it over, they looked at Hawk, "So now what?" Chris asked.

"Exactly my point, Chris. Now what? It is why I asked Bill to come in on this. We could move for a directed verdict or mistrial. Collucci is intimidating witnesses, hell he is suborning perjury. My feeling is if Rodericks grants the motion for a directed verdict, we win. If he denies the directed verdict, but grants a mistrial, the US Attorney will have trouble re-trying the case. We can ruin his credibility."

Symonds interjected, "Here is the issue as I see it. Clearly, you have grounds for a mistrial; the directed verdict is a stretch but not totally out of the picture. Get either one and this case is dead in the water."

Josh looked at the document again, "but where does that leave me. I would be the cop that beat the rap on a technicality. People will think I shot and killed an unarmed man because he was black. I do not want that. It's not the truth."

"That's what I anticipated, Josh," Hawk answered, "that's why I wanted Bill to be the neutral here. Personally, I want to run with it and crack the son-of-a-bitch over the head with a Not Guilty verdict. I believe we can get that.

Nevertheless, my obligation is to insure you make the best decision based on the rules of law. My competitiveness may be clouding my responsibility to the best legally viable course."

"Chris, what do you think?"

"Oh, Josh, I don't know. If we can end this now I would be inclined to go with that. Nobody really believes you did anything wrong, well, nobody that matters. I understand you want to see this through. However, at what cost? Suppose the jury buys into some of this bullshit. Collucci is an evil bastard, who knows what other shit he might try and pull."

"Bill?"

Symonds paused for a moment, and then stood, "Let's think this through. A directed verdict is a stretch; let's take it off the table. Our best course is a mistrial. Two things can happen. Collucci regroups, uses his political skills to turn the mistrial into a case of judicial activism, the standard 'courts denying justice on technicalities'.

He turns Josh into the 21st century equivalent of a lynch mob killing innocent black men and the court condoning it.

He then re-indicts, garnering a completely new round of publicity, and we are in the same situation. Only this time, the Government will be better prepared, they'd have seen our game plan, which we won't really be able to change very much."

Walking over to the window, he continued, "Or, he decides not to retry the case. Does the same angry cry to the world for justice denied, effectively destroying Josh's career and likely yours as well, Lieutenant. He then assassinates the reputation of a good Police Department, the local FBI office, and rides that wave to Washington."

Chris stood up, "Wait a minute, you don't expect Josh to risk his freedom just to derail a political campaign do you, come on. That's not fair."

"I am merely laying out various scenarios should we file either motion and win. However, there is one more scenario to entertain. This one, now that I've taken some time to consider it, seems the best course for Josh to emerge from this with his reputation, and career, intact."

Symonds looked at Hawk and smiled, "a little disinformation campaign my friend."

Hawk smiled.

"I will provide notice that Bill is coming aboard as co-counsel. If Ms. Fleming is as smart, and as honest, as I think, she will see this for what it's worth and use it to poison Mr. Collucci's brave demeanor. It will put him off-balance."

"And why would that be, for all we know this is Collucci's idea." Chris asked, looking around the room.

"Wow, who's the conspiracy queen now?" Josh said.

"Bill here is the master of the motion and appellate process. Collucci will read this, I hope helped by some poisoning of the well by our secret friend, as our refocusing on motions because we have learned something about his inner workings. It will put him on the defensive, perhaps overreacting, digging a deeper hole in his case."

Hawk walked to the computer and turned the monitor to get a better look, "Bill" he said, 'look."

Symonds came over and smiled, "Once again my friend your intuition is remarkable. That, my friends, is Special Agent Frank Wilson, FBI Boston office. One of the most honest and trustworthy people in the bureau. Came there from Boston PD. He was a real cop for a while and never forgot his roots. I bet Fleming reached out to him as a bit of protection for the niece and her mission."

"Not very good at undercover work," Chris said.

"On the contrary, that wasn't a disguise, it was a message. They hoped you'd figure it out." Hawk answered.

"That still doesn't answer the question, what do we do?"

"Yes it does, Chris," Josh said, "We see this thing through, I testify. Collucci will have to be extra cautious he does not provide us any other avenue for a motion. I want to do this. Hell, I am going to do this."

Hawk walked over to Josh, "are you certain, there are no guarantees here. This can all go bad and we will really have to use Bill to write an appeal on your behalf. Maybe you need to think about it a bit."

"No, I thought enough. I have to live the rest of my life second-guessing my decision to shoot Machado. If I wiggle out of this without a verdict, it will make it all that harder. I know what I have to do and this is it."

Josh and Chris left Hawk's office and walked over to O'Reilly's Cafe. Dark, classically low key, the Cafe was a nice place for a beer and corned beef sandwich. As they sat at the bar, Josh looked at Chris "I am sorry you went through that, today"

"What?"

"You know, adjust the facts to fit the truth."

"Josh, I may not agree with your philosophy very often, but having seen the effect politics has on this case, I am starting to wonder if you may be right." Lifting her beer, tipping the glass to Josh.

"You know, Lieutenant, I am starting to think your philosophy makes more sense." Staring into his beer.

Chris looked stunned. "And what might that philosophy be?"

"Well," smiling broadly, "dump one lover, find a new one. Waste no time. I saw you drooling at Symonds."

"Fuck you, Josh, Fuck you," laughing, as she drained the beer.

Josh continued to look into the glass, he hoped he was kidding.

63:   Adding to the Team

Hawk sat talking with Josh as Collucci and Fleming entered the courtroom.

Not waiting for Collucci to settle in, Hawk walked over handing Collucci the notice of Symonds' addition to the defense team.

Collucci looked at the document, dropped it on the desk, and glanced at Fleming, "apparently our brother at the bar has now recognized his limitations and called for assistance."

Looking back at Hawk, "too little, too late I fear."

"Actually, I was just taking the opportunity to share the imminent demise of the unremarkable, and completely in-admirable, career of one more self-righteous, pompous egomaniac." Walking backwards to the defense table and smiling at Collucci.

Collucci ignored the comment, but he did take notice of the brief smile by Ms. Fleming.

"Did you find something amusing, Ms. Fleming?"

"Yes, I did. Bennett is a piece of work. I don't think he very much cared for your comment." Picking up the notice, "this worries me though. Symonds is a very bright guy. He may see something here we do not. We need to tread carefully."

Collucci thought about that for a minute, "What could they have? There is no way the priest went to them. This is all bluster. Let'em file the motions, there is no way Rodericks will grant any of them."

"Robert, I know you have things under control, but there could be someone working against us, from inside."

"Like who?" Collucci waited for the answer, thinking, *Perhaps you my idealistic asshole of an AUSA. Why did I appoint you in the first place?*

"The local office, they have not been exactly thrilled with the DC guys running things. They can feed things to Bennett."

Sometimes, all it takes is a little nudge.

"Look, you just follow the plan," staring at her for a moment, "at any time you want out, I can make it happen."

Collucci started to write something on a notepad, put the pen down, watching Fleming.

"Is there something else?" she asked.

"Keep in mind, sweetheart, I can make it happen even if you don't want out."

Arrogance knows no limitations. There was no way she would let that happen. She needed to make this right.

Rodericks entered the courtroom, "Mr. Bennett, I see we have a new addition at the defense table, care to elaborate."

"Yes your Honor, I served notice on the Government and the Court informing them that Mr. William Symonds, Esq., will be assisting me as co-counsel."

Rodericks glanced over to Symonds, "Welcome aboard Mr. Symonds, perhaps you will be able to keep a leash on Mr. Bennett. The court would be most appreciative."

Symonds stood, "Thank you, your Honor, I fear that may be a Sisyphean task."

Rodericks shook his head, "I see you understand my dilemma. Ah well, we shall persevere. Mr. Bennett are you ready for cross?"

"I am, your Honor."

As soon as the jury took their seats, the marshal announced, "Lieutenant Hamlin."

Chris retook her position in the witness box. As she sat, the juror she remembered leaned over to the juror next to him. A moment later, they both nodded towards Chris. *Not sure if that is a good thing, but I better tell Hawk about this. Might be useful.*

"Good morning Lieutenant Hamlin."

"Good morning sir"

"Now, Lieutenant, I'd like to have you recall the moments just prior to encountering Mr. Machado. You heard a radio broadcast, is that correct?'

"Well, we heard several but the one I believe you're referring was reporting a robbery with a shooting at the Cumberland Farms on Taunton Avenue."

"Yes, my apologies, we will confine this to the radio traffic and your actions regarding the incident at the Cumberland Farms. Do you recall what information was broadcast?"

"Yes I do. The dispatcher reported multiple calls for a robbery and shooting at the Cumberland Farms, Taunton Avenue. She broadcast a description of a suspect seen leaving the store, cautioning he was armed with a sawed-off shotgun."

"Lieutenant, help me understand, what significance is there to multiple calls?"

Chris smiled a moment, and then continued. "There is a distinct correlation between the number of calls, particularly for a critical incident as this, and the likelihood of it being true."

"I see, so in this instance, the dispatcher reporting multiple calls made the incident more likely to be true, not another false call?"

"Yes, exactly. I believed this call to be a real one."

"And did the dispatcher provide a description of the suspect?"

"Yes, the suspect was described as a black male, wearing a blue hooded sweatshirt armed with a sawed off-shotgun. Last seen running from the store to the Six Corners area."

"I see. And where were you as this information was being sent out?"

"Sergeant Williams turned onto Grove Avenue. As we came to the intersection of John Street, we spotted a person matching the description of the suspect."

"How close a match, Lieutenant?"

"There was no doubt in my mind this was the suspect."

"So, you've spotted the suspect what do you do?"

"Josh was already out of the car, the suspect turned away, running towards Saint Domenicks. I radioed into dispatch our location and the pursuit, then went after Josh and the suspect."

"If I may Lieutenant, go back a bit. When you saw the suspect, he fit the physical description correct?"

"He fit it perfectly."

"Did you see a weapon; I believe it was reported to be a sawed-off shotgun?"

"No, I did not see a weapon, but such a weapon, a sawed off, is easily concealed."

"Easily, how easy can it be?"

"Objection, calls for a conclusion," Collucci said.

"A conclusion by this seasoned police officer which, if I recall, you yourself made much of her vast experience."

"Overruled," Rodericks made the extra effort to look at the jury, "the witness will answer the question."

"Perhaps it would be helpful to explain what a sawed-off shotgun is, for those of the jury that may be unfamiliar with such weapons, Lieutenant?"

Collucci started to stand, Fleming grabbed his arm, "Christ Robert, she's got thirty three years on the job, not to drag up the ghosts of Viet Nam again, she's pretty well qualified to describe a sawed-off....."

Collucci glared at Fleming, then back at Chris. "Fine, fucking fine," he muttered.

Hawk saw a better road to follow.

"A sawed off shotgun is essentially one that has been altered, typically by shortening the barrel, sawing it off, thus the name. There are federal firearm standards that proscribe the legal length of a barrel. A shotgun is a devastating weapon, a sawed off is even worse since it is easily concealed.

"So Lieutenant, let me understand, the suspect fit the description, acted in a manner consistent with, in your experience, someone trying to avoid contact with the police, yet you did not see a weapon, but you acted as if he did, Why?"

"It is how cops do their job every day; expect the worse, hope for the best. Mr. Bennett, cops all over this country survive to go home by that philosophy." Chris turned to look at the jury.

"And the fact that the dispatcher reported the subject armed with a sawed-off shotgun, did that do anything to contribute to your decision to consider him armed?"

"Yes," looking directly at the friendly juror, "he held his right hand under his sweatshirt, there was an awkwardness to his running, and I believed he carried a weapon concealed on his person. It was consistent behavior for someone hiding a sawed-off shotgun."

"Couldn't his behavior have been consistent with something else?" Hawk trusted the instincts of the Lieutenant to follow his lead.

"In a dynamic situation such as this, Police Officers are trained to do everything they can to apprehend the person with minimal force, while protecting themselves, the public, and the suspect as far as humanly possible. Their training teaches them to look at the totality of the circumstances as a guide to their actions. In this instance, there are several elements which, taken as a whole, lead to a reasonable conclusion that this was the suspect in a robbery and shooting."

"Could you be more specific?"

"Certainly, the suspect fit the physical description broadcast by the dispatcher obtained from multiple witnesses, he ran from the police in spite of our clearly identifying ourselves and ordering him to stop, he held one arm concealed beneath his sweatshirt consistent with someone trying to hide an object, and a sawed-off shotgun could easily be concealed in such a manner. Taking all of that into consideration any officer would believe this to be a dangerous individual and act accordingly."

It was apparent to all the jury was warming to Chris.

"Now, Lieutenant, let me take you to the scene at the church. Josh radioed he was going in the front door after the suspect, correct?"

"Yes, that is correct."

"As a seasoned officer, did anything about his decision to enter the church in this manner seem inappropriate or against normal police procedures?"

"Not at all, as I described earlier, this was a dynamic, dangerous situation. There is never one way to handle such matters. In some circumstances, it may be appropriate to wait for additional manpower, in others, such as this one, the risk to innocent people that may have been inside the church, outweighed the choice to wait. It was common knowledge that the church welcomed parishioners inside during the day. Father Swanson himself was often in the church as well. Sergeant Williams's decision to enter was reasonable when balanced against that risk."

"Lieutenant, how long have you worked with Sergeant Williams?"

I first worked with Sergeant Williams when he was a rookie patrol officer assigned the midnight to eight shift. I was his direct supervisor.

Over the course of time, Sergeant Williams and I worked together many times. Now he is my assistant commander of the Special Investigations Unit. I selected him personally for that position."

"And why was that Lieutenant?"

"Because he is one of the most conscientious, dedicated, honest, determined, and caring officers I have ever worked with. I trust him with my Special Investigations Unit, which was my idea from the beginning, and I have trusted him many times with my life, and would not hesitate to do so again."

Hawk watched the jury as they took in her testimony. The damage done by Collucci forgotten.

"Now Lieutenant, turning your attention to the Church, you testified that you heard the shots fired and then entered the church, is that correct?"

"Yes, as I was making my way in the side entrance, I heard the shots and went into the church."

"And as you entered the church, you saw Sergeant Williams, what was he doing?"

"He was performing CPR on Mr. Machado."

"And what did you do?"

"I came over, bent down to assist, and then recognized that Mr. Machado was beyond saving."

"Were you surprised to see Sergeant Williams doing CPR?"

"Actually, I was relieved. Until I entered the church I didn't know if anyone was shot, I was afraid it may have been Sergeant Williams, so I was relieved."

"Once you saw Sergeant Williams was okay, were you surprised he was performing CPR?"

"Not at all, it's what I would have expected from Sergeant Williams."

"Were you surprised Sergeant Williams was doing CPR on a black man?"

"Objection, asked and answered," Collucci argued.

"Your honor, this is a different question than the previous one, race goes to the very heart of this matter. I think it reasonable that Lieutenant Hamlin, through her long association with Sergeant

Williams, can answer the question. And it is relevant to one of the very elements of the charge against Sergeant Williams."

"Overruled, you may answer the question, Lieutenant." Rodericks reluctantly ruled.

"I was not surprised at all. Sergeant Williams has never exhibited any racist attitude since I have known him. He'd perform CPR on anyone that needed it, regardless of the color of their skin"

Collucci began to rise, then thought better of it. This Judge was not going to help him at all. He would find another way.

"I have nothing further your honor." Retaking his seat, patting Josh on the back, Hawk smiled at the jury.

Rodericks asked to have the jury taken to lunch.

Once the jury was out of the courtroom, Rodericks could not resist one last shot at Chris. "Lieutenant Hamlin, in my twenty years on the bench I have never been more offended by such evasive, self-serving, insincere testimony by a Police Officer. I will be contacting the Department of the Attorney General to look into this matter on the state level, and should they find anything unlawful I will have the Justice Department review this testimony as well."

Chris knew better but could not help herself, "Your Honor, I never lie, not in any courtroom or out in the real world. Frankly, I am offended you would make such a statement from the bench. I would welcome any inquiry from anyone into anything I have ever done as a police officer. If such an inquiry takes place, and the results come back that I did nothing unlawful, I would hope you'd be as quick to apologize." Standing slowly she walked toward the defense table, put her hand on Josh's shoulder as she passed by, and walked out of the courtroom.

Rodericks was glaring, but unable to respond before the door closed behind her.

Hawk smiled, noticed Rodericks looking at him, shrugged his shoulders, and continued organizing his notes.

Rodericks motioned for the US Marshall to come to the bench, handed him a note, and sent him from the courtroom.

64: I Have a Complaint

Rodericks came into the courtroom after lunch, loudly dropping his files onto the desk he said, "Gentlemen, please approach the bench, now!"

Hawk looked over at Collucci, and then followed him to the bench.

"I have been informed that Lieutenant Hamlin has filed a notice of complaint with the Chief Judge of the Circuit Court," looking at Hawk, "were you aware of any of this Mr. Bennett?"

"No sir, your honor. I know she was upset about your comments from the bench but if she told me of her intentions I would have discouraged her from such a course." Hawk answered.

"Well, if her intention was to intimidate me it failed. This trial will go on. I would suggest, Mr. Bennett, that it would be better for all concerned, particularly the defendant, if Hamlin did not appear in the courtroom for the remainder of the trial."

Collucci could not help smiling at this little turn of events. Hamlin may have unintentionally turned the Judge to the Government's side.

"Well, your Honor, I can convey that message but I don't see how I can force her to comply. She's a rather determined individual."

"And so are you Mr. Bennett, do your best to keep her from my court." Rodericks replied, dismissing them with a wave of his hand.

When Hawk returned to his seat he leaned over to Josh, "Our friend Chris decided to light a fire under the Judge."

Josh looked confused.

"She filed a complaint with the Circuit Court," taking in Josh's smile, "I am glad you find this amusing, this Judge is not exactly a fan of ours. This isn't going to help."

"You know what, fuck him," Josh answered. "The prick deserves it for what he said about her. I'm glad she did it."

"Well, we'll see how glad you are when you're up there and he gets a shot at you. This isn't going to make it any easier."

Collucci interrupted their conversation announcing, "The Government calls Cheryan Pincince."

The young woman entered the courtroom. She looked around nervously. The clerk motioned for her to come to the front of the courtroom. As she stood there taking the oath, she kept glancing over at Josh. Settling into the witness stand, she appeared terrified.

Collucci walked to stand near her. "Now, Miss, would you please state your name and occupation for the record?"

Cheryan glanced around and in a barely audible voice said, "My name is Cheryan."

The clerk interrupted and asked her to speak louder.

Rodericks looked over at her, "Young lady, there is nothing to be nervous about. Please speak loud enough so we can hear your answers. If you do not understand the question just ask them to clarify it for you. Do you understand?"

"Yes, sir," she replied gaining a little confidence and relaxing.

"My name is Cheryan Pincince. I am eighteen years old. I am unemployed. I decided working at a convenience store is not for me. I am enrolled in a Certified Nursing Assistant program."

"Thank you," Collucci said, "you are doing fine. Now I am going to ask you some questions about the incident at your former place of employment. Just answer as best you can, and like the Judge said, if you do not understand the question let me know and I will try to help you. Okay?"

Cheryan nodded, and then quickly said, "Yes, I understand."

Collucci could see the jury was taken by this young woman. He was going to make some major points with her.

"Now Ms. Pincince, were you working at the Cumberland Farms, Taunton Avenue on March 15th of this year?"

"Yes, I was"

"How long have you been working there?"

"I got there around 9 AM."

"Ah, I mean, how long have you been employed there?"

"Oh. About a year. I started right after my Sixteenth birthday."

After Collucci took her through the preliminaries, he asked "Now on that day, did anything unusual happen?"

"You mean beside Mr. Subedar and CK being shot?"

Bits of laughter in the court until Rodericks' glare calmed the noise.

"I will ask this another way, please describe when you first realized something was wrong?"

Fleming shook her head at this performance. *She thought. How does a person like this become the US Attorney? He cannot even do a decent job of questioning his own witness. Maybe it was time to consider a change.*

"Well, like I told the officers, I thought it was weird that CK was there. He and I never work at the same time."

The response caught Collucci off guard, "Okay, go on."

"Then Mr. Subedar told me if anything went on I was to just hide behind the counter. That was really weird." She looked nervously at the jury then put her head down.

Collucci was frustrated. "Okay, Ms. Pincince, let me try it this way. When did you first see Ventraglia and Machado enter the store?"

"Well, first I saw Machado, I didn't know his name then," She began to answer, "I found out later they call him JoJo, but anyway he was wearing a blue hoodie and he was standing at the end of the parking lot looking up and down the street. He looked back at me and then started walking towards the store. That's when Ven...Ventrag..."

"Ventraglia?" Collucci offered.

"Yes. Ventraglia came in and yelled something. Mr. Subedar was at the end of one of the counters and he started yelling. I heard a shot and I dove down. I heard a real loud noise and then I heard CK yelling. Right after that, I heard another loud noise. I think it was the shotgun. Then the guy JoJo was on top of me," Pincince started to sob, "he, he told me he wouldn't let anyone hurt me."

Collucci nodded as he watched the jury, "Okay, now take your time. What did Machado, ah JoJo, do?"

"Well, he got up and I heard him and Ventraglia saying something about getting the money. That's when Ventraglia saw me. He started to point the gun at me," pausing to take a breath, "JoJo told him to stop but he said 'the bitch is a witness'. Sorry, but that's what he said," looking up at the Judge.

"That's fine, you just continue along. Don't worry about the words." Rodericks said.

"JoJo was arguing. Telling him not to do it. JoJo grabbed the shotgun and hit Ventraglia. He went down to his knees. He came back up yelling and I saw JoJo karate kick him in the head. I think it knocked him out."

"Okay, then what happened?"

"JoJo came over and told me to run." She replied.

"And what did you do?"

"I ran, faster than I could even imagine." Bringing more laughter to the court.

"Did you see JoJo after that?"

"No, I just ran and called 911 on my cell phone. I wasn't even thinking straight. I ran up the street and then around the back of the store. I don't know why. As I was going by the store, a car came flying at me. I stopped; the car turned, jumped the curb, and hit a pole. The driver fell out and I realized it was Ventraglia. He was lying on the ground. I lost it. I ran over and started kicking him. I know I shouldn't have," shaking her head, sobbing, "but he tried to kill me. The cops got there and pulled me away."

"No need to apologize, Ms. Pincince. I think we all might have reacted the same way," smiling at the jury.

Fleming sat in her seat thinking, *no, you would not. You don't have the balls. You would have shit your pants.*

"I have no further questions, your Honor."

"Mr. Bennett, would it be a problem if we took a 20 minute recess to let the witness compose herself?" Rodericks asked.

"Not at all your Honor, not at all."

"Very well, 20 minute recess," banging the gavel. Pincince almost jumped out of her seat at the noise. Fleming came over and took the young girl to a conference room. Collucci ignored the gesture and continued writing notes.

Hawk and Josh were talking when Josh made a head motion for Hawk to look at the back of the courtroom. Chris Hamlin came in and sat in the back row.

Hawk motioned for Chris to come over. As she did, she could see Josh smiling and making a throat slashing motion behind Hawk.

"Well, well if it isn't our idiot ally that decided making a complaint against the sitting Chief Judge of the United States District Court of Rhode Island, mid-trial I might add, was a good idea." Hawk said, "What the hell were you thinking? Or more to the point, why did you stop thinking before you did something stupid?"

"If you thought for one minute I was going to let that pompous son-of-a-bitch condescend to me like that you should be the one using your brain. I am going to make his life miserable. Cranky old self-righteous bastard." Chris replied.

Josh added, "Do you mean Hawk or Useless, which cranky old bastard?"

"I am glad you find this amusing, perhaps it will be different when Chris is delivering the discount soap she gets as a new employee of CVS, formerly of EPPD, to the Federal prison selected for you with the influence of Judge Useless." Hawk said.

"Well, it's done. Nothing you can do about it now. The prick had it coming." Chris replied.

"Okay, okay. I know he probably overstepped his bounds there, but couldn't you have waited until after the trial?"

Chris just stood staring, not even blinking.

"No, I suppose not." Hawk said. "Okay, but you do have to do one more thing I say."

"I suppose I can do that," Chris answered.

"Really? You agree to do this right?" Hawk asked

"Within reason, and it doesn't involve you being naked at any point." Chris smiled.

"I am going to puke," Josh said, "there's an image I didn't need."

Hawk shook his head, "remind me to be busy next time you two come looking for help. Okay, here is what you do. Get the hell out of this courtroom; get the hell out of the building. Now. Please."

"But..."

"Nope, that's the deal, now go!"

Chris looked at Josh who nodded, "it is probably best for now. After the jury is out you can come back and torture Rodericks if you like."

"Okay, I'll go. For now." Chris said, "But if that bastard does anything else I will be sitting in the front row staring him down." Turning around, she walked out the door.

"I love that woman," Hawk said, "but she is the biggest pain in the ass."

"I know exactly what you mean." Josh concurred.

As Chris left the courtroom, the Marshal announced the Judge's return.

"Mr. Bennett, I see I can depend on you to follow directions. I noticed Lieutenant Hamlin leaving the courtroom. Please keep it that way."

Hawk nodded, and then leaned over to Josh, "If our friend heard that she'd march right back in, wouldn't she?"

"No doubt," Josh replied, "No doubt."

Chris was a very private person, there was much about her only a few people knew, and no one knew it all. In addition to being a great cop, she was very well off financially. Actually, she was more than that; she was rich beyond most cops' wildest imagination.

While she may have been a disappointment to her family in the grandchildren department, she paid attention to her father's investment advice. Between her own investments, and her inheritance, she could afford to challenge Federal Judges. She would not even notice the missing money if she left the PD.

Judge Rodericks might take some satisfaction in her absence, but it was nothing to do with her being the least bit intimidated. She knew how to pick her battles. She would undoubtedly win the war.

65: *Something Wasn't Right*

"Okay, Mr. Bennett, shall we recall Ms. Pincince to the stand?" Rodericks asked.

"Yes sir," Hawk replied.

Cheryan retook the stand. Rodericks reminded her she was still under oath.

"I understand," she answered, the break obviously having its intended affect.

"Good afternoon Ms. Pincince, I only have a few questions for you." Hawk said gently.

"Okay."

"Now you testified that you saw Machado standing near the road looking up and down the street. Is that correct?"

"Yes."

"Why did you notice this?"

Pincince paused a moment then said, "Well, I noticed him right after Mr. Subedar told me to just hide if something happened. I thought that was weird. Then I saw this black guy, I mean JoJo, standing there like he was watching for something. I just thought it was all weird, I don't know. I never saw anybody stand there and do that before."

"Okay, now was the fact he was black part of the reason you thought it was odd?"

"Well, no, I mean, not really. Mr. Subedar always said to watch the black guys when they came in, but I never really paid him any attention. He didn't trust anybody. It's just, I don't know, I can't explain, between Mr. Subedar telling me to hide if something happened, and then a guy acting weird at the end of the parking lot, just made me nervous." She looked over at the jury then back down at her hands.

"Okay, now you said he, Machado, started walking towards you?"

"Yeah, he looked at me and seemed surprised to see me. He started to walk towards the store. That's when Ventraglia came in and started yelling," she paused a moment, taking a deep breath, "that's when I heard the shot and ducked down."

"Now, I want to call your attention to after Machado entered the store. Did you hear him say anything?"

"There was a lot of yelling and I couldn't really hear anything because of the two really loud noises, I guess they were from the shotgun. JoJo was on top of me and he told me he wouldn't let anyone hurt me."

Pincince started to sob again, "He saved my life."

"You're doing fine," Hawk tried to soothe her, "I only have a couple more questions."

Cheryan looked up, "Thank you, I'll be fine."

"Okay after Machado stood up did he say anything?"

"He was arguing with Ventraglia. Ventraglia pointed the shotgun at me. JoJo took it away and knocked him out. That's when he told me to run."

Hawk paused a moment, looked over at Collucci, then back at Pincince.

"One or two more questions if I may," looking at Pincince's statement to the police. "Have you ever seen Machado before this happened?"

"No, I don't think so. A lot of people come in the store but I don't remember him."

"How do you know they called him JoJo?"

Cheryan looked up nervously, looking at Collucci. Hawk noticed him shaking his head, so did some of the jury. Hawk moved to block her view.

"I am not supposed to say." She replied.

Rodericks beat Hawk to the punch, "You're not supposed to say? Young lady, unless the answer to the question is against your interest in a criminal matter, you will answer the question. Do you understand?"

"Yes, yes I do. But, I want to answer, well when I was talking to Mr. Collucci about my testimony, he told me to call him JoJo. He said it made him more of a nice guy for the jury. He told me not to tell anyone about this."

"Thank you, nothing further." Hawk turned, looking a Collucci, winked at him, and returned to his seat.

"Re-direct, Mr. Collucci?" Rodericks asked.

"No sir, noting further."

"You are excused, Ms. Pincince."

Cheryan stood and walked out. She glanced briefly at Josh and smiled, quickly making her way out of the courtroom.

Fleming watched with bemusement as the jury exchanged glances with each other.

"The Government has nothing further your honor. At this time the Government rests." Collucci slumped into his seat.

"Very well, Mr. Bennett?"

"Your Honor I have a motion to argue before we present our case. With the court's permission I'd like to argue now and, depending on how the court rules on the motion, begin with our first witness this afternoon."

"First things first, Mr. Bennett." Turning to the Deputy US Marshal, "Will the Marshal remove the jury please." Rodericks ordered.

As the door closed behind the last juror, Rodericks looked at Collucci.

"Please explain to me how your coaching of the witness doesn't equate with suborning perjury?"

Collucci stood. "Your Honor, the witness must have misunderstood me. I never said any such thing about how she should characterize her knowledge of Mr. Machado."

Reaching for a drink of water, he continued. "In my trial preparation with her, I referred to Machado as JoJo to make it more comfortable. She was never told to misrepresent those discussions."

Rodericks stared at Collucci for a long moment, "The court is not entirely persuaded by the government's characterization of these discussions. We will take this under further advisement for potential future actions." Rising from the bench and heading into chambers.

Hawk smiled at Collucci, "Oh my, Robbie boy. I think you may be the first guy Useless actually sanctions. That wouldn't be a helpful campaign boost, would it?"

66: *The Defense*

"Okay Mr. Bennett, proceed." Rodericks began shuffling papers, looking them over, ignoring Hawk.

"You honor, the defendant moves for a directed verdict. The Government failed to prove their case; they have not even managed to establish that a crime was committed. All the government has produced is conjecture and innuendo by so-called experts with a specific agenda, namely enhancing their own reputation.

The only thing clear here is that an unfortunate incident took place and a young man killed. Not an innocent young man, a young man who was directly and intentionally involved in a robbery leading to two deaths at the store, and his own death several moments later.

The evidence shows that Mr. Machado was not only involved in the crime, but that he held the murder weapon. A fact, let me remind the court, which the government tried to conceal.

That is all the government has managed to establish.

We would have stipulated to all of that in the beginning. They demonstrated no evidence of any crime committed by the defendant to support allowing this case to go to a jury. There is no established pattern of behavior by Sergeant Williams that shows him motivated by prejudice towards blacks. There is no clear and convincing actions by Sergeant Williams showing a callous indifference to blacks. There is nothing here.

The case law is clear, in the absence of any evidence of criminal action or intent by the defendant, a directed verdict is required. To send this case to the jury would be a travesty. The defendant moves for a directed verdict of acquittal. Thank you, your honor."

Hawk paused to look at Fleming, then Collucci, shaking his head he rejoined Josh at the defense table.

Collucci stood and walked to the gap between the defense and government tables, "Your honor, there must be some sort of a void in the sound between this table," gesturing to where Fleming was seated, "and this one," pointing to Hawk and Josh. "Mr. Bennett either did not hear, did not listen, or did not understand the significant amount of evidence submitted by the government in support of this charge. I submit that there is overwhelming proof that this defendant shot and killed an innocent man simply because he was black."

Walking to stand in front of the jury box, he continued. "Even if the government were to concede much of what Mr. Bennett contends, which we don't, but for arguments sake, the incontrovertible evidence of a dead, young, albeit troubled, combat hero, who was unarmed, shot by the defendant while he flagrantly disregarded normal police procedures, is enough for the jury to render a verdict of guilty.

Mr. Bennett too easily dismisses the expert testimony.

It is powerful, compelling, and on point.

There was no legitimate reason for Williams to enter that church and execute that man. In the absence of a legitimate reason, we are left with an illegitimate reason, a criminal one in this case. A police officer, acting under the color of law, intentionally depriving Mr. Machado of his civil rights.

Moreover, he did this for no other reason than the color of Mr. Machado's skin.

For that reason, we would ask that this court deny the motion and the matter allowed to proceed, ultimately to a jury. Thank you."

Rodericks looked up from his note taking, "Thank you Mr. Bennett, Mr. Collucci. I will take this matter to chambers and rule at 2:00 PM when court resumes, we stand adjourned until then." Banging the gavel, leaving the bench.

Hawk began gathering papers, Josh helping. Collucci walked over, hands raised as in surrender, "hear me out, no need to get angry, just trying to do my job."

Hawk turned to face him, "What?"

"Suppose I amend the charge to Civil rights violation, no jail, he'd have to resign from the department but that's much better than fifteen years of protective custody. Just wanted to put it out there. I am not unreasonable."

Josh started to come around Hawk, who blocked the move and stepped in front him. "Mr. Collucci, the very idea that you would make such an offer to a person you know full well is innocent speaks volumes about your integrity. You bring this bullshit case, tear apart this good officer's life, and now want him to go along in some face saving act for you. I tell you what, you are a piece of work."

Looking over at Fleming standing behind Collucci, "How do you go to work every morning knowing this is the caliber of people running that office?" Shaking his head and turning away.

"Come on Josh, let's get out of here before some of whatever the hell is wrong with this guy infects us," pushing Collucci aside, Hawk winked at Fleming, and walked out of the court.

67: *Spinning the Media*

Hawk and Josh stood outside the courthouse talking to Chief Brennan. Chris came over to join the conversation. The Channel 12 reporter spotted the group and came over.

John Peterson was the quintessential reporter. Starting out in print media out of college, he recognized the warning signs. Even though he was not the young flashy type, his cool demeanor, handsome face, and slightly graying hair gave him a quality that people trusted and, more importantly, would open up to.

"Chief Brennan, I wonder if I might have a word," smiling at Josh and Hawk. "I know better than to bother with you two, although maybe Lieutenant Hamlin would also join us?"

"No thanks, John, after the trial perhaps." Chris replied.

"John, I'd be happy to talk to you." Brennan said and walked over to the cameraman.

"Do we want to hear this?" Hawk asked.

"Probably not, plus they'd cut over to get us in the background, let's head in." Josh suggested.

As the trio walked behind the camera operator, they caught part of Brennan's statement, "...and I will tell you this, I am damn proud of all of the members of my department, but none more than Sergeant Williams and Lieutenant Hamlin. I don't think anyone, let alone a Federal Judge, should stick his nose into things when he does not have the whole story. I have a good mind...."

Hawk pulled Josh and Chris in close and said "It's a good goddamn thing ole Useless won't hear this until after the Chief testifies."

"I think it'd be funny," Chris said, "Our old Buford versus Useless, my money's on Brennan."

"How about we get through his testimony first, then he can have his feud with the Federal Judiciary." Hawk replied.

Chris laughed, "Okay, but I'd still love to see someone jam it up the old coots ass."

"Who's," Josh asked, "Useless or Hawks?"

"Very funny, two comedians, remember there is the matter of the trial." Hawk started to lead the way into the courtroom, "Where are you going, Lieutenant?"

"I'll just sit in the back. He won't see me there."

"I don't think so. You go run along and keep up your end of the bargain. Stay away from this, Chris. Please."

68: *Not That Easy*

Rodericks took the bench and wasted no time. He removed his glasses, rubbed his eyes, and then said, "The motion for directed verdict is denied, as soon as the jury is brought in, the defense will call its first witness."

Looking towards Hawk, "your objection is noted for the record and preserved should there be a need for an appeal." Turning his gaze to Collucci. Rodericks just could not help himself.

Once again, the jury paraded in, this time it was clear several were looking at Josh and smiling.

Hawk rose as if nothing transpired, "Your honor, the defense waived its right to an opening statement at the beginning of the trial, reserving it for this moment. I have decided that an opening is unnecessary. The defense calls Chief Winston Franklin Brennan.

Chief Brennan, wearing his full dress uniform, came into the courtroom. His mere physical presence captivating the jury and spectators. As he walked to the witness stand, he made a point of looking at Rodericks the whole way. He then turned and faced the clerk as she administered the oath.

Taking his seat in the witness box, he could almost look the Judge in the eye. Rodericks tried to ignore him.

"Good afternoon, Chief, for the record would you state your name and position?"

"Certainly, my name is Winston Franklin Brennan; I am the Chief of Police for the East Providence Police Department. I have been a member of the department for thirty-six years, the last twelve as Chief."

"Thank you Chief, were you also in the service?"

"I was, I served six years in the United States Marine Corps," smiling towards the jury and adding, "Semper Fi"

"Yes thank you for that, now sir, in your capacity as Chief do you have occasion to review the service records of the officers that serve under you?"

"I do, I make it a habit to review each officer's file annually, time permitting."

Hawk retrieved a file from the table, showed it to Collucci, and then turned to Rodericks, "Your Honor, may I approach?"

Rodericks nodded.

"Chief can you identify this file?"

"Yes, it is the standard personnel folder we use in the police department. This one is Sergeant Williams's file," looking at Josh, nodding slightly.

"The defense moves to have this exhibit marked as Defense A in full."

"No objection," Fleming said, Collucci seemingly engrossed in the file. Fleming was constantly amazed at his arrogance; he did not even bother to read the file beforehand. She did. This was not going to be helpful for the case, for that she took some satisfaction.

"Chief, would you read the section of the file where Sergeant Williams has been disciplined?"

Brennan looked confused at first, and then the light went on, "Sergeant Williams has never been disciplined for anything."

"Well, Chief that's a rather thick file, are there any letters of reprimand?"

"No"

"Letters of complaint?"

"No"

"Well then can you tell us what the file contains?"

"It contains standard family contact information, training records, firearms qualification scores, promotion letters, and a number of departmental and external commendations."

"How many commendations?"

Brennan was in the game now. He counted the pages, individually, and announced, "There are twenty-eight departmental commendations, including one for the Medal of Heroism, the highest award given by the department.

There are eleven commendations from outside agencies, including the Rhode Island State Police, FBI, DEA, ATF, and Royal Canadian Mounted Police.

There are two commendations from the United States Attorney's Office in Rhode Island, one signed by William Strain, who went on to be Governor, and one by Mr. Robert Collucci, the current US Attorney, for outstanding support of the United States Department of Justice," watching as Collucci heard his name, looked at Fleming, trying to figure out why.

"Chief, you mentioned a Medal of Heroism; can you read a portion of that commendation?"

"I'd be happy to," shuffling to find the document, "Detective Sergeant Joshua A. Williams is awarded the Medal of Heroism for actions above and beyond the call of duty. On the night of July 29, 2005, Sergeant Williams responded to a reported house fire. Upon arrival, neighbors reported a small child on the second floor of the residence. Sergeant Williams, at great personnel risk, entered the building, located the child, age 4, as well as an unconscious female, later determined to be the mother, on the floor in a rear bedroom.

Sergeant Williams picked up the unconscious woman and young child taking them to safety.

Sergeant Williams exhibited the highest example of courage and selflessness, risking his life to safe innocent people. His actions are in the best tradition of the East Providence Police Department."

"Thank you, Chief. One more thing, is there anything in that file regarding a complaint against Sergeant Williams for conduct of a racist or prejudicial manner?"

"Nothing, not one thing. I will add that I do not tolerate that behavior on my department. We have done a great deal to combat those attitudes. Sergeant Williams has never engaged in such behavior."

"Chief, what is the normal departmental procedure for an officer involved shooting?"

"Well, first we make sure the officer receives any necessary assistance in dealing with the situation; it is always difficult to take a human life regardless of the circumstances.

He or she is immediately placed on administrative duties while the matter is investigated. Since I have been Chief, we always ask for assistance from the Rhode Island State Police to insure impartiality. The result of the investigation then submitted to the Attorney General for review. Typically, the matter is placed before a Statewide Grand jury."

"How many times has this happened under your command?"

"Thankfully only three times, including this one, in each of the two prior cases it followed the track I just described."

"Chief are you aware of any other case taken over by the US Attorney's Office?"

"Objection," Collucci jumped from his seat. "Any other cases, where, the state, New England, nationwide? There needs to context here, although I fail to see the relevance."

"Your Honor, I am merely demonstrating how these matter are normally handled. Chief Brennan can certainly testify to that. I will rephrase the question to put it more in context." Hawk argued.

"Overruled, rephrase the question and the witness can answer." Rodericks ruled.

"Chief, in your experience in the State of Rhode Island, are you aware of any other cases of an officer involved shooting taken over by the US Attorney's office?"

Brennan directed his gaze to Collucci, "No sir. As a matter of fact, I spoke to every Chief in the state and the Superintendent of the Rhode Island State Police; no one could recall any such action by the US Attorney."

"Now Chief, are you familiar with the Rhode Island Police Officers' Bill of Rights?"

"Yes, of course."

"And is it true that the law says an officer 'charged with a felony may be suspended, without pay, at the discretion of the Chief of Police?"

"Yes that is true." Brennan was now sitting straight up, he knew where this was going, knew how much it irritated the political hacks, and some other Chiefs, but he did not care.

"Did you suspend Sergeant Williams once he was indicted by the Federal Grand jury?"

"No," placing his hands on the railing and looking the jury, "I did not."

"And why is that Chief?" Hawk took a step back bringing him next to Josh.

"Because I have absolute faith in Sergeant Williams, I reviewed the investigation, done by the members of my department, assisted by the Rhode Island State Police, and I found absolutely no evidence whatsoever to justify suspending Sergeant Williams. I believe in the concept of innocent until proven guilty, I will never suspend an officer just because it is politically expedient. I stand behind my officers when they are doing their job and acting within the requirements of the law. Sergeant Williams's actions met that standard."

"Thank you Chief. I have nothing more your Honor."

"Mr. Collucci, do you wish to inquire?" Rodericks asked, looking hopefully that he wouldn't.

"May I have a moment, your Honor?" Collucci replied.

"Of course."

Collucci and Fleming engaged in a brief conversation. Fleming pointing out several of the documents in the file. Collucci nodded, rose, and said, "Your Honor, I have no questions for this witness."

"Very Well, Chief Brennan thank you for your testimony, you are excused."

Brennan rose up, nodded to Rodericks, smiled at the jury, and strode out of the courtroom.

"Your Honor," Hawk said, "I would like to amend my witness list. The original list called for an expert witness to testify, we have decided not to call that witness."

"Very well, Mr. Bennett," Rodericks looked at the computer on his desk, "We will adjourn for the evening. Reconvene at 9:00 AM. Will Sergeant Williams be testifying?"

Several members of the jury leaned forward at this.

"We will be discussing that very subject this evening, your Honor. I have two other witnesses on my list before we get to that point." Hawk smiled, "We will have our decision for you in the morning," allowing the tension to simmer and build slowly.

Hawk knew he would have to shoot Josh to stop him from testifying, but no need for everyone to know that quite yet.

69: No Walk in the Park

Bill Symonds, Josh, and Hawk sat in the office eating pizza. They ordered two large and one small one since Josh insisted on having anchovies.

"How can you eat those things?" Bill asked.

"It ain't pizza without anchovies." taking a swig of Beck's beer.

As Hawk opened one of the beers he said, "Did you take these out of evidence as well?"

"Nope, deducted the expense from your fee."

"Nice, which leaves me enough to buy one more pizza. At this rate I'll be paying you."

Josh tipped his beer and smiled.

"Okay," Hawk settled into his desk and propped up his feet, "which part of Josh's anatomy is Collucci going to try and cut off first, his head or his balls?"

Josh laughed, "I am ready for him, I got this. He isn't going to do anything to me on the stand I can't handle," taking a long drink from his beer, not noticing the look between Symonds and Hawk.

Symonds put his pizza down, walked over, and picked up a file, tapping the outside of the folder repeatedly. "Sergeant Williams, does it say in your report that you cataloged and placed in the evidence safe the six bottles seized during the arrest for the Sale of Alcohol to a Minor, yes or no?"

Josh looked at Hawk, then back at Symonds, "What's this?"

"It's a yes or no question, Sergeant," looking over at Hawk, "your Honor would you instruct the witness to answer the question please."

Hawk sat up, bang his fist, "Sergeant, you do understand the concept of yes or no, answer the question."

Josh shook his head, "okay, you want to practice, fine. Yes, that is what it says."

Symonds continued, "Does it not say you removed one bottle, packaged it, and delivered it to the Rhode Island State Toxicology Laboratory for analysis, also yes or no?"

"Yes," Josh sat up. *These people think they can rattle me, fine, go for it, I have been playing this game a long time.*

"Now Sergeant, is it your testimony that the evidence you produced in the court hearing on that matter was in fact the same evidence you seized at the time of the arrest?"

Josh smiled, gotcha, "No, I did not testify to that."

"Ah, what did you testify to?"

"I was asked if it was the same beer seized that night and I answered yes it was. It was Becks Beer."

"I see," Symonds paused a moment, "was there an evidence tag attached to this same beer?"

"Yes" Josh replied, starting to wonder where this was going.

"And was it the same evidence tag you prepared the night of the arrest and evidence seizure?"

Josh thought to himself, okay, I see this now, not going to work. "It was the same evidence tag, same bag seized. I never said it was the same evidence," his confidence growing.

"Did you alter the tag?"

"No"

"Did you indicate that the evidence contained therein was not the original evidence seized?"

"No, that's not what I was asked." Enjoying this game.

"Is it normal practice to substitute similar items for missing evidence?"

Josh hesitated, Symonds continued

"When did you discover the original evidence was missing?"

"When I received the subpoena, I went to retrieve the evidence out of the locker and found it was misplaced"

"And who has access to this evidence storage area?"

"The members of SIU, the Captain of Detectives, and the Chief of Police."

"Who did you report the missing evidence to? Did you prepare a report, did you notify anyone, Sergeant? How many times have you testified on court with exhibits that were substituted for evidence you lost? Did you drink the evidence, Sergeant, is that what happened? You have such a callous disregard for this, or any court, that you believed you could slide by because of some poorly structured questions that failed to uncover your lying to the court? Is that it Sergeant?"

Josh was staring blankly.

"After admitting here you've lied under oath in the past, or in your version altered the facts to fit the truth, do you now expect this jury to believe you? Why is that Sergeant? Is lying in a minor case that, at worst, if you told the truth about the missing evidence, might have resulted in a dismissal of charges, perhaps a minor reprimand to your spotless record acceptable? Yet you would have the jury believe you would not lie about something that could put you in jail for a very, very long time? Is that what you want us to believe?" Looking over to Hawk, "I am threw with dis guy."

Josh was rattled.

Symonds opened another beer, walked over, and handed it to Josh. "Look, don't be fooled by Collucci's soft-pedaling this with Lt. Hamlin. It is you he wants to fry in front of the jury. He is going to try to make it so they will doubt anything you say. He will try to cover the lack of evidence by building his case on destroying your credibility. That is what we have to deal with. We need to get this out, take the bite out of it, before Collucci uses it."

Walking back and sitting. "My advice is don't give him the opportunity to do this just to satisfy that ego of yours. If you let him destroy your credibility, the lack of evidence will not matter. All the jury will see is a liar on the stand. A liar who shot a war hero that saved the life of a seventeen year old girl."

"Josh, listen." Hawk added, "I can tell this jury likes you. Collucci put Chris in the hot seat about this and the jury did not care. They want to hear what you say about things in the church. I can lead them away from letting this affect your credibility. However, you are going to have to listen to us and lose that 'I've been doing this a long time' attitude. You have just lucked out that most lawyers do not prepare properly. For all his arrogance and faults, Collucci knows where his opportunity lies, and it is here, with this. We need to neutralize it."

Josh stood, walked to the window, and looked out on Weybosset Street. "Okay, you made the point. What do I, I mean we, do about it?"

As the discussion continued, Chris Hamlin arrived. Josh looked up at her, searching her eyes. She just shook her head.

Hawk noticed the exchange, "not to be cold my son, replacing is more efficient than repairing."

Chris turned to face Hawk, "You really can be an asshole. You know that?"

"I do, I freely admit it, that's why my experience is that it is easier to start with a blank sheet, so to speak." Chuckling as they continue to discuss the plan.

70:   *The Fifth Commandment*

"The defense calls David Anthony Ventraglia," Hawk's voice resounded through the courtroom.

The door at the side of the courtroom opened. Ventraglia, dressed in a plain white shirt and khaki colored pants, entered the court. The marshal directed him to the witness stand. Two other marshals, trying to be inconspicuous, took up positions near the exit doors.

"Please raise your right hand," the clerk said.

"Why? I ain't saying shit," came the reply.

Rodericks glared. "Mr. Ventraglia, you should be aware that I can make your time within your present living arrangement even less pleasant. I will not tolerate such language or attitude here. Is that clear?"

"Whatever," Ventraglia replied, slightly raising his right hand.

The oath was administered.

Ventraglia's responded, "I ain't testifying, so everything I say will be true." Looking up and smiling at the judge.

Hawk, watching the jury's reaction to this, thought this is even better than I hoped.

"Would you state your name, Sir?"

"Nope, I ain't stating nothing, I am pleading the fifth." Rising from the seat and heading back toward the exit, "thanks for the day trip but it was a big waste, bye judge."

Rodericks said, "Mr. Ventraglia, you will remain in that seat until such time as the court instructs you otherwise. Now sit down or you will be held in contempt."

Ventraglia sat back down.

"Now," the Judge continued, "Mr. Ventraglia, are you invoking your right not to testify under the Fifth Amendment?"

"Yes, I am," Ventraglia nodded and smiled at the jury, "I know under the Fifth Commandment I don't have to say shit, I mean, sorry, I don't have to say anything."

However, no one on the jury, or in the court, was paying much attention. They were laughing too hard.

Rodericks motioned for the Marshals to take Ventraglia back to the holding cell.

As soon as Ventraglia left, Rodericks ordered the jury removed.

"Mr. Bennett, was that really necessary?"

"Your honor, under the best evidence rule, since Mr. Ventraglia will not testify, I intend to call Detective Joseph McDaniel to introduce the video of Mr. Ventraglia's statement regarding Mr. Machado's participation in the robbery."

"Objection, your honor," Collucci said, "It would be hearsay and should not be allowed."

"Well, isn't this an interesting twist, the Government objecting to the defense motion for the introduction of a video statement, obtained by the police. They didn't mention this in Law school that I recall."

"This would hardly be hearsay. Mr. Ventraglia gave a very detailed statement, against interest, regarding the robbery. It goes to the very essence of this matter. The jury needs to see the whole picture. Sergeant Williams had good reason to put a great deal of weight on the validity of information he received from the dispatcher. Ventraglia's statement merely confirms the basis of the information."

Hawk looked at his notes for a moment.

Collucci stood and interjected, "Your Honor, if I may, Mr. Ventraglia's statement has no bearing on the matter before the court. The defendant in this case knew nothing of the details surrounding the robbery, other than the broadcast by the dispatcher. The Government's contention is that information was insufficient to justify Sergeant Williams's actions; his innate prejudice was the motivating factor. Whether or not Ventraglia's statement is consistent with the information broadcast is immaterial and prejudicial. The jury would be compelled to give information not available to the defendant inordinate probative weight. This matter hinges on what actions the defendant took based on what was available to him at the time he took them. Any subsequent information, learned after the fact, is immaterial and will confuse the jury," Collucci argued.

Rodericks wrote a few notes, looked over to the computer monitor, and said, "I will take an hour to review this matter. We will stand adjourned until 10:00 AM."

71: *A Different Truth*

Rodericks returned promptly at 10:00, catching everyone by surprise.

"The court has considered the arguments in this matter, Detective McDaniel will be allowed to testify about, and introduce, the statement made by Ventraglia." Holding his hand up as Collucci rose to his feet, "subject to the normal standards of evidence and subject to wide latitude in cross-examination," looking over at Bennett. "Call your witness Counselor."

"The defense calls Detective Joseph McDaniel."

The door at the rear of the courtroom opened and Joe McDaniel walked in. Wearing a nicely tailored, dark blue suit, his short gray hair, deep blue eyes, slightly ruddy complexion, glasses hanging around his neck gave him the appearance of a grandfather walking into a school performance. McDaniel spent so many hours in courtrooms he lost count. As he walked to the witness stand, he nodded at Josh, smiled at the jury, turned to face the clerk, and raised his right hand.

"I do," he said in response to the oath and took his seat on the stand. "Good Morning, Your Honor," he added.

Rodericks nodded.

McDaniel knew how to play a courtroom. His calm friendly demeanor always put people, good and bad, at ease. You could not help but like him. Many a bad guy took this nice guy persona as a sign of weakness, vulnerability. Most of them served, or were still serving, long sentences for their mistake. Defense attorneys gave him much respect as well; experience taught them he was not one easily tripped up. If he adjusted the facts to fit the truth, as was all too common in the insular world of cops, he did it flawlessly. Experience is a great teacher and McDaniel had decades of it.

"Good Morning Detective McDaniel, would you state your name and occupation for the record?" Hawk began.

"Good morning to you Mr. Bennett," turning to the jury he looked at the first one on the left, top row.

"My name is Joseph McDaniel, I am a Detective with the East Providence Police Department. I have been a member of the department for thirty-seven years," pausing a moment, slight smile crossing his face. "If I recall correctly I was assigned a dinosaur as my first patrol vehicle," causing laughter throughout the court.

Continuing, he said, "I have been assigned as a Detective in the Major Crimes Squad for the past twenty two years." When he finished he had looked each juror in the eye.

"Thank you Detective, now let me call your attention to the March 15, 2006 were you working that day?"

"I was."

"And did you have occasion to be involved in the robbery-homicide investigation at the Cumberland Farms on Taunton Avenue?"

"Yes sir, I was the lead investigator for this case."

"And, in your capacity as the lead investigator, did you conduct an interview of Mr. David Anthony Ventraglia?"

"Yes, I did. The East Providence Fire Department rescue brought Mr. Ventraglia from the scene to Rhode Island Hospital. He was treated and released to our custody. I and Detective Doyle took him to the East Providence police station."

"And what did you do once you arrived at the station?"

"We brought Mr. Ventraglia into the interview room. I got him something to eat and a coffee," McDaniel saw the surprise on some of the Juror's faces. *TV has created such a skewed version of what we do and how we do it.*

McDaniel looked back at Hawk, "After he finished, I read him his rights from the standard Rights Form. I asked if he understood his rights, and if he wanted to make a statement."

"And what did Mr. Ventraglia do?"

"He told me he knew the form better than I did and signed the form."

"Objection, hearsay." Collucci said.

"It was all recorded on the video. You can see it for yourself." McDaniel said before Hawk could reply.

Rodericks looked at McDaniel, "Detective McDaniel, please do not say anything else after an objection is made until I rule."

"Yes sir, sorry." McDaniel replied, looking to the jury for their reaction. He knew they wanted to see the video now.

"The objection is overruled. Mr. Bennett, why don't we move on?" Rodericks said.

"Gladly your honor." Hawk moved to the table and held up an envelope, "May I approach the witness your honor?"

Rodericks nodded.

As Hawk passed Collucci, he showed him the envelope.

"Now Detective McDaniel, can you identify this item for me?"

"Yes, it is the original DVD recording of the interview I conducted with David Ventraglia. The DVD is in a sealed case with my initials on the seal dated March 15, 2006 with the time 15:45. The case was then placed in the plastic evidence bag, sealed, time and date stamped, and placed in the evidence vault at the East Providence Police station."

"Your Honor, we'd like to have the item marked as a full exhibit."

"No objections," Collucci said.

"So marked," Rodericks ordered

"Now Detective McDaniel, would you please open this item," Hawk asked.

Removing the DVD from the sealed envelope, McDaniel handed it to Hawk. Hawk handed it to the court clerk and waited for the DVD to play on the screen.

The initial video showed Ventraglia sitting at a table holding a cup of coffee. His head was bandaged and one eye was somewhat swollen. McDaniel appears on camera and sits across from Ventraglia.

The audio portion began "David, my name is Joe McDaniel. We know each other pretty well, don't we?"

Ventraglia just nodded.

"David, I am going to read you your rights from this form," placing a copy in front of Ventraglia, "would you follow along with me please?"

Ventraglia picked up the paper and listened as McDaniel went through the rights form.

"Now David, do you understand these rights as I've read them to you?"

Ventraglia nodded.

"David, if you would, please say yes or no if you understand these rights." McDaniel smiled, his voice sounding as if he was a schoolteacher helping with homework.

"Yeah, I understand. I know the form better than you do. I know the drill, I want to talk, I don't need a lawyer, I didn't do anything. I didn't know that nigger was gonna rob the place. I never saw the shotgun. He hid it under his jacket when I went to pick him up."

"Okay, David, we'll get to that. I want to hear the whole story but let's make it all nice and legal," handing Ventraglia a pen McDaniel continued, "would you initial each line and then sign and date the bottom for me."

Ventraglia quickly went down the list, signed it, and pushed the form over to McDaniel. "You guys should just keep these on file for me, I always sign them, don't I?"

McDaniel smiled, "Yes David, you are always cooperative with me, I appreciate that." Taking the form and sliding it under his notebook. "Let's start from the beginning, when did you first meet Machado?"

"You mean yesterday, or when I first met him before that?"

"Let me put it this way, how long have you known him?"

"I don't know, awhile. I've just seen him around. We've partied once in a while," Ventraglia kept glancing towards the camera, "but other than that, I don't hang with him, I don't really know him that well."

McDaniel took some quick notes, "Now let's talk about yesterday. When did you meet up with JoJo?"

Ventraglia never missed a beat, painting a beautiful tale of just happening to see Machado outside the complex at 25 Gemini Drive, not recognizing him at first, and Machado asking him for a ride to the Cumberland Farms.

"Why were you at Gemini?" McDaniel asked.

Ventraglia hesitated, "Ah, I was just passing by, I go that way sometimes. I have friends that live there."

"Who else do you know lives there?" McDaniel continued

"Just some guys, that's all, people I see around." Ventraglia was starting to fidget.

"Did you know JoJo lived there?"

"Ah, yeah, I think so, I'd been to a few parties there and saw him."

"I see," McDaniel replied, "So you pick him up and take him to Cumberland Farms?"

"Yup"

"How did you drive there?"

Ventraglia looked up, "In my car," smiling at McDaniel.

"Which road did you take?"

"South Broadway, to Broadway to Grosvenor. What other way is there?"

McDaniel made another note, watching Ventraglia's feet moving in a shuffle, back and forth, knees shaking. "Did you go anywhere else before getting to Cumberland Farms?"

Ventraglia looked up at the ceiling, "oh yeah, wait a minute, I just remembered, he asked to go to Rite Aide. I took him there first."

"And you did this why, out of the kindness of your heart?" McDaniel asked.

"Okay, you got me," came the answer, "He offered me some weed, I think he deals but either way he had a couple of bags and offered me some. Call DEA they'll want to take over now." Ventraglia leaned back, fold his arms, and smiled.

"I think DEA has better things to worry about. Now, just so I have this straight. You go to Gemini for no particular reason, see JoJo, a guy you barely know, he asks for a ride to a couple of places, and you drive him, right?"

"For the weed, yup. It saved me the trouble of going downtown to get some later. I had a few bitches coming over to party later. I do that a lot you know. You must have done that back in your day, huh? A few centuries ago?" laughing at his own attempt at humor.

"David, I am so old weed was something I pulled out of the lawns I cut for pocket money," smiling right back.

Ventraglia visibly relaxed. McDaniel had that effect on people.

"Now, when you get to the Cumberland Farms, what happens?"

"JoJo asks me to pull around back, so I do."

"And you didn't find that strange?"

"Nah, I figured he wanted to get in the store and back out quick cuz he was carrying weed. If cops happened by they might decide to fuck with him and he could run. If they saw him get in a car they had better control over him. Your fucking uniforms are always messing with the brothers, you know. It ain't right. You guys are always prospecting people."

"You mean profiling?" McDaniel replied.

"Whatever, just messing with people for no reason."

"Okay, so then what happens?" McDaniel asked.

"I decided I needed cigarettes, so I get out of the car and walk to the front of the store. JoJo is standing there. He says 'Take this', hands me the shotgun, and pushes me in the store. I tried to go back but he pushes the door closed. So I am standing there, like, what the fuck man, what do I do? I look and there's some dude yelling at me. JoJo comes in, takes the shotgun and blasts the guy, and then another guy comes running with a knife and he blasts him. I am like, what the fuck dude? He then sees a girl behind the counter and he jumps on her like he's humping her or something. It was un-fucking-real man. I started to yell at him. He jumps up and clocks me with the shotgun. I went down man, I saw stars. I came to and ran out the door."

Ventraglia paused, his head slumped on his chest, "I just wanted to get out of there."

McDaniel nodded, "Go on, what happened next?"

"I ran to my car, I heard sirens and wanted no part of the cops. I got in the car, fired it up, and jetted out. As I started out of the lot, someone ran in front of the car. I turned the wheel, the car shot forward, and I hit a pole. After that, I don't remember much," pausing a moment, looking at McDaniel "as a matter of fact, I ain't really sure about any of this. They say I have a concussion and that can cause memory loss. I probably have that."

This continued for another thirty-five minutes with Ventraglia continuously changing the story as he remembered new facts. The point made, Machado participated in the robbery. He held the murder weapon, corroborated by the FBI fingerprint report. The jury now possessed a better idea of the 'victim' in this case.

As the video ended, Hawk moved back over to the jury. "Detective McDaniel, after you completed the interview, what did you do?"

"I brought Mr. Ventraglia down to the holding cell to await transportation to the ACI, ah the Adult Correctional Institution, Intake

Center. Secured the DVD in the evidence bag and placed it in the evidence holding locker for permanent filing by the BCI detectives." McDaniel replied.

"I have nothing further your honor." Hawk returned to his seat.

"Just a few questions, your Honor," Collucci rose.

"Detective McDaniel, isn't it true that before being transported to the Intake Center, Mr. Ventraglia was taken back to Rhode Island Hospital?"

"Yes, that's true." McDaniel calmly answered.

"Do you know why that was necessary?"

"No, I was not involved in the transport."

"Did you notice anything about Mr. Ventraglia's physical condition when you placed him in the holding cell?"

"Yes, he was bandaged from the injuries suffered in the car accident, one of his eyes were swollen. I assume he was trying to avoid the prison and spend the night at the hospital." McDaniel answered.

"I am not interested in assumptions, only facts Detective. Now isn't it true you inflicted a beating on Ventraglia as soon as the camera was turned off." Collucci looked to the jury for their reaction.

"No," McDaniel answered calmly, "Mr. Ventraglia was handled in accordance with the law. I take that very seriously, sir."

Collucci spun around, "Are you testifying, under oath I might add, that you didn't beat Ventraglia. A man responsible for two murders, a person you have personally arrested numerous times, one you considered responsible for the situation Sergeant Williams finds himself. Is that your testimony, Detective?" Collucci was losing his composure.

McDaniel was not.

"Yes I am," McDaniel sat up and looked at the jury, "my job is to interview and gather evidence. Mr. Ventraglia's statement was sufficient to show his involvement in the robbery and shooting. He tried to spin a tale, but the contradictions and physical evidence say otherwise. I do not beat prisoners to get confessions. There is no need. That's television cops. Here in the real world I talk to them, and they talk to me. Frankly, sir I resent the implication. That's not how good cops work." McDaniel saw half the jury nodding in agreement.

"Nothing further your Honor." Collucci said.

Hawk loved watching the man self-destruct.

Rodericks looked at Hawk. Hawk shook his head. Rodericks said "Detective McDaniel, you are excused. Thank you for your testimony."

McDaniel smiled at the jury, rose from his seat, and walked out of the courtroom, patting Josh on the back as he past him.

72: On the Stand

Hawk rose slowly from his seat, moved to stand between the two opposing tables, "the defense calls Sergeant Joshua A. Williams."

There was a slight buzz in the courtroom. Rodericks quickly moved to contain it, "there will be no outbursts in this court. Anyone," looking directly at the three rows of uniformed Police Officers from several different departments," anyone that violates this will be removed from the courtroom. Please continue, Mr. Bennett."

Josh stood, walked to the stand, and took the oath. Dressed in a dark gray suit, he projected an image of confidence and trustworthiness. The jury, to a person, was looking intently at him. This was exactly what Hawk wanted. Chris told him about the juror she recognized. He would play to that hidden ace. Emotions drive most decisions, use it correctly, and it will overcome almost anything. Even the truth.

Hawk paused a moment to let the jury take their measure of Josh. This is where he earned his money and he was going to make it memorable.

"Josh, or more appropriately Sergeant Williams, would you please tell the jury about your current employment?"

Collucci was on his feet, "Your Honor, in the interest of saving time, the Government would consent to having Sergeant Williams's personnel file submitted as a full exhibit for the jury to review." He was not going to give Hawk any opportunity to Canonize Saint Josh before the jury.

"Your Honor," Hawk began.

"Save it, Mr. Bennett," Rodericks interrupted, "While the court appreciates the Government's thoughtful gesture I have no intention of denying or restricting this defendant's opportunity in front of the jury. He may testify as to his experience and position," pausing to look at Collucci, "and we will so mark and submit the personnel file as a full exhibit."

Collucci sat down, glaring at Fleming as she tried, but failed, to conceal a smile.

Hawk looked at Josh, indicating he should continue.

Josh looked at the jury, "As you know, my name is Joshua Williams. I am a member of the East Providence Police Department and have been for ten years. My current rank is Detective Sergeant, assigned as the Assistant Commander, Special Investigations Unit. I have been in this position for three years."

"Now Sergeant, Chief Brennan testified as to the content of your personnel file. He testified that there were no disciplinary actions against you, is that accurate?"

"Yes, there are always complaints, but none of them were ever substantiated. It goes with the territory; any good cop doing his job will have people complain. I learned a long time ago, from cops like Joe McDaniel, to treat people fairly, no matter the circumstances. It has always worked for me." Josh looked at the jury again; some of them were nodding their heads.

Collucci was on his feet again, "Objection, this is storytelling your honor. Narrative and commentary is not appropriate on direct."

"Overruled," Rodericks quickly replied, "However, Sergeant, please confine your answers to the question asked without editorializing. You may continue, Mr. Bennett."

"Thank you, your Honor. Sergeant, I'd like to turn your attention to March 15, 2006, were you on duty that day?" Picking up a paper then putting it down, Hawk made a quick note.

"Yes. Lieutenant Hamlin and I were returning from court."

"At what point did you become aware of another incident in the city?"

"As we were coming off the highway onto Warren Avenue, dispatch put out a radio call for shots fired at Kent Farm. I immediately began to head in that direction. Before we got to the intersection of South Broadway and Warren Avenue, Lieutenant Ackerly called in that he was at the location and there was nothing showing. He told dispatch to cancel all but two uniform cars to the scene."

"Then what happened?"

"I turned onto Broadway and headed north to check out information we had on a fugitive. Dispatch put out another call for a shooting at the Cumberland Farms, Taunton Avenue. The dispatcher reported receiving multiple calls on this one. I realized the first call to Kent Farm was a diversion. I turned onto Grove Avenue heading towards the scene." Josh paused a moment, looking at Hawk to see if he should continue.

"Sergeant, how did you know the first call was a diversion?" Hawk asked.

"Experience. It has happened a number of times in my career. Lieutenant Ackerly even asked how many calls they received on the shooting. There was only one. The bad guys think by diverting officers away from the area they will improve their chances to get away. To be honest..."

"Excuse me, your Honor. I didn't hear that, what did he say about honest?" Collucci was going to go big on this.

Rodericks looked at Collucci, "perhaps you should pay closer attention." Looking at the clerk, "would you please read the last response by the witness."

Reviewing the transcript, the clerk read, "Question, Sergeant, how did you know the first call was a diversion? Answer, Experience. It has happened a number of times in my career. Lieutenant Ackerly even asked how many calls they received. There was only one. The bad guys think by diverting officers away from the area they will improve their chances to get away. To be honest." pausing to look at the Judge, "The witness did not finish the answer."

"Are you up to speed now, Mr. Collucci?" Rodericks asked.

"Yes, thank you, the honest part threw me."

"Objection, your Honor, do we really have to tolerate childish editorializing by Mr. Collucci?" Hawk asked.

"Sustained, please approach." Rodericks ordered.

Sliding the microphone away from the bench Rodericks said, "Mr. Collucci, you'll have ample opportunity to impeach this witness. I will not tolerate such tactics during direct by Defense counsel. If you cannot contain yourself, I will have you removed and let Ms. Fleming take over. Is that clear?"

"Of course, your Honor. I intend no disrespect. I simply did not hear the answer." Collucci answered, desperately trying to sound sincere.

Hawk laughed, "Oh that certainly makes it all acceptable."

"Enough," Rodericks said, "resume your questioning Mr. Bennett and as for you Mr. Collucci, take my words to heart."

Both lawyers returned to their respective tables.

"Do you recall the question I asked Sergeant?"

"Yes, I heard you perfectly well." Josh answered, watching as some of the jurors caught his sarcasm.

Hawk raised his eyebrow at the response, "Continue with your answer."

"As I was saying, to be honest," staring down at Collucci, "sometimes the tactic works. In this case it didn't."

"Objection, witness is assuming facts not in evidence." Collucci interjected.

"Your honor, if I can get through an entire answer, those facts will be in evidence. This is an experienced officer, he's been through these situations, he can certainly testify to his experience." Hawk challenged.

"Overruled, continue." Rodericks offered no explanation.

"Thank you, your Honor." Hawk, in a parade rest stance, continued. "Now Sergeant, if I recall correctly, you said you turned onto Grove Avenue as you headed to the scene. What happened next?"

Josh turned back to the jury, "Dispatch broadcast a description of a suspect, black male, blue-hooded sweatshirt, armed with a sawed-off shotgun, last seen running toward Six Corners.

As we came down Grove, near John Street, I saw a person that matched that description. As soon as he saw the unmarked car, he turned away, running toward Saint Domenicks."

"Were you certain that this was the suspect?"

"Yes, I was. He matched the description and it appeared to me he held something concealed under his sweatshirt and pants. I believed it was a weapon."

Collucci started to rise, and then reconsidered. *I'll let this play out, he thought, when I am done with him they won't believe anything he's said.*

Fleming watched his indecision and wondered if she was missing something. She did not enjoy being in this position but her conscience would not let her allow Collucci's political agenda to thwart justice. She needed to know what he was going to do.

"What did you do?"

"I yelled to Lieutenant Hamlin to call it in and took off on foot after the suspect. He ran around to the front of Saint Domenicks, up the stairs, and in the front center door. I came up the stairs, drew my weapon, called on the portable radio I was entering the church, and asked the responding units to set up a perimeter. I then went in the left side front door. As I..."

"Let me stop you there for a moment," Hawk interrupted, "Please explain to the jury why you decided to enter the church at that point."

Josh looked over at the jury; they were all watching him intently. "I knew this was a very popular church. The doors, unlike some churches, are open during the day for parishioners, and others, to come in." Pausing a moment, he continued.

"I also know the Pastor of the church very well, Father Swanson. He is often inside the church during the day. I was concerned that someone, perhaps Father Swanson, was in there. I believed this suspect already shot two people and wanted to prevent anyone else from being shot."

"But why not wait for assistance? Wouldn't that make more sense?" Hawk asked, also watching the jury's attention on Josh.

"Under the circumstances, I believed getting inside to assess the situation was a better choice. In these circumstances, the suspect is panicked and not thinking clearly. I wanted to be able to evaluate the situation and keep him off-balance. Most of the responding officers were a few minutes away. Going in made the most sense to me. Protecting anyone inside overcame the risk."

Hawk let the jury digest that for a moment, then continued. "There was a risk to yourself as well, correct?"

Josh replied, "I wasn't concerned about myself, it goes with the job."

Hawk continued, "okay, as you came inside, what happened?"

"I came in low and went to the left, down behind the last pew. I quickly scanned the inside. I didn't see anyone, but it was very dark. I caught movement out of the corner of my eye and saw the suspect crawling behind the altar."

Clasping his hands together, he continued. "I looked around again to make sure no one else was there, then moved up the left side of the church until I could see the whole altar."

Josh looked down for a moment, recalling the scene in his mind. "As I gained a better view of the suspect, I could see he was crawling slowly towards the Sacristy."

"For my benefit, the Sacristy is?" Hawk asked.

"It is a room off the altar. The priests and altar boys use it to prepare for Mass." Josh answered.

"Thank you, okay so the suspect is moving what do you do?"

"I put myself behind the lectern on the altar, identified myself as a Police Officer. I ordered the suspect to stop moving."

"In those words? Sergeant, we are all adults here. I know the rush of adrenaline is coursing through your body. Please tell the jury the exact words you said." Hawk waited for the reaction. Several of the jurors leaned forward.

"Well, I said, stop right there you motherfucker or I will blow that fucking hood off with your black head in it." Josh looked a bit shocked by the words himself.

There wasn't much reaction by the jury, a few side-glances.

Hawk continued. "Sergeant why did you say those words?"

Josh glanced at the jury, back at Hawk, then once again to the jury. "I wanted to get his attention, I wanted him to know I was a Police Officer, I had my weapon drawn, and I wanted him to comply with my order to stop moving. It is important in these situations to get their attention right away. Using loud commands, sometimes laced with profanity, makes the point emphatically."

"And why did you say quote 'your black head' unquote?"

"Because I wanted there to be no doubt in his mind I was talking to him," Josh answered quickly.

Looking at the jury, Hawk said, "Okay what happened next, did he comply with your command to stop?"

"No, he looked back at me, and then continued to crawl. He was saying something but I could not make it out at first. I could only see one hand, his left hand, and I was concerned he held a weapon in the hand that I couldn't see."

Hawk watched as the juror pointed out by Chris kept nodding. As he did this, he would look to the Jurors seated to his left and right and they joined in this silent agreement. Time to go for the hard part. This jury was with him now.

"Okay, now Sergeant, I want to take you through the next few moments step by step. Now you're in position behind the lectern, correct?"

"Yes, sir"

"Using it for cover, right?"

"Yes, trying to minimize the suspect's view of me. I didn't want to give him a clear shot at me."

"Okay, does the suspect keep moving?"

"Well, he moves a bit, but I can see he's struggling, trying to decide what to do..."

"Objection, the witness is testifying as to the intent of someone else, he can't know what was going on in Mr. Machado's mind. It was just as likely he was terrified, lying there, unarmed, with the white cop pointing a weapon at him. Threatening to blow his black head off." Collucci interrupted.

"Your Honor, Sergeant Williams is testifying to what he was thinking, his perception of what the suspect was doing, not what Machado was thinking. He can certainly testify to that. Intent is the whole basis of the Government's fantasy of racial motivation here. And he's putting words in Sergeant Williams's mouth."

"They are his words," Collucci replied, "I am just refreshing the jury's mind about them."

"They are out of context and you know it." Hawk responded angrily. "You're trying to twist this testimony because it clearly contradicts the government's whole case."

Rodericks held up his hand to stop the argument, "All argument and discussion will be to the bench, not a shouting match between counsel. The objection is sustained, in part, and overruled, in part. Mr. Bennett, ask the question so it is clear you are eliciting Sergeant Williams perception and thoughts. Mr. Collucci, the jury will have the record available to them. They do not need your assistance in recapping it. Is that clear?"

"Yes sir," Collucci replied, sitting down quickly.

"Go on Mr. Bennett." Rodericks motioned with his hand.

"Thank you, your Honor. Now Sergeant, getting back to the moment leading up to the shooting. You testified Machado kept moving. He did not follow your command to stop. Is that correct?"

"Yes."

"And he was looking back at you and then towards the Sacristy, is that correct?"

"Yes."

"How far away from you is he at this point?"

Josh paused a moment to visualize the scene, "I would say fifteen to twenty feet."

"And could you see both his hands at this point?"

"No, I could only see his left hand. His right hand was under his body. I believed he was holding something in that hand," Josh's head dropped slightly and he looked toward the floor, then back up at the jury, "I thought it was a weapon."

Hawk studied the looks from the Jurors. Some were clearly taken with Josh's words, but there were two that seemed doubtful. One of them kept glancing at Collucci for his reaction. Collucci, apparently aware of this, kept shaking his head and writing notes.

Hawk thought, if people only knew how big a part theatrics play in trials they would be disheartened by the Justice system. Now, this was his stage and he intended to command it.

"Okay, Sergeant. What happened next?"

Josh inhaled deeply, "Machado kept looking towards the Sacristy. I became concerned that someone might be in there. Perhaps, someone saw Machado rush in and was trying to hide. I was worried Machado was trying to get to the Sacristy and take a hostage."

Hawk said, "What did you do?"

"I told him again to stop, the exact words were," pausing a moment, "which part of don't move motherfucker aren't you getting, asshole. Stop moving now or you're a dead man." He could not help a glance at the jury for their reaction.

"Did he stop moving?"

"No, he slowed a bit. That is when I understood his words. He kept saying them over and over," Josh stared at his hands again, "he said 'I tried to get him to stop, I tried to get him to stop...' Josh's voice trailed off a bit.

Hawk quickly continued, "What happened next?"

Josh looked at Hawk, sat up a bit, and said, "His right arm started to move from underneath him. He was looking right at me. As the arm started to move, the hand came into view. I could see a black object in his hand. I couldn't make it out but his arm continued to move and he pointed his hand right at me," Josh took another deep breath to calm himself, "I saw a glint of light, a reflection off the object, then I heard a loud metallic noise, it sounded to me like a weapon misfire. Machado started to raise himself up, continued pointing what I now believed was a weapon at me."

Josh stopped again to compose himself. He looked directly at the jury. "I believed he was pointing a weapon at me, I believed he was firing at me but the weapon misfired. At this point, I made the decision to fire my weapon. I fired three times. I saw Machado fall on his back. Just before he stopped moving, he said, "I tried to get him to stop..." Josh stared up, away from the jury, quickly wiping his eyes, trying to hide the tears.

"Sergeant, I realize this is difficult for you, what did you do next?"

Josh sat a moment staring blankly ahead, then answered, "I went to Machado, tried to stop the bleeding, and performed CPR," turning to the jury, "I didn't want him to die."

Hawk could see tears in the eyes of some of the jury.

After a moment, Hawk asked, "Now Sergeant I want to turn your attention to another matter. The incident involving misplaced evidence in a Sale of Alcohol to a Minor. Do you recall the case?"

"Yes, sir, I do." He could not help but notice the reaction by some of the jurors.

"Now much as been made about the exhibits used in that hearing, can you explain that?"

"I can. I made an error in judgment. When I couldn't locate the evidence, I brought a similar container with the same brand of beer. My intent was only to show the court the type of items seized. I never testified or intimated that it was the actual evidence. The defense lawyer never asked me if they were"

"Why didn't the prosecutor ask?"

"Because there is no prosecutor, so to speak, the police, in this case it was me, presents the case."

"I see, so you never testified that it was the actual evidence?"

"No, sir."

"How did you establish the charge then?"

"We introduced the Toxicology report from the Rhode Island State Toxicology lab. In fact, the defense agreed to the validity of the toxicology report. It was never questioned."

"So, let me get this straight. You brought a similar item to the court because the actual evidence could not be located. You never testified that it was the actual evidence seized. Is that correct?"

"Yes sir. I realize I should not have taken that path. We introduced the toxicology report and that was unchallenged. I suppose I was embarrassed we could not locate the evidence. I made an error in judgment."

"Did you inform Lieutenant Hamlin about this?"

"Yes sir, I did. She made it clear I was to inform the court about the exhibit. It never came up in the testimony."

"So you didn't misrepresent the exhibit as evidence?"

"No sir."

"And you didn't lie under oath?"

"No, sir. I never would."

Hawk a moment, returning to the table, stood in front of the chair, "One more thing Sergeant, did you shoot Mr. Machado because he was a black man?"

"No," Josh replied, "I fired because I thought he was trying to kill me."

"But if the circumstances were the same and the suspect white, or a woman, would you have done the same thing?"

Josh looked at the jury, "I fired at Mr. Machado because I believed he was trying to fire at me. I perceived him as a threat. I waited until the absolute last moment. I never wanted to kill anyone. Mr. Machado forced me to take action because he would not comply with my telling him to stop. I believed he was a threat to others and me. I did what I needed to do. If he stopped he'd be alive today." Eyes brimming, "I wish he listened to me. I tried to get him to…" The last words directed at the friendly juror.

Hawk looked at each of the jurors, catching their eyes, nodding his head. "Thank you, Sergeant. I have nothing further your Honor."

Rodericks looked at his computer screen, "I see it is 1:50, let's take a short break and reconvene at 2:30."

"All rise."

The jury left the courtroom. Hawk, Symonds, and Josh headed to the conference room.

"Well?" Josh asked.

"Bill, you watched the jury what do you think?" Hawk passed the question to Symonds.

"I think you did well. I did not get the sense the jury cared much about the other case. They were more interested in the shooting. I think saving the question about shooting him because he was black for last was perfect. If any of them cared about the creative testimony, it took their attention away from it. Collucci will try to leave that as the last thing they hear from you and he'll try to make you look like Richard Nixon covering up Watergate but overall I think it went well."

"I agree" Hawk said. "Our friend on the jury was acting like a cheerleader. They seem to like you Josh. Collucci will have to be careful not to attack you too much or it will backfire with them. However, we all know Collucci isn't subtle. It is going to be a long, painful cross for you. Just keep calm and don't let him rile that Irish temper of yours."

Josh smiled, "I will be the quintessential model witness."

"That's what scares me," Hawk replied, "your idea of quintessential."

The door opened and Chris Hamlin came in.

"Are you nuts?" Hawk said, "If Rodericks sees you he'll pop that vein in his neck."

"I'll be quick. Our insider friend called me." Registering the shock on their faces.

"Fleming? She called you?" Hawk asked.

"Yup, said she couldn't wait. Collucci found another case that Josh testified in and the Judge found him less than credible. She is trying to learn which case but Collucci will not tell her. He's starting to doubt her loyalty."

"With good reason I might add." Hawk answered. "Josh, any ideas?" Hawk asked.

"No, I don't recall any such thing. Unless," he paused for moment.

"Unless what?"

"Unless it was that informant case. You remember, Chris. Santiago shooting. The judge in the case ordered us to reveal the name of the informant we used on the Search Warrant. He ruled the informant was a witness and subject to cross-examination by the defense."

"Okay, so why did he find you less than credible?" Hawk asked.

"The Judge gave me twenty-four hours to produce the name of the informant. I told him I didn't need twenty-four hours and would reveal it right then. The prosecutor tried to object but was overruled. So I told him." Josh smiled.

"I can tell by that look I am not going to like this," Hawk added, "You told him what?"

"The name of the informant, Orlando Bueno."

"And?"

"And the Judge ordered us to bring him to court. I told him I'd be happy to, except he was dead."

"Oh, Christ." Symonds exclaimed.

"Nah, he is most likely not with him. Bueno was a real bad guy." Josh replied, laughing. "So the Judge ordered us to produce the death certificate. Which I did. Apparently, the Judge found that a little too convenient. If I recall correctly he said something about us mining the daily obituaries. I was very offended."

"Okay, well. Isn't this nice." Hawk said, "I'll try to argue as to relevance and such but I bet Rodericks lets it in. Are there any more war stories you'd care to share before I learn of them along with the jury?" Shaking his head.

"Nope, he was the only dead informant. But I did follow the Judge's advice and checked the obits anytime I testified about a search warrant after that." Josh and Chris were both smiling now.

A moment later, there was a knock on the door. Chris slipped off to the side, out of sight. Hawk opened the door, Deputy Marshal Murray stood there, smiling.

"Mr. Bennett, the US Attorney asked me to deliver this package to you." Handing over the folder.

"Thanks, Steve." Hawk replied.

"You're welcome. Oh, and tell Lt. Hamlin she can come out of the closet now. The coast is clear."

"Thanks, smartass," Chris called out, "everybody is a comedian."

Chris headed towards the door, Hawk grabbed her arm, "The dead informant was your idea wasn't it?"

Smiling back, Chris said, "Now counselor how was I to know Bueno would check out a few days before the trial. I was shocked when DEA called me and asked if we knew anything about him."

Hawk looked at her for a moment, "Did you tell them he was a snitch?"

"We prefer the term, cooperating individual, but yeah I told them. I knew it would piss them off that we hadn't shared that info."

"And this was before the trial, correct?"

Chris caught on, "Why yes it was as a matter of fact."

"DEA told you he was dead, you didn't conveniently find this info yourself?" Hawk paused a moment, thinking, "Find that agent and get him here, I may be able to derail this little surprise attack."

"On the way." Leaving quickly, she was on her cell as soon as she hit the street.

Bill Symonds reviewed the package, "It's notice he intends to modify discovery due to newly discovered, previously unavailable, information. It contains the relevant trial transcripts of Josh's testimony and case precedent references."

"Okay then," Hawk clasped his hands together, "let's go ruin Mr. Collucci's surprise party."

73: *Character Assassinations*

"Your Honor," Collucci said, "before I begin my cross-examination of Sergeant Williams, I'd like to make a motion to amend discovery."

Rodericks eyes narrowed, "At this point in the trial? I find it troubling that the Government, with all its resources, is just now finding new information. Mr. Collucci, your record of accomplishment on discovery in this matter is a disgrace. But go on; let me hear the Government's position on this matter."

"Thank you, your Honor. The Government has recently uncovered trial transcript material that impeaches the credibility of Sergeant Williams. A Superior Court Judge, Judge Julio Martinelli, made a specific reference to finding Sergeant Williams, and I quote from the transcript, "less than credible." Since the transcript from the other trial that casts serious doubt on Sergeant Williams's credibility is conveniently absent, the relevance and material applicability of this transcript is evidence of a pattern of deceptive behavior by this Officer under Oath. Thus critical to the Government's case.

The material was not available until recently due to a failure of the computer system used by the State of Rhode Island to archive court transcripts. As soon as this system was available to the Government, I ordered FBI agents to review all relevant cases involving testimony by this defendant.

I provided appropriate notice and copies of the material to defense counsel as soon as practical.

For these reasons, the Government moves to introduce these transcripts and use them during cross-examination.

This case hinges on credibility. This transcript is clear and convincing corroboration of a pattern of behavior by this defendant of lying under Oath."

Rodericks wrote some notes and then looked at Hawk, "Mr. Bennett, what do you say?"

Hawk rose. He looked over at Symonds covertly monitoring his cell. Symonds shook his head.

"Your Honor, I also find it hard to believe that the Government is just now finding this. The system Mr. Collucci is referring to has been back in service for over two months. To insinuate that the Government has not had adequate time is laughable. That's not to mention the fact of Judge Martinelli's rather abrupt retirement from the bench in light of the allegations of his accepting bribes."

Hawk glanced again at Symonds. He was writing a note and sliding it to Josh to hand to Hawk. Taking the note he continued, "However, in the interest of fair play, I would be willing to agree to the introduction of the material as long as the defense is given similar latitude in adding a witness to my list. Should the court rule to allow the Government's motion, I have a rebuttal witness I would call."

Collucci was looking at Hawk, trying to guess what was in play here. Once again, he went with his instincts without any idea of the consequences.

"Your Honor, if it pleases the Court. The Government has no objection to the additional witness sought by the defense." Once again, leaping off the ledge.

"No, Mr. Collucci, it doesn't please the court. These last minute tactics of yours very much displeases the court. In addition, Mr. Bennett, this is not let's make a deal, quid pro quo. I find these trial theatrics troubling."

Rodericks looked at the computer screen then back at counsel, "with that said I will allow the government to introduce the transcript and the defense's additional witness. But keep it relevant gentlemen, or it will be as quickly excluded."

"Thank you, you Honor. The Government is now ready to proceed with the cross-examination."

"That is pleasing to the court," Rodericks replied, "bring in the jury."

As soon as the jury returned, Josh resumed the witness stand.

Collucci stood looking at him for a moment, then said, "Before we get to the specifics of the execution of Mr. Machado."

"Objection, your honor, this is highly inflammatory." Hawk interjected.

"Sustained. Mr. Collucci I have warned you about such tactics. This is the last time. The jury will disregard the last remarks of the US Attorney. Proceed cautiously, Mr. Collucci."

"Very well, before we get to the specifics of your shooting and killing Mr. Machado I want to clarify these testimonial issues you seem to have. In the matter of the evidence presented to the court as part of your Sale of Alcohol to a Minor case, you knew it was not the actual evidence is that true?"

"Yes, that is true." Josh was going with the short and sweet on these questions.

"And you intentionally concealed this from the trial Judge, is that not also true?"

"No, that is not true. There was never a question about it at the hearing."

"There was never a question, since you orchestrated the manner in which the exhibit, as you called it, was presented, is that not true?"

"No, that is not true."

"Well, Sergeant Williams, did you display the exhibit in the courtroom?"

"Yes, it was on the table, but never introduced. I introduced the Toxicology report."

"But, as you just testified, the exhibit was on the table is that true, yes or no?"

"Yes."

"Why?"

Josh looked confused, "I don't understand the question."

"Why did you bring this item to the court knowing full well it wasn't evidence?"

"Because, because I would use it if asked about the evidence." Josh put his hands on the rail in front of the seat.

"Isn't it true you did this to intentionally mislead the court and the defense counsel into believing the evidence still existed?"

"No that is not..."

"And isn't it true," Collucci interrupted.

"Can I finish my answer?" Josh asked.

"As soon as I hear an answer, not an excuse," Collucci argued.

"Objection your honor, the witness is entitled to answer even if counsel doesn't get the answer he wants." Hawk interjected.

"Sustained. Mr. Collucci let the witness finish before asking the next question." Rodericks ordered.

"Of course your honor. Sergeant you placed this so-called exhibit on the table in full view of the court, is that correct?"

"Yes, sir."

"And did you inform the court that this was an exhibit, not the actual evidence?"

"No..." Josh started to explain, but caught Symonds' subtle shake of the head.

"Please explain to the court why you did this?" Collucci stood, arms folded, glancing between the jury and Josh.

"As I testified earlier, I believed it would be helpful should the question arise regarding the evidence. It was an error of judgment on my part. In hindsight, perhaps if I considered it more in depth, I would not have done that. I should have just informed the court of the evidence being misplaced." Josh answered.

"So you admit it was an ill-considered decision on your part?" Collucci followed up.

"I wouldn't say that, it was an error in judgment."

"Are you prone to that Sergeant?" Collucci smelled blood in the water.

"No, sir. But I am not perfect."

"Perhaps you are prone to making hasty, ill-considered decisions such as entering a Church, alone, and creating an unnecessary opportunity to shoot an unarmed black man?"

"Objection," Hawk said, "Is there a question here or another of Mr. Collucci campaign slogans?"

"Sustained. Ask a question or sit down, Mr. Collucci." Rodericks said. The annoyance on his face apparent.

"Sergeant, was your decision to enter the Church alone an ill-considered decision?"

"No Sir, I believed at the time it was the right decision." Josh replied, looking again to the jury.

"And do you still believe that?" Collucci followed-up.

Josh hesitated a moment, looked at his hands, then directly at Collucci, "Police Officers don't have the luxury of time to consider all possibilities, to weigh all the options." his voice gaining a rhythm, "We make decisions as best we can at the time. That's what I did."

Collucci started to speak again and Josh interrupted, "We also have to live with those decisions. Then we have to deal with the Monday morning quarterbacks of the world who spend hundreds of hours constructing creative and appealing alternatives to a decision I had seconds to make. So if your question is would I make a different decision the answer is no, not with what I knew at the time. If your question is do I believe there was a better decision to make, the answer is also no. I did what I was trained to do, Sir. Do I wish there was a different outcome? Of course I do."

Collucci tried to regain control, "So you're saying that even if you obtained more information, you'd have done the same thing, made the same rash decision?"

Hawk was on his feet, "Objection, your Honor, argumentative."

"Overruled," Rodericks replied, "continue Mr. Collucci." The bent against the police rising once again in Useless' court.

"It wasn't a rash decision," came the answer.

"That's what you'd like this jury to believe, sir, but isn't it a fact that your decision went against standard police protocol?" Collucci was all over the place now.

"No, it did not." Josh answered, the words coming out in a slow, individual stream.

"Well, this all goes to credibility doesn't it, Sergeant?"

"Yes, sir it does. My decision was sound under the circumstances." Josh replied.

"Now then, Sergeant Williams, I'd like to discuss another case in which you testified, the matter of State of RI vs. Javier Delgado. Are you familiar with that case?"

"Yes sir." Josh replied

"And do you recall testifying in that matter?"

"I recall testifying, I testify in cases all the time so I may not recall all the specifics." Josh continued to stare at Collucci, following his every move around the courtroom.

"I'd like to draw your attention to the pre-trial suppression hearing regarding the Search Warrant you prepared and executed in that matter, do you recall that?"

"I do, I prepared a search warrant and during the execution of the warrant we recovered a large amount of cocaine, heroin, cash, and three weapons. One of which was later identified as the murder weapon used to shoot and kill Olivia Santiago, age 15."

"Yes, thank you for that history lesson. Now as to the suppression hearing, during your testimony did the trial judge rule that the informant mentioned in the affidavit was required to appear as a witness?"

"Yes."

"And what did you do?"

"I don't understand the question; I didn't do anything at that moment." Josh answered, glancing over to Hawk, then back at Collucci.

"Did you produce the informant?" Collucci asked, facing the jury as he prepared for the climax.

"No."

"But weren't you ordered to do this by the court? You ignored this lawful order?"

"No, I informed the court that I was unable to comply with the order due to the fact the individual, Orlando Bueno, was dead. Having been shot, stabbed, and dismembered by rival gang members."

"And how did the court react to this information?"

"I can't answer for the Judge's reaction."

"Perhaps the transcripts would refresh your memory." Turning to the bench, "Your Honor, per your earlier ruling I would move for the introduction of the court transcript in this matter."

"No objection," Hawk rose, "but I would hope this won't require reading the entire transcript for the jury."

Several members of the jury visibly reacted to this. Collucci was losing them with his nonsense.

"No, of course not," Collucci replied, "I will have the court clerk read the relevant section."

"Continue," Rodericks said, "But be brief on this Mr. Collucci."

Handing the transcript to the clerk, with the particular section marked, Collucci asked her to read it.

Judge Rodericks motioned for the clerk to wait a moment, "Ladies and Gentlemen of the jury, certain abbreviations are used in trial transcripts. When the clerk says, for example, Martinelli J, the J stands for Justice as in the Judge. In this transcript section, you will hear two such abbreviations, J and P. The J is the Judge and the P is the Prosecutor. Are there any questions? No, okay the clerk will now read the transcript."

The clerk brought the transcript up on the computer and began.

Martinelli, J "Sergeant, the court has determined that you must release the name of the informant and produce him, or her, in court. Do you understand?"

Williams, "Yes, sir. I do"

Martinelli, J. "The court will allow you twenty-four hours to provide the name and bring the informant to court. Is that clear?"

Williams, "With all due respect, I don't need twenty-four hours. I can provide the name, but I cannot bring him before the court."

Campbell, P "Objection, your honor, the State objects to compelling this disclosure."

Martinelli, J "Overruled, Sergeant the court order was not open for negotiation. Both rulings must be complied with."

Williams, "Well, your honor, as I said, the part I can comply with the informant's name is easy. His name was Orlando Bueno. Producing him in court will not be so easy. He is dead."

Martinelli, J "Sergeant, the court finds your testimony and demeanor in this matter to be less than credible. A great deal of the court's time has been spent with your refusing to release the name of the informant. Now you inform the court he is conveniently dead. I suspect you mined the local obituaries as an insurance policy. I will be seeking a Justice Department inquiry into this matter. You are dismissed."

Collucci waited for the clerk's words to fade, turned to Josh and said, "Now, Sergeant, hearing the transcript, is your memory refreshed?"

"Yes, sir, it is."

"And you recall the judge determining you to be less than credible?"

"I recall his saying that, it wasn't accurate, but he did say it."

"Sergeant, a Superior Court Judge, from the bench ruled on the record he found you to be less than credible, is that not true?" Collucci was now glaring back at Josh.

"Sir, just because he made the statement doesn't make it true. Judge Martinelli resigned from the bench amid allegations of accepting bribes from the defense attorney in that case for favorable rulings. That fact doesn't make those allegations true either." Josh replied, looking to see both Symonds and Hawk cringe.

"Your Honor," Collucci was apoplectic, "move to strike as unresponsive."

Hawk never moved, the words were out there, nothing was taking them back.

"The jury will disregard that last answer and it will be stricken from the record. Sergeant, confine your answer to the question asked."

"I thought I did your honor," Josh replied, quickly adding, "I understand and apologize to court."

"I ask you again Sergeant Williams, is it true that Judge Martinelli ruled from the bench that he found your testimony less than credible?'

Hawk thought, just let it go Josh, let it go.

Josh looked over at the jury, "It is a fact that former Superior Court Judge Martinelli ruled from the bench that he found my testimony less than credible."

Symonds leaned over to Hawk, "the boy has more balls than brains, but the jury is eating it up."

Collucci stood, waiting for Rodericks to say something, and then realized the son of a bitch didn't even hear the answer. No matter, point made with the jury. Now to bring out the truth in the shooting.

"Okay, Sergeant now that we've addressed the issue of your past testimonial performances in various courts I'd like to go over a few items regarding the killing of JoJo Machado. Help me understand something, when you were standing outside the church, after you saw JoJo enter, did you know anyone else was inside?"

"I wasn't sure." Josh answered.

"So for all you knew at that moment, the only one inside the church was an unarmed black man?

"I didn't know whether he was armed or not, I believed he was armed, and I didn't know if there was anyone else inside."

"Well, Sergeant, there's apparently a great deal you didn't know and we're not dealing in beliefs here. Did you know for a fact that the black man, JoJo, was armed?"

"I had no way of knowing that, he was running from the police." Josh answered, looking at the jury.

"Sergeant, yes or no, did you know for a fact that JoJo was armed?" Collucci asked again, moving in front of the jury.

"No, however in my line of..."

Collucci interrupted, "You just answered my question, no need to explain."

"I didn't finish my answer."

"Your Honor, Mr. Collucci is badgering. The witness is allowed to complete his answer, "Hawk said, "fully and in its entirety."

"Your honor, the witness is not entitled to give a speech. I asked a yes or no question. He wanted to provide excuses. That is not allowed." Collucci argued.

"Overruled, it was a yes or no question. The witness answered. Sergeant Williams, if you cannot answer a yes or no say so and the Court will assist you, is that clear?"

"Yes, sir, " Josh answered.

Collucci picked up document and moved in front of the jury again. "Sergeant, what made you decide to enter the church alone? Why not wait for backup?"

"Objection, your Honor," Hawk interrupted, "can we have one question at a time please?"

"Sustained," Rodericks replied, not bothering to look up, "one question at a time Mr. Collucci, please?"

"My apologies to the court" Collucci answered, smiling at the jury. "Sergeant, why did you enter the church alone?"

"There were several factors, Mr. Collucci." Josh replied, looking at each member of the jury, "First, I believed he was a suspect in a double shooting, second, as you brought out, I didn't know for a fact if Mr. Machado was armed, and third, since I was equally unsure he was unarmed, I decided the best course of action was to enter the church." Turning his gaze to Collucci, he continued "I was concerned he might shoot someone else should it turn out he was armed."

Hawk glanced at Symonds, who smiled and mouthed the words, "Big balls"

Collucci turned to gauge the jury's reaction, he could not get a read on them but he suspected he was slowly stripping away the shine of Sergeant Williams. "Now, Sergeant, once you entered the church did you see anyone, besides Mr. Machado?"

"No. I quickly scanned the inside but didn't see anyone. However, it was dark and my eyes hadn't fully adjusted to the reduced lighting. I wasn't certain that no one else was in there."

"Did you see anyone, yes or no?" The frustration rising in his voice.

"Yes."

"You did?" Collucci seemed surprised. "Where was this person?"

"On the altar, trying to hide." Josh answered.

"Aside from Mr. Machado, aside from him. Do not play games with me, Sergeant. You understood the question." Collucci argued.

Hawk began to rise but Rodericks cut him off with a wave of his hand, "Mr. Collucci, ask the question more clearly. I wasn't sure what you were getting at. And do not argue with the witness."

Collucci tried to recover, "Sergeant, other than Mr. Machado, was anyone else in that church?"

"Sir, I do not understand the context of the question. Do you mean did I see anyone then, or did I later learn that someone was in the church?"

Collucci looked at the bench, seeing no sympathy there he said, "As you were in the church did you see anyone else there? Besides Mr. Machado."

"No, sir. I did not."

"You testified it was dark and your eyes hadn't adjusted, correct?"

"Yes, it takes time for the eyes to adjust from bright sunlight to the darker interior."

"You could see Mr. Machado, correct?"

"I already testified to that, yes."

"Yet you would have this court believe you weren't sure anyone else was there, is that correct?"

"I testified I wasn't sure, because I wasn't sure. The altar was lit; the rest of the church was not." Josh replied emphatically. "I could not be sure no one else was in there. I cannot make it any plainer than that."

Hawk looked to Symonds. Symonds leaned over and said, "Let him go, he's holding his own. I cannot believe Collucci is this naive. High school mock trials have better cross."

"Sergeant, if you couldn't tell whether or not anyone else was in there, why did you move closer to Mr. Machado instead of maintaining your position, observing his actions, and waiting for backup?"

Josh looked at the jury, almost incredulous, turning back to the US Attorney, "Mr. Collucci, perhaps I am not explaining myself well enough for you to understand. I moved closer to Mr. Machado precisely because I wasn't sure if anyone else was there. If there was, they could be at risk from a suspect I believed just shot two people. I wanted to draw his attention to me. I wanted him to see that I was a police officer."

"When did you realize Mr. Machado was a black man?" Collucci asked, changing tactics.

"I realized he was a black man before I learned his name. When I spotted him on Grove Avenue, he looked right at me. I clearly saw he was a black male matching the description of the suspect in the shooting. Right down to the color of his sweatshirt."

"So right from the beginning you chased him because he was black?"

"No, sir!" Josh raised his voice a bit. "I chased him because he fit the description of the suspect in a double shooting. One aspect of his description was that he was black. He ran from the police, another suspicious action. He seemed to be concealing something in his sweatshirt, another suspicious action. It was for all of these reasons I went after him."

Collucci paused a moment, then picked up the cell phone recovered from Machado. "Sergeant, do you recognize this?"

"Yes sir. It is the cell phone Mr. Machado pointed at me." Josh dropped his gaze a bit, then looked up.

"Well Sergeant, since I am about, what would you say, twenty-five or thirty feet away from you? Yet you have no trouble seeing it for what it was at this distance. How is it you mistook this for a weapon?"

"The conditions were entirely different, darker. The circumstances altogether different, more dynamic." Josh was becoming visibly angry.

"You mean the skin of the person holding this cell phone was darker, and therefore in your mind more of a threat, isn't that true Sergeant?"

Josh knew enough to pause a moment. Taking a deep breath he again turned to look directly at the jury, "The color of Mr. Machado's skin didn't matter to me. At that moment, the only consideration was whether he posed a threat to others or me. I believed he did."

"Sergeant, let me draw you attention to your own earlier testimony. You testified that you said 'stop right there you motherfucker or I will blow that fucking hood off with your black head in it.' Is that not true?" Turning to face Josh directly.

"Yes, that is what I said."

"So, by your own words, the fact that Mr. Machado was black was important enough for you to include that in your threat to kill him, is that not true?"

"That was not a threat to kill him; it was to get him to stop moving, to comply with my commands to give up." Josh was becoming agitated again.

"Did he stop moving?"

"No."

"Did you kill him? Withdrawn," sensing Hawk rising to object. Collucci moved toward the jury, turning to Josh.

"So you shot him because the black man wouldn't stop moving?"

"Absolutely not!" Josh replied.

"Then why did you shoot an unarmed man?" Collucci was rising to this. He wanted Josh to crumble. This would make great press.

"I didn't." Josh answered.

"Excuse me?" Collucci turned, staring at Josh.

"I didn't." Josh repeated.

Looking over at the jury, he could see the confusion on their faces. "Sergeant Williams, are you testifying here that you didn't shoot Mr. Machado?"

Josh waited a moment, looked at the friendly juror, and then answered, "Sir, you asked me if I shot an unarmed man. At the time I pulled the trigger, after I did everything I could to get Mr. Machado to surrender, I believed he was armed." Pausing to look at his hands, then back to Collucci, "When I shot Mr. Machado I believed he was pointing a weapon at me. I believed he was trying to shoot me. What I learned after didn't alter that fact."

"Sergeant," Collucci said, walking quickly back to the table, "this is what prompted you to execute Mr. Machado!" Holding the cell phone in the air. "This is what that Marine hero threatened you with. Is that what you'd have this jury believe?"

"It is." Josh paused, "He may have been a hero, but I had no way of knowing that."

"Sergeant, you have to admit, that is a pretty flimsy justification for taking a man's life." Collucci replied.

"I am not making excuses. I am telling you what I did and why. I have to live with this decision for the rest of my life. I have to..."

Collucci interrupted, "At least you have that option. You took that away from Mr. Machado just because of the color of his skin. Your rationalizations don't hold water in light of the evidence!" Collucci went back to his seat and sat. "One more thing Sergeant, since you'd have this jury take your word on this. Isn't your testimony here less than credible as your track record demonstrates?"

Josh felt himself starting to rise up. He regained control. Hawk and Symonds were both on their feet, "Objection," Hawk said, "The Prosecutor has gone beyond badgering. This is for all intents and purposes an assault."

"Sustained," Rodericks looked over at the jury, "Ladies and Gentlemen you will disregard this last statement by the Government. It is stricken from the record. Mr. Collucci are you through, now?"

"Just one more thing, Your Honor. Sergeant Williams. You've testified here that you yelled 'stop right there you motherfucker or I will blow that fucking hood off with your black head in it. Is that correct?"

"Asked and answered," Hawk objected. "This is all in the record."

"if I may, you honor. There is something the jury needs to see is not in the record. My next question will address that." Colluci responded.

Rodericks waved his hand for Hawk to sit, "Continue sir, But get to the point."

"Sergeant, is that what you've testified to?"

"Yes." Josh answered.

"Were you in uniform?" Collucci asked

"No, I was in plainclothes. My badge was displayed on a lanyard around my neck."

"So, you're in civilian clothes, pointing a weapon, threatening to kill Mr. Machado. In an area you described as dimly lit.. Yet you never identified yourself as a police officer. You never said that did you?"

Josh hesitated, "He knew who I was."

"He certainly did when you shot him, didn't he." Collucci said, "Withdrawn. The Government has no further questions, your Honor."

"Mr. Bennett, re-direct?"

Hawk looked at Symonds, "May I have a moment your honor?"

"Yes, of course." Rodericks answered.

Symonds leaned over, "I'd let it go, Collucci made some points but the jury still likes Josh. I'd put the DEA guy on about the dead informant then call it a day."

Hawk rose from his seat, "Your Honor, the defense has no questions for Sergeant Williams. We'd like to call Special Agent John Washington, US Drug Enforcement Administration to the stand."

Rodericks nodded. Josh stepped down and returned to the defense table. As he sat down, Symonds patted him on the back, "You were going to punch him out weren't you?" He whispered.

"I still might." Josh replied.

"After the jury comes back my boy, after the verdict." Symonds said.

Special Agent Washington took the stand. Hawk stood and walked over to the jury.

"Special Agent Washington, I just have a few questions." Hawk then led the agent through his professional background and current assignment.

"Now Special Agent Washington, are you familiar with a subject by the name of Orlando Bueno?"

"I am." Washington answered.

"Would you tell the court how it is you know this individual?"

"Well sir, knew the individual would be more accurate. Mr. Bueno was a documented cocaine and heroin distributor and the victim of a brutal homicide."

"I see, and did you have occasion to discuss this with the Sergeant Williams and Lieutenant Hamlin?"

"Yes sir, I contacted Lieutenant Williams and all three of us met. Sergeant Williams told me Bueno was been cooperating with the East Providence Police Department and provided information on the Delgado murder case."

"And do you recall the date of this conversation?" Hawk asked.

"I do, it was February 21st, 2005." Washington replied.

"You have a remarkable memory, why do you recall the date?"

"Because it is my wedding anniversary and I would be the victim of a brutal homicide if I forgot it." Bringing the courtroom to laughter.

"I understand" Hawk said. "So during this conversation you informed Sergeant Williams and Lieutenant Hamlin that Bueno was dead?"

"Yes sir."

"And this conversation took place several days before the start of the Delgado murder trial, which I believe you also testified at. Is that true?"

"Yes sir."

"Thank you, nothing further your Honor." Hawk sat down.

"Mr. Collucci?" Rodericks raised his eyebrows, looking over his glasses at the US Attorney.

"Nothing for this witness your honor, thank you." Collucci answered.

Rodericks said, "The witness is excused. We will stand in recess until 9:00 AM tomorrow. At that time, I will consider any motions after which we will hear final arguments. Please escort the jury."

"All rise."

Rodericks left the courtroom.

Josh glared at Collucci.

Fleming saw the look and motioned for Deputy US Marshall to come over. "Keep an eye on him, Steve. Don't let him near Collucci."

Murray leaned down and whispered, "But he'd be doing us all a favor."

Fleming looked annoyed.

"Okay, okay, just saying." taking a position to block Josh out from Collucci.

Noticing the movement, Symonds came over and took Josh by the arm, "Everybody here would love to see you kick his ass, including Rodericks so he could order you held without bail until the next trial. Let it go."

Josh smiled and pulled away, "I was only going to scare him."

Hawk came along his other side, "Yeah right my boy, and I am taking up celibacy and abstinence. Move on out of here, now. Or I'll show you another, more painful, move."

74:   *Divergent Roads*

Josh left the courtroom, alone. He needed time to think. Going to find her was hopeless. He'd gone down too many divergent roads.

He didn't know how to fix this, or even if it could be. So he wrote Keira a letter and sent it to her office.

He loved her more than his own life, yet acted like an idiot. Why would she forgive him, how could he expect her to?

Keira,

Sometimes, goodbye is all that is left. No matter the depth, no matter the breadth, no matter the sincerity of the desire. Life presents some opportunities that are just mirages of illusions of unattainable desires.

I have come to believe that in many things we are in full control, in some things we have influence, but there is one overarching aspect of life over which we have no control, no input, no say. It is the ocean of our life.

We are merely a ship afloat in this ocean, we direct it to islands, guide it through a storm, rest on deck and enjoy sunset, but life is the ocean, always in ultimate control. It allows our ship to float, to gently ride the calm seas and brave the roiling storms; ultimately, life determines the course.

The ocean teaches us, challenges us, sustains us, and frightens us. Sometimes icebergs, sometimes gentle breezes.

We can fight the wind, tack back and forth resisting its force, continue in the face of insurmountable obstacles, but inevitably, life directs us, and when it suits its whim, forces us in a different direction or reclaims us in the depths.

There is a joy in this. Driven before a storm, we suddenly come upon a gentle wind, a following sea, moments of happiness and contentment, still surrounded by the reality of life. We pass alongside others, share the wind, climb the peaks, and face the troughs, together.

Creating a bond that cannot be broken, knowing no limit of the distance it can bear in separation.

You are my gentle wind.

There are those who resist to the point of damaging their ship, colliding against others, taking both down.

This, I have done.

I have fought against the currents, ruined rudder and rigging, lost my course, damaged the one I care for most.

I will not be responsible for this anymore.

I have taken this ship as far as it will go off course; I am compelled to return to the direction set for me. I wish there were a different compass setting facing me, but it is not to be.

So the ocean turns my ship, sets my heading, and the wind's beginning to rise. Our experiences embedded in my mind, changing me forever, leaving me a better man.

180 degrees away from where I hoped.

Sometimes, goodbye is all that is left.

Josh

75: *Points of View*

"All Rise," announced the Deputy Marshall, as the Judge entered the courtroom.

"Good morning" Judge Rodericks mumbled, ignoring the crowded courtroom, taking his seat on the bench.

"Be seated," the Marshall exclaimed, taking a position near the jury entrance.

"Okay, there are a few rules I want clear before we bring in the jury." Looking first at the Government table, Fleming and Collucci, then to the defendant's table with Hawk.

"This is the final phase of this trial. So far, I have not been pleased with much of your conduct here. I have no tolerance left. Consider yourselves forewarned. This is not a political commercial," pausing to glance at the US Attorney, "nor is it a soapbox or Crusade" looking to Bennett, "at the moment any of this begins to take on either of those patinas, I will removed the jury and you will be held in contempt. Necessitating your immediate replacement as Counsel of record. Is that clear?"

Collucci and Fleming nodded.

Bennett rose from his seat, "If I may, your honor…"

"Mr. Bennett" the Judge interrupted, "for once, just once, can you acknowledge a simple instruction with just an affirmation of your understanding and consent," shaking his head, "but I know it is too much to hope for. Go on."

"Thank you, your Honor, I have reconsidered. I am fine with your instructions."

Sitting down Hawk looked to Josh and whispered, "Collucci already turned this into a political sideshow, making pronouncements instead of following trial protocols, making public statements, poisoning the jury pool. His Honor's instructions, of which I endorse and concur, are too little, too late, and likely to be ignored by my able brother at the bar." Smiling over at Ms. Fleming, he continued, "The Judge is just going to have to learn to tolerate me. I am not letting the political cocksucker off the hook that easy."

Josh smiled, "My, my Hawk. Is that appropriate language for the US District Court?"

"If there is nothing else, Ladies and Gentlemen," the Judge asked, turning to the Marshall, "Bring in the jury"

The jury filed in. They focused on the Judge.

Josh thought of all those talking head analysis of juries about things to look for, signs of a jury's intent. It played on Josh's mind the whole trial. They did not looked at him as they came in. Hawk was not doing his count. Then again, they did not look at Collucci either. Josh did not know what to make of it. He leaned over and whispered to Hawk "they aren't looking at me, is that a bad indication?"

Hawk looked up at the jury, back at Josh, lifted a large binder and dropped it on the desk.

The jury all turned as one.

"They're looking now," Hawk mumbled out the side of his mouth, shrugging his shoulders, and smiling at the jury, "feel better?"

A moment of silence ensued as the Judge reviewed some notes then, turning to the jury, began to speak.

"Ladies and Gentlemen. The presentation of evidence and witnesses by the Government and the defense has concluded. Each side will now have the opportunity to summarize for you their positions on the strengths, and weaknesses, of the case. This is not evidence, and is not to be considered evidence. It is the right of the defendant to have his counsel present their interpretation of the matter before you. The Government will have the same opportunity. I ask you to be attentive, respectful, and open-minded about each summary statement. You may give it any value you see fit, but I caution you; it is not evidence.

After both sides have an opportunity to make their summary statement, I will provide further instructions to guide your deliberations. Do not take anything I say, or any ruling I make, during these statements as indication of my favoring one side or the other. It is not for me to judge, in spite of my title," causing laughter among some of the jurors.

"That is for you. I am merely a referee; so to speak, making sure each side has a fair opportunity. As during the trial, any rulings I may make are about the law in this matter, not the merits of the evidence or witnesses. That is your responsibility.

The defense will proceed first. Thank you for your attention this morning and in this whole matter. Mr. Bennett, proceed."

Hawk rose from his seat, stepped behind Josh, placed his hands on Josh's shoulders, and looked at the jury.

"Ladies and Gentlemen. I have the privilege of representing Sergeant Josh Williams. Sergeant Williams, no," Hawk's voice rising, "No, his name is Josh; you need to think of him as a person, not just a police officer, or defendant, but a human being. This is a man of respect, decency, courage, and integrity. He is not perfect, who among us is? This is a good man." Stepping around Josh and moving to the podium.

"What the government, your government, my government is trying to do to this good man is a travesty. They have tried to build a case on innuendo, political correctness, racial stereotypes, and emotion. They have subverted the criminal justice system for purposes other than what it was intended, a search for the truth.

They have twisted, perverted, altered and trampled on that noble purpose and now they want you, each of you, to be complicit in that nefarious miscarriage of Justice. Do not let them do that."

Hawk looked at Collucci and then back at the jury.

"The choice for you is easy," banging his hand on the lectern.

"Do you know why?" Arms outstretched, palms up, "There is no evidence. Not one single bit of evidence was presented that supports the government's contention that this police officer, this hero, this man who has placed himself in harm's way for all of us, is guilty of any crime, let alone the charges he has faced in this courtroom.

Mr. Collucci is trying to ride this fairytale to another job!"

"Objection, you honor" Collucci interjected, rising to his feet.

"Back to the point Mr. Bennett," the Judge commanded.

Hawk continued without missing a beat, "the government, represented by Mr. Collucci, has demeaned our justice system. They have shown their disrespect for this court, this defendant, and most importantly, you, the members of this jury.

"The government thinks, by virtue of the fact that they are the Government," his tone rising, walking to the jury, "that you will assist them in this process. They believe by having so called "experts" in race relations, police profiling, and prejudicial behavior testify, it will conceal from you the lack of hard evidence.

We are all guilty of furthering stereotypes or holding prejudices. How many of you have told, and laughed at, Blond jokes, or an Italian joke," looking at Collucci," or even a Lawyer joke, well, okay, those are mostly true."

The jury, and most of the courtroom, laughed.

"See," Hawk continued, "we all hold some aspects of stereotypes within us. It does not control us. It does not make us do things against our own common decency. It certainly does not compel a trained, competent, compassionate, experienced Police Officer to shoot someone. If that were the case, we'd all be in trouble."

Walking back to the defense table he began shuffling papers, rummaging through his brief case, reading and discarding documents.

"Mr. Bennett, have you lost something?" the Judge asked.

'Sorry, your Honor, I am looking for something." Hawk replied, continuing his search.

"And what would that be, perhaps the court can assist?" the Judge answered.

"It's the evidence, your Honor," turning to the jury, "I am looking for the evidence in this matter, there is none. Well, let me rephrase that. As you all know, Josh was under no obligation to present any evidence in this matter, he was under no obligation to testify before you. I advised him not to. It was not necessary. The government's case was smoke and mirrors. Josh insisted. Josh wanted you to hear from him the truth about what happened that day."

Turning back to look at Josh he continued "that took extraordinary courage. Josh knew the government would stop at nothing to try to discredit him. However, they could not do it. They made much of some insignificant hearing, some in-artfully posed questions, but they could not show anything other than Josh answering them truthfully.

That is hardly credible evidence of anything. Mr. Collucci will undoubtedly make much of that. He has no choice. It is his whole case.

However, more importantly, Josh answered the most difficult questions the government threw at him. His answers were truthful and complete.

The Government tried to bring out inconsistencies. They failed

The Government tried to get him to change his story. They failed

You know why? The truth is easy to remember, lies are hard. Josh told you the truth. The truth the government tried to hide from you. They failed.

There is one actual piece of evidence, interestingly enough, introduced by the Defense, though available to the Government, I want you to consider. The prints on the shotgun. The shotgun used to kill two people. Whose prints were on it? Mr. Machado's. He may have tried to right a wrong. He may have reconsidered his involvement in the robbery. His actions with the young clerk may have been heroic. We know he suffered because of his experiences in the Marine Corps. While that is admirable, it is not pertinent to this matter.

Josh was facing an individual who was an accomplice to robbery and murder. Mr. Machado took the risk. Things went bad. He may have prevented one death but his actions leading up to that contributed to the deaths of two others.

Josh told you he tried to get Machado to stop moving. He gave Machado every opportunity to surrender. Father Swanson confirmed this.

During your deliberations, you must put yourself in the mind of Josh. You must see the circumstances leading up to the church through his eyes. You have to base your analysis of Josh's actions by what he knew at the time, what he believed at the time, and what he saw at the time. All the things we know about Mr. Machado, all the information we have about the robbery after the fact does not matter.

It is all about what Josh knew at the time and what actions Machado took, in the church, when he knew Josh, a Police Officer, was ordering him not to move.

He did not comply.

His actions were consistent with an armed individual trying to escape. Keep in mind the shotgun fingerprints, he was, at some point armed and a willing participant in a robbery.

His movements were consistent with his being an imminent threat to Josh and others."

Walking to the table, he reached into his briefcase, retrieved an item, turning quickly, he raised his hand, pointed it at the jury, then put it in his pocket.

"What did I just point at you?" he asked the jury, "how many of you can tell me what that object was?"

The jurors looked at each other, then to the Judge.

"You do not need to answer that." The Judge responded, "Mr. Bennett, to your point please"

Hawk nodded "My point is, that here in this courtroom, in full light, in a controlled, safe, nonthreatening environment, given a moment to look at an item pointed at you from a few feet away, I venture to say all of you have doubts as to what you saw in my hand".

Hawk paused, looking each juror in the eyes.

"Now, put yourselves in Josh's position, chasing a man he believed to have shot two people, one who was refusing to comply with his orders" slipping his hand back into his jacket pocket Hawk lifted his arm, flipped open his cell phone, and pointed it at the Jurors.

Several of the jurors jumped.

"Gun, or no gun?" he asked, closing the phone

"Objection, your honor" Collucci rose to his feet, "this is supposed to be summary not show and tell."

"Overruled" the Judge replied, "I'll extend Mr. Bennett the benefit that this will be the sole demonstration."

"It is your Honor, merely trying to illustrate the point." Hawk replied.

Turning back to the jury, Hawk continued, "Now to the point of racial bias or prejudice as motivation for Josh's action. There is no motivation other than an officer facing a horrible situation, making decisions based on what he knew, and the actions of a suspect refusing to comply.

Josh acted as his training, experience, and facts available at the time warranted, not by any prejudice or ill intent."

Hawk looked at Collucci.

"This case is not about racial prejudice, this case is solely about political gain. Ask yourselves these questions. Is every interaction between a person of color and the police racially motivated? Does that make sense?

The government is trying to turn a tragic incident into an intentional racial one. It failed."

Moving to the podium again, Hawk lifted the trial transcript.

"Josh was very clear in his testimony that his actions were based on Mr. Machado's failure to comply with his commands to stop. Read this testimony again if you need to. I know you'll concur."

Hawk looked at each member of the jury, shaking his head slowly, eyes down. "Stop. So simple. All he needed to do was stop moving, and none of this would be necessary."

Lifting his head again he looked at Collucci.

"You will also recall Mr. Collucci spent a great deal of time trying to get a different answer during cross-examination. He tried to elicit some racial bias in Josh's actions that day. He failed. So much so the Judge stopped him."

Collucci and Fleming jumped simultaneously "Objection!"

"There is no choice but to find Josh not guilty." Hawk continued.

"Approach the bench," the Judge commanded

"Mr. Bennett I warned you," pointing a finger at Hawk, hand shaking with rage.

"Your honor, this is outrageous. Mr. Bennett has prejudiced the jury beyond repair. I demand you declare..."

"Counselor, nobody demands anything in my court. Mr. Bennett, you will limit your remarks to the facts and evidence before this jury. Do not make this mistake again."

"Your honor, I was pointing out what the jury would see in the record if they asked for it during deliberations. It was about the facts and evidence, or lack thereof, before this court."

"Away, get away from the bench and continue." The Judge dismissed them.

As Collucci stormed back, he could not help but notice a smirk on one of the juror's faces. *We will see about this Bennett, Collucci thought, two can play this game and my turn is coming.*

Hawk returned to the front of the defense table and continued as if the interruption never happened.

"Ladies and Gentlemen, ask yourselves this question. If you found yourself in a situation such as Josh did, would your first reaction, after shooting them, be to try to save them? Does that sound like the actions of a person holding a racial prejudice?

The whole basis of the government's case is, according to the so-called experts, white cops cannot help themselves but to act in a prejudicial manner when confronted by a black person.

Therefore, Josh shot Mr. Machado because he was black. However, he then tried to save the life of that same black man.

Does that sound like the actions of a prejudiced white cop?

Recall when I asked each of these 'experts' none could explain the conflicting actions." Looking at each of the jurors.

"Now, Ladies and Gentlemen, we are well aware that Mr. Machado was a combat veteran who came home from the war with horrible physical and psychological damage.

We recognize his service. We also recognize that the good part of him, for a brief, shining moment, rose to the surface as he stopped Ventraglia from killing the young store clerk.

Mr. Machado was a troubled young man. A victim of molestation by a member of the clergy, a difficult childhood, the wounds he suffered in the service of this country, all contributed to serious psychological issues. Mr. Machado found himself back at the scene of his molestation, after witnessing the brutal killing of two people during a robbery he agreed to commit. His actions were irrational and clearly posed a danger.

Nevertheless, do not let your natural feelings of empathy for Mr. Machado cloud the fact of his participation in the robbery. His last words were 'I tried to get him to stop.'

Raising his hands clasped together, "He did not say 'I didn't do anything. He did not say I don't have a gun. He said nothing of the sort." Letting that sink in.

"He may have succeeded in saving the young clerk, but he played a willing part in the robbery, resulting in the deaths of two people.

Remember those were the exact same words Josh said to Lieutenant Hamlin, moments after the shooting, 'I tried to get him to stop." The evidence is clear, Josh did everything in his power to get Mr. Machado to comply with his order to stop moving.

Mr. Machado's own actions caused his death."

Pausing a moment as his words took hold of the jury.

"Josh did everything in his power to get Mr. Machado to stop. He tried to get him to give up.

When it became evident the Mr. Machado was not going to comply, when it was evident Mr. Machado was a risk to Josh and others, when Machado's actions posed a threat, when there was no other choice, Josh did what we asked him to do. To protect us all.

It is a terrible burden to put on a person. We ask our Police Officers to do this all the time."

Walking back to stand behind Josh he again put his hands on Josh's shoulders. "Ladies and Gentlemen, the government is now going to try to salvage their case. It would be easier to find the Loch Ness monster. It is not possible. Nevertheless, they will try.

They will try to mask the lack of evidence by fueling the fires of racial inequalities. Do not let them demean or denigrate the history and progress of the civil rights movement for their own political gain. This case is not about race. This is not about prejudice. Do not let the government turn this into something it is not solely for political gain.

Don't let them turn you into a tool that turns back the clock on racial relations."

Holding his hands out to the jury, "Don't let them. It will soon be in your hands to do that.

The commonality of our humanity depends on it."

Hawk looked at the Judge, then at Collucci, and finally back at the jury.

"When you adjourn to your deliberations, I want you to remember the things I said, and I want you to remember this man. This good man. Unlike the situation Josh found himself," pointing at Collucci, "you can make him stop."

"Find Josh not guilty. Repair the damage done by Mr. Collucci. End this abuse power of by government. That would be justice for everyone.

Thank you for your attention."

Judge Rodericks ordered the jury excused for lunch. As soon as the door to the jury room closed, he exploded.

"Mr. Bennett, in as few words as possible I want you to give me a reason not to hold you in contempt."

"Empathy," Hawk replied without hesitation.

"Empathy? That's the best you can do?"

"Your honor, you said in as few words as possible, I used one."

"If its empathy for your client, I do, if its empathy for you, not so much. You intentionally ignored my instructions. You actions border on contempt. I am struggling for a reason not to hold you as such."

"On my behalf, your honor, I can only say I was trying to provide my client the vigorous defense he is entitled to, without crossing the border. I may have approached that line, but I do not believe I violated the spirit of your instructions.

If I did anything inappropriate, please do not let it adversely affect my client. If you find I am in contempt, so be it. But I implore you to withhold that determination until the trial's conclusion."

Rising quickly to his feet, Collucci interjected, "Your Honor, Mr. Bennett...."

"Sit down" Rodericks ordered

"I want to note for the record...,"Collucci continued.

"Sit down, Mr. Collucci, or the record will reflect you being found in contempt."

Hawk tried to conceal a smile.

"Mr. Bennett, I do not find this amusing, nor do I intend to tolerate this any further." Rising from the bench, "From this point forward if you so much as walk into my courtroom showing even the slightest misunderstanding of my instructions, not only will I jail you for contempt, but I will notify the State disciplinary counsel of your flagrant disregard for proper procedure. Is any of this unclear?" Rodericks glared as he rose, storming off the bench.

"No your honor." Hawk replied as the door to the Judge's chambers slammed shut.

Outside the courtroom Josh said, "Look, I know you're the expert here, but is pissing off a Federal Judge really a good trial strategy?"

Hawk smiled, "My boy, remember the good Judge's moniker, Useless Rodericks. He got that because he threatens to find every lawyer in contempt. Hasn't done it yet. His efforts are..."

"Useless," Josh finished the sentence, "but still, I am not sure about this."

"Okay, listen, let me sweat the contempt stuff, we have more important things to consider," Hawk said, "Collucci is going to go for the jugular on this. We need to focus. No matter what he says, you have to appear calm, in control, but angry. If I know him, he's about to make you look like a Ku Klux Klan Grand Wizard.

The jury likes you. It is going to be a leap for them to believe that about you, but not impossible. They'll look to your reactions, read your emotions."

Hawk, Symonds, and Josh walked over to the alcove off the courtroom.

"I need you to be offended, angry, pissed off. None of this shaking the head nonsense. You have to convey genuine offense at Collucci's words." Hawk said.

"And how do I do that?"

"Do you hate niggers?" Hawk asked.

Symonds looked as shocked as Josh.

"What? What the hell are you talking about?" Josh said, angrily.

"Do you hate those low-life, welfare grubbing, food stamp fed, fat ass, baby making machine, drug dealers? It's a simple question."

Josh glared, "where the fuck do you get off asking me something like that. I have never, ever..."

Hawk smiled. "That's how you do it. You were pissed off at me for saying that. Show the jury that face when Collucci piles on the bullshit. Show genuine revulsion being called something you've never been."

Hawk started to walk away, turned back, and added, "When Collucci starts talking, you remember that anger. Show the jury you aren't that man."

Josh just stood shaking his head.

"He's a real piece of work," Symonds said to Josh, looking at Hawk checking out two court stenographers as he walked back to the courtroom, "a genuine fucking piece of work."

76: *The Government Spin*

While the jury settled into their seats, Collucci sat at the table reviewing notes.

Hawk leaned over to Symonds and whispered something. Symonds shook his head, smiling, and said, "I suppose at this point you can't make the Judge anymore pissed off at you than he already is. Even so, why don't we see if Collucci scores any points before we go nuclear, okay?"

Judge Rodericks looked over at Collucci, "Is the Government ready for Summary?"

"We are your honor, if I might have a moment?"

"Fine, but please be brief. I'd like to move on quickly."

Collucci, ignoring the Judge, scribbled on a note pad. After several moments, he rose, returned to his seat, wrote more notes, than rose and addressed the court.

"Your Honor, if it pleases the court, the government is ready to proceed."

"The Court cannot express its pleasure at this moment, proceed."

Symonds leaned over to Hawk, "disarm that nuke. The Judge is going to do your dirty work."

"I'll be the judge of that, so to speak," Hawk replied, "I am keeping all my options on the table."

Collucci walking toward the podium, looked to the jury, and began.

"Ladies and Gentlemen, you have before you a case of troubling magnitude. The Government, by compelling and overwhelming evidence, established beyond any reasonable doubt criminal, racially motivated actions by a police officer." Turning and pointing to Josh, "This Police Officer, a man sworn to uphold the law, took the law into his own hands. He summarily executed Anthony Machado, a Marine war hero, simply because he was a black man.

I want you to think about that for a moment. Mr. Machado was shot to death because he was a black man."

Collucci paused, put his hands on the podium and looked at each of the jurors.

"Killed because he was black, by a Police Officer acting under color of law" Pausing again and shaking his head.

"I know each of us would like to think the days of lynching a man due to the color of his skin are over. However, the evidence in this case shows, sadly, they are not.

First, let us review the testimony of the retired FBI agent, an acknowledged expert in use of force and tactical situations. His clear and incontrovertible testimony was the Sergeant Williams made a series of errors in his handling of the situation."

Collucci lifted has hand, counting the points.

One, he pursued Mr. Machado into the church without securing adequate backup.

Two, he placed himself in the situation that, if Mr. Machado was armed, caused the deadly confrontation.

Three, Sergeant Williams's actions created the circumstances wherein he found himself.

It begs the question. Why?

Why would a highly trained, experienced officer do that?

I will tell you why. He decided he was going to shoot Mr. Machado because, if Machado was black, he must be guilty.

It is the logic of the bigot.

A running black man equals guilty."

Shaking his head, he looked at the jury. "You heard the Government's expert clearly explain the tactical errors, improper procedures, and disregard of accepted police procedures committed by Sergeant Williams.

We know these were not merely errors of judgment.

The evidence shows they were intentional acts by the defendant; resulting in the execution of Anthony Machado.

The testimony of this witness is absolutely convincing. Your review of this evidence will leave no doubt in your minds. In and of itself, it is enough to convict."

"But wait," lifting his hand signaling a stop, "there's more."

Collucci smiled at his own attempt at humor.

"The government's case didn't end there. We presented another witness, Dr. Kingston.

You will recall Dr. Kingston's detailing of the comprehensive study he conducted of Police Departments throughout the country.

You will also recall his analysis of the activities of the East Providence Police Department as being consistent with the national trends.

The police show a demonstrable prejudice towards people of color. They act with more scrutiny, more frequent detention, and more frequent searches of black individuals.

His testimony was also clear and convincing. It complimented the testimony of the FBI Agent.

Taken as a whole, the testimony of these two experts proves beyond any reasonable doubt that Sergeant Williams's actions were in direct conflict with accepted police procedures. Keeping in mind, Sergeant Williams himself acknowledged his training in such matters.

His actions, inasmuch as they went against the proper procedures, were clearly motivated by a prejudice towards people of color. There can be no other explanation."

Taking a moment to let his words sink in, Collucci looked again at each Juror.

"Let me put it another way. When one looks for an explanation, generally speaking, the simplest one is the correct one. In this case, by the process of eliminating any other explanation, the truth is apparent.

There were no mitigating circumstances justifying Sergeant Williams's entry into the church.

There was conflicting information as to Mr. Machado's involvement in the robbery.

Sergeant Williams did not report seeing a weapon, shots fired, or even threatened by Machado.

Given the list of circumstances I just described, all of which conceded by Sergeant Williams himself, what we have can only lead to one conclusion.

Sergeant Williams, acting under the color of law, summarily executed Mr. Anthony Machado in clear violation of Federal Law.

The evidence is voluminous and convincing.

Your responsibility in the matter is clear.

You must find Sergeant Williams guilty of each of the counts against him."

Collucci looked about the courtroom, stopping to stare at Josh and Hawk, and then turned back to the jury.

"Do not be fooled by the defense in this case. Nothing they did in questioning the Government's witnesses did anything to alter their testimony. Facts are a stubborn thing. Despite the theatrics, they remain.

I have the utmost confidence in the ability of this jury to see through the defense façade. In your deliberations, I know the facts will lead you to the correct verdict. Justice demands it.

Thank you. The Government rests."

Judge Rodericks announced there would be a one-hour recess. When court resumed, he would instruct and charge the jury.

Surprising all involved, Rodericks was back on the bench precisely at the end of the hour. His instructions to the jury, reviewed by the defense and prosecutors, did not sway from the script.

The jury sent to their deliberations, and the waiting began.

77: *Anticipating Final Judgment*

Hawk, Josh, Bill Symonds, and Chris sat in Hawk's back office. An uncomfortable silence cast a pall over the room.

"Okay, listen. I've spent half my life waiting for juries to get their heads out of their asses and vote." Hawk broke the stillness. "Sitting here mulling over things isn't helpful. Let's plan the celebration party."

The others ignored him, lost in their own thoughts.

"Oh for God's sake," Hawk said. "There's not a chance this jury will do anything but find you not guilty. Stop worrying and start thinking about how far up Collucci's ass we are gonna ram this decision, as soon we get it."

Chris looked at Josh then at Hawk, "I'm glad you're so confident. I hope you are right. But what happens if..."

The phone ringing in the outer office interrupted her. She looked at Josh.

"There," Hawk smiled, "I told you they'd be quick." Answering the call, feigning a British accent, "Why hello, this is Attorney Harrison Bennett how can I help you?" Smiling at Chris.

Nodding his head, "Hmm, I see, oh fine, we'll be right over." A look of concern on his face caught everyone's attention.

"Well?" Josh asked.

"The jury has a question." Hawk replied, glancing at Symonds. "I am sure they are just biding time so they can get lunch out of this. The judge wants us back over right away."

Symonds went to his briefcase, looking at Chris with a half-smile. "I agree with Hawk, nothing to be too concerned about."

"Too concerned?" Josh replied. "You're not the one facing prison."

"Nobody is going to prison." Hawk said. "Let's go hear what they have to say before anyone gets their panties in a bunch," turning to smile at Chris. "Unless you aren't wearing any?"

Drawing a laugh from Josh and Symonds, and a glare from Chris.

"That's the attitude my boy."

Once all parties were in the courtroom, Rodericks returned to the bench.

"I have received a question from the jury regarding a point of law. They wish to have clarified the definition of what constitutes intent. The specific question they sent to the court is *"We do not fully understand whether intent is necessary as part of the charge. Can this be explained further?"*

Rodericks looked up, "Does the Government wish to be heard before I recall the jury?"

Collucci looked at Fleming. She wasn't returning the look, focusing on her notes. Rising, he replied, "No, your honor. We are confident the court will be concise in its response to the jury."

"Mr. Bennett?" Rodericks continued.

Hawk stood, "For once I concur with the Government. We have every confidence in the Court your Honor." Looking over at Symonds as he retook his seat.

As the jury filed in, all but two of the jurors looked at Josh.

Hawk leaned over to Symonds, "You don't think its hung do you?"

"Who knows? I don't put too much stock in that 'jurors looking at the defendant nonsense', but if there are two holding out they may be able to stand firm."

"Christ," Hawk replied. Looking at Symonds for a moment, "Do you think Collucci got to them?"

Symonds raised his eyebrows, "Well, I wouldn't put it past him seeing his performance in here."

Hawk shook his head.

Josh tapped Hawk on the shoulder and whispered, "You want to let me in on this discussion? Should I be planning a trip to a country with no extradition treaty?"

"No." Hawk answered, then turned to listen to the Judge.

"Ladies and Gentlemen of the jury, the court received your question and will provide the best explanation it can." Moving around some notes, he continued.

"If I understand your question, you wish to have what constitutes intent clarified. Is that correct Mr. Foreman?"

"Yes your honor."

"Fine, in order for an act to constitute intent it must meet the following criteria. The person committing the act must foresee the consequences of the act, or omission that result from their doing something or failing to do something. Black's Law Dictionary and People v. Moore, 51 Cal 4th 386-2011..." Pausing a moment, and looking over his glasses at the jury. "The legal reference there is for the benefit of Defense and Government Counsel. It has no bearing for your purposes."

Resuming his explanation, "As I said these references state the definition of Criminal Intent as 'The intent to commit a crime: malice, as evidenced by a criminal act; an intent to deprive or defraud the true owner of his property.' Or, this case, to deprive one of his civil rights."

Rodericks looked at each of the jurors, "I hope the explanation aids you in your deliberations. Please return to the jury room and continue with the task at hand. Thank you again for your time and effort."

Once the jury left the courtroom, Rodericks said "Well, Mr. Bennett, I did not see you writing furiously as I spoke. I take it you saw nothing of an appellate nature in the explanation?"

"Nothing at all, your Honor. I couldn't have said it better myself."

"Mr. Collucci?"

"It was fine, your Honor. I am sure the jury understands now."

Rodericks rose and left the bench.

Collucci started towards the defense team, Hawk raised his hand. "Don't bother. We are not entertaining any offer from the government except a dismissal. I wouldn't take too much delight in this unless, of course, you know something about some of the jurors that we don't."

Symonds shook his head.

Collucci was incensed, "What are you implying?"

"I am not implying anything. Just wondering aloud just how far you are willing to go to subvert Justice."

"Listen, you sanctimonious bastard..."

"Now, now boys," Deputy US Marshal Murray interrupted, "play nice or I'll have to let Rodericks know. And he would enjoy that."

78: *Waiting and Wondering*

"Well, what do you think?" Hawk asked Symonds.

"It's hard to read this. I think they may be having a hard time with the fact that Machado was not armed. The store clerk, what was her name, Pincince. She made him a pretty sympathetic character. And then there's the two jurors we think are problematic."

"I know."

Josh came into the office. "So, now do I head for the hills?"

Symonds looked at Hawk and nodded.

"Josh, Bill and I are concerned with two of the jurors. I am wondering if Collucci got to them somehow. That's why this is taking so damn long."

"What does that mean?" Josh asked.

"Well, the good news is the worst case scenario is a hung jury. I don't think they could persuade the other ten to vote along with them. But it means another trial."

"Maybe I should take a plea. He said no jail time. I'll just do something else. I mean, I did kill Machado."

"No pleas. If we have to do this all over again, nothing will change. Collucci will be a little wiser to our approach, but it won't matter. Let's go get coffee and wait this out."

Symonds and Chris begged off the offer, Chris said she was heading back to the station and Symonds wanted to do some research.

The convenient timing of the excuses raised Hawk's level of suspicion, and envy.

"Our friends have become awful friendly haven't they?"

Josh wasn't listening.

"Hey, Josh. Aren't you the least bit interested in this sudden need for both of them to deal with other things?" Hawk chided.

"I have my own problems right now, remember.' Josh answered, walking ahead of Hawk, and into Café 101.

79: *Final Act*

The call, coming so quickly on the heels of the return to the courtroom, surprised everyone.

Josh and Hawk walked quickly back from Café 101 to the courthouse. Hawk was ebullient. "This is in the bag, Josh. I am certain of it. Once we have that verdict in our hands, I am going to hold a press conference that will ruin that son-of-a-bitch forever."

Josh had his doubts. He liked Hawk. Hell, he just trusted him with his life, but he hated that everything was a crusade to him. Josh just wanted this over. There wasn't much left of his life that really mattered anyway.

Symonds and Hamlin met them outside the courthouse. Hawk tried to dissuade Hamlin from being there, but it was to no avail. She did not care what Rodericks said, she was going and that was the end of it.

Hawk, Symonds, Hamlin, and Josh entered the courtroom. The court was once again full of uniformed police officers, several agents from the local FBI office, and other law enforcement agencies.

One person was not there. The one that would have made a difference.

As they took their seats, Fleming walked over. "I hope you understand," she said, "I am truly sorry for this." Turning, she went to her seat.

The Marshal announced Rodericks entry as he took the bench.

Looking over to the Government table, then at the defense he said, "Are we ready, gentlemen?"

Hawk answered, "Your Honor, I have been ready since this whole charade started."

Rodericks shook his head, "True to form Mr. Bennett. I would've expected nothing less." The Judge examined a few documents, and then motioned for the jury to be brought in.

As the jury took their seats, Josh noticed no one was looking at him. *What the hell*, he thought, *what the hell?*

Rodericks addressed he courtroom. "I want to remind everyone that this is a court of law. No outbursts will be tolerated. Heed my words."

There was no reaction from the crowd; they learned to pay little attention to this judge.

"Mr. Foreman, has the jury reached a verdict?"

The foreman rose, glanced briefly at Josh, and then said, "We have, your Honor." He then handed the verdict form to the Deputy US Marshal.

The Marshal took the document and handed it to the Judge. Rodericks opened the paper, read it, and then returned it to the Marshal.

The Marshal returned the document to the foreman.

In the back of the courtroom, the door opened. Josh looked to see, but his view was blocked.

Rodericks looked out at the courtroom and said, "Mr. Foreman on the count of Violation of Civil Rights while acting under Color of Law, how do you find the defendant?"

"We, the jury, find the defendant Not Guilty."

Josh hung his head. Hawk slapped him on the back and shook Symonds hand. Hamlin let out her breath, tears in her eyes.

The foreman read off two more verdicts of Not Guilty. Collucci asked to poll the jury. The not guilty verdicts rang out in the courtroom.

In the back of the court, the door opened once again.

Reporters rushed from the court to report the verdict.

Rodericks motioned for quiet and addressed the jury. "Ladies and Gentlemen, thank you for your service. The willingness of people such as yourselves to serve on a jury is the cornerstone of our judicial system. You are dismissed. Thank you again for your time."

Turning his attention to the court Rodericks said, "The defendant's bond is released. Are there any other matters Mr. Bennett?"

"Not for the moment, your Honor, not for the moment."

"All rise."

Josh heard those words for what he hoped the last time.

Epilogue

The Note

Josh stood looking out the window onto Kennedy Plaza. He heard Hawk speaking to the reporters, turning Collucci into evil incarnate. He did not have the strength to care enough to listen.

He wanted no part of it.

Chris came into the room, walked over, and put her arm around him, "She hasn't called?"

Josh just shook his head, continued to stare, "Why would she? I doubted her. The one person in the world that never gave me a reason..."

"She'll be back, she loves you Josh. You don't walk away from that...."

"She isn't walking away, I pushed her."

"Look, give her time. I know her Josh. I tried to get you to listen to me. She will be back. I know it."

Josh walked to the desk, opened the briefcase, and took out a letter. He handed it to Chris.

"Can you give this to Chief Brennan for me?"

"What's this?"

"My resignation. I can't stay here, no reason for me to try."

"Bullshit Josh, you can't go. Look, you're a good cop, this never should have happened to you... The department is better with you on it. You cannot let this take you away from us. We want you, Josh. I don't know what will happen with Keira, but you will have a chance to deal with that. You resign and that is it. Even Brennan will not be able to get you back. The political whores will see to that."

Chris took the letter, tore it up, and threw it in the trash.

Josh smiled, "I'll think about it, but I can just print another one if I decide to go."

"Fine, I take out all the printers in the office first thing tomorrow." Chris replied. "Look, take some time off. Go hike, or fish, or whatever it is you do in the woods. Take time to think it over. Then come back to work. That last part is an order."

Josh looked at Chris, "Thanks, Lieutenant. It means a lot to me."

"Oh, now it's Lieutenant. Not Cheeks, or Swiss Cheeks? All I needed to do was get you indicted, tried, found not guilty and that would housebreak you? Jesus, why didn't I think of this before?"

A moment later, Hawk came walking into the office with one of the many news bunnies covering the trial, "Josh, this is Candace Ferguson. Candace, this is Josh Williams and Lieutenant Chris Hamlin, two of the finest officers you'll ever meet."

"Sergeant, Lieutenant, it is a pleasure to meet you," Candace said, flashing a perfect smile.

"Josh, Candace would like to do a feature story on the trial, the emphasis, of course, being my brilliant legal tactics and maneuvering. She'd also like to focus on the impact this miscarriage of justice has taken on you personally, and the department as a whole."

"I don't know Hawk, I'd rather pass."

"Josh, listen to me. This is your opportunity to get the full story out on what the government is capable of doing when it lacks restraint."

Josh looked to Chris. Chris shrugged her shoulders.

"Okay, but can we hold off a few days, I just want to get away from here for a bit."

"Listen my boy, we are all done talking about anything trial, or police, or law related. Tonight we are going to the Capital Grille, my private dining area, and celebrating."

Chris saw the look on Josh's face, "Hawk, we appreciate the offer, but not tonight. Josh and I need to get back to the department and deal with a few things," expecting an argument.

"Are you sure?" Hawk replied, "Well, okay I understand. However, as soon as you are ready, the offer stands. Candace, why don't you and I go? We can discuss my trial strategy."

Candace smiled, "That sounds lovely Mr. Bennett."

"Hawk, please. Hawk, we are among friends."

"Josh, you and Chris stay as long as you like. You know where I keep the Scotch." Turning to the reporter, "Shall we, my dear," gesturing to the door.

"Did I mention I was a Green Beret in Vietnam, Candace? Perhaps you could use that as an aspect of my tenacity..." Taking her by the arm, walking out the door, a perfectly formed thumbs up behind his back.

Josh started to close his briefcase; it slid off the desk, onto the floor, contents everywhere.

Chris helped him gather things, noticed a small envelope on the floor, picked it up, looked at the 'J' on the outside, and showed it to him.

"Hmm, I forgot about this," taking the envelope, examining the partially opened flap, "Steve Murray gave it to me at the beginning of the trial. I was going to open it, Hawk came over. I threw it in the briefcase and forgot about."

"So?"

Josh looked at her, and then opened the envelope...

Josh,

I wish I could find words....you hurt me.....but now that I've taken time to truly look at myself.......I hurt you as well.

I wrote this one night waiting for you to come home. I wanted to surprise you by being there.

Not expecting me, you didn't come home until long after I was asleep, unsuspecting I had been there for hours, waiting.

You didn't know.

I gave you no reason to believe.

I know you will come out of this okay. You are the most caring, loving, honest man I have ever known.

Taking a human life is the worst thing that could happen to a sweet man like you. You'd never do that unless you saw no other choice.

It is why I love you...

****

She looked out over the dunes to the ocean for a ship, a sign, anything. Would he come? Why haven't I heard? Why was he so distant?

This was the part she hated, The intensity of the feelings, all of them, love, hope, doubt, distance, despair, delight, resolve, and resignation.

It had always been as this. Was it her obsession?

Was he really that different? Was he really so sweet, and caring, and tender, and distant, and difficult?

Does it have to be thus?

But she kept looking, kept hoping, every day; whenever she could, watch the sun fade, steal her heart, pulling it down below the horizon, inevitably, undeniably.

Broken, she would return inside.

Surrendered to her life.

Morning sunrise would return hope, renew her spirit, buoy her heart...and the pattern would repeat, day in and day out.

There came a time when she no longer went.

She believed now that his absence wasn't a delay, or a deferral, it was a decision.

She thought never to look out again.

Resigned to feigning happiness, taking consolation in consistency, undeniably familiar but never fulfilling, irrevocably there but not theirs, numbingly comfortable but not comforting.

She medicated her soul into submission.

****

He steered the ship through the storm, made little progress. He turned back over and over only to return, and try again. He was unprepared, unequipped, unsure of the way.

But there was something compelling him. Something drove him, despite objections to his leaving the safe harbor.

The waves chilled him, blinded him, impeding his progress. He was moving forward, approaching the coast. Coming closer to that which held him together for years.

The storm receded, the sun appeared, and set. Would she be watching? It had been so long, so much time lost, so many times he'd disappointed her.

Sea calming, wind relenting, mists of rain fading.

He could see.

He looked to the shore, felt the guilt rise, felt the shame of his cowardly delay consume him.

How could he have expected her to wait? After all he'd done and failed to do, how dare he think himself worth it.

He returned to the tiller, a gentle turn away from the coast. Tears blinded him, he couldn't imagine life alone.

And then, he heard the voice, tried to see, saw only motion. She was there, she had always been there, it was his doubts that blinded him.

Her gentle, loving, honest heart wouldn't let her abandon the shore.

All men seek love, some have it presented to them, the rare man embraces it.

It wasn't where, how, or when they came together, it was always that they would.

The journey continues.............

I hope you will let me back in your life,

Keira

Josh dropped the letter on the desk, looked at Chris, tears streaming down, "I am an idiot, how could I do this...."

Chris picked up the letter, "Go. Go find her."

Memory of Love

Watching a sunset at Sachuest Point was a favorite of Josh and Keira. They came here for the first time after dinner on their second date. They returned here many times since.

Sachuest Point is one of Rhode Island's best-kept secrets. A national park encompassing several hundred acres of land at the mouth of Narragansett Bay, overlooking Newport to the west and Sakonnet Point to the east. Home to deer, migratory birds, hawks, falcons, osprey, and myriad other creatures, it also was one of the best fishing spots in the state, and virtually unknown.

Sometimes, Josh would fish while Keira would lie in the sun, sometimes they would both just sit and stare at the water, and sometimes they made love, hidden in the many rocks, out of view of the rangers that patrolled the park.

It became cathartic when there were those difficult times every relationship endures. It was a place of refuge from the horrors of their intimate view into the hell of other's lives. It renewed their strength, reminded them of their original feelings for each other, and added to the quality of their mutual existence.

It was the only place he could come to decide, the one place he could be free from outside influences, the place it started all those years ago.

Where would they go from here? Could it even be they? He went everywhere he could think of to find her. He came up empty. He was too late.

Josh walked down the path, to the furthest point from the parking lot at the spot where he liked to fish, and sat on the rocks.

How did it come to this?

As he sat there, the Jane Olivor song 'You', the one they fell in love to, played in his head.

"You are the one who makes me happy

When everything else turns to grey

Yours is the voice that wakes me mornings

And sends me out into the day

You are the crowd that sits quiet

Listening to me
And all the mad sense that I make
You are one of the few things worth remembering
And since it's all true
How could anyone mean more to me
Than you?"

He lost sight of the very thing that made him happiest.

It was better this way, he had gone too long to save things now. He wanted to, tried to think of a way, he did not know how.

The 9mm Sig was one solution. He knew it was the coward's way out. He thought of himself as a coward, he could not face his own problems, could not just explain. He spent his time immersed in work, avoiding reality, missing the parts of life that matter.

"I knew I'd find you here."

For once, Josh appeared startled.

Keira stood there, smiling. "Josh, all you needed to do was ask."

Josh stared out at the sea. "But I doubted you, the one person who never gave me a reason to, the one person that..." He began to sob.

Keira pulled him close, held him to her, held him like the first time she realized she loved this man.

"Josh, Josh. I never expected you to be perfect; I just wanted you as you were, as you still are. I was as difficult for you as you were to me. There are things I have done that hurt you. I think the intensity between us is also a curse."

She smiled, and took his hand.

"There is one more thing."

Josh looked up, how was it he deserved this woman, how was it he was so lucky?

"Anything, Keira, anything..."

Smiling, gently kissing his forehead, "You owe me a car."

Sitting there, holding each other, starring at the sea. *"...one of the few things worth remembering..."*

Made in the USA
Charleston, SC
10 April 2015